BLACK HEAT

BEX HOGAN

Orion

ORION CHILDREN'S BOOKS

First published in Great Britain in 2023 by Hodder & Stoughton

1 3 5 7 9 10 8 6 4 2

Text copyright © Rebecca Hogan, 2023
Illustration copyright © Leo Nickolls, 2023

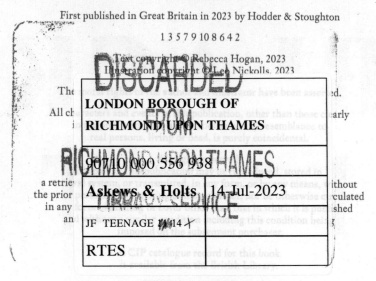

The moral rights of the author and illustrator have been asserted.

All characters and events in this publication, other than those clearly
in the public domain, are fictitious and any resemblance to
real persons, living or dead, is purely coincidental.

All rights reserved. No part of this publication may be reproduced, stored in
a retrieval system, or transmitted, in any form or by any means, without
the prior permission in writing of the publisher, nor be otherwise circulated
in any form of binding or cover other than that in which it is published
and without a similar condition including this condition being
imposed on the subsequent purchaser.

A CIP catalogue record for this book
is available from the British Library.

ISBN: 978-1-51011-096-0

Typeset by Initial Typesetting Services, Edinburgh

Printed and bound in Great Britain by Clays Ltd, Elcograf S.p.A.

The paper and board used in this book are made
from wood from responsible sources.

Orion Children's Books
An imprint of
Hachette Children's Group
Part of Hodder & Stoughton
Carmelite House
50 Victoria Embankment
London EC4Y 0DZ

An Hachette UK Company
www.hachette.co.uk

www.hachettechildrens.co.uk

For my wonderful grandmothers,
Enid and Marjorie,
and everyone else who has ever been underestimated.

MARZAL

There are two things my father loves in this world.
I am not one of them.

My mother warned me – long before I was old enough to truly understand – that he cares only for power and prophecy. And she should know. The second of the Emperor's many wives, she did what the first could not and bore him a son, but the boy was sickly and didn't live beyond his first week. Then she had me – and that was worse than a dead son. A daughter is no use at all.

The Emperor does not forgive failure and so, when I was only weeks old, I was sent with a wet nurse to be raised in a convent far away, where I've lived ever since.

Until now.

I always knew that once I turned eighteen, I would be summoned back to the palace, to take my place among the women of the inner court and await whatever marriage my father deemed appropriate.

I have waited my whole life for this.

The carriage bumps along the track, and Ama, my governess, knocks into me. Holding back a glare, I think instead of my mother, pulling her face into my mind. I couldn't bring myself to say goodbye to her, it hurts too much. Besides, she knows what lies ahead and has done all she can to prepare me.

As we get closer to our destination, Ama starts fussing with my clothing, but I push her away, eager to catch my first glimpse of the Imperial Palace where my father, the Emperor, commands his reign of terror.

'Child, sit still,' Ama says. 'You must look perfect for your arrival.'

'I do look perfect.' This is not a boast, simply the truth. I am beautiful. I was raised to be modest and without vanity, but I also have eyes to see my own beauty, and ears to hear others whisper of it. Despite their best efforts, the nuns couldn't hide *everything* from me.

My governess knows when she's fighting a lost cause and sits back with a pointed sigh.

Free of her interference, I look out of the window. The journey has taken us over a week, and Ama has been fretful the whole way, worried that the repercussions of war would reach us on the road. Though the battles are being fought on the enemy's territory, our own country has nonetheless been left in tatters. With many men and boys away fighting, settlements have been left unprotected and thieves take what pleases them. People are afraid, you can smell it in the air along with raw sewage and decomposing flesh. And fear never leads to anything good.

Even in the convent, we weren't entirely safe. With no regard for the sanctity of the building, men came to take what they wanted from the kitchens, leaving us close to starvation last winter.

From the looks of the country as we've passed through, many others are close to starvation now. I've seen shrunken bodies begging at the side of the road, women clutching dead babies in their arms, mules that have been left to rot where they fell, with virtually no meat for the scavengers to steal: their protruding bones, the viscera crawling with maggots, mesmerised me.

Ama is looking out too and clicks her tongue in disapproval. 'War is an expensive business,' she says, as if lives are a currency. 'And yet I wager we'll find those at the palace have full bellies.'

I say nothing, but look away, an unexpected flutter of nerves in my stomach. My whole life is about to change. In the convent, I was the most important person – no matter what Mother Superior protested. But in the palace, I will be just one of many women who belong to the Emperor, and finding my place will undoubtedly be a challenge.

My father has eight wives, one mistress and ten daughters. Three of his empresses did provide him with sons, but none have survived past infancy. I'm sure he's also had many other lovers and fathered dozens of other children, but only the official ones matter. Seven of his daughters are away from the palace, being raised elsewhere just as I was, but my eldest half-sister lives back at court now, having returned when she came of age. One of my younger half-sisters will be there too – she is the only one of us girls to have lived her whole life in the palace as she was not deemed important enough to be raised in the conventional way, being merely the daughter of his mistress rather than a wife.

Wives, mistresses, daughters.

I doubt any of them will welcome me with open arms.

'There, child,' Ama says, poking me in the ribs. 'There it is.'

Her voice has gone up in pitch – she's excited to be returning to her former home. Ama craves luxury and frequently bemoaned the lack of it at the convent, blaming me for costing her the comforts she was accustomed to. She has willed me to age as strongly as I have fought it.

I peer out once more and, despite myself, I gasp. The palace is vast. It looks as though it's been dipped in gold, and glimmers back up at the sun like a pale reflection.

The Emperor clearly has never been taught the merits of frugality by a convent full of nuns.

'Now, remember to address the wives as "Aunty", to show respect. And you'll need to bow to them all too, of course. And your sister. And the Imperial Empress is to be addressed as "Highness".'

Ama rattles on, repeating etiquette I've had rammed into me since I could walk, and her incessant waffling is irritating beyond belief. The temptation to take a needle and sew her thin lips shut is strong. But a good friend taught me long ago that silence can often be the best weapon. So much can hide in the unspoken, while a loose tongue is a liability. And so I say nothing and let the old woman keep on prattling.

'We'll be safer in there, that's for sure,' Ama is saying, with a look of approval at the palace.

I don't agree with her. Being inside those walls will bring its own dangers. Just new ones.

The palace stands behind a vast stone wall, the elaborate gates of which are now opening. As our carriage passes through, it's as if I've suddenly fallen asleep and entered a dreamworld. The darkness of the grim reality outside the gates is obliterated by the overwhelming gleam of gold inside, the orderly streets free of filth and waste. Even the air here smells clean of fear.

Gone are the bumpy dirt tracks; now we travel across stone-paved roads flanked by pencil-thin conifers. Instead of small huts made from wattle and daub, with timber frames supporting roofs made from mud and straw, the towering villas here are all stone and tiles. Instead of shit and death, I can smell fresh bread and flowers. The marketplace dazzles with colourful fruits, sumptuous pastries, exquisite fabrics, glittering jewels. Outside a brothel, three overweight old men are groping a pair of beautiful, young, half-naked girls. As we pass, the Madam appears to usher them back inside.

This is not a world for commoners. Only the rich and powerful are considered worthy to dwell behind the palace walls, and share the luxury and bounty within.

Ama lets out a girlish giggle. 'Oh, it's even more wonderful than I remember.'

'Wonderful' isn't the word that comes to my mind. More like 'obscene'. But I tuck the thought away with many others. I need them to like me here. It's important they like me.

The carriage winds through the outer streets until we reach the heart of the Imperial city: the palace. We pass through the immaculate grounds, where an army of gardeners are trimming box hedges to within an inch of their lives and several more men are lying on the grass, skimming razor blades across the surface to achieve perfection. At last, the carriage comes to a halt in the gravelled space before the golden palace, and I take a deep breath as I wait for the door to be opened. Ama gives me a nervous smile, and her anxiety frees me of my own. I will be stronger than her. Stronger than all of them.

So when the door swings wide, I shun the hand offered to escort me out and step down by myself. Waiting outside the palace doors is a tall man of imposing stature. His sunken cheeks frame a large, hooked nose which looks to be permanently tickled by the bushy moustache beneath it. Both the moustache and his dark hair are peppered with silver. All his finery tells me who he is. This is Imperial Advisor Rom, the most important man in the country – after my father, of course. I had not expected to be greeted by someone of his importance, but show no sign of my surprise, instead striding elegantly but purposefully towards him, leaving Ama struggling to keep up behind me.

I curtsey low before Rom. 'All hail the Emperor,' I say, the customary greeting.

'All hail the Emperor,' he says, with a nod of his head. 'Princess Marzal, welcome home. Your journey here was a comfortable one, I trust?'

'Yes, perfectly, thank you.'

His lip flickers at the side in a way I can only assume is his attempt at a smile. It isn't successful. 'Allow me to escort you to your chambers.'

I follow him, fighting to keep my eyes fixed straight ahead, despite how desperately I want to look around. Who knows who may be watching me? First impressions are everything, and mine needs to show that I am unfazed by my new surroundings, though my body aches from days in a carriage and the grandeur of my new home seeks to swallow me whole and spit out my bones.

The palace is massive, the corridors ornate with high ceilings, yet somehow it feels airless inside – stale and stifling and hot – so that beads of sweat begin to trail down my back and between my breasts. Rom leads me towards the west wing; from my studies I know this is where the women live together, separate from the men. I'm used to living solely among women, but I suspect the hierarchy here will be quite different from the convent.

We meet no one on the way. I do not think it's coincidence. When new girls arrived at the convent, Mother Superior always made sure they only met who she wanted them to, and when. She called it *managing* the situation. It seemed more like *manipulating* the situation to me, and I'm certain that's what's happening now. I glance up at Rom and ponder again why he has been the one to greet me.

My mother told me many stories about the palace and its inhabitants when I was little, and she spoke of Rom. He was someone she trusted when she lived here. As I stare at his back, I wonder whether he remembers her. Just thinking about my mother sends a sharp pain through my chest. I miss her terribly. How I wish she were with me.

Eventually we reach a doorway, and Rom opens it, standing aside so I can pass through.

'Your chambers,' he says.

The space is everything my room at the convent was not. For one thing, it's huge – chiffon hangings dividing the large space into multiple rooms, sprawling from living quarters at the front to a bed chamber at the back. But it's the sheer opulence that I find staggering. Scatters of velvet floor cushions, silk draped from the ceiling – every inch designed for luxury and comfort. I'm used to a cold cell and a hard bed.

'Your father commands you to attend him on the hour,' Rom says, as Ama pushes past both him and me, and gasps at the sight before her. 'Be ready.'

'I will, thank you,' I say with a respectful nod.

He holds my gaze longer than necessary, as if he's trying to decide something, but in the end he merely nods back and then he's gone.

The moment we're alone, Ama drops the bags she's carrying. 'So!' she huffs. 'They put you in your mother's old quarters after all.'

I'm too tired for one of Ama's rants, and besides, we've discussed this already. Several times. 'We thought that would be the case,' I say, my voice emotionless.

'Yes, but still,' she says. 'How thoughtless of them to remind you of her absence here.'

It isn't thoughtlessness. It's *spite*, of that I'm sure. But if their intention was to hurt me, they've failed. I'd hoped they'd put me here. I am glad to share the space my mother has told me so much about, feel comforted to sleep where once she did. Later, I'll write to tell her all about it.

But for now, I must prepare myself to meet my father.

Spread out on the bed is a clean outfit, a dress made of expensive silks, dyed in deep pinks and blues. It's a far cry from the scratchy brown wool I've worn my whole life, and I can't wait to peel the tunic off, flaying my old life from my body like a snake shedding its skin. The girl in the convent no longer exists. Every part of me tingles with excitement and fear, a delicious blend that makes my heart beat faster.

Ama has never been happier to assist, taking great satisfaction in changing me from meek to magnificent. My golden hair shines beneath the sheer veil that's attached to my hairpiece, my ivory skin is radiant and flawless. When Ama finally holds up the looking glass after endless tweaking, I'm not surprised at my reflection, but I am pleased. I look every inch an Imperial Princess.

My transformation complete, there's nothing to do now but wait until I'm summoned. Ama leaves me to find her own quarters and, for the first time in over a week, I'm alone.

I can finally breathe.

'I made it, Mother,' I whisper, as if she can hear me over such a distance. 'I'm back.'

Glancing around the room, I try to imagine her here. My gaze falls on the small altar, a shrine to my father. At the convent, we offered prayers for the Emperor alongside the Gods, something that I know bothered the Mother Superior, but my father declared himself a demi-God not long after his first conquest as ruler, and demands to be worshipped as such. Here, my father has apparently forgotten the other Gods altogether; this altar is designed for him alone.

There's a portrait of him set behind the candles. It's the same one you'll find in every household throughout Vallure, though slightly bigger than the one we had at the convent. The only image I have ever seen of my father. In it, he's young, strong and handsome. Frozen in time. Unless he really is a God and has remained immortal while the rest of us have aged. I guess I'll find out for myself soon enough.

Since I can remember, I've hated my father: for the way he treated my mother; for sending me away; for everything. When we lit candles at his altar, it wasn't prayers I offered, but curses. That he would choke on his food, that his bones would splinter beneath his skin, that his prick would shrivel to nothing. Yet his reign only went from strength to strength. Though he remains without a male heir, so perhaps my efforts haven't been entirely in vain.

Soon, I will stand before him for the first time and must disguise every trace of my dislike. My life will depend on it. Thank goodness not even his soothsayers can see the truth concealed in my thoughts, or I'd be hanged for treason.

I think of my beloved friend at the convent, Sister Kala. She taught me how to make the face do one thing while the mind does another. Without her, I wouldn't be prepared to enter this den of vipers, and I whisper a blessing over her name.

Ama returns, changed into clean clothes, her eyes bright with happiness. She prattles on about her room, my room, the fruit laid out for us, while my eye strays to the vast tapestry hanging from the wall. It's old, the thread faded from the light, and I remember my mother telling me about it.

'Child, are you listening?'

My gaze reluctantly leaves the tapestry and turns to Ama instead.

'Of course,' I lie.

She narrows her eyes. 'Pay attention,' she says. 'This is serious. When you're presented to your father . . . well, we don't know . . . he could . . .'

Despite myself, I take Ama's hand. 'I shall be on best behaviour, I promise,' I say, with a reassuring smile.

She gives me a withering look. 'You haven't been on best behaviour since you entered this world. You know you have to grow up now, or he'll send you away again.'

'I know.'

He'll send me away eventually, no matter what I do, once a husband is chosen. But until then, I want to make every minute of being in the palace count. 'You have my word, Ama. You won't recognise me.'

There's a brisk knock at the door. 'This is it,' Ama says, squeezing my hand before hurrying to open it.

Taking a deep breath, I welcome Rom back with a smile.

His eyes widen a little as he drinks in my appearance,

which clearly pleases him. His gaze lingers a little too long on the swell of my breasts, and may the Gods forgive the pride that bursts inside me. I wonder whether any of my sisters are quite as beautiful as I am, and find it hard to believe. There are few women as stunning as my mother, and I've inherited all her best attributes.

Rom clears his throat. 'Your father is waiting.' But as Ama begins towards the door, he holds up a hand to halt her. 'Not you. Just the princess.'

We weren't expecting that, and Ama's face creases with worry. I offer her a reassuring smile in return. I can do this alone.

Following Rom through the palace, I memorise every turn we take, creating a mental map should I ever require it. A knot is forming in my chest, pulling tighter with every step that takes me closer to my father.

Despite my loathing of him, I still want to impress him. Pathetic really, but there it is. I want his approval. And as he values beauty over almost everything else, I'm hoping to be enough.

We reach an imposing doorway, tall and ornate with engravings, and Rom pauses. 'Ready?'

I nod, too nervous to speak, and Rom pushes the door open.

The hall dwarfs anything I've ever seen. The ceiling soars above us and, like the walls, it's covered in exquisite murals, which from a quick glance look to depict my father and the stars he worships. The air is dense with perfumed smoke, the burning incense so overwhelming it stings my eyes.

There are so many guards, it's as though half an army flank my walkway and the throne where the Emperor sits.

The women of the palace stand to the left of my father. The sheer material of their veils cannot conceal their curiosity and judgement. I have no veil to hide behind; my face is exposed for all to see.

I fix my eyes on the Emperor to steady myself as I start the long walk towards him.

Only the fact that he sits on the throne identifies him to me, for he is nothing like the image we're commanded to worship.

He looks even older than his years, and a lifetime of indulgence has left him fat and sallow. He is buried in furs and weighted in jewels and gold, and I wonder how long it would take him to get to his feet, let alone move around the room. Legend declares him a warrior, an immortal; I see a decaying old man.

I hadn't thought it possible to be any more disappointed in the man who sired me, but I was wrong. The legend is a lie. And his deception disgusts me.

But when I reach him, I bow deeply.

'All hail the Emperor.'

Keeping my head low, I wait for his response. None comes.

Confused, I raise my eyes, just enough to see that my father is eating honeyed fruit. Noisily.

Uncertainty crippling me, I remain bent, knowing to stand without permission would be considered an insult to the Emperor. But still, no words are offered.

There's a smattering of laughter, and only then do I realise what's happening. I'm being ignored. Deliberately humiliated. My cheeks burn scarlet with rage.

But I do not move, though my thighs and back begin to ache from the effort of remaining in such a position, though I struggle to breathe through the sweet, sickly smoke, which I now suspect is used to disguise the reek of my father himself. I will not allow him to succeed in this attempt to embarrass me.

I risk a glance at the Emperor, but he's not even looking in my direction. He's beckoning Rom to join him.

And he starts talking about the weather.

While I wait like a fool, the Emperor embarks on every kind of petty conversation, ranging from how wet the season is, to hunting, to training the guards. All of it clearly designed to make me feel small, to remind me how insignificant I am.

I'm painfully aware of the women watching me. I shall be forced to meet them later, and they won't let me forget this. It takes all my effort to hold my position and my expression just right – not too haughty and defiant, not hurt and wounded. Just accepting of my situation. Humbled.

When my whole body is screaming for release, my father finally grunts the command, 'Up.'

I stand, willing my limbs not to shake.

'What is this?' He speaks as if I were nothing more than a stray dog, wandered in off the streets.

'The Imperial Princess Marzal, your Highness,' Rom says. 'Now of age and returned to us.'

For the briefest of moments, our eyes meet. Mine and my father's. His are cold and cruel, devoid of any feeling. I mean less than nothing to him, and my own hatred swells deep inside me. I always knew this to be true, but somehow to see it hurts more than I expected.

He looks away, bored. 'Indeed,' he says, and this time dismisses me with a wave. He's done playing with me.

I bow deeply once again. As I promised Ama, I'm on my best behaviour, appearing outwardly calm, while the fire blazes internally, so hot that my insides blister.

Rom steps down to accompany me, and just like that it's over. I've officially arrived at the palace.

We walk in silence back to my chambers, but before he opens my door, Rom hesitates.

'Has anyone ever told you . . . you look so like your mother.'

I smile at him. 'I shall take that as a compliment.'

'It was meant as one.' His voice rasps low as his eyes roam my body once more.

I study him carefully. This is unexpected. Could he be a possible ally? Or does beauty just temporarily blind a man?

'Will I see you again soon?'

He makes another attempt at a smile, no more successful than when I'd first arrived. 'Undoubtedly. Tomorrow, I shall introduce you to the women of the inner court, but for now, I shall leave you in peace. You must wish to rest after your long journey.'

'Thank you.' I give him my most appreciative smile, and then disappear behind the door.

I have no time to collect my thoughts before Ama unleashes a barrage of questions. It's easiest just to let her speak, and I set about unpinning my hairpiece.

When she finally draws breath, I say, 'It was fine. Quick, but fine.'

'And the women? Did you see them?'

'Only through their veils.'

'And?'

I lie back on the bed, wondering at how soft it is. 'And what, Ama? There's nothing to tell, really.'

I don't want her to know how little the Emperor cared for me, or how amusing the spectators found it. It'll only upset her and she's so happy to be here.

'You need to rest,' she says, hearing my unspoken weariness. 'Shall I undress you?'

'I'm sure I'll manage.' I just want her to go. 'Come and see me in the morning though. I must look my best.'

Ama nods approvingly. 'Quite right, and sleep is essential. Sensible girl. Now remember, I'm just next door if you need me.'

'Sleep well,' I say to her. Though she may be deeply irritating, I'm glad to have someone here who's on my side.

But more than anything, I just want to be on my own.

When she's gone, I slip into my nightdress and offer my prayers to the Gods, requesting their help and guidance. I wait for the moon to rise and until I can hear Ama snoring through the wall.

And then I go to the tapestry.

It's thick and heavy, and when I finally manage to lift it, I am showered in dust. Behind it, low down on the wall, is a grate.

My mother discovered it when this was her room and told me about it. It's the entrance to a narrow tunnel, part of a labyrinth that runs hidden behind walls, a way for air to circulate around the building. For years, she explored the concealed passageways, desperate to find a way to escape.

I have my own plans for them.

It takes some effort to prise the metal away, but two chipped nails and a sliced finger later, I'm able to lift it off and consider the size of the tunnel beyond. I've never been more grateful for my slight figure – shrunken further by countless nights of going to bed hungry – because without it, I couldn't possibly fit. But my nightdress is too thin, too delicate for what I have in mind.

Hurrying back to my bed, I search underneath for where I'd stowed my convent dress. No doubt Ama would like to burn the itchy garment, but it serves my current purpose perfectly.

Once changed, I return to the tunnel armed with a candle stub and I wriggle into the tight space on my front, warily pulling myself along on my elbows.

As best I can with little to no room, I hold the flame up and run it over the walls, searching for what I know is there. Eventually, I find it. A map. Scratched into the clay with a hairpin long ago, by my mother. A guide to the maze before me. Just as she said it would be.

For a few minutes, I study her chart, looking for the route I want to take. I'm fortunate to have an almost perfect memory for detail. It doesn't take me long to choose the way I want to go, and once I do, I blow the candle out and leave it behind, needing both hands free to pull myself along.

It's cold in the tunnel, and thick cobwebs cling to my face as I break through them. I can't even see my hands in front of me, and I suspect it's just as well I don't know what else might be crawling alongside me.

I can't move fast, and my body aches after only minutes, but I persist, navigating my way through the turns and twists, wondering how long it must have taken my mother to explore this place. How many wrong turns did she take before she figured out where each way led? Did she feel as scared as I do, trapped in this dank, airless space that feels like a burial pit? Or did her desperation drive her as fiercely as my determination does now? The thought of her being here before me pushes me through the darkness, but even so, I'm considering slithering back the way I've come when I hear voices echoing in the air.

Men's voices.

Smiling to myself, I carry on, the voices growing louder. Then, around a turn, I finally see what I've been looking for. Another grate. Light from a room beyond is casting a patterned shadow through it into my tunnel, and I shuffle along as far as I dare go without revealing myself, and drink in the image before me.

The room I'm looking up into is more opulent than anything I've ever seen. It is filled with men – important men.

And sitting on a gilded throne in the centre of them all is my father.

MARZAL

If I'm discovered here, my life is over. But I knew the risks and came anyway, because in this room of men is an opportunity to learn all the things denied to me because of my gender. From this tunnel, I can discover secrets and truths, information that will give me power. The knowledge stolen from these walls may help me survive.

So I stay where I am, barely breathing, keeping my face in the shadows so no one can see me. The position of the grate, low down at the side of the room, a little behind the throne, affords me a surprisingly good view, even if I do have to contort my neck and strain my gaze.

They're discussing military strategy. My father is poring over papers, while fluttering around him, like decorated birds, are his advisors and soothsayers. They twitter and flap, all wanting their voices heard by their ruler, all competing with each other to stand out. I see Rom among them, but he's lingering back from the flock, distinguishing himself by separation.

'Have we got that pissing leverage yet?' my father growls, and he's apparently unimpressed with what's on the papers because he pushes them away, scattering them over the floor.

'I'm waiting for confirmation,' Rom says. 'But our contact assured me it would be done, and he's a man of his word.'

'You'd better be right,' the Emperor says. Watching the men, I realise how afraid they all are of him. He may be past his physical prime, but something about him still claims power over them and that intrigues me.

Since I was a child, I've been fascinated by the dynamic of power. I would watch the nuns for hours, observing how some commanded total respect and obedience, while others garnered natural affection. I learned early on that love was more effective than fear if you wanted true loyalty, something my father clearly hasn't grasped. People will go beyond all reason for love.

'I want to have control of Eron before the year is out,' the Emperor says. 'This war is costing a blood-blazing fortune.'

Typical of him to measure the cost in money. The lives of his subjects mean nothing.

'Wheels are in motion to achieve all we want,' Rom reassures him. 'You must be patient.'

In a fit of rage, the Emperor flings his goblet of wine across the room. 'I've been patient long enough. I am the godsdamn Emperor. I *win* wars. Naperone will fall to me, and soon. Do you understand?'

Rom nods, but I can see his jaw clench, his teeth grinding.

One of the soothsayers leaps on Rom's silence. 'Majesty, you will indeed have victory, for the stars have spoken of it. In fact, I read them myself only this morning. There can be no mistaking their message.'

It was common knowledge at the convent that the Emperor relies as much on his soothsayers as he does his Generals. Their readings are an obsession for him. I can see from his face that Rom thinks little of the soothsayers and their prophecies. He's not alone. I used to wish the stars would side with me. That they would whisper to my father and remind him of my existence. But the stars forgot about me, just as he did.

The Emperor on the other hand seizes on the soothsayer's words. 'You see, Rom? You can't argue with destiny. Now, get me my godsdamn victory.'

'As you command,' Rom says with a bow. I don't miss the scowl he gives the soothsayer, nor the smug grin he receives in return.

This room, this inner sanctum, is nothing more than a vicious rats' nest.

Rom attempts to change the subject. 'Majesty, if I may . . . we need to discuss the issue of marriage.'

The Emperor laughs. It's an empty, hollow sound. 'Finally realised your bed is too cold, have you? Need more than the occasional whore to wet your dick?'

The other men join in, laughing at Rom's expense. He looks unfazed by the taunt, but I can see the tips of his ears are burning red. I recognise the effort to disguise rage; I've been doing it my whole life.

'I was actually referring to the Princess Marzal,' he says coolly.

I jolt at the unexpected mention of my name and hit my head on the roof of the tunnel, only just managing to stifle a gasp.

'What about her?' the Emperor asks, utterly bored.

'Now she has returned, should a suitable match not be considered?'

Long fingers of panic tear at my chest. I didn't think they'd plan my marriage so quickly, thought I would have months before I was packed up and sent away again. I need more time.

My father yawns. 'Does the scorpion care what happens to the ant? Don't bother me with such trivialities, Rom. You decide. Just ensure he has deep pockets.'

If I'd been in any doubt before, I'm not now. I am here purely because tradition dictates it, not because I am wanted. Who knows what kind of husband I might end up with? I think of the men I saw at the brothel, all rich enough to satisfy my father and all repellent enough to disgust me. My skin crawls at the mere prospect of lecherous hands pawing possessively at me, of a limp, ancient cock attempting to invade my body.

Rom opens his mouth to respond, but before he can speak the door swings wide and a man dressed in long, trailing robes hurries in, his arms full of scrolls. My father meets his gaze and, with one look, the atmosphere changes. Whatever the newcomer has to say, it's not good.

'Leave us,' my father says to his advisors. When they hesitate, he shouts, 'I said leave, you festering heap of shit-swillers!'

They scurry out, all apart from Rom, who stays by my father's side.

Once the others are gone, my father leans forward to the newcomer. 'The stars have spoken again?'

The robed man must be the chief soothsayer, the most trusted of them all.

'A new prophecy, Majesty.' He casts Rom an anxious look.

'A *new* one?' My father sounds annoyed. 'The stars have assured me of victory. Gofford just confirmed it. What's changed?'

The chief soothsayer shifts uncomfortably. 'Well, there

21

are, as you know, many ways to interpret the stars, Majesty. Their meaning can be difficult to decipher—'

'Tell me.' My father's tone is threatening, and I pity this man for having to be the bearer of bad news.

The soothsayer glances once more at Rom but, receiving no help, he unrolls the scroll, clears his throat and begins to recite.

> *'The child born on a winter's night,*
> *when moon is full and land is bright,*
> *will set the earth and sky alight,*
> *when all your enemies unite.*
> *And he who mighty fires would burn,*
> *must clear the embers in their turn.*
> *Then in the ash his fate will learn,*
> *a blade of blood and death discern.'*

The room falls quiet, and my own blood runs cold. Despite my scepticism, the prophecy carries an undeniable sense of fate.

'Does that mean what I think it does?' My father sounds agitated, and more than a little afraid.

The soothsayer says nothing, just hangs his head.

'Rom, bring that prick weasel Gofford back.' My father's voice has dropped to a dangerous snarl.

Rom bows his head in acknowledgement and hurries out of the room. He returns moments later with the soothsayer who minutes ago had assured my father of his victory.

Gofford looks less certain of himself now. 'Majesty?'

My father's tone is sweetly sinister. 'Gofford, you were just telling me of the reading you did, the one in which I win the war, is that right?'

The man nods, eager to please. 'I was indeed, Majesty.'

'And you also said there could be no doubt of the stars' meaning, did you not?'

Now Gofford falters. He steals a glance at his superior, but the chief soothsayer refuses to meet his gaze.

'That's correct, Majesty,' Gofford says slowly before adding, 'Of course . . . one can never be entirely certain, but in my opinion the stars were hard to misread this morning.'

'Do you think I want your *interpretations*?' The Emperor seems to have grown in stature, his presence somehow filling the entire room. I shrink back a little despite myself. 'Do you suppose I give the smallest turd what you *think*?'

'No, of course not,' Gofford stammers. 'I aimed only to give you the certainty that you require.'

My father puts a hand on Gofford's shoulder, but not to comfort him. 'Then explain to me,' he says, as his voice crescendoes to a roar, 'how you foresee victory when Loris prophesises my blood-blazing death.'

And without awaiting an answer, my father reaches under his layers of clothing for a concealed dagger and plunges it into Gofford's guts. My father pulls the man towards him, forcing the blade in further.

'I don't like liars,' he says, before twisting the dagger free and letting the man drop to the floor. He returns to his throne, pausing briefly to wipe the blade clean on Rom's sleeve.

Loris swallows hard, but Rom remains emotionless. For my part, I'm struggling to remember how to breathe.

'Loris, you will confirm the prophecy and then decipher its meaning. If I'm to stop it, I need to understand it.'

The chief soothsayer bows obediently. 'Immediately, Majesty.'

'Rom, clear up this mess.' My father gestures to Gofford's body and the blood pooling around it.

It's time for me to leave.

Slowly, I back up, trying to remain calm by focusing on finding my way safely to my room, and only once I'm there, sliding out from the tunnel like an infant from a womb, do I begin to shake.

I replace the grate, and stash my tunic safely under my bed once more.

Finally, I climb under the sheets, and stare at the ceiling. I was hoping for a sliver of information, something I could use to my advantage. Instead, I saw a man murdered in cold blood.

But when I close my eyes, it's not the sound of the apprentice choking on his last breath I hear. It's the fear behind the bluster in my father's voice. And in spite of what I've just seen, I smile to myself. I got *far* more than I hoped for. I heard a prophecy. And not just any prophecy.

One that told of my father's death.

MARZAL

I'm slow to wake the next morning, even as Ama shakes my shoulders to rouse me.

'Heavens, child,' she chides, when my eyes finally open. 'You act as if you didn't sleep a wink last night.'

I suppress my smile as I think of my adventures in the tunnel. 'It is the comfortable bed,' I say, yawning. 'It's seduced me.'

Ama places her hands on her hips and I sit up, shaking sleep from my head. 'Well, I can understand that. Our old beds were hard as nails. But you have a busy day ahead of you. Come now.'

She passes me a cup of tea and I take a sip.

'Oh, what *is* that?' It tastes very much how I'd expect donkey piss to taste.

'The Imperial blend,' Ama says, though her expression leaves me in little doubt that she too finds it revolting.

'I think we can live without that, don't you?' And I put the cup aside.

The first opportunity I have, I will find the palace gardens and see what herbs they grow. I've always enjoyed making my own teas, and spent many an hour happily with the Sisters as they talked me through the various properties of plants and their many great benefits. The perfect brew can fix any problem.

Ama takes hold of my nightdress and, obediently, I raise my arms so she can remove it. While she dresses me like I'm her doll, I think about what awaits me today. I am to be presented to the women of the inner court and, as is the case any time an outsider is introduced to the pack, I'm expecting blood to be shed. It's just a question of whose.

'Whatever happened here?'

Ama's holding up my hand with the chipped nails, the finger I sliced trying to open the grate last night still red.

'It's nothing,' I say. 'I must have caught it on the carriage, that's all.'

She doesn't believe me, I can tell, but I don't really need her to. I just need her not to ask more questions, which she doesn't.

'Of all the days,' she mutters under her breath.

'My sleeves will cover it,' I say, which is true. And I'm confident the women won't be looking at my hands.

Eventually, I'm dressed, decorated and veiled, all in red and gold today. The exquisite fabrics are as much an armour to me as any soldier's. I too am preparing for battle.

As we wait for my escort to arrive, Ama fusses nervously.

'Be guarded today,' she warns unnecessarily. 'But be friendly. They're your family, after all.'

Family is the last word I would use to describe these women. As Ama continues prattling, I focus. The Emperor's treatment of me yesterday will not have been forgotten by the women, and I must be prepared for the attack that will surely come my way.

'Pass me my embroidery, would you?'

Ama gives me a questioning look but does as I ask. I slip it into my pocket and smooth my dress down.

When the guard arrives, I'm ready. Ready for the way

his eyes drink me in. Ready for the silent walk through a maze of empty corridors. Ready for my judgement. And when the guard pushes the door open to reveal a room full of women, I am ready for every head to turn towards me.

But no one so much as lifts an eye in my direction. The silence is deafening. Clearly, they've decided to follow the Emperor's example and act like I'm invisible.

I can play their game.

Thanking the guard, I walk to an empty chair across the room, positioned so that I'm forced to walk past them all and endure their coldness.

Once seated, I take the embroidery from my pocket and begin stitching, with the same ease as if I were in my own chambers. I had a reason for bringing it. The Mother Superior hated idle hands, but I found the only way to survive the long hours of enforced silence at the convent was to have something for my mind to do, along with my hands. I became a master at surveying a room while appearing not to. The embroidery is today's weapon of choice, a shield to hide behind as I size up my enemy.

The first thing of note is that the hall is large – far bigger than needed as the women occupy only a third of the space, near the door. The floor is tiled but layered with many tapestries to soften the ground. Perhaps the women's feet are deemed so delicate they require the extra comfort. The ceiling is high and, while in the corridors it made little difference to the suffocating airlessness, in this room it serves to expose: the smallest whisper is hard to keep private. At least the incense is more bearable than the cloying sickliness of the Emperor's. A floral scent that reminds me of summer in the convent, of jasmine in bloom, of rose petals as soft as Kala's skin.

The women are split into three distinct groups, which tells me everything I need to know about the power dynamics between them.

The smallest pairing is two young women, alienated from the others. I expect that they are wives five and seven, Aelia and Fausta. Apparently, the older wives have little time for them, perhaps deeming them insignificant as neither was Empress for long – both only provided my father with one worthless daughter, and were replaced shortly after.

The next group centres around one woman. I know who she is, can identify her by the dark streak of black through her otherwise pale hair. Roselle, the only mistress ever elevated to the inner court. In her time, she was extremely powerful, and now she sits with a woman I suspect is Cassia, the sixth wife, along with several courtiers, and a girl about my age who I'm certain is Roselle's daughter. My half-sister, Sennan.

The third group belongs to the woman who ranks the highest in the pecking order. Though it's been a long time since she was the official Empress, Izra still commands the authority due to the first wife of the Emperor and is, undeniably, Empress in this room. Of all the women, it is her I need to win over. Gaining Izra's approval means gaining everyone's approval.

Seated beside Izra are two women I guess are Oona and Vita, the third and fourth wives respectively, as well as a handful of women who are married to the more influential men in my father's court, and of course, Izra's daughter, Urso.

The current heir to the throne.

Not that she'll be given it. Though the law deems

succession to apply to either gender, and there have been many great Empresses in the past, my father's extreme lack of regard for women means he will never allow a daughter to succeed him. He will continue until the day he dies to try and sire a healthy, living son. And failing that, he will marry Urso to someone he views worthy of the throne. Once married, a female has to submit to her husband's authority, meaning any power the law might give us by birth is stripped away by marriage.

I'm curious why Urso, who has already turned twenty-one, hasn't been married off. Is she pledged to someone, and if so, how much longer will she be at the palace?

The minutes tick by and still no one so much as glances my way. I can see the effort it's taking them, the strained expressions and raised veins, but they are determined to succeed in their isolation of me.

I feel for them. They do not realise my determination outstrips all of theirs.

My embroidery is coming along nicely when the door opens once more. This time, every head does turn, and the women rise quickly, if somewhat resentfully, to their feet, curtseying to the woman standing there.

The current Empress. She is beautiful. Her raven hair runs down her back in a long plait beneath her veil, which in turn is held in place by an ornate crown, and her dress is exquisite, a bright-orange fabric which makes her dark-brown skin glow. But her eyes betray her misery. Barely older than me. I feel disgusted on her behalf that she has to lie anywhere near my father.

Izra sweeps forward to address the Empress, presumably seeing it as her role to welcome the young wife into the inner court.

'Highness,' Izra says in a tone that sounds far from sincere. 'What an honour it is to have you join us today. Won't you have some tea?'

'Thank you, but no,' the Empress says.

The refusal leaves Izra furious – she tries to hide it but fails, her nostrils flaring and her lips thinning. But the Empress pays no heed. She searches the room and when she sees me, she walks over. There is a small, collective gasp from the other women. To reject Izra in favour of me is an outrage.

I drop deeply into a curtsey as the Empress approaches.

'Princess Marzal,' she says, her voice soft and warm as she extends a delicate hand to help me up. 'It is an honour to have you home with us once more. I trust you're settling well?'

I won't deny it is a surprise to have my father's current wife greet me in this fashion. Certainly I hadn't anticipated it, but it is welcome, nevertheless.

'Thank you, Highness. Yes, everyone's been most kind to me.' The lie sits easily on my tongue.

'Won't you take a turn with me?' The Empress gestures to the quiet end of the vast room.

I smile my agreement and she slips her arm through mine. Together we turn our backs on the wide-eyed stares of the other women.

'I do hope you weren't offended by your father yesterday,' the Empress says in barely a whisper. 'He has been so very distracted by the war, I fear his attention was elsewhere.'

It is both kind and dangerous to make excuses on the Emperor's behalf, and I regard her with surprise. She may be young, but she has some courage. Or is it foolishness? It is perhaps unwise to risk such talk to a stranger, one who could use it to their advantage. Fortunately for her, such trust in me is not misplaced. I have no intention of betraying her.

'Of course,' I say. 'All hail the Emperor.'

'All hail the Emperor.'

Neither of us say the words with much conviction.

'It can be hard,' the Empress says after a while, 'to find your place here. Especially . . .' She pauses, searching for the right words. 'Especially without a mother to guide you?'

I say nothing. She's the first person to mention my mother's absence, but thankfully she does not expand on the circumstances that have prevented her from being here with me. I do not wish to relive the scandal with a perfect stranger, even one who's being kind.

When I do not speak, the Empress continues. 'Should you need a friend, I am always here. I fear Izra may not be quick to extend such an offer.'

I glance back at the first wife, who's watching us like a hawk.

'Has she been as welcoming to you as she has to me?' I ask with a smile.

'Oh, every bit.' She chuckles lightly before saying, 'I wanted you to know you're not on your own.'

'Thank you.' And I rest my hand on her arm to express my sincerity.

She flinches, and our eyes meet for a moment before she lowers hers to the ground. Anger flares up inside me as I imagine the bruises on her skin beneath her clothes. Vessels broken by the rough hand of my father. I wonder what unforgivable act she had supposedly committed to receive them.

'Neither are you,' I say, so quietly she only just hears me. 'Alone, I mean.'

And we share an understanding. The Empress nods in gratitude as our walk nears its end.

'We will speak again,' she says.

'I shall look forward to it, Highness,' I say, bowing my head.

When she leaves, the atmosphere once again shifts. I return to my chair and resume my embroidery, contemplating what just happened. It's possible the Empress came to see me purely out of the goodness of her heart. She certainly seemed genuine. But we're all playing the same game here, one of survival. What then, could be her motive for befriending me? Or is she using me? Maybe my father sent her in as a spy. It's too soon to tell and so, for now, I shall play along until her reasons become clearer.

If nothing else, my visitor has broken the wall of silence from the other women, who now openly stare at me. I wonder who will be the first to make a move. My money is on Izra – she wouldn't want someone else to beat her to it. Someone other than the Empress, of course.

It isn't long before I'm proven right. Izra strolls over with an indifference that would make my father proud. Her fan raised between us, she chooses to look at the empty space of the room rather than at me when she speaks.

'You are well, Marzal?' She sounds bored.

'I am, thank you, Aunty.' I bow my head like a subservient child.

'And the Empress? You know her?' As casual as she is attempting to be, there's no disguising her suspicion.

'Not as well as you do, I'm sure.' My words are intentionally submissive. I do not want Izra to feel threatened by me in any way.

'Indeed. You will join us?'

'You are too kind,' I say, rising to my feet.

Izra makes a dismissive noise and sweeps in front of me to reach her group first.

'Everyone, this is Marzal. Marzal, everyone.'

I do my best to smile at the others without seeming forward. Like wild animals, they must be allowed to come to me in their own time.

Roselle, the mistress, moves to stand beside Izra, and looks me up and down.

'You look awfully like your mother,' she says. Unlike when Rom said it, it is not intended as a compliment, so I say nothing. 'Don't you think, Izra?' Roselle waits for an answer.

'The resemblance is strong,' Izra agrees, barely looking at me.

I know exactly what the two of them think of my mother. How they treated her when she was Empress. But to speak my mind would be beyond foolish, and besides, they wish to provoke me. I shan't give them the satisfaction.

'I see your own daughters have inherited your beauty also,' I say, with a respectful nod at Urso.

Izra can't disguise her pleasure at such flattery. 'Yes, it's a shame the Emperor has not found himself a wife so handsome,' she says.

I'm not sure what I find more astonishing: that Izra can suggest the Empress is not beautiful, or the disdain with which she speaks about her. Her manner seems to have power over the other women, who shrink slightly under the bite of her sharp tongue. But I see something different. In her jealousy, I see weakness. And I tuck that knowledge away.

'Marzal, fetch us tea, won't you?' Roselle commands me

with a flick of her hand.

I dip into an obedient curtsey and walk over to the tea table. The request is a reminder that I am at the bottom of the pack, not worthy enough to *be* served, but useful only *to* serve.

Lifting the teapot, I swirl the contents around, before starting to pour. The smell rises with the steam, and I am glad to be the one pouring, not drinking. It's more of the repulsive Imperial blend.

'She won't be Empress much longer,' Roselle is saying as she drapes herself elegantly over a chaise longue.

'How can she help herself?' It is Urso who asks.

Izra considers her daughter. 'Why should I care?'

'Not the Empress then,' Urso says, blushing slightly. 'But how does any wife keep her husband happy?'

In that moment, I'm certain my father has already promised her to someone, but she doesn't seem at all pleased about it. More like afraid.

Izra seems surprised at the question. 'Give him a male heir, of course. Nothing else matters.'

Roselle glances over. 'You'll need to conceive under a quarter moon.'

As I pass the teacups around, the other women start offering their opinions too, firing advice at poor Urso.

'You have to be standing up. Lie down and you'll conceive a girl.'

'Make sure you're facing north.'

'Surround yourself with images of men, and men alone. Your imagination dictates gender, so if you see men, you'll produce one.'

'And drink blessed thistle tea just before he comes to your chamber.'

Urso looks mortified and overwhelmed, and far from reassured.

'And have any of these things helped you all have sons?' I ask it pleasantly, but Izra clearly hears the sharpness underneath it and casts me a glance.

'I had a son,' Oona says, her voice a hollow whisper.

'And it was a sickly thing that died.' Roselle's cruelty silences the room.

Eventually, Izra speaks, addressing Urso once more. 'You'll do what you must, to give yourself the best chance.'

'And as for your own pleasure?' Roselle flashes a wicked smile. 'Well, it's best you take care of yourself.'

The women all laugh, and it eases the tension slightly, but I do not smile. Nor does Urso.

I lean in to pass her a cup and speak, my voice barely audible above the laughter. 'I think perhaps they're trying to scare me, for surely I will be found a husband of my own soon.'

Urso appears taken aback that I am talking to her, but once she recovers, she offers me a small smile.

After that, the women settle down, sipping their tea before returning to embroideries, and largely ignoring me again. But it doesn't matter. I've moved from outside the group to sitting with them in a single day. And when it's time for me to go back to my room, Urso comes over to me, pulling me slightly away from the others.

'Perhaps one day we could take tea together, if you would like?'

'It would be my honour,' I say, with a warm smile.

'Very well.' She looks nervous. 'Good day, sister.'

I hide my pleasure until I've returned safely to my room, where Ama pecks me for details of the day.

Truthfully, I couldn't have hoped for a better start.

RAYN

There's so much mud. Mud for miles around. When I joined the regiment, I expected battle, blood, death. It never occurred to me I'd have a more immediate enemy.

It's in my boots, in my socks, up my legs, splattered on my arms, dried into my hair, creeping into crevices I'd rather not mention, and constantly in my mouth. It's wet, it's cold, it's miserable. A misery that burrows under your skin and drives you mad.

All the world has turned to mud.

It does nothing for my already sour mood. I'm tired of war, tired of trudging around the country fixing up broken weapons and shoeing horses, with only a piss-poor travelling forge to work from.

I miss my forge back home, with its roof and space. But it was my choice to come, so I've no one to blame but myself. No one makes a woman join the army. The same can't be said for the others. I'm not a soldier, of course, though I'm good enough to be, probably better than most of these boys I travel with. My master taught me that to make a perfect sword, you must know a sword perfectly. And you can't do that without being able to use it perfectly. None of that matters to the men in charge. They don't see past my sex and in their eyes, girls aren't fighters. To be honest, the only reason they let me come at all is because they were desperate. Blacksmiths tend to end up killed or captured, which makes me a valuable commodity.

Not that I like to call what I do on the road 'forging'. It's been a long time since I had the luxury to make something new, from scratch. The best I can manage here is essential repairs, trying to keep the men alive when they're on the battlefield. Even the horses' hooves receive a half-hearted job, as simple as I can make it without them going lame. A file here, a trim there. I take no pride in what I do any more.

Still, I'm alive, with a hammer in my hand. Things could be worse.

I glance over at Luc, my apprentice. He's seen fewer than eight winters, but if this war lasts another two, he'll be sent out to fight with the others. Arrow fodder. I told the Commander I didn't need any help, that I could keep this piece-of-crap-forge running myself, but he wouldn't listen. Plucked Luc away from his family and assigned him to work for me.

Luc hates me. Of course he does. I'm the reason he had to leave his mother, I'm the reason he's up before the sun, and the reason he's awake long after it sets. Because if he is going to be my apprentice, even for a short while, I want to make damn sure he can use a sword before they send him out to slaughter, give him some chance of defending himself. But while I'm used to only a couple of hours' sleep, Luc is not. One day he may thank me for my tough teaching, but it won't be today.

It doesn't help that he has no interest in pumping bellows, or learning the trade, which makes him resent everything I ask him to do. An apprentice must want to forge. To endure the heat, the thankless task of keeping the fire burning for hours upon hours just to catch a glimpse of how something is done, you have to really want it.

Luc couldn't give a shit.

He shouldn't be here. He's too young to stand on the edge of battle, never knowing if the fight will reach the camp where we wait. And what's worse is I see him watching the men. He admires them, wants to be like them. He doesn't realise what he's wishing for is a painful and early death.

There's no point saying anything though. I'm the last person he'll listen to. So instead, I try to protect him the only way I know how.

'Put your back into it,' I say. 'There's more heat coming out of your arse than the coals.'

Luc glares at me but pushes harder. He's already been at it for three hours but there's plenty more to do.

I'm reforging a spear head, damaged in its last fight. As I slide it into the orange heat and wait for the iron to glow, I sweep my rebellious hair away from my face. I should have chopped it all off long ago, once I realised it refused to be tied back, but my mother had hair just like this and a passing resemblance is the only thing I have left of her. So the hair remains, the ends permanently singed from one accident or another.

When I pull the iron out, it sizzles with fire, and I rest it on my anvil, immediately striking it to form the desired shape, the hammer acting as an extension of my arm. Every beat steadies me, strengthens me. This is what I know. In a world of chaos, here I have control.

The regiment has been travelling all day, but when they stop for the night, ready to rest, that is when my work begins. Though I was up and forging before the sun rose, though I've ridden for hours alongside the exhausted men, I am expected to get straight back to work and forge until the sun is long forgotten.

I have already tended to all the horses. Several lost their shoes, while others had loosened them. Once they were taken care of, I'd started on weaponry. Swords have been sharpened, arrows repaired and now I'm fixing spears. Before I can rest, there's some armour to tend to as well.

Blacksmithing is not for the faint-hearted.

It's not just the hours that are punishing. There are the injuries too. Burns are a given, and my fingers, hands and arms are covered in welts ranging in both size and age. Most are well-faded scars, but there are always fresh ones joining them.

My worst injury is one only I know about. It happened years ago, when I was still an apprentice. A spark flew straight into my eye. It can't have been anything more than the smallest sliver of metal, but it lodged in there and has never left. Over the years my sight has deteriorated in that eye and now I have virtually no vision left in it at all. I've had to train hard to compensate for its loss and am only grateful that my partial blindness isn't visible to anyone else. I don't want to draw attention to anything people could see as a weakness and take advantage of. Being a girl *and* being blind? May as well paint a target on my back.

But my work doesn't suffer, and so this secret remains safe.

All of them do.

Despite my warning, Luc continues to do a poor job with the bellows, and I have to scold him several more times before our work is finally finished. When the last piece of armour is beaten back into shape, I cuff Luc around the ear.

'You need to work harder,' I say to him, not unkindly. 'I know it's exhausting, but you make my job more difficult if you don't keep the coals hot, understand?'

He nods, though I can tell he wants to tell me what he really thinks of me. There's no need. I know exactly what he thinks of me.

As I'm tidying up, Luc starts on preparing the fire to cook our food. By the time I take my leather apron off and sit down, it's ready, and Luc dollops a spoonful into a bowl for me.

I look at the sludge with dismay. It's been the same thing for days now, ever since our bread ran out. A handful of oats mixed with water. Tasteless mush, but better than an empty belly.

'Thanks,' I say, before forcing it down.

We eat in silence; we've nothing to say to each other, and I'm relieved to be distracted by the sight of a horse and rider approaching.

'Looks like we have a visitor,' I say, nodding in the direction of the figures.

Luc follows my gaze and we watch as the soldier rides up to our camp and exchanges words with the men on lookout.

'Who's he?' Luc asks.

I shrug. But as he dismounts, my heart sinks, because if he's getting off his horse, that means he'll probably rest here overnight and want his horse shod in the morning. As if I don't already have enough to do.

'Eat up,' I say. 'We still have sword training to do.'

'Please,' Luc groans. 'Not tonight. I'm exhausted.'

I'm about to argue with him, remind him why I push so hard, but I feel the unmistakable weight of someone staring at me and glance up.

The man who just arrived is walking past and is looking this way with far more interest than I'm comfortable with. Our eyes meet and I hold his gaze, though every part of me is sensing danger.

Finally, he looks away and carries on past, but the last thing I want to do now is draw more attention to myself by sparring in the moonlight.

'All right,' I say to Luc. 'Just this once. You can clean the bowls instead.'

His reaction would make you think I'd just asked him to clean the latrines.

I ignore it. 'And then get some rest. We're going to be up early.'

Despite my own advice, I can't sleep. It's not because I'm not tired. I am. Exhaustion seeped into my bones long ago, welded into my very fibre, and yet no respite comes. Maybe it's simply because I know I have to be awake again soon. Or perhaps it's because the dread that has been a restless itch within me since I came on the road settled in my stomach like a solid weight the moment my eyes connected with that soldier.

I'm certain he knows who I am.

I've travelled a long way and given up everything that was important to me, in order to disappear. To become a nobody. But I always knew one day, the past would catch up with me. I can't escape who my family are, and what they did.

What happens now all depends on what the stranger's intentions are. Instinct tells me they're not going to be good.

'What's the matter?'

I hadn't realised Luc was still awake, despite the fact that we're sitting back to back, leaning against each other for warmth – and so we don't have to lie in the mud.

'Nothing,' I say. 'Go to sleep.'

'Can't.'

It's barely audible, but I hear it. The slight quiver to his voice, the merest hint of fear. Night-time can be a bleak and lonely place on the road, and I don't want him to feel alone.

'If I tell you what's wrong, do you promise to keep it secret?'

'Yes.'

'I'm just afraid,' I say. 'All the time.'

I want him to know it's OK to be scared, that it's normal. It's also the truth.

He's quiet for a moment, but then, in barely a whisper, he says, 'Yeah. Me too.'

We fall silent then. No more words are needed. Every person in this regiment knows it's only a matter of when, not if, we die.

War is desolate. It takes everything from you: your hope, your dignity and, eventually, your life. It's a permanent winter that sucks the warmth from your flesh and bones.

What's worse is that we did not ask for this war. For centuries, Naperone and Vallure were peaceful neighbours, but everything changed when Vallure got their boy Emperor nearly six decades ago. He was young, ruthless and ambitious, and immediately set about invading the smaller countries east and south of his. With every success his army grew, and as smaller targets capitulated to his power, we knew eventually he would come for us. For our gold. And so he did, nine years ago when I was little more than a child.

I hate him, the Emperor, the faceless demon who's stolen my life from me. And as I cling to that hatred, it soothes me like a dark lullaby, until finally I drift into oblivion.

RAYN

I had hoped I was wrong. Had hoped the stranger's arrival was nothing to do with me, that all my fears of the previous night were unfounded. Always hoping.

Always wrong.

He brings his horse to see me just as the sun bleeds over the land. I've already been working for a good hour, but when he approaches I stop what I'm doing, still holding the iron in one hand, my hammer in the other. My heart sinks as I see how highly he's ranked.

'So you're the blacksmith. A woman.'

I'm not impressed. 'It's no wonder you made General with such keen observational skills.'

He smiles, revealing crooked teeth. 'What's your name?'

I don't want to tell him, I really don't, but he can ask any one of the men if I refuse. 'Rayn.' It's as specific as I've got with anyone, but right now, I'm regretting using my real name at all.

He stares at me and I feel like a mouse being tossed about by a cat. His bushy beard covers most of his face, but what skin I can see appears to be permanently flushed red, and etched with deep lines. His green eyes are sharp though. I sense they don't miss much.

'And where are you from, Rayn?'

He's playing with me. I'm certain he already knows

the answer.

'Did you need something?' I fix him with my sourest glare. 'I'm pretty busy.'

My attitude only seems to amuse him. 'As a matter of fact, yes I do. My horse threw a shoe yesterday, need you to sort him out.'

'I'll have to check,' I say. 'With my superior. You understand.'

He laughs, though it's a cold sound. 'I *am* your superior.'

'Yes, but you're not part of the regiment.'

'I'm a General of the Naperone Army,' he says. 'You'll do as I say.'

'And if I don't?' I'm being foolish, I know that, but I can't help it. Fear makes my tongue sharp.

His humour is all but evaporated now. 'You're very outspoken for a woman. It's as if no one ever taught you your place.'

'Actually, my father taught me to know exactly who I am.'

'Your father the master blacksmith?' he says, with a hollow smile.

I walked right into this. Idiot.

'Or your father, Lord Arlan of Grynn?'

I don't move my face, not a flicker of my eye, or a quiver of my lip.

The General raises an eyebrow, and glances around us. 'Not quite where I'd expect to find the Lady of the Manor.'

'What do you want?' My voice is like stone.

His smile returns, though his eyes are serious. 'We need to talk.'

I feel cornered, uncertain of the safest way to respond.

I'm saved from having to make that decision by someone calling my name. Loudly.

Both the General and I turn towards the noise and see some altercation taking place. My name is shouted again, and this time I run over, momentarily pushing the General aside in my mind.

One of the soldiers is clinging to the rope around his horse's neck, while some of the other men are trying to pull him off.

'What's going on?'

My appearance causes the soldiers to hesitate, and the two commanding officers who are arguing turn to me. Turner and Hark. I realise now it was Turner who called for me.

'Need you to settle a dispute, Rayn,' Turner says.

'What's the problem?'

'Horse is lame,' says Hark. 'She's no use to us, and we need the meat.'

The soldier who owns the horse looks to me, his eyes pleading. Jarith, that's his name, and the thought of his beloved mare being eaten by the troops is clearly more than he can bear.

'She's lame?' I fix Hark with my most unfriendly glare. He nods. 'Says who?'

'Says me.'

'And you're an expert, are you?' I reach to take the rope from Jarith. Reluctantly, he hands it over.

'Don't need to be an expert,' Hark says. 'It's bloody obvious.'

'Well, why don't you let me decide? You know, the one who spends half her life sorting out horses' hooves.'

Hark narrows his eyes at me. 'It's cruel to keep a lame horse working, you know that.'

'I do. And if nothing can be done, then I'll put her out of her misery myself. You have my word.' I ignore Jarith's cry of protest.

Hark glares at Turner, who shrugs.

'I say it's up to the blacksmith,' Turner says.

Eventually, Hark gives in. 'Fine. She's all yours. But you better keep your word.'

'Always do.'

I lead the mare back with me to the forge, Jarith beside me.

'Thank you,' he says.

'Don't thank me yet,' I say. Because I'm watching the horse closely, and her limp is pronounced. She's reluctant to put weight on her left foreleg.

The General is still at the forge, and he raises an eyebrow when I approach.

'You'll have to wait,' I say to him. 'Priorities, you understand.'

'Oh, I'm in no hurry.' And the General folds his arms. Clearly, he intends to watch.

Ignoring him, I run my hand down the mare's leg and lift the hoof. The smell of infection hits me harder than I'd like, and I cast my eyes over the sole, quickly identifying the problem. There's an abscess nestled beside the frog, and though it's not big, I'm certain it's painful.

'Is it bad?' Jarith asks, holding his horse still for me.

I look up at him. 'It's not good.'

'Please.' His voice is barely a whisper. 'Help her.'

I release the leg and straighten up, thinking. The General continues to stare at me, entertained by my predicament.

'All right,' I say, not entirely sure I'm making the right decision. 'I'll do my best.'

I grab our cooking pot and fill it with water, before placing it on the coals.

'Keep it hot,' I shout over to Luc, who's already red and sweaty though the day's barely begun.

While the water is boiling, I search through my limited supplies, gathering all the bits I'll need for a poultice, and when I've done that, I walk over to the hedgerow and pull out several handfuls of ribwort leaves.

'You almost look like you know what you're doing,' the General says as I head back over.

Ignoring him, I pull on a glove to lift the water from the heat. I pour half into a bucket and then add some cold water and a handful of salt to it – my entire provision until we can restock. The rest of the water I return to the fire, throwing in the ribwort leaves to boil down.

'Right,' I say. 'I'm going to lance the abscess. You'll need to hold her tight.'

Jarith does as I ask. I lift the mare's bad leg once more and, using a hot, sharp blade, I slice into the mass, allowing the pus to run free. The mare shudders, but doesn't object, as if she knows we're trying to help her. Using my fingers, I squeeze out some muck, and finally discover the cause of the abscess – a large thorn. I feel a certain amount of relief. Once it's out, the hoof should heal reasonably quickly.

'Pass me my tongs,' I say to the General, who once again raises his eyebrows at my tone, but does as I ask.

The tongs give me a better grip on the thorn, and seconds later, it's out. Immediately, I plunge the mare's hoof into the bucket of salted water and hold it there.

'What are you doing?' The General almost sounds genuinely interested.

'The heat will help draw out the rest of the pus and the salt will fight the infection,' I say.

'And the leaves?'

'They're for a poultice.'

The General laughs. 'It's a lot of effort just for a horse.'

'She's not just a horse,' Jarith says, momentarily forgetting his place. 'She's my friend.'

The General's smile disappears, and my irritation with him reaches breaking point.

'What are you still doing here?' I hiss.

'Told you,' he says. 'My horse needs shoeing. And we need to talk.'

Fear bubbles up again. I don't want Luc or anyone else to hear what he has to say.

'What's your name?' I ask. 'It's only fair that you tell me. Seeing as you know so much about me.'

'Drake,' he says. 'General Drake.'

'Well, General Drake, I can't talk right now. I'm busy.'

'Yes, wasting your time on a lost cause because some soldier has grown overly attached to an animal.'

I sweep the hair from my face. 'We're at war. Small things matter. *She* matters to him and he asked for my help. If we stop helping each other, what are we even fighting for?'

He holds my challenging gaze, but necessity forces me to break it first, and I lift the mare's hoof out of the water.

'That's long enough,' I say to Jarith. 'Can you hold it off the ground?'

He takes my place, and I fish out the wilted leaves from the hot water with my tongs and pack them against the sole of the horse's hoof, before wrapping some old sacking around and securing it with a thin stretch of rope.

'There we go,' I say. 'All done. Don't ride her today, just walk with her, and tomorrow I'll change the poultice.'

Jarith exhales with relief. 'Will it work?'

'I don't know,' I say honestly. 'But we've done our best for her. Nothing more we can do.'

As Jarith leads his mare away, I reluctantly turn to Drake. 'All right, I'll look at your horse now.'

'How gracious of you,' he says.

'You didn't happen to have the presence of mind to pick up the thrown shoe, I suppose?' I say as I'm examining the hoof.

When I glance up, he's holding the shoe in front of me with a smug expression.

I snatch it from him. 'This shouldn't take too long.'

He doesn't stop staring at me the whole time I work; the heat of his gaze burns my neck.

My heart is beating too fast as I try to think what to do. He knows who I am. But how? He says he wants to talk, but no part of me trusts him. It's possible he means to blackmail me, otherwise why not tell everyone? There's not a man in this regiment who wouldn't want to kill me if they knew my truth.

As I hammer in the final nail, I realise I have no choice but to hear what the General has to say.

Releasing the hoof to the ground, I stand up straight, pushing my hair back with my arm.

'There, that wasn't too hard, was it?' Drake says.

I ignore his smirk. 'We can talk,' I say. 'But not now.'

'Of course not. Meet me tonight, once your camp is asleep. You'll find me at the ruins you'll pass today. Come alone.'

I'm mad to even consider this. 'And if I don't?'

The General mounts his horse.

'Oh, you will,' he says. He tips his hat to me. 'Until later, my Lady.'

And then he rides away, as if our conversation was the most mundane in the world.

Once we're packed up and back on the road, the hours pass slowly as dread and anticipation build in my gut.

There is no doubt this is about my father and brother.

They are traitors.

I find what they did hard to stomach. There was a chance, a real chance to end this war, but they betrayed us all. Peace talks were in place, and an envoy was sent from Vallure to meet with our Governor Franklin in our capital, Eron. My father was in charge of escorting the Vallurians there safely, but they never made it. The whole party was murdered in their sleep. Everyone apart from my father and brother, who were nowhere to be found.

They are the most hated men in our country – even more than the Emperor of Vallure, because it was a crime against their own people.

I should have known I couldn't escape the association for ever, not with so many people looking for them. And now this Drake has come for me. There are only three things I can think he might want. The first is to use me as bait to bring my family out of hiding, thus allowing him to capture them and claim the bounty on their heads. The second is to hand me over to the authorities, in the hope they'll reward him for finding a member of the family – if not the ones who matter. And last, but by no means least, is the possibility that he wants to vent his hatred for my father on me, out of some sick sense of vengeance.

I don't mean to let any of those things happen.

By the time the day is over, I know what must be done. I will have to kill Drake if I am to silence him.

I have never taken a life before. I've disarmed, wounded, even maimed – you don't survive in the army as the only woman without having to teach the men to leave you alone – but I'm yet to actually kill anyone. Tonight is as good a time as any to start.

When we have settled at our new camp and the night is thick with darkness, I make my move. Taking my sharpest blade, I skulk away into the shadows. If I take a horse I'll surely be seen, and so once I'm past the others, I run. It will take me a while to reach the place where Drake awaits me, and I'll need to have some energy left to fight.

I'd seen the ruins he'd spoken of when the regiment passed earlier, and paid attention to the path so I'd find my way back. He's chosen a clever location to meet. Close enough for me to get to without raising any suspicions, but far enough away that no one will hear any screams – though if there are any, I don't intend for them to be mine.

The moon is hidden behind a blanket of cloud, and I'm grateful for the cover tonight. I do not want a light shining on the sins I must perform to keep myself safe.

When I'm close by, I pause and catch my breath. I need to be sharp and fast; my life depends on it.

Sword drawn, I creep towards the abandoned huts, whose occupants must have fled at some point from the violence of war. I hear Drake before I see him, coming up behind me, and I spin around, my sword raised so that it's pointed straight at his chest, the blade brushing his jerkin.

He raises his hands in surrender, and I'm confused to see his own sword remains in its scabbard.

'Easy,' he says. 'You could hurt someone with that.'

'And I will, if you don't start talking,' I say. 'What am I doing here?'

'You mean to kill me.' It's not a question. 'I don't blame you. I would be planning the same in your position. But those reasons I'm sure you've come up with for why I'm here? They're all wrong.'

'Horseshit.'

His response is to offer a smile, which is entirely unsettling. This isn't how things were supposed to go.

'Well then, why *are* you here?' I ask.

'Because I made a promise to your brother that I would find you and tell you the truth.'

He may as well have stabbed me in the chest, for all the air leaves my lungs. Drake reaches forward to steady my arm, my sword now lowered.

'You know my brother?'

Drake nods. 'And your father. And neither of them were the men the country thinks they are.' He pauses, watching me closely. 'They were set up.'

I'm staring at him. I know I should say something, but the world is falling away beneath me.

'Come,' he says. 'Sit with me. There's much I have to tell you, and none of it will be easy to hear.'

I perch on a slab of rock, dimly aware that my opportunity to kill him has gone and I may well live to regret that, but something about the way he speaks of my father suggests sincerity. I need to know what he has to say.

'Go on.' I brace for what's coming. He said 'were'. Not 'are'. 'They're dead,' I say. 'Aren't they?'

Drake bows his head. 'I'm sorry. I wish I could give you different news.'

Cold spreads up from the granite through my clothes,

chilling me to the bone as much as his words. I think I've known this for the longest time. I just didn't want to admit it.

'How?'

'Let me start from the beginning. You know of their mission to accompany the peace envoy?' I give him a scathing look and he quickly continues, 'Of course you do. But what you can't know is that your father suspected that something was wrong. He couldn't put his finger on it, but he asked your brother to split from the party and follow at a distance.'

'He wanted Graylen to look for signs of trouble?'

'Exactly. But Graylen kept too much distance. Three days before they reached Eron, your father and the envoy were attacked at night. By the time Graylen reached them, everyone was dead. Except the man who initiated the talks in the first place, Captain Occius. Your brother tried to help him, but it was too late. Before he died, Occius told Graylen they had been attacked by his own men. Vallurians. He told your brother not to trust anyone. To run.'

He pauses, watching me closely. I'm fighting to keep my emotions buried.

'And that's exactly what Graylen did. But he made a mistake. He took your father's body with him. He couldn't bear to leave him there to be torn apart by animals, but the absence of them both made it far too easy to blame them for the atrocity. It turned *both* countries against them, and Graylen learned what it was to become hunted.'

I stare straight ahead, not wanting to make eye contact with Drake. 'He told you this himself? Graylen?'

Drake nods. 'He did. When we met, I was already

working with other rebels who are seeking to expose the truth.'

'What truth?'

Drake sighs. 'We know the Emperor is corrupt. We all know he wants our gold, and therefore that peace talks would have stopped him getting what he wants. It's obvious why he might sabotage the envoy. But there are those in our own government who seem to want the war to continue too, and many of us have been asking why.'

'You believe our government is corrupt?' I ask, struggling to make sense of what I'm hearing.

Drake fixes me with his most sombre expression. 'I do. I think some are working with the Emperor, for their own gain. And what's more, I believe they were equally to blame for the attack that killed your father. So did your brother.'

I steel myself for what's next. 'What happened to Graylen?'

'As I told you, he was being hunted. Sadly, a month ago, they finally found him. They think by silencing him, they've protected themselves. They're wrong.'

I should cry. Should weep for the loss of my father and brother. But instead, I can feel myself hardening, anger battering me as if it were metal and my heart the hammer.

'What do you want from me?'

Drake hesitates, as if reluctant to continue. 'Graylen told me to find you, so you would know what really happened. So you would join us.'

My eyes narrow. 'Join you? What could I possibly do to help you?'

'We need more people on our side if we are ever to uncover the truth. If we're ever to end this damn war.

Graylen told me you could fight, and being a woman means you could go places, talk to people without raising suspicion.'

He could be lying – I have no reason to trust this stranger – but . . . if he wanted to kill me, or trade me, then there are easier ways than this. Still, there's one way of knowing for sure.

'If you really knew Graylen, if he truly told you to find me, he would have sent a message, so that I would trust you.'

'He did, though it makes no sense to me. He said to tell you when he found your father, your mother was no longer by his side.' He pauses, watching for my response. 'Does that mean something to you?'

It does. Which means it's true. It's all true.

'They took his sword,' I say softly, fighting back my grief. 'My father's killers took his sword.' That's as much as I'm willing to tell Drake. For now, at least.

He looks confused but doesn't press me. 'So now will you come with me?'

I'm so cold. Frozen from the inside out. 'I can't.'

Drake frowns, displeased by my answer. 'Why not?'

'Because there is a boy in my charge.' I will not abandon Luc, not when it's my fault he's with the regiment in the first place. 'It's my duty to watch over him – I won't leave him.'

'Bring him with you. What I'm asking you to do is more important than bashing out armour.'

I bristle at his words. 'What I do is more than just "bashing out armour". What I do makes sure those men have the best chance of survival.'

'Their best chance is not having to fight at all.'

He's angry with me and I'm not really surprised, but he won't change my mind. I get to my feet, the rush of blood aching through my legs. 'I'm grateful that you found me and told me the truth about my family, I am. But I cannot come with you, I'm sorry.'

I turn and start walking away, suddenly desperate to be back to the normality of the regiment, to the familiar sour stench of unwashed men and horseshit and festering wounds. I even long for the comfort of my bed of mud.

'If you change your mind, just say the word,' Drake calls after me. 'I'll be keeping my ear to the ground.'

I don't look back, and only once I'm away from the ruins do I break into a run. My head is too full, pounding as hard as my feet on the ground. Of everything that Drake told me, all that's been said, there is one simple truth that won't stop running through my mind: my father and brother were innocent. And I didn't defend them. I should have known better than to think them capable of betraying their country, their people, but I thought them traitors like everyone else.

I'm the one who betrayed them, and guilt coils through my insides like creeping ivy, strangling my organs, tightening around my heart. I should have stood alongside my family, no matter what. Now Luc is the only thing approaching family that I have left, and I won't make that mistake again. Not even for a chance to continue the fight my father and brother died for.

As I reach the regiment, I slow to a walk, wanting to sneak back in unnoticed and put this evening behind me. But as I approach, the smell of acrid smoke carries towards me, filling my nostrils so I choke. I know fire, I know smoke. And something has contaminated the smell I love.

Something terrible. A horse whinnies, a fearful sound that makes my stomach lurch.

Drawing my sword, I creep closer, keeping low to the ground, until I'm at the perimeter line of the camp. There's no noise, save for the solitary horse whose cries still carry on the wind. I stand up, realising there's no one here to harm me, and step through the bodies lying still. This isn't the quiet of the sleeping. It's the silence of the dead.

The ruins were too far away for me to hear the fighting, though the sound must have been deafening. All the horses have been taken, supplies and weaponry plundered, but I'm not thinking about any of that as I stumble towards my travelling forge, towards the screaming horse, towards the body I dread finding.

Luc lies slumped against the wagon, his blood emptied on to the ground around him from a wound in his guts. It is my horse that's screaming, his eyes wide from terror. I'd left him hitched to the wagon overnight, for my own ease in the morning, and I guess whoever attacked couldn't be bothered to free him. I do it now, and the horse gallops away, wanting to escape the horrors he's witnessed.

I want to run too. But instead, I sit beside Luc and take his cold hand in mine. For all my talk about wanting to protect him, I'd left him to see Drake. Perhaps if I'd stayed, I could have saved him. I could have at least died trying. Now I have nothing.

*

The sun is starting to rise when I see someone riding towards me. I don't move. Let them come and kill me too. I have failed everyone I love, and I cannot bear it. I deserve to die.

It's only when Drake stands before me that I realise my penance won't come today.

'Any survivors?' His voice is heavy with emotion.

I shake my head.

Drake sighs, his breath spiralling like smoke in the air. 'We shouldn't stay,' he says. 'It's not safe.'

And he reaches his hand out to me.

I stare at it for a moment and wonder at what point during this night did my heart turn to stone.

Grasping his hand, I pull myself to my feet and I look him in the eye.

'I'm ready to join you. Let's make them pay.'

ELENA

Aliénor once told me I emerged from my mother with a sombre mouth and haunted eyes. Like I knew that my life was causing my mother's death. That was why she let me live, when so many times before she'd been forced to smother orphaned arrivals. She saw in me someone who understood the violence of the world and accepted it with a fatal resignation. Someone who could be her apprentice.

There are times when I understand that was not a decision Aliénor made lightly, and this is one of them. The weather is unseasonably cold, and though no snow has fallen, the air stings my skin like a thousand wasps. Trying to keep the water warm enough is a challenge, my fingers curling into unwilling claws as I prepare the cloths for Aliénor. If the wind outside has settled or the rain has stopped, we wouldn't know – nothing can be heard over our patient's screams.

Sitting on the birth stool, the woman, Claris, strains under the agony of labour, while Aliénor crouches in front of her. Things aren't going well. Claris is carrying twins and they seem intent on staying in the warmth of their mother's body. But Claris has been struggling for hours now with no progression, and time is running out for all three of them.

Aliénor's eyes meet mine. We both know how this

could end. It's our job to deliver babies, but just as often we are forced to bury them. Aliénor has taken me into birthing rooms all my life, allowing me to breathe in their atmospheres so that I would instinctively know the smells, the sounds – and the dangers. Life and death all rolled into one devastating act of nature. And it worked. By the time I was five, I knew what scent signified infection, and worse. I was able to distinguish between the types of howls and wails the women made, knew what noises produced healthy babies and what heralded dead ones. And I knew what a woman's eyes looked like as the life drained out of them for ever.

I snatch the bottle of oil, some cloth and a clean blade, and squat beside Aliénor. Death may be forever hovering in the corner of the birthing room, but I'll be damned if he steals our patients from us tonight.

Aliénor takes the soaked cloth and smiles at me, seeing my stubbornness has set in. 'That's my girl,' she says, and gives me a nod of encouragement.

She pats Claris on the knee. 'Right then, my dear, let's get these babies born.'

I place a cloth over Claris's forehead and then hold her hand while Aliénor sets to work. To Claris's credit, she doesn't protest too much when Aliénor makes the cut which will enable her to pull the babies out, though undoubtedly the abundance of oil helps minimise the damage. At this point, my job is simply to comfort the mother and keep her as still as possible while Aliénor reaches inside for a head to guide down.

Claris's cries soon turn to pitiful whimpers as she begs us to stop. But there is no stopping. One way or another, this has to end. Aliénor's eyes are tight at the corners, the nearest she ever gets to a frown, and I know the delivery is imminent.

'Come on, Claris,' I say. 'You're so close. Push now, as hard as you can.'

She obliges, giving so much effort I worry she'll have nothing left, but it's enough.

The first baby slips out in a pool of blood, and I grasp it from Aliénor's hands so she can concentrate on tying and cutting the umbilical cord. The little boy is tiny and lifeless; blue like he was born in ice. Once severed from his mother, I rush him to the dwindling fire, wrapping him in one of the blankets I've been heating there, and rub his back as vigorously as I dare. The body remains limp and unresponsive, even as my efforts grow more desperate.

And then the cry of the second baby fills the air and it seems to carry across into its sibling's lungs. The first stir of life moves through the boy, just as Aliénor places his brother in my arms.

I smile at her, but Aliénor isn't ready to celebrate just yet.

'She's bleeding badly,' Aliénor says, and hurries back to Claris, who is now horribly quiet.

With both babies breathing and pinking up nicely, I bundle them in the same blanket and carry them over to their mother.

'You did it, Claris,' I say, holding the twins so she can see them. 'Now keep fighting, you understand?'

'Can you be spared?' Aliénor asks me.

I place the babies carefully into the cradle. 'What do you need?'

'Her placenta's retained.'

Damn it. She'll bleed to death before her sons are even an hour old.

'Do you want the counterweights?'

Aliénor shakes her head. 'Let's try the angelica first.'

As I fetch the syrup made from the crushed root, I'm reminded how lucky I am. How lucky these mothers are. Though Aliénor carries all the tools necessary to deliver babies, the more barbaric methods are always considered an absolute last resort. Where other midwives may rush in to cut the limbs from a dead child stuck in the birth canal, or attach weights to pull placentas out, Aliénor prefers to rely on calm experience. In the hundreds of deliveries I've witnessed, I can count on one hand how many times she's used such extreme practices. She has an exceptional gift, and I know I am privileged to be benefiting from her wisdom.

Claris's skin is deathly pale and clammy. I force several spoonfuls of the medicine into her mouth. There is nothing to do but wait and see if it works.

The room is too quiet and too cold. Ordinarily, we overheat in the birthing room, with multiple bodies and the raging fire, but Claris has no one left but her husband and he's away fighting. In this eerie silence the presence of other women is sorely missed.

While we wait for the tonic to do its work, I massage Claris's belly with oil, encouraging the placenta down. Aliénor doesn't move, her focus unwavering. The babies start to cry, hungry already, and the lanterns swing in the draught, creaking hypnotically. Time seems to stand still, but it can't take more than ten minutes for the angelica root to weave its magic; the afterbirth comes free.

Aliénor and I inspect it closely and, satisfied that it's complete and that the uterus has begun to contract, Aliénor sets about stitching Claris up. The danger has passed – for now – but our night's work is far from over. While Aliénor tends to our patient, I clean the twins and rub salt on their skin, before smearing some honey on their gums, though it doesn't seem as if their appetites need any stimulation.

Between us, we care for the family through the long, dark hours, until dawn breaks. Seeing I'm struggling to stay awake, Aliénor pats me on the arm.

'We're nearly done here. Why don't you head home and get the fire burning?' she says. 'I can finish up on my own.'

'Are you sure?'

Aliénor nods. 'Be certain to clean our tools straight away. We must always be ready.'

I smile. Barely a day passes when she doesn't say that to me. 'I'll see you soon?'

'You will.'

I lean in and kiss her lightly on the cheek, her skin cool against mine. 'I'll have breakfast waiting.'

It takes only a few minutes to gather up our things and, wrapping my shawl around my head, I brace myself for the cold morning air.

To my relief, the day has brought fairer weather, the storm of last night now a faded memory. The light is beginning to rise over the town, and from here I can see the river at the bottom of the valley, glistening a dusky pink as it reflects the early morning sun. The smell of rain mixed with dust rises from the cobbles, a welcome freshness after the stale air of the birthing room.

The town is stirring into life. Familiar faces greet me as I traipse through the filthy streets, dodging manure and fresh streams of urine. The smell doesn't bother me – you get used to natural odours in my profession – and, anyway, the far more alluring scent of fresh baked bread is reaching my nose. Though I'm so tired I could collapse, I turn away from home, up towards the church where the baker lives.

To her credit, she doesn't flinch at the sight of me, still bloodstained from my night's endeavours, but then I've helped safely deliver all five of her offspring. She knows enough of what happens behind closed doors not to judge me.

I buy two of her cheapest rolls and head home enjoying the stillness of the morning, the bracing air giving me a new lease of life.

Our house is down a narrow lane, bordered by several large trees so that in the autumn we're flooded by an ocean of leaves. But as the heat of summer progresses, I know we'll be grateful for their shade. By the time I reach our door, dust clings to the blood on my tunic, and I'm tempted to walk down to the river and just dive in.

Though the space we inhabit is tiny, we squeeze a lot in. Hanging from every spare inch are herbs and plants, all drying before they can become ingredients for various ointments and salves. There's usually a pot boiling; Aliénor and I are constantly creating both new and tested brews and tonics to soothe our patients. The intoxicating aroma is heavenly and encapsulates everything I love about our home.

After a quick change of overgarments and a splash of water to my face, I start the fire. Once it catches, I scrub the delivery tools in lemon juice and vinegar, and am just finishing as Aliénor returns.

Wordlessly she enters and sits at the wooden table, dragging a dish of arnica roots towards her, which she starts to crush absently.

'Are you all right?' I ask.

She doesn't look it. Not at all.

'I'm weary, child.'

I lay the last of the tools down and wipe my hands on a clean cloth. 'You should rest.' I'm not sure when Aliénor last slept, but I know it's been a while.

'Don't fuss,' she says. 'I'm old. I'll be in an eternal sleep soon enough.'

She often jokes about her age, but today she sounds different. Serious.

I reach to touch her arm. 'Don't say such things,' I whisper. The thought of being without Aliénor is unbearable. If it wasn't for the silver streaks of hair against her brown skin, I could imagine she was impervious to time, bound to be with me always.

Her mouth pulls into a small smile, but her eyes don't follow. 'I received a letter yesterday.'

I take the chair next to her, bracing myself for the bad news I can sense coming.

'I was going to share it with you sooner, but then Claris sent for us and it had to be forgotten. But today it cannot be.'

She pauses, tears welling in her eyes.

'Artemis is dead.'

My hand clasps around hers. Aliénor had never met her nephew, her estrangement from her sister preventing it, but I knew that had never stopped her loving him and thinking about him as he grew.

'What happened?'

'Died in combat.' The fire in her eyes seems to extinguish the tears from them. 'He was only sixteen.'

Here in the south, we have largely remained unscathed

66

by the war. Though the number of men in town has slowly dwindled with each new conscription for the army, the women have risen to the challenge, doing the work required. And life has carried on as normal. Most of the people here are immigrants, having crossed the border from Metée during the famine fifty years ago. That's when Aliénor and her sister came to this country with their mother to start a new life – before the Emperor took advantage of the famine and invaded Metée, claiming it as part of his empire. This hidden corner of the country, filled with people who no longer know where they truly belong, has always seemed forgotten by the Emperor and we've always been grateful for it. We are supposed to worship him as both our ruler and our God. But to most of us, he is nothing more than a name who, once a year, sends men to claim our taxes. It's hard to adore a man when the only thing he cares about is your money.

But the death of someone we know is real. Makes it real. I think about Artemis, wonder how he died. Was it quick and painless? Or did he die slowly and alone, dreaming of his mother, his home, the future he'd never have?

I blink the horror away and focus on Aliénor.

'I'm sorry,' I say, hating the emptiness of the platitude. 'I know he was the closest thing you had to your own child.'

The look she gives me is as full of astonishment as it is of bewilderment. '*You* are the closest thing I have to my own child. And it is you I fear for, Elena. The war is growing, like a disease. It spreads from town to town, reaching even these quiet extremities.'

At any other time, her declaration of affection would have made my heart sing, but now I can only think about how I've never heard Aliénor afraid of anything before. She is always so confident, so self-assured. The change disconcerts me and so it is fear, not warmth, that wraps its claws around my heart.

'My sister has lost her son,' Aliénor says. 'I do not wish to live to see the day I lose my daughter.'

ELENA

O ver the next days, fresh rumours of the war circle us like vultures. Whispers of the Naperones' continuing resistance, and the Emperor's anger. Word is, he expected to have conquered them by now, but still they fight. It seems inevitable that soon the Emperor won't want only our men, but also our boys to fight for him and, while it makes some afraid, it makes others dangerous.

Too many of the boys in the town have never experienced true hardship, or witnessed death, and the thought of war excites them. Makes them arrogant. Makes them feel invincible.

While there have always been a few who call Aliénor and me names, recently the whispers of 'witch' have grown louder, the young men emboldened by the prospect of carrying swords in their hands.

I've been up all night tending to a young woman whose milk was struggling to flow. Hot cloths and cabbage leaves placed on her swollen breasts have done the trick, and now I hurry home, thinking only of my bed and perhaps a morsel to eat.

The group of boys are in my peripheral vision, and too late I see the danger. They're striding towards me before I have time to change direction, and when one of them throws a stone, it hits me on the side of the head with pinpoint precision.

My hand moves to the wound and I stumble off balance.

'Look, it bleeds,' one of the boys jeers.

'Don't be stupid,' another replies. 'Witches bleed. It's just their blood is black. I've seen it on her dress before.'

I glare at him. 'That's dried blood, you idiot. From other women.' I hold up my hand, glistening wet from my cut. 'See? Red, just like yours.'

'I heard you eat the dead babies to give you powers,' the first boy says, causing the others to laugh.

'Can you fly too? Or do you need a broomstick?'

Not wanting to listen to any more, I start walking again, desperate to get home. But I've barely taken five steps when I'm grabbed by the arm. The boys aren't finished with me yet.

'Don't ignore us, witch.'

'Look at it. Filthy whore.'

As I attempt to break free, a handful of manure is smeared on to my face, the sweet acidity burning my nostrils telling me it's fresh.

'What man is ever going to want you?'

'Shitwitch.'

Their hands are holding me tight as the insults fly, and I bow my head, hoping if I don't react, they will get bored and let me go. Then I realise they'll never stop. Not until they grow older and have wives. They'll leave me alone then. But for now, if they think I'm a witch, then perhaps I'll give them what they want.

I begin to growl. Just a low murmur to start with, before I let it crescendo into a fierce roar. I can sense their uncertainty, their grips loosening, their bravado wavering, and I start gnashing my teeth, like I could devour them all.

They let go simultaneously. The fear on their faces would be funny if I weren't standing there covered in shit, forced to act like a madwoman to escape their taunts.

Giving them my scariest scowl, I walk away, fighting the temptation to run. My head's throbbing, my hair's damp with blood, but I don't stop as I weave my way through the lanes, dodging horses, ignoring the looks I'm receiving from those I pass. I fight back the tears that beg to spill down my cheeks. I won't give them the satisfaction of crying.

Aliénor looks up with a start when I burst through the door. She takes in my appearance and immediately fetches me a damp cloth.

'Thank you,' I say, wiping the manure from my face.

'Let me look at that,' Aliénor says, gesturing to my cut.

Feeling stupid, I sit down at the table with her, while she examines my head.

'It's not deep,' she says. 'I'll clean it for you.'

We sit in silence for some time while she works. Not once does she ask me what has happened. She doesn't have to.

One of the first things Aliénor ever taught me was that women like us frighten men. They don't understand what we do, and people fear what they can't comprehend. And then they hate what they fear. I wonder how many times she was cornered, threatened and abused before she learned that lesson.

Eventually she says, 'How did you get away?'

'I growled at them.'

Aliénor chuckles under her breath. 'Did you, indeed.'

'Pretended I wanted to bite them.'

Now she laughs broadly. 'Good! Stupid ingrates. I

probably delivered all of them safely into this world and this is the thanks we get.'

She's wiping some ointment on my skull now, which stings, but I say nothing.

'Remember what I told you,' she says, her voice gentle. 'Men have strength for war and fighting, but they can't fathom the strength of women. I see it every time I'm in a birthing room. The strength to survive, the strength to live. The strength of love so great that it surpasses all reason. They can't take that away, no matter the power they think they have over us. Just remember that.'

Our eyes meet, her smile filled with sadness.

'All done,' she says, and to my surprise she takes my hand in hers. 'Better?'

I nod.

'Good. Then go and bathe yourself because you stink.'

This time, I laugh too.

I really was incredibly fortunate the day Aliénor took me home. Though she is not traditionally maternal, she has loved and cared for me in her own way as if I were her own blood. She has taught me everything I know, and I adore her.

How different might my life have been if my mother hadn't died that day? The woman who bore me remains a stranger. Aliénor has been able to tell me little beyond the fact that I've grown up to look remarkably like her, with my mousey hair, grey eyes and full figure. During her troubled and fatal labour, my mother had told Aliénor nothing of herself, beyond having no husband or family. She had begged Aliénor with her last breath to keep me safe, and for some reason, Aliénor had. I am eternally grateful to them both for that.

If my mother had lived, I would probably be married already, most likely to a man twice my age or older. Many times I've assisted girls as young as thirteen deliver their babies, while their husbands wait outside, praying for healthy sons and caring little for the fate of their wives. Without fail, these girls are terrified, and every time I witness those births, I thank Aliénor for saving me from that path, for giving me a life of independence. She worries that she's condemned me to a lonely existence, but for every happy marriage, I see a dozen that aren't. A lonely existence is preferable to what many girls endure.

When I've changed my dress, I return to the kitchen where Aliénor has some bread and warm milk waiting for me.

'It's my own fault,' I say, tiredness reaching my bones. 'I knew they'd started hunting in packs and I should have been more aware. I just thought we were safe here. That the men of the town respected us enough. That maybe they saw us not as a threat, but as equals.'

Anger flashes in Aliénor's eyes. 'The problem is men and women *aren't* equal. There is something that women can do that men cannot, and that is grow life. From two seeds, they can make a person. That is a power men envy, and their response is to take life away. That is how they exhibit *their* power. The Emperor himself lusts after power. He has conquered many countries already and seeks to conquer another, all the while building an empire to worship him. And for what? Why should we worship a man who has only caused death? Mark my words, Elena, the idea that women are equal is dangerous. Because if women were allowed to believe they were truly capable of anything, we would be unstoppable. And we would destroy the Emperor and all he stands for.'

I stare at her in surprise. I've never seen her like this before. 'You really think men hate women that much?'

She waves her hand dismissively. 'Oh, I'm sure there are many good men out there. But yes, I believe what I said. Even a "good" man will side with their Emperor when it comes down to it.'

A loud bang at the door makes us jump, as if the Emperor has somehow heard Aliénor speaking such blasphemous words. We look at each other, frozen with fear, momentarily convinced that his reach could actually stretch this far. But then Aliénor recovers herself.

'It'll just be a woman in labour,' she says matter-of-factly, and moves to open the door.

Aliénor is rarely wrong, yet this time it's no woman before us. The man swaying in the doorway is holding a swaddled baby, which he thrusts into Aliénor's arms. And then he promptly collapses in a heap on the floor.

For a second, we're too startled to move, but our instincts soon kick in.

I'm on my feet just as Aliénor says, 'Quickly, get him inside.'

He's hardly light, but I manage to drag him in far enough that he's out of the way of the door, and I slam it shut, pushing a chair in front of it.

I'm not sure what makes us so certain we don't want him found here, but we both sense this needs to remain a secret.

'Is the baby well?' I ask Aliénor, as I check the man for injuries.

'Yes, a little dehydrated, but nothing we can't remedy. What of the father?'

So far, all I've established is that he's well armed. Then

my hand reaches wet material, and as I lift his shirt I see he's been gravely injured, and though he's done his best to patch himself up, I think he's probably lost too much blood already.

'He's hurt. Badly.'

Aliénor gently puts the baby down on the floor, and hurries to my side. Casting her more experienced eye over him she says, 'I would say he's been hit by an arrow. Look.' She points to the ragged edges of the wound. 'I think he's pulled it out. He should have left it in there.'

'Will he live?'

'I doubt it,' she says, and she's worried. If he dies here, how do we explain the body?

'Let's clean that wound as best we can and hope he wakes up. Until then, no one's to come in here, understood?'

Together, we manage to drag him into a back room, where he'll be hidden from any callers who might appear at our door. And then I start work on his injury, while Aliénor tends to the baby.

After only a few minutes, the man regains consciousness and grabs my arm.

'You the healing woman?'

'I'm . . . yes, I'm Elena.'

'You have to help me.'

I try to smile through my fear. 'Yes, I am. I'm cleaning your wound—'

He shakes his head. 'Don't bother. I'm a dead man anyway. Where's the baby?'

'Aliénor?' I call, and she comes in, cradling the infant while staring at the man suspiciously.

'Who are you?' she asks.

'I'm a mercenary,' he replies, and his honesty is as shocking as his answer.

'What do you want?'

'You have to protect that child. He wants him dead.'

I see Aliénor's grip tighten around the baby. 'Who does?'

'The Emperor, damn it, who else?'

Aliénor and I exchange a look. It's possible he's delirious. Or it could be a trap.

The man's fingers dig deeper into my flesh. 'You have to listen to me. I was sent to steal the child on the Emperor's orders. Leverage, they said, but I knew they would kill him. What did I care? Until I had to look after him on the road.' He groans, struggling to speak. 'Godsdammit, hell of a time to grow a conscience. I couldn't do it. Tried to disappear, knew they'd be looking for us. And they found me, one of their damn arrows got me a few days ago. I'm not going to make it . . . You have to get that child to safety. Get him home.'

'And where is his home?' Aliénor is somehow managing to keep all emotion from her voice.

'Eron.'

I frown. 'In Naperone?' Eron is the capital city there, a place that, according to war whispers, sits on huge reserves of gold, which the Emperor wants for his own coffers.

The man nods. 'He's the Governor's son.'

I look over at Aliénor once more; her eyes have narrowed like a hawk's. 'What does the Emperor want with the Governor's baby? Why does he want him dead? Does he wish to blackmail his enemy?'

The man nods his head, grimacing in pain. 'That's exactly what he wants. To force Governor Franklin to surrender. But once he does, he'll kill the boy anyway.'

Aliénor steps towards him. 'You're taking a great risk

coming here and telling us this. What makes you think we aren't loyal to the Emperor?'

The man stares at her. 'I've been watching you both since I got hurt. Been looking for someone I could trust. Someone who would put the life of the baby above all else. Please tell me I'm not mistaken.'

I believe him. His despair is entirely genuine. But I don't know how he thinks we can possibly help. 'We can't travel to Eron,' I say. 'We'd never make it.'

'You have to try,' he says, coughing. 'The Emperor ... this war ... none of it is as it seems. If this baby dies, Naperone will stop at nothing to exact revenge ... there will never be peace. And the Gods may forgive me for my part, if only I can make this right.'

'What do you mean, none of it is as it seems? What do you know, soldier?' Aliénor is urgent now, the threat to our safety putting her on the defensive.

But the man ignores her, directing his pleas to me. 'Please, keep him safe. And trust no one.'

He starts to cough again, and this time he doesn't stop until the last breath has been expelled from his body.

Aliénor and I stare at each other, the enormity of what's just happened sinking in.

'Do you think ...?' For a moment, I'm too afraid to finish my sentence. 'Do you think he was telling the truth?'

A grim certainty has settled over Aliénor. 'Yes. I think he was.'

'What should we do? We can't go to Eron.'

'No.' Aliénor looks down at the baby. 'But we can't abandon him either.'

Dread wraps around my shoulders like a shroud. In a heartbeat, everything's changed.

'We'll decide tomorrow what we will do,' Aliénor says. 'It's always wise to sleep on troubling news.'

'And in the meantime?'

Her lips purse tightly together. 'We have a body to bury.'

MARZAL

Though I've been here almost a week now, I'm still not used to the sheer vastness of the palace and its grounds. For the first time since I arrived, the sun is warm, and so instead of sitting for hours in the same room, stitching embroidery that no one will ever look at, the women are outside, taking a turn around the gardens. The aunties walk in front of me, relishing the heat while simultaneously shielding themselves from it with parasols.

I do not carry one. It's a joy to feel the sun on my skin, the fresh air in my lungs, and despite my dislike of the Emperor's inappropriate opulence, I can't help but admire the landscaping. Every tree, every hedge, every blade of grass has been clipped to perfection, most in straight, formal lines, but some in the image of animals. So far, I've seen a dog, svelte and streamlined like the ones used for hunting, a horse rearing on its magnificent back legs, and a bird with wings spread wide as if trying to soar away, though it is forever tethered to this place.

I know how it feels.

Behind me, I hear the crunch of gravel beneath hurrying feet and brace myself for company. Moments later, I have a sister on either side, as Urso and Sennan fall into step with me.

'Sister, you really should take this,' Urso says, thrusting a parasol into my hand. 'Think of your skin.'

'I hardly think a little sunshine will trouble me,' I say, returning it to her.

'I told you it was pointless trying to help her,' Sennan says to Urso. 'Besides, the damage is already done. I can see lines appearing on her face.' Then she looks at me with an insincere smile. 'I imagine you had to spend a lot of time working outside at the convent, am I right?'

Clearly Sennan has as much love for me as her mother had for mine when they shared their time here all those years ago. Fine. I do not require her approval, nor do I want it. Though I *would* like to rip a handful of the manicured lawn and shove it into her mouth until her lungs turn to dirt and grass sprouts from every orifice.

Instead, I return the smile with equal sincerity. 'I was fortunate enough to spend time in the garden with one of the nuns. Perhaps the lines you notice are from smiling, for my friend was kind and made me laugh often. Maybe your absence of lines is less to do with shade and more because friendship is a gift you are yet to receive.'

Sennan's face twitches with silent rage, but she says nothing. I turn to Urso.

'Perhaps you could point me in the direction of the herb garden? If I'm to be responsible for making tea, I insist on preparing my own blend for you all to try. I hoped to pick some ingredients later.'

Urso still seems to be recovering from my exchange with Sennan, but by the amusement on her face, I suspect there's little love lost between them either. 'Yes, of course. It's over there.' And she points beyond the pond to our left.

'Thank you,' I say. 'Perhaps you would like to come to

my quarters some time to try one of my blends? I have one that is most refreshing and has restorative properties.'

The invitation is very deliberately aimed at Urso and not Sennan.

Urso hesitates, but only for a moment. 'Yes, thank you. That would be nice.'

'Good.' And I give her a real smile. 'Come tomorrow morning? We can get to know one another.'

She nods while Sennan glares at us both, and then I bid them farewell as I make my way towards the herb garden, smiling in satisfaction.

I know I've just made an enemy of Sennan, but she was never going to be my friend. Better she knows early that should she seek to harm me, I will fight right back. I may have been raised at a convent, but I am no nun.

However, I am glad to cultivate a friendship with Urso. She was discussed briefly last night by my father and Rom, and it was the most interesting thing I overheard during my spying in those late hours. She is to be wed to a cousin of ours, Prince Junus, a mere boy who, as far as I can tell, has only one redeeming quality – he's obscenely rich.

It seems to be an unspoken decision that, should my father be unable to sire the male heir he so desperately wants, the next best thing would be to have a puppet who will do as my father wishes, even from beyond the grave. A man with no thoughts of his own, no cares beyond his own comfort and needs. This, to my father, is preferable to having a woman rule.

I sincerely hope that the Emperor's propensity to underestimate the abilities of women will one day be his undoing.

As I turn a corner away from the other women of

the court, I see the Empress walking towards me, her entourage trailing behind her.

If I pity Urso, it is nothing to what I feel for the Empress. To have to endure the company of the Emperor, until such time as he grows tired of her and replaces her with someone even younger, cannot be a pleasant way to live.

When we reach each other, we stop and I curtsey.

'All hail the Emperor,' we say to one another.

'Princess Marzal, how nice to see you again,' she says, smiling sincerely. 'Are you enjoying the fine weather?'

'Very much,' I say. 'I was just on my way to discover what herbs you're growing here.'

'Allow me to accompany you?'

She asks it as a question, but really it's not. To refuse her would be the highest insult. Fortunately for me, I'm more than happy to have her company.

We walk together in awkward silence at first, neither of us sure what to say.

The Empress speaks first. 'You have an interest in plants?'

'I do, Highness. I was fortunate enough to have a good teacher at the convent who made me see how valuable they are to us.'

'I'm afraid I am unable to distinguish between them,' the Empress says. 'To me they are simply pretty, or not.'

'I would be happy to show you, if you like,' I offer.

'You say they're valuable to us . . . In what way?'

I sense she has a specific reason for asking – I just need to put her at sufficient ease to be honest.

'Health benefits mostly,' I say. 'There's little the right blend of tea cannot fix.'

'Indeed.'

The silence resumes, the only sound our feet on the path, though we occasionally exchange smiles.

'Perhaps,' she says, as we pass a bench, 'we could sit for a while before you commence your work.'

I do as I'm told and sit beside her. Her guards position themselves close by, but with discretion.

I take a moment to look at them. They are all older men and I wonder if that's because, despite them all being eunuchs, my father doesn't want the Empress to even *see* beauty. My eyes drift beyond the guards and my gaze falls on a group of men walking briskly across the way, deep in animated conversation. One in particular catches my attention, a man who is only a little older than we are and incredibly handsome. Perhaps he feels my eyes on him, because he looks over and holds my gaze, giving the slightest hint of a smile.

I instantly look away, wondering if my face is flushed.

The Empress is watching me with, I think, a little amusement. But she doesn't comment.

'The teas you spoke of,' she says instead. 'Is there a blend that would help a woman to fall pregnant?'

There it is. The reason we're sitting here together.

'Absolutely,' I say. 'Depending on what I find in the garden, we could blend raspberry leaf with some red clover. Perhaps some nettle leaf. If there's any chasteberry, then all the better. I'd be happy to make you something, if you wish?'

To my surprise, the Empress clasps my hand. 'Thank you, yes. I would be most grateful. And if I can impose on your kindness a little further—'

I interrupt her gently. 'I would, of course, do it with complete discretion. No one else need know of our conversation.'

The Empress exhales a little with relief. 'Thank you. I am indebted to you.'

'Not at all. We women have to stick together.'

She laughs. 'I fear that view is not shared by anyone else in the palace. In fact, the others seem to hold the complete opposite opinion. Every woman for herself.'

'That is their mistake,' I say, and though my tone is light, I mean it wholeheartedly. 'You can rely on me.'

Her eyes cloud over with emotion. 'I will not deny that the prospect of having a friend again is most desirable.'

'You miss your family?'

'Terribly. When I came here, I came quite alone, at the Emperor's command. It is more ... difficult than I expected, to be separated from one's mother and friends.'

'I understand.' I truly do.

'Perhaps,' she says hesitantly, 'I could do something for you, to show my appreciation for your help?'

I raise my eyebrows, intrigued. 'Such as?'

The Empress tilts her head ever so slightly in the direction of the handsome man, just visible now on the other side of the gardens. 'I noticed you admiring Zylin. I could arrange for an introduction, if you wish?'

I'm certain I blush now. 'I was simply noticing that he's much younger than most of the other men. Is he one of my father's advisors?'

'Yes, his father used to be one of the Emperor's favourites, and so he was provided a good position as a favour.'

'His father is dead?' I keep my voice even.

'No, but unwell. Apparently, the only thing keeping him alive is his pride in his son.'

'I see.' And I do, because although I say nothing to the Empress, I know who his father is. In fact, I knew exactly who Zylin was the moment I saw him. Ama had already fed me all the gossip about the young man and his family.

'Word of advice though,' the Empress says, oblivious to my thoughts. 'Flirtation with a member of the court is not something to do publicly here. Privately, however? Well, why shouldn't you enjoy a little beauty before you're married off to an ageing reptile?'

I have the strong impression that last comment wasn't about me, and I understand why she wants to fall pregnant quickly. Once she's carrying his child, the Emperor won't demand she lies with him any more. Also, if she gives birth to a son who lives, then she might be rewarded with the presence of her family, and I can't blame her for wanting that.

Her request made, the Empress gestures for us to stand and we walk in companionable silence until we reach the only part of the garden I'm truly interested in.

'I will see you again soon, I hope?' she says, as I turn to the herbs.

'Indeed you will. I shall bring you your tea as soon as it's ready.'

And then finally, I'm alone. The first thing I do is follow the path, my eyes skimming over the plants, assessing what is growing, what is thriving. It is an impressive collection, far bigger than the convent's, which I suppose is to be expected. Once I've surveyed everything that is here, I start to pick handfuls of leaves for various blends, relishing the sensation of touching the earth once more and the way it grounds my spirit in a way nothing else does.

It's so peaceful that, for a short moment, it's hard to imagine a war rages on beyond the palace walls, with death on all sides. It would be easy to forget that innocent people are suffering while we are shielded from the horror, and it's no surprise that most of the women here care little for anything but their petty dramas.

But not me. I've seen too much. Heard too much.

I will not forget.

MARZAL

Ama is outraged I've invited Urso for tea without consulting her first, and has been up long before sunrise fussing over the room's appearance.

'Don't you realise everything you do – every move you make – is under scrutiny?' she says, plumping up pillows with unnecessary violence. 'Urso is their spy and they will feast on every last detail she brings back to them until all your privacy has been devoured.'

It irritates me that after all these years, Ama still doesn't credit me with an ounce of intelligence. But then again, I've deliberately hidden most of it from her, so perhaps I'm being unfair.

'They'll do that anyway,' I say. 'May as well feed them some truth, rather than all their fodder being lies.'

'If you insist on it, then at least make an effort for the truth to be presentable. I mean, look at the state of you.'

I assume she's referring to my choice of outfit, which is slightly crumpled, due to my negligence last night. I knocked it from its carefully placed position when I emerged from the hidden tunnel and lost my balance.

'Urso's not going to care about what I'm wearing.'

Ama scoffs. 'If you believe that, then you're even more stupid than I thought. And what are you doing, messing about over there?'

I'm far from messing about. I am, in fact, preparing a fresh blend of tea for my sister as promised. How anyone could fail to grasp the power of tea drinking escapes me. It is so much more than the consumption of fluid – it forms the foundation of social interaction, it denotes the order of family authority. It opens conversations, furthers friendships, puts people firmly in their place. Ama may be oblivious, but I understand the huge significance of this taking of tea today. Everything from here on hinges on this.

Fortunately, I'm saved from any further scolding by a knock at the door.

'Make yourself scarce,' I hiss at Ama, tired of her moaning at me. 'If she sees your miserable face, she really will have something to gossip about.'

Ama glares at me, but slips out through our adjoining door with a frustrated sigh nonetheless.

Taking a deep breath of my own, I smooth out my skirt, and my expression, before opening the door.

'Good morning, sister. Thank you for coming.' I gesture for Urso to enter my chamber.

'Thank you for inviting me,' she says, and I sense she's a little nervous to be here. I wonder how often she's been without the safety of a group, without several others to fill the silence. Maybe she feels vulnerable being alone with me, a virtual stranger. Or perhaps she's relieved to escape for once.

She's looking around my room, probably comparing it to her own chambers. I'm certain hers will be bigger.

'Please, sit down,' I say, gesturing for her to take a seat. 'Tea?'

'Yes, thank you.' Urso smiles at me. 'What a sweet room.'

I smile back, though I know in this case 'sweet' means small.

'Have you settled in well?' she asks, kneeling on the cushions as I place the tray between us.

'Very,' I reply, adding a measured emphasis to my gratitude. 'Compared to the convent, this is heaven.'

I pour us both a cup of herbal tea from the pot and offer one to her.

'It's my own blend,' I say. 'Made fresh this morning.'

She takes a sip, and despite her immaculate manners, pulls a face.

'A little bitter?' I ask with a smile.

Urso laughs. 'Yes, a little.'

'You get used to it,' I say. 'Trust me, the wonders these herbs do for your skin, it's worth every sip.'

'If you say so.' And she takes another hesitant taste. 'Mother will be pleased; she wants me looking my best for the wedding.'

Although I've heard all about her betrothal while spying on my father and Rom, I feign ignorance. 'Oh! Have you been matched already?'

Urso nods, though without enthusiasm. 'To Prince Junus.'

I watch her carefully. 'Is he nice?'

'I've only met him briefly,' she says. 'He seemed pleasant enough. Young.' She pauses and then adds, 'And short.'

Our eyes meet and we both laugh. I can tell it was a relief for her to admit that to someone.

'He wasn't the Emperor's first choice,' she says, surprising me, 'for my husband. I should have wed two years ago.'

Fascinating. Both the information and the fact she feels comfortable confiding in me.

'I confess, I did wonder why you weren't already wed,' I say, quickly adding, 'though I am grateful for it, or we shouldn't have met.'

'Yes, I am quite the old maid now,' she says, only half joking. 'The man I was to marry was a General in the army. It was decreed that our wedding should take place after the war was won, as celebration of the victory. The Emperor thought very highly of him, to consider such an honour.'

I imagine it was his wealth, not his merits, that commended him to our father.

'Alas, he died on the battlefield several months ago. And I have had to wait an appropriate time to mourn, and for a new match to be found. The General was a hard man to replace.'

Yes, I'm aware of the criteria our father requires.

'Did you love him? This General?' I ask sympathetically.

'I barely knew him. He was older than Prince Junus. And taller.'

'Well then,' I say comfortingly. 'I'm sure all will work out well. The Emperor must have had good reason to choose the prince, and a kind husband is surely the best we can hope for,' I say, refilling her cup.

'Yes.'

Urso is hopelessly easy to read. Her face tells me everything, all her fears about marriage, her lack of desire for the man – the boy – she's to wed.

'Tell me about your life before you returned here,' I say to distract her from unpleasant thoughts, and to learn more about her.

Now she becomes animated. 'I was at the Winter Palace,' she says, her whole face lighting up at the mere mention of the place. 'It was wonderful there. I was very happy.'

Jealousy needles me at the thought that she grew up

in the luxury of the Winter Palace, while I was sent to a convent. But I will not let her see it bothers me.

'Did your mother visit often?'

'As much as she could,' Urso says. 'The Emperor gave her a small residence about a day's carriage ride away, and she would come and stay there from time to time.'

'But she preferred to live here? With the other women?'

'I think so. You'll come to learn that it's important to my mother that everyone remembers she was here first.'

She says it lightly, but I am already well aware of this fact. I know how Izra seized every opportunity to bully my mother, jealous to the point of madness at her beauty, furious at being replaced. It's not hard to imagine that with every successive wife, the insecurity has grown until all she has left to cling to is a memory.

'Is she pleased with your engagement to Prince Junus?' I know I'm prying, but Urso seems happy to share.

'She says it's a good arrangement and that, as he is my cousin, we should produce strong children.'

I watch as she parrots back to me all she's been told to think and say. She clearly doesn't mean a word of it.

'Was there ever . . . someone else?' I test a hunch I have. 'Someone at the Winter Palace who was dear to you?'

Urso's cheeks flush red, telling me all I need to know.

I reach to touch her arm. 'I'm sorry, I'm being too forward. You need share nothing with me.'

My words seem to offer her the reassurance she was seeking. 'You see everything,' she says, tears glistening at her eyes. 'There was someone. But . . . it is impossible, we both know it. We always did.'

I raise my eyebrows. 'You loved each other?'

'As much as any two people can,' she says. 'I've known

him since I was a child, but he is only a groom and I am to marry a prince.'

I pity her in that moment. To know the one you love still lives while you are forced to be with another must be an exquisite pain.

'But surely there is no harm in continuing a friendship?' I say, swirling my tea around the cup like a tempest.

Urso looks at me, her expression both questioning and hopeful all at once. 'What do you mean?'

'Well, could you not write to him? Take comfort in his words, if not his presence?'

She frowns. 'I do not think it would be appropriate . . .'

'You said yourself you have known each other since you were children. Surely there is nothing inappropriate about a childhood friendship?'

Urso's hand starts to shake, rattling the cup upon its saucer.

I reach forward. 'Forgive me,' I say quickly. 'I was simply trying to help. Do not concern yourself, it was merely a suggestion.'

She nods, but I can see I've planted the seed of the idea. Now I simply need to give it water.

'Forget I said anything,' I insist. 'I just fail to see the harm in corresponding with a friend.'

It's the last thing I say on the matter and we move on to safer topics, gossiping harmlessly about the palace fashions and agreeing that Roselle dresses indecently. But by the time she leaves, I'm certain of one thing.

Urso will be writing to her love.

*

Ama takes longer than usual to leave me that night at bedtime. I'm eager to climb into the tunnel and visit my father, but I can't tell her that, so listen impatiently as she airs her grievances.

'And that snooty upstart of a worm refused to give it to me, can you believe it?'

She's complaining about Izra's handmaiden, Lilah, who wields as much control in the servants' quarters as her mistress does with the wives.

'It doesn't matter,' I say to calm Ama. 'I can make my own powder easily enough.' Honestly, I'd much prefer to do that than accept anything from Izra or her lackey.

'But you shouldn't *have* to,' Ama says, as if it's the worst crime imaginable. How quickly she's forgotten the perils of war afflicting everyone outside of this haven.

'I don't mind. Truly. Do not let it trouble you.'

Ama sighs, but I can tell my lack of outrage is diminishing hers. 'It's just not right, is all. A princess being denied powder by a nobody.'

'You know it's Izra, not her,' I say. 'She just wants me to look different to everyone else.' She doesn't know I can easily crush up some chalk with my pestle and mortar, alongside some lilyroot, rice flower and rosewater to beautify myself. I look forward to seeing her confusion when her plan to humiliate me fails.

Eventually, Ama accepts I'm right and slopes off to bed like an injured animal needing to lick her wounds. But she'll live.

I, on the other hand, still have work to do, and once I'm sure Ama's settled, I change into my filthy tunic and remove the grate.

The dark isolation of the tunnel no longer leaves me in

a cold sweat, but it's still not pleasant. In parts it's slimy, in others it stinks, and it's infested with the sort of creatures who thrive in such cold, inhospitable places.

The conversation reaches my ears long before I see them. Angry voices of men who have nothing but violence in their hearts.

The lateness of my arrival means I've missed the discussion with the wider group of advisors, but my father is still conversing with Rom and Loris, the chief soothsayer. The three of them are huddled around a table covered in scrolls. From the expression on my father's face, it seems that Loris has brought more unwelcome tidings.

'. . . and this *child* . . . will kill me?'

Loris sighs. 'I believe the stars are warning that this *could* happen, yes. But it is a future we can now plan for and avoid, thanks to the stars.'

'And the child was born under a winter moon?' Rom sounds sceptical.

'Again, yes. Though I cannot guarantee precisely which one, my reading suggests within the last year.'

'So my assassin is merely a baby?' The Emperor laughs. 'Then I have nothing to fear.'

'Not until the child grows up, no,' Loris agrees.

'Then it's simple. I cannot have the little bastard rise up against me in a matter of years. So we don't allow the boy to grow into a man.'

Rom and Loris exchange a glance of uncertainty. 'But how do we do that?' Rom asks. 'We don't know his identity.'

'Kill them all.'

There's a hollow silence. My blood runs cold because I know my father by now. I know what's coming.

'Majesty?' Loris looks stunned.

'All boys born this past year must die, for the sake of the empire. Rom, see it is done.'

Rom hesitates for a moment. 'Majesty, I do not think what you ask is possible—'

'I am Emperor. Everything I ask is blood-blazing possible.'

'You're talking about killing babies. *Innocents*.' Even Rom is having trouble believing what is being asked of him. I don't blame him. 'If you do this, Majesty, your people will turn against you. There's no forgiving such an act.'

My father has no interest in the warning. 'Then make them think it's the Naperone army committing atrocities. Fuel their hatred towards those swine-sniffers. Must I think of everything?'

I lie in my dark, cramped tunnel, enveloped in horror. To command the murder of thousands of babies – his subjects – with such casualness, just to save his own miserable neck? I had known my father was a despicable man. I had not known until this moment how evil. He has no soul; hollow him out and all there'd be is fat and gristle.

Rom tries again, at length, to dissuade my father from such madness, but to no avail. He will not be deterred.

'And when you've done that, find this blade of blood. Round up every blacksmith in all the world if you have to. I want that godsdamn weapon in *my* hand, not my enemy's.' He looks at the soothsayer. 'Then will the prophecy be avoided?'

Loris clears his throat. 'I believe so, yes. It says a child born on a winter's night will kill you with a blade of blood. So if you kill the child and possess the blade – the prophecy cannot be fulfilled.'

'Then what are you waiting for, you skinshit?' the

Emperor positively snarls at Rom, who bows his head before hurrying out of the room.

I hurry too, sliding as quickly as I can away from the wickedness that clings to my skin like a stain. By the time I'm safely tucked into my bed, I'm shivering – though not from the cold. There has to be some way to stop him, to prevent such a barbaric loss of life.

As I lie there, a plan forms in my mind. A dangerous one, to be sure. But I didn't come here expecting things to be easy. Creeping from my bed, I wrap a shawl around my shoulders and pick up my quill. Ink pours from the feather like blood from my heart as I explain my intentions to my mother, sharing with her my fears and my hopes, my tears mingling with the words, making them unreadable at times. Unburdening myself in this way strengthens me, reminding me of the resolve I have.

When I'm done, I return to bed. Tomorrow, I will find a way to have my letter delivered safely. Knowing I have a plan soothes my spirit, and sleep creeps in at the corner of my mind.

My father forgets it's not only boys who are born under winter moons.

I was too.

RAYN

Corsets are horseshit. A method of torture designed to keep women quiet. I have never been more strongly of this opinion than I am now as I stand outside the château, my ribs threatening to crack and puncture my lungs at any moment. My body is angular, carved by the work I do, and resents being squeezed into another form.

I barely recognise myself, I'm so far from the filthy mess that Drake pulled from the mud. I'm certain no one else will either, which is just as well as I'm on my first mission for the rebels: infiltrate the château and find evidence that the owner, Lord Norvill, is working for the Emperor. I'm not surprised the rebels think he's a traitor; his château is untouched by the war and the extravagant soirée I'm about to gatecrash is far from a common sight in our country these days.

The guests are dripping with money, from their lavish clothes to their ornate carriages, and after years on the road with the regiment, I hadn't realised anyone still lived like this. I feel sick to my stomach, and not just because my whole body is locked in a vice.

Of course, I have no invitation, but apart from my skin being far more sun-browned than most of the ladies who spend their days indoors, I look the part and I'm armed with my wits. I only hope that's enough.

Before I'm truly accepted as one of the rebels, privy to all they've uncovered, I must demonstrate both my loyalty and my usefulness. If I fail . . . No, I cannot fail.

I watch as people arrive, waiting for someone who'll serve my purpose. When I spot an older gentleman, with a bad limp and an even worse moustache, I smile to myself. He'll do perfectly. I set my course towards him, keeping my head down until, inevitably, we collide.

'Oh, forgive me,' I say, resting my hand on his arm with a beseeching gaze.

As predicted, he takes a moment longer than necessary to look me over with invasive eyes, and then smiles. 'Not at all.'

'I'm distracted,' I say, by way of explanation. 'But I really should look where I'm going.'

I say it with just enough distress that his interest is piqued.

'Are you quite all right, my dear?'

I shake my head, dabbing a handkerchief to my eye, pressing my hand to my breast. 'Foolish, I'm afraid. I've travelled all this way without my invitation. All this effort for nothing.'

He behaves exactly as I'd hoped, which is simultaneously pleasing and disappointing. With a lecherous lick of his lips, he says, 'Perhaps I can be of some assistance? I'd be more than happy to escort you in as my guest.'

My display of gratitude is finely balanced, so as not to be overeager, but excessively effusive. 'Oh, I couldn't impose . . . unless . . . you're sure you don't mind?'

'It would be my pleasure.' And he raises his arm for me to slip mine through.

At his side, it's all too easy to walk unquestioned into the château. No one suspects a thing; they see only what they want to see.

Now I just need to find a way to free myself of the old man.

'Would you excuse me?' I say, extracting my arm from his once we're inside, standing in the grand foyer. 'I must just go and freshen up.'

Leaving him open-mouthed, but too polite to protest, I push through the busy corridor, using the crowd to disappear until I find myself alone.

Hurrying, I move from one room to the next, searching for somewhere locked and private. I'm not going to find anything interesting in a public room. If I'm discovered, I shall simply say I was lost and return to join the guests.

With no luck on the ground floor, I have to take a flight of stairs before I find a locked door. Checking there's no one around, I reach into my bodice for the narrow key I forged for this very purpose, a key that will open almost any door.

It fits the lock perfectly and I carefully turn it, more than a little satisfied to hear the click that allows me entry.

The walls are lined with books from floor to ceiling, and there are cupboards, chests of drawers and – most promisingly – a vast writing desk. I could be disturbed at any moment, so I know I need to be quick. The desk readily opens to my key, and I scan through papers, searching for anything incriminating.

But I find nothing in the drawers beyond accounts for Lord Norvill's home and land, records of his tenants and what they owe. There has to be *something* of use though. Drake is certain Lord Norvill has made a deal with the devil to save himself. And I have no reason to doubt him. Then I remember my father used to have hidden compartments for the secrets he didn't just want to keep, but needed to.

I run my fingers over the desk, seeking a chink in its armour. And I find it, a tiny latch in the bottom drawer. I flick it open to reveal a scroll. Though the seal is broken, I recognise the insignia. It's from Eron. The note itself is hardly damning. It simply reads, 'Your assistance was most appreciated and will not go unrewarded. Until next time.' It isn't signed.

There is no obvious reason to think that this is important, other than the fact that such care was taken to hide it, but I take it, carefully slipping it down the front of my corset.

Quickly checking the desk looks just as I found it, I leave the room. There's no sign of anyone, only the noise from downstairs floating up like the distant hum of bees around a hive. It's time I rejoined the party.

The guests are mostly assembled in the grand hall now, where musicians play merrily, and an extravagant banquet stretches along one wall. My belly growls at the mere sight of such abundance, though I doubt I could stomach even a bite in this corset. Instead, I decide it's time to leave before anyone can question my presence.

'May I have this dance?'

The man who steps in front of me, blocking my escape, carries such an air of authority I daren't refuse him.

Painfully aware of the stolen paper tucked between my breasts, I smile at him. 'Of course.'

It's been years since my father taught me to dance, and a failure now would certainly reveal me as an imposter. Fortunately, the music triggers enough memory that my legs and feet move when they are supposed to.

'I do not recognise you,' he says, as we glide across the floor. 'Who did you come with?'

I scan the room, never more hopeful to spy the old man I abandoned. I see him watching me grumpily from the side and lift my fingers in a small wave. Luckily, between the wave and my sweet smile, he softens and waves back.

'Oh, Lord Crouchley. Family or friend?'

I decide to play it safe. 'Just a friend.'

'And your name?' It doesn't escape my attention that he's questioning me. I wonder whether he saw me sneaking about, and only then does it occur to me that he could be Lord Norvill himself.

Drake and I had talked about how it was unlikely anyone would recognise my first name here, and lying might cause other complications, so some portion of the truth was simplest. 'I'm Rayn. And you are?'

'Someone else who shares your concerns.'

I look up at him sharply and he grins back at me. 'It's disgusting, isn't it? Such a shameful display of wealth when most of our countrymen are struggling to survive.'

When I fail to disguise my surprise, he says, 'You're not as good at hiding your feelings as you think you are.'

Quickly gathering my thoughts, I decide to proceed with caution and laugh lightly. 'That obvious, is it?'

'I'm afraid so,' he says, then he lowers his voice. 'In fact, the only reason *I'm* here is to instruct Norvill to cease such frivolity when our country is under siege.'

Right. So he's *not* Lord Norvill then.

'Ah, there is our host.' My dance partner's lips purse dangerously thin. 'Would you excuse me?' He releases me and strides over to a haughty-looking man near the door.

I'm more than happy to be released from his hold, and

eager to escape this place, but on my way out I attempt to linger by them for a moment, in the hope of hearing their conversation.

But to my frustration, I see Lord Crouchley targeting me like a hunter does his prey, and have to hurry past. All I'm able to make out is that whoever my dance partner is, Lord Norvill is afraid of him, for when I pass, his skin is as white as if he's seen a ghost.

The last thing I see before I flee the building is the two of them skulking off into the shadows together, Lord Norvill looking over his shoulder nervously, as if he didn't want to be seen.

Outside, I put them from my mind because getting safely away is my priority. I left my horse in the woodland beyond the château, and fortunately there aren't many guests gathered in the courtyard, making it easy enough for me to slip away unnoticed into the treeline.

The sound of revelry fades fast once I'm under the canopy of trees. It reminds me of being left behind at camp when there was a battle. All I could do was wait for the soldiers, hoping they would return, and listen to the distant sound of death. In some ways, I find the revelry more disturbing.

My horse nickers gently when it sees me, presumably glad it hadn't been abandoned. Again, I can relate. I was always so relieved when the troops rode back, even if they were bloody and broken and with repairs for me to do. Not because I particularly felt attached to any of them. I was just so desperately afraid of ending up on my own.

I untie my horse and mount, trying to ignore the way the corset cuts into my guts. I can't wait to rip the bloody thing off. But for now, all I want to do is put as much distance between myself and this place as possible.

We ride fast through the woodland, and I have to lean low against the horse's neck to avoid being torn apart by branches.

It takes all night and most of the next day to return to Drake's camp, partly because I have to double back on myself and follow some decoy routes, just in case anyone's tracking me. But by the time I ride into camp, I'm certain I'm alone, just me and my exhausted mount.

Drake and the other rebels move frequently, never staying in one place for too long, since the rebels are constantly hunted by those who wish to silence them. For now, they're hiding out in the ruins of an ancient castle, far from any inhabited settlements. There's only about a dozen men here, but Drake told me there are other groups of rebels scattered across the country. It's too dangerous for them to all travel together.

When I ride up, a warning arrow is fired at me, landing just shy of my horse's hooves. I raise my left arm, holding my second and fifth finger up; the signal to the lookout that I'm one of them. Cautiously, I proceed, but no more arrows greet me.

Drake is waiting, and takes hold of my reins as I jump down.

'Well?' No preamble.

'I'm fine, thanks for asking,' I say.

Drake shrugs. 'You're alive, aren't you?'

I reach into my corset and pull out the scroll. 'This was all I could find. If there was anything else, it wasn't in his study.'

He takes it from me and nods. 'Understood. Leave it with me. Get some rest and I'll come and find you soon.'

I watch his retreating back with irritation. Apparently, the rebels aren't big on emotion.

'Come on,' I say to the horse. 'Let's get you some water.'

After I've tended to the horse's needs, I go in search of my forge, which I find exactly where I left it. My clothes, though worn from my time on the road, have never looked more appealing and I change eagerly, not caring who might see. I lost any modesty years ago. The bones of the corset seem almost fused to my own, but I force them apart. Such clothes do not belong to me now. Lady Rayn of Grynn is nothing more than a ghost of a life long gone. I would not wish to be her again, even if I could be.

I'm not sure what will happen next, or when Drake will seek me out. All I know is I'm exhausted and, as night closes in, I decide to get some sleep.

I rest leaning against the wheels of the cart, guarding my forge. However, as tired as I am, the spokes offer none of the warmth of Luc's back, and sleep evades me.

No one comes. I imagine Drake discussing the scroll with the other men, none of whom have spoken much to me since I joined them. Will I be deemed valuable enough to stay? Or have I failed? Am I liability more than an asset?

I blink my doubts away. Being on my own is too horrible to contemplate.

'When did you last eat?'

I look up from my muddy seat to see Drake standing over me, two small jugs of ale in his hands.

'I'm not hungry.' I passed the point of hunger long ago.

'Then drink at least. It takes the edge off.' He pushes a jug into my hand.

To my surprise, he then sits down beside me in the filth and takes a long, deep swig of his own ale.

'So?' I ask, when he offers nothing but silence.

He removes the letter from his pocket and sighs as he rubs his thumb over the broken seal.

'What do you think it is?' I prompt. His silence is unsettling. 'Do you think it's important?'

He takes another long drink. 'Could be something. Could be nothing.'

'If it's nothing, why hide it?'

'Why, indeed.'

He pulls another scroll from his pocket and passes it to me. 'See this?' He points to where Governor Franklin's name is scrawled at the bottom.

I look at the penmanship, noting the disparity in style and flair between this signature and the words on the scroll I found. 'The writing's different.'

Drake finishes his ale before answering. 'Exactly. Whoever sent Norvill that note, it wasn't the Governor.'

'But they used his seal.' I finally take a sip of my ale. It tastes repulsive, but my body is grateful for anything it can get these days.

'It's not evidence of wrongdoing . . . but it's suspicious enough to make me want to investigate further. I have a contact in Eron who can do some digging.'

I look at him hopefully. 'So I found something worth finding?'

Drake nods. 'You did. Not bad for your first try. Graylen would be proud.'

Trying to ignore the pain that blossoms at the mention of my brother, I quickly ask, 'So what's next? Is there anything else I can do?'

'Actually, yes.' Drake looks longingly at my ale. 'But it's something a bit more . . . dangerous than before.'

His tone of voice suggests it's actually a lot more dangerous than before. In fact, he sounds distinctly reluctant to even describe it.

'What is it?'

'The Emperor has started targeting blacksmiths. Capturing them, killing them. We're not sure why, but you can be certain he has his reasons.'

And I can be certain those reasons aren't going to be good for me.

'A General well known for his loyalty to the Emperor has been spotted not five miles from here, and we don't think he's marching towards battlelines. He seems to be rounding up smiths.'

It doesn't take a genius to see where this is going.

'You want to let them capture me?'

Drake nods. 'Exactly. You're in a unique position to find out what we need to know.' He licks his lips and nods at my ale. 'You going to finish that?'

I hadn't been planning on it, but then I hadn't been planning on becoming a prisoner of war either. I down it in one go.

Drake looks at the ground. 'You don't have to do it. We don't know their intentions and I can't guarantee you won't be killed on sight.'

Sighing, I lean my head back against the wheel. 'We're at war. Every day we wake up with no guarantee we'll make it to sunset.'

It's not like I have anything left to lose. My family are dead. Luc is dead. Every day I wake up with a dread in my stomach that cannot be eased, even by all the ale in the world.

In the end, it's not even a choice.

'What's the plan?'

RAYN

I'm halfway through making a sword when the soldiers arrive.

I've been stationed in this village for the past two weeks, since the rebels found an unmanned forge for me to claim. I brought a few tools with me, but whoever owned the forge had left it in a hurry, and most of what I needed was already here.

The villagers have accepted me as a displaced blacksmith looking for trade and asked few questions. It's been wonderful to work a proper stone forge again, one of the young village boys pumping the bellows for me with an enthusiasm that Luc never had. If it wasn't for the haunted air about the village, the emptiness left by the men who went to fight and haven't returned, I could almost pretend that everything was normal.

But of course, nothing is. And every day I've waited to hear the approach of horses, always on edge. When they finally find me, it's almost a relief.

They're spotted approaching by a lookout who sounds the alarm, and the villagers scatter back to their homes, fearful of being killed . . . or worse.

'Run home,' I tell the boy at the bellows, whose name I've deliberately not learned. I cannot get attached again. 'Don't come out until the soldiers have gone.'

He does as he's told, his little face etched with fear.

And then I wait, hammering the sword as if nothing in the world is wrong.

'You, blacksmith!' The words are shouted at me and I turn to see who spoke them.

Four men are riding towards me. Four soldiers. Enemy soldiers. I lift the blunt blade I'm working on and raise it so they can see I'm not entirely unarmed.

I squint in the sun and raise my arm to shield my eyes. 'What can I do for you?' Acting like I'm not expecting them. Like I'm an ordinary blacksmith happy to take passing trade. Like I'm not wondering if I'm about to die.

'You can come with us.' The man who speaks has a cruel glint in his eye.

I laugh humourlessly. 'I don't think so.'

'Emperor's orders.'

Every part of me bristles. 'He's not my Emperor. This isn't his country.'

'Not yet. But either way, you're coming with us.'

'Touch me, and I'll kill you,' I warn them, and I'm serious. I can't make this too easy for them.

The man who's been talking to me clearly doesn't rate the threat and dismounts. 'I love it when they're feisty, don't you?' he asks his companions, and they nod and jeer.

I stoop to grab a poker with my free hand and stand with weapons raised, but they don't seem the least bit concerned.

The man's almost laughing as he brings his blade down on to mine, but he's not expecting the force with which I meet it. In his second's hesitation, I use the poker to trap his sword and spin it out from his grip, flinging it to the floor.

He stares, disbelief quickly turning to humiliated rage. He throws himself at me, knocking me backwards, and then his friends join him and together they wrench the weapons from my hands. I can smell their desire for pain, and wonder if this is it, if this is when I die.

'Enough!' A commanding voice cuts through the mayhem and the men release their hold on me, making way for their superior to approach. I straighten myself, lifting my chin defiantly.

The Commander is tall, with hair that looks almost as untameable as mine. He has a scar which looks to be from an old burn on his left check, but it is his startling blue eyes that dominate his light-brown face, drawing all attention to them. And he's surprisingly young for someone of such a high rank; he barely looks older than me.

'*You're* the blacksmith?' he says with surprise. 'A woman?'

'You soldiers never cease to amaze me with your talent for observation.'

'I didn't think women were skilled enough for such a trade,' he says.

'And I didn't think idiots were allowed to become commanders, but here we are.'

To my surprise, he smiles. Not cruelly, but a genuine smile as if my insult amused him.

'I need you to accompany us, Mistress,' he says.

'I would,' I reply, 'but I don't want to.'

His smile fades. 'It's not a request.'

'What could you possibly want with a mere woman, lacking in skill?'

The Commander steps towards me now, only stopping when his face is inches from mine. 'What do you know of a blade of blood?'

It's as if he's stuck a knife into my chest, and part of me forgets how to breathe, even while another part of me is saying, 'Nothing. Never heard of it.'

'No?' He raises an eyebrow, suggesting he doesn't entirely believe me.

'No.' I cannot be more emphatic.

The Commander is trying to read my expression; I can practically feel him attempting to prise my mind open with his stare. I give him nothing.

'No matter,' he says after a while. 'We can discuss it more when we reach the camp.'

'Don't you wanna kill her?' The other soldier sounds disappointed. 'If she don't know nothing?'

The Commander doesn't take his eyes off me. 'She may be of use yet,' he answers, before adding, 'and it would be a shame to waste such a sharp tongue.'

He signals for one of his men to put me in iron cuffs and this time I don't fight. So that's why they've been capturing blacksmiths, because of a 'blade of blood'. I will have to tread carefully. Because I lied to the Commander. I do know of a blade of blood.

I made one.

*

We ride hard for the rest of the day, heading north-east. I try to pay close attention to our path, so that when I escape – *if* I escape – I can find my way back to the rebels. Interestingly, it wasn't only me the Commander took from the forge; he gathered most of the tools too. I didn't ask why. I have a feeling I'll find out soon enough.

I wasn't trusted with my own horse and am forced to

ride with the Commander, his arms pressed tightly into mine as he reaches around me for the reins. He smells of sweat and war.

As the light begins to fade, we still haven't reached their camp, and he soon signals to his men to stop.

'We'll rest there tonight,' he says, gesturing to the woodland running parallel to the road. 'Fetch some wood for a fire.'

While his men set to work, the Commander dismounts before helping me down, never releasing his grip on my arm.

'Don't even think about trying to run,' he warns, drawing his sword and holding it to my neck.

I give him my most scathing look. 'You're going to run me through with that sorry excuse for a sword? It's half blunt. At least let me sharpen it for you first.'

He withdraws the blade from my skin, and if I didn't know better, I'd say he was embarrassed. 'You'll have to forgive our less than perfect weaponry. We've had some trouble with blacksmiths lately.'

'Can't find any good ones?'

'Finding them isn't the issue,' he says. 'It's that we have to keep killing them when they fail to prove useful.'

If he hopes to scare me, he's mistaken. I've lived with the threat of death for too long to care now.

'Only a poor soldier blames someone else for the state of his blade,' I say as he guides me towards a clearing. 'You should take better care of yours. One day, your life may depend on it.'

'Yeah, well, I've been busy lately,' he says and though his voice is light, he can't entirely disguise the weariness beneath it. 'Now, are you going to stay put or do you plan on doing something stupid?'

'I haven't decided yet,' I say as I sit down on a tree stump. It isn't true, of course. I have no intention of running. But I don't want him to relax. Let him have a sleepless night wondering what I might do.

The men prepare a meal, and apparently it doesn't matter which side you're fighting on, all food on the road is foul. Still, I force down the tasteless slop I'm given. It barely quietens my angry stomach, but at least I am fed. The Commander offers me a sip from his flask and, though I have no idea what liquor it is, it's strong enough to burn through me, bringing warmth and relief.

'The ground is too wet to sleep on,' the Commander says, crouching beside me. 'Here, use this.'

He takes off his travelling cloak and lays it on the damp earth.

I look at him with suspicion. 'What about you?'

'I'll manage.'

'We could share the cloak if we sit and lean against each other,' I say, wondering instantly why I suggested such a thing.

He raises his eyebrows in surprise. 'Us?'

'I'm just being practical,' I add quickly. 'Last thing I need is for you to be sleep deprived and grumpy tomorrow.'

A smile tugs at his mouth. 'Fine. But if you want me to turn my back on you, I'm going to need some assurances.'

He gestures for my hands and begins to undo one of the iron cuffs. Then he attaches it to his own wrist.

'Commander,' I say, unable to hold back the tease rising. 'We hardly know each other.'

This time his smile spreads wide. 'Don't get excited, Smithy. It's simply so I don't wake up with my back in the dirt and you long gone.'

'Smithy?' I glare at him. 'I'm a person, not a building. Smith will do just fine, or you could ask for my actual name.'

Now the smile reaches his eyes. 'No, Smithy suits you.'

What he means is, it annoys me. So I won't give him the satisfaction. What does it matter what he calls me?

We sit and press our backs together, the ground soft beneath us. The Commander's whole body is tense, ready to move at a moment's notice. I'm not sure if that's because I'm there, or if that's how he always is. Braced for danger, day or night.

The rain starts soon after we settle, though the trees offer protection from the worst of it. The rhythm of the falling drops is just lulling me to sleep when the Commander speaks. It is barely a whisper, but I hear it all the same.

'Does nothing frighten you, Smithy?'

I remember confessing my fear to the night a time not that long ago. But then it was Luc at my back. The Commander is my enemy. He'll get no honesty from me.

'Just your men's snoring.'

His body shakes with his chuckle. 'Wait till you hear mine,' he says.

But I never find out whether he's telling the truth, because I'm asleep long before he is.

*

We're on the road at first light. As before, I'm riding in front of the Commander, my wrists bound again. It's far from the most comfortable journey I've ever had and the further we go, the harder I'm finding it to track our direction. Making my way back to the rebels won't be easy, but I'll worry about that if I'm ever in a position to escape.

By late afternoon, we finally reach their camp, nestled in a sheltered valley.

'Take her directly to Tygh,' the Commander orders his men as we dismount. 'I'll be along shortly.'

The two soldiers who assume responsibility for me insist on shackling my feet in addition to my hands, as if I'm somehow capable of fleeing and outrunning their horses. I'm escorted to a large tent bearing the Emperor's insignia, where I assume the men of importance reside in comfort. Gods forbid they endure the same conditions as the men whose lives they hold in their hands.

A handsome but battle-worn man awaits me inside the tent. He's perfectly groomed, his expensively tailored clothes distinctly impractical for the road; I get the impression it's been a long time since he actually fought for his country. Perhaps he's a diplomat, but the nasty glint in his eyes suggests diplomacy is of little interest to him.

'Ah, the blacksmith. You're here at last.' He dismisses my guards with a sharp nod, then gestures for me to take a seat.

'I'd rather stand, if it's all the same to you.'

'Sit. Down.'

His voice is a challenge and I am tempted to defy him, but manage to tame my tongue and my temper long enough to do as I'm told.

'There,' he says, his sourness instantly replaced with an unsettling sweetness. 'That wasn't so hard, was it?'

'Who are you?' I ask.

'My name is General Tygh.'

'General?' I raise an eyebrow. 'Aren't you a little well dressed for a soldier?'

'A sharp eye,' he acknowledges with an appreciative smile. 'My orders come directly from the Emperor himself, and such a position affords certain luxuries.'

'I'm sure your men are very understanding while they starve and freeze to death.'

'My men understand the chain of command and the importance of respect. Something you clearly do not.' There is such bite to his voice, it makes me flinch inwardly.

He strides over to sit opposite me, rather too close, and leans in. 'You're strong, I can see that.'

I hold his gaze, though his breath is warm on my face. 'I've spent my whole life working with iron. It's taught me a thing or two.'

He smiles and reaches out to touch my cheek. 'Then you know even iron can be bent to another's will. All you need to do is apply sufficient heat.'

His words are carefully chosen; the threat obvious.

Despite it, I raise my bound hands to push his from my face. 'What do you want?' I won't give him the satisfaction of knowing he's scared me.

For a moment, his anger burns so brightly I think he's going to hit me, but then someone walks into the tent, and Tygh moves quickly away, dusting his trousers down casually.

'Ah, Commander, there you are.'

The man who captured me is watching us closely, frowning uncomfortably at the scene before him.

'Have you two been properly introduced?' Tygh asks, as if it's normal to be exchanging pleasantries at a time like this. 'Commander Stone, this is . . .'

And he looks at me expectantly.

'The blacksmith,' I finish.

Tygh glares at me and something in his gaze warns me not to push it. Eventually, I give in. 'Rayn. My name is Rayn.'

'And do you know why you're here?' Tygh asks, leaning back in such a relaxed fashion that we might simply be discussing the weather.

'Because you need some forging done, and I'm the best there is?' Oh, me and my smart mouth. I gesture to the Commander. 'He said something about a blade of blood.'

Tygh presses the tips of his fingers together. 'Ah, that is it precisely. Tell me, do you know of anyone who has ever made one?'

I shake my head. 'No.' The lie hangs effortlessly in the air.

I can feel Commander Stone's eyes boring into me. I refuse to meet his gaze.

Tygh nods, mulling my answer over. 'All right, let's try this. Have *you* ever made one?'

It's as if he's reached his hand down my throat and tied knots in every organ I possess. But I simply shrug. 'No.'

'I thought you were the best,' Stone says, one eyebrow raised.

'I am,' I snap back.

'Well, here's the thing,' Tygh says, leaning towards me once more. 'The Emperor is looking for this "blade of blood" and has sent me to find it. I've captured and tortured a great many blacksmiths in my search, and they all proved useless. The Emperor grows impatient.'

Now I lean towards him. 'Not my problem.'

Our faces are practically touching, and I can smell the

rage on his breath. 'If you think I won't kill you because you're a woman, you're sadly mistaken.'

'And if you think I won't fight because I am a woman, then you're the one who's mistaken.'

'Could you make one?' The Commander's voice interrupts our stand-off and we both turn to look at him.

'What's that, Stone?' Tygh asks, resuming his charm again.

'The Emperor wants a sword and we can't find it. So let's make one instead. Get her to make what the Emperor needs. And Gods know we're in need of a blacksmith anyway – she can do some other repairs while she's here. That keeps everyone happy.' He looks at me. 'If you think you can do it?' The challenge in his voice is clear.

'It's possible,' I say, after a while. 'I have heard rumours of how it's done.'

Tygh gets to his feet, weighing up his options. 'All right,' he says in the end. 'Do it.'

'And if I refuse?'

'Remember what I said earlier about bending iron to your will? It would be a shame if any harm were to befall the peaceful settlement we found you in. So unprotected, with so many children. Wouldn't it?'

My fists clench in rage. 'You bastard.'

'It's been said before,' Tygh says with a satisfied grin, before he clicks his fingers and the guards return to drag me to work.

ELENA

For two women who spend their lives delivering babies, you would think we'd be more prepared for the disruption one would bring to our lives, but nothing could be further from the truth.

After wrapping the mercenary's body in a blanket and carrying it to the river in the dead of night, weighting it down so it wouldn't reappear, Aliénor and I returned home in a state of shock. Neither of us could sleep, and so we sat up, drinking warm milk with lavender to calm our nerves. With no wet nurse at our disposal, Aliénor fed the baby by dipping milk into a clean rag for him to suck. Fortunately, he is a quiet, sleepy thing.

We'd debated long and hard about what we were to do. Neither of us could be sure that what the mercenary had said was true, and certainly none of the rumours we've heard mentioned anything about a stolen baby. But then, perhaps they wouldn't, as it was our side doing the stealing.

'There's only one thing we can do,' Aliénor had decided as the dawn began to rise. 'We'll keep him with us. We have a responsibility to keep him safe, but we also have a duty to this town. Gallivanting across a war-torn country with a baby will only get us all killed.'

'People will ask questions,' I'd said, fear poisoning me with uncertainty.

'People always do.' Aliénor had frowned. 'We'll say exactly what I said when I took you in – that his mother died and we took pity.'

But as the days pass, I feel no more comforted than I did that first night when my darkest thoughts consumed my mind. I see the man's body, remember the urgency in his voice, and wonder whether we can really keep the baby safe here.

I think Aliénor fears it too. Whenever there's a knock at the door, she jumps, momentary alarm in her eyes.

It's a blessing that the baby is very quiet. Aliénor has mused that perhaps the trauma of being snatched away from his mother and carried across two countries by a stranger has dulled his senses. Either that, or he might be mute. Whatever his story, Aliénor seems to have become quite fond of the little boy, which surprises me. It's not like her to get attached.

Still, neither of us have named him, perhaps because we both understand by doing so we really would be forming a bond. I think maybe we're both still in denial.

'He can be my apprentice,' I say to Aliénor one morning while we work on remedies together. 'When he's older.'

Aliénor chuckles, glancing over at the sleeping bundle. 'The women would love that. Mind you, bet he'd be a darn sight more biddable than you ever were.'

I gasp with mock indignation. 'I was never anything but perfect.'

To my surprise, Aliénor brushes a soft kiss on my cheek. 'True enough. I'd have wished for no other.'

The tender moment is interrupted by an urgent knock on the door. Aliénor and I exchange a worried glance, and my pulse starts to race.

'Who is it?' Aliénor calls.

'Claris.'

Aliénor frowns, but hurries to the door. 'Is it the twins? Is something wrong?'

I join Aliénor and am concerned to see Claris looking pale and drawn . . . and afraid.

'A messenger just arrived from the next town. Said soldiers are on their way. That they . . .' Her voice cracks, her eyes fill with tears. 'That they are killing children. Babies.'

Aliénor and I look at each other, a sense of foreboding settling upon us.

'Get to the temple,' Aliénor says to Claris. 'Hurry, and spread the word. You'll be safe there.'

Once Claris is gone, Aliénor shuts the door. For a moment she is still, I can almost hear her mind searching for every possible option. I do as I always do. Wait for her guidance.

'Pass me my shawl.'

I do as I'm told, and then reach for my own.

'No,' she says, so firmly it makes me jump. 'You need to stay here. I'll go and see what's happening.'

'I'm coming with you.' I shake my head in confusion. Where she goes, I go. It's always been that way.

'Not this time. I will get the women to the temple with their little ones. They'll be safe there. The Naperones are not monsters.' But the look on her face tells me she isn't certain of that. 'You must hide, do you hear me?' she goes on. 'Take that boy and hide until the danger has passed. You are the closest thing that child has to a mother now. Your only job is to protect him, as best you can.'

'I can't hide here while you go to help. Please, Aliénor.'

I'm begging, not because I really want to go, but because I'm afraid she won't come back. 'I can be brave too.'

Her eyes are full of pity as she looks at me. 'Don't mistake recklessness for bravery. Now wait here, look after the boy and let me go and help those who need it.'

'Why don't you stay with him and let me go? It would be cowardly of me to stay here while you face the soldiers.'

She touches my cheek with such tenderness it hurts. 'Oh, my dear. There is no cowardice in wanting to survive. Sometimes it takes more strength to live and fight another day.'

'But what if something happens to you?'

'Then I've lived a good, long life. And you were the best part.' She presses a firm kiss to my forehead, filled with so much love I could weep. 'My dearest girl. Keep making me proud.' And then she rushes out into the street, as if it was simply another day's work.

For a moment, I stare at the door. Then I run to her room and pull up the loose floorboards that hide a small storage space. I hurry to fetch the baby from my room, where he sleeps, and gather him tightly to me. With some difficulty, I scramble into the cramped space, and after settling the baby beside me I pull the floorboards back into place, the dark hole becoming instantly suffocating.

And then we wait.

Aliénor said to stay here until the danger has passed. But how will I know, stowed away in this hole? *Because she will find you*, I remind myself. She'll return when it's safe and everything will go back to how it was. *But what if she doesn't?* The thought creeps in and takes root.

The fear that's been building inside me since the mercenary shattered our quiet peace intensifies. My whole world up to this point has been made safe by Aliénor. Even when the mercenary lay dying on our floor, I trusted Aliénor would know what to do. In the birthing room, it is she who's in charge. I don't know how to do this without her. Any of it.

Please come back.

I wait. The baby sleeps. Time passes, fast or slow, I don't know.

And then I hear the screams. The thundering of hooves. The soldiers have arrived.

Above us, the door is kicked open, and I'm frozen with fear as heavy footsteps thud over our heads. Soldiers are in the house. Pots clatter as they're thrown to the floor, glass smashes, bowls break. The sound of my world shattering.

Please don't cry, I silently plead with the baby. *Please.*

'There's no one here,' a harsh voice says eventually. 'Come on.' And the men leave my home, though the sharp cold air that invades our hiding place tells me they didn't bother to shut the door.

I can't breathe, terrified they'll realise their mistake and return. But they don't. Instead, the screams outside build, layer upon layer, until it's the only sound in the world. I know this sound. Have heard it before, though usually as a solitary voice. The sound of a grieving mother.

I reach for the boy's little hand and hold tight. Aliénor's words finally start to sink in. *I have to protect him.*

It feels a lifetime before the noise dies away. My tears have fallen silently, staining my face, and I'm shaking in a way I didn't know was possible, as if my very bones have failed to withstand the trauma. But if I don't want to die in this hole beneath the floor, then I'm going to have to emerge eventually. And I have to find Aliénor.

Mercifully, the baby has slept through it all, blissfully unaware of the danger. Leaving him swaddled in his blanket, I slowly raise a floorboard and peer into the room above. There is no sign of anyone, so I climb out, carefully replacing the floorboards to try to keep the boy as safe as possible, and then tiptoe towards the open door.

Cautiously, I look out, but the narrow lane beyond our home is deserted. There is no movement, and more than that, in fact, there's no *noise*, like the town itself is holding its breath, waiting for danger to pass. I clutch hope close to my chest as I walk cautiously towards the temple, praying all is not lost just yet, that I will find Aliénor there and all will be well.

And then I see them.

The square outside the temple is littered with bodies. Women and children, their blood still running over the cobbles. I walk past them all, heading into the building, sick with fear for what I'll find there.

For once, Aliénor was wrong. The Naperones *are* monsters. They entered a sacred temple and murdered both babies and anyone who shielded them. My eyes search for Aliénor, falling on woman after woman who lost her life trying to save her child. My feet slip in blood as I hunt desperately for my mentor. My mother.

And then I see her. Aliénor died defending five infants, her body spread out to protect them, even in death.

My legs give way, and I reach for something to steady myself, sobs choking me as I clamp my hand over my mouth to muffle the rising scream.

I have to get out of here. The need for air is overwhelming, but being outside the temple brings no relief. There is horror everywhere I look.

For a moment, I am frozen, unable to think let alone move. They're all dead. Aliénor's dead. Slaughtered. What do I do? *What do I do?*

Still in shock, I stumble back towards our house.

I hear the baby's cries as soon as I open the door, and hurry to retrieve him from beneath the floor, cradling him close to my chest. The ragged sobs that consume his whole body tear into me, opening my own wounds fresh with grief. We are two lost souls, bound together by tragedy.

'It's OK,' I whisper against his soft, hot head. 'I'm here, I'm here.' Slowly, my voice calms him. I realise it's been hours since he's eaten, so I fetch some milk and while he feeds, I think.

We can't stay here. There's nothing left to stay for. And though nowhere feels safe now, anywhere is better than this.

'We're going to be all right,' I say to the boy, who's sleepily sucking on the milky rag. 'I promise, I'll keep you safe.'

Once he's asleep again, I start packing. I'll have to travel light, so only take essentials, reserving most of the space for as many of Aliénor's supplies as I can. Things that will be hard to replace or replicate. I'll need to earn a living if we're to survive the journey.

There's only one place I can think of to go: Aliénor's sister's home. She lives in the north, and it won't be easy getting there, but she's the closest thing I have left to family. If Anaïs won't take us in, then I don't know what I'll do. But that's a problem for another day.

When I can carry no more, I lift the boy to my chest and fasten him in place with a long strip of cloth. Then I wrap my travelling cloak around us both, hoping to hide him from unwanted attention. And casting a lingering look round my home, I walk out the door for the last time.

Grief is a heavy burden on my heart. It cannot be shaken, cannot be lost, but right now I cannot afford to think about it.

As I leave the town I've lived in my whole life, I tell myself I'm running towards something. But really, I'm just running.

MARZAL

The sun has graced us once more with its presence today, and I intend to make use of it. I want my introduction to Zylin, the handsome young advisor to my father. I've observed that on a pleasant day both he and the Empress will likely be outside soaking up the warmth. Timing will be everything to make it appear entirely coincidental that I should happen upon them, rather than meticulously calculated.

I'm almost at the gardens when someone appears before me, blocking my way. Izra. I'd wondered how long it would take for her to seek me out.

'Izra, what a pleasure to see you,' I say.

'I'm sure,' she says, her voice a nasal drone. 'I think it's time we had a little chat, don't you?'

I bow my head obediently and follow her silently to her chambers. My mind is racing, trying to figure out quite what the purpose of this talk will be. I strongly suspect I'm about to be put very firmly in my place.

When we reach her chambers, I struggle to contain my amazement. If Ama could see this, she'd faint fair away with jealousy and indignation. I thought my mother's old quarters were large, but they are positively dwarfed by Izra's – in both size and luxury. I doubt even the Empress's rooms are better than these.

'Sit down,' Izra says, like I'm nothing more than a servant.

I perch on the edge of a couch draped in furs.

'Tea,' Izra orders, as she elegantly positions herself on the chair opposite me, and immediately Lilah, her handmaiden, hurries over with a tray.

'I hear my daughter has been kind enough to take you under her wing,' Izra says, once the tea is poured and she has waved Lilah away.

Interesting that she phrases it like that. As if Urso is the one doing me a favour, when it very much feels the other way around to me.

'She has,' I say, wanting to maintain the illusion that I'm simply happy to be here, that I'm content at the bottom of the pack, especially if they throw me a few scraps. 'She's been very kind to me.'

Izra continues to glare. Her dislike of me is palpable. 'My daughter was raised well,' she says, as if I were not. 'It has made her altogether too trusting. But I'm no fool, and I see you for what you really are.'

I arrange my features to convey only confusion. 'I don't know what you mean.'

She arches a perfect eyebrow. 'I think you do. And if you imagine I will let you use Urso to claw your way into my favour, then you are sadly mistaken.'

Internally, I breathe a sigh of relief. She knows nothing of my true intentions and only judges me by her own dismal standards.

Feigning the utmost innocence, I say, 'I imagine nothing of the sort. I am simply enjoying getting to know my sister.'

Izra leans forward. 'I don't believe you.' Each word is clipped and cruel. She leans back again, running her hand along the velvet seat. 'You see, I understand the bond between mothers and daughters. I experience it every day. I know how alike Urso and I are – she has inherited my beauty, yes, but it's more than that. A daughter is like a living reincarnation, like looking in a mirror that reflects the past. And if you are anything like your mother, then *you* are a nasty, vindictive bitch.'

How dare, *how dare* she insult my mother like that. I want to pin her down to the couch and pluck every single perfect eyelash from her lids, one by one, wishing for her slow death as I blow each one on the wind.

But I give no outward sign of my rage. Instead, I pretend to be mortified, lips trembling, eyes wide with fright.

'I'm sorry if my mother offended you so,' I say, sounding suitably simpering with my quivering voice. 'But I can assure you, I am nothing like her. I'm just grateful to be here. Urso's friendship is a kindness I don't deserve.'

The look of disdain on Izra's face suggests she believes me entirely.

'Perhaps I have overestimated you,' she says, her nose crinkling as though my existence offends her. 'You are a far simpler, stupider creature than I expected.' She almost sounds disappointed.

Izra rises to her feet now, so that she towers above me, asserting her authority in every physical way. 'However, the fact remains that your mother stole my husband from me. It was because of her I was cast aside, and so for that reason alone I shall make sure you are miserable here – from this day, until the one you leave for a loveless marriage. Your husband can ensure your misery from then on. You see, I do not forget and I do not forgive. So I hope you enjoyed your tea with Urso, for it will not happen again.'

I allow tears to gather in my eyes under her imposing gaze and nod my understanding. I can only assume from her silence that I've been dismissed and so, bobbing a little curtsey, I hurry out of the room, leaving her to her self-satisfaction.

Once I'm clear, I wipe my eyes dry and straighten myself. So she doesn't forgive or forget, does she?

Oh, Izra. Neither do I.

*

After being derailed by Izra, I resume my original plan and head towards the gardens. It's possible I'm already too late and may have to wait for the next clement day, but there's no harm in trying. If nothing else, I can enjoy the sense of freedom only fresh air can bestow on one's soul.

To my relief, I quickly locate the Empress, who is walking with her handmaidens today, and as I have a legitimate reason to approach her, I do so without hesitation.

'All hail the Emperor,' I say as I draw near, and when she sees me, the Empress looks genuinely pleased.

'All hail the Emperor,' she responds. 'It's good to see you, Marzal.'

'And you, Highness. I was hoping we'd cross paths as I have a gift for you.'

She understands my meaning perfectly and addresses her maids. 'Princess Marzal shall accompany me now.'

They nod obediently and drop back to give us privacy.

Once we're alone, I reach into the purse hanging from my wrist and remove the tea leaves I'd prepared, wrapped carefully in muslin.

'Soak this for an hour before you drink it,' I say.

'Hopefully this is all you'll need, but if it's not fruitful, I can make more.' And I place it back into the purse and hand it over to her.

The Empress exhales most gratefully as she takes it from me. 'I cannot thank you enough,' she says. 'My greatest desire is to make the Emperor happy, you understand.'

I understand perfectly that the only happiness she cares about is her own – but that this can only be achieved by satisfying my father's demand for a son.

'Of course.' Wanting to change the subject, I say, 'It's another lovely day.'

The Empress embraces the new topic with an appreciative smile. 'Isn't it? I do enjoy being outside.'

I glance over at her, trying to read her expression. 'Did you spend a lot of time outside with your family?'

'I did. My parents' home had huge gardens where I would run with my brothers and sisters. Nothing as grand as here, of course, but there was an orchard and we'd shake the trees until we couldn't carry any more apples.' She's smiling at the memory, but it slowly fades.

'Maybe you should suggest to my father that he plant an orchard here for you?' When she doesn't answer, I glance at her and add, 'To honour the birth of his son, perhaps.'

The Empress squeezes the bag of leaves I gave her and nods. 'Yes, maybe I should.'

A flash of colour catches the corner of my eye, and I turn to see a man striding briskly through the gardens on a different path.

The Empress notices him too. 'Oh, how fortuitous,' she says. As if it was fortune and not my calculations that had led to this. 'Advisor Zylin,' she calls, catching his attention. He immediately changes course and heads towards us.

'All hail the Emperor,' he says, bowing to the Empress.

I parrot the welcome back and curtsey.

'It's a fine day, is it not?' he says, smiling broadly at us both.

'The finest,' the Empress says. 'Tell me, have you been introduced to the Princess Marzal?'

Now he bows before me. 'It's an honour to meet you.'

I give him my sweetest smile in response.

'Would you ladies care to join me?'

The Empress accepts eagerly, but then says, 'Oh, but I've just remembered I have matters to attend to back at the palace. But please, you two go on without me.'

I hesitate slightly, knowing I should show reluctance, even though in reality I am grateful to her for finding a way to leave us alone.

She sees my concern and adds, 'I shall instruct one of my attendants to chaperone you, of course.'

'Perfect,' Zylin says. 'We wouldn't wish to be accused of any impropriety.' And then he gives me a look that suggests, in fact, that the very opposite is true.

The Empress smiles at me as she takes her leave, and then I find myself alone with Zylin – well, alone apart from the poor woman made to trail at a safe distance behind us as we stroll around the gardens.

We smile at each other tentatively.

'How do you like the palace?' he asks.

'Very well.' It's the only acceptable answer I can give.

'I do believe the air has been a little sweeter since your arrival here.'

I blush accordingly and lower my eyes, acknowledging his flattery.

'It is simply the season's change,' I say, before daring

to glance up at him and adding, 'Or perhaps it is your continued favour with the Emperor that has brightened your view.'

Now it is his turn to bask in the compliment. His pride at his achievements is written all over his handsome face.

'Your accomplishments are the talk of the women's chambers,' I say, daring to venture further. 'We're all most impressed by how high you've risen at such a young age.'

So far, I've had little opportunity in my life to talk to men, but Kala taught me that what they love above all things is themselves, and that to win their hearts, you simply need to stroke their egos. I never asked her how she knew such things, but the lesson was accompanied by such bitter certainty that I didn't dare question her. Zylin's giving me every reason to believe Kala's advice was entirely accurate.

'That is most kind of you to say.' He seems to have swelled in stature. 'I wouldn't have thought you'd have heard of me, Princess, let alone spoken of me.'

I blink slowly, my eyelashes beckoning him to me in as great a seductive invitation as I dare. 'The dashing young advisor? Of course we speak of you.'

Zylin smiles broadly at me. 'Then I consider myself honoured.'

'It is I who am honoured. I shall be the envy of the others for taking a turn with you.' I pause for a moment. 'Though it shall be my secret. Others would use it against me if they knew.'

He glances at me with concern. 'What do you mean?'

I smile to reassure him. 'Just that I know my place, and it's beneath many others.' When he looks confused, I add, 'You men aren't the only ones with a hierarchy.'

'That I can believe,' he says. 'What I struggle to comprehend is why you aren't at the very top.'

I laugh. 'And why is that? I am the newcomer.'

'But you are the most beautiful.'

We are near the palace now and, with an embarrassed smile to acknowledge the compliment, I say, 'I should go. My aunties will be expecting me.'

Turning to face me, he says, 'Of course. I do hope to see you again.'

'I would like that very much.' I hesitate. 'But I fear it would be best if we did not.'

Zylin's forehead creases with concern. 'Because of the other women?'

I look to the ground and nod.

'Then they need not know. Surely there are places within these walls we mightn't be disturbed?'

I raise my eyes to meet his. They are hazel, flecked with gold. 'I do believe the herb garden is rarely frequented by anyone but myself.'

His eager eyes flash with excitement. 'Very well.' He bows his head. 'Until then, I am your servant, Princess.'

I smile warmly at him and, bidding him farewell, start towards the palace. I can sense him watching me as I go, and my smile only grows. Zylin was everything I hoped for and more.

*

Over the next few weeks, Izra launches her campaign against me. The other women quickly fall into step and the atmosphere in the hall has grown frostier towards me. She seeks to punish me, but really she just makes things too easy. By allowing Izra to believe she is succeeding, I can linger invisibly at the bottom of the pack, where my actions will pass easily unnoticed.

Today, as every day, I finish serving the tea and then take the only unoccupied seat, smiling meekly at my companions. No one smiles back, and, seeing this, Izra smirks openly. Urso looks fixedly at her lap. She has seemed uncomfortable since Izra increased hostilities, but she's far from brave enough to defy her mother.

The victims of this morning's gossip are Aelia and Fausta, who sit at the far end of the room with expressions that tell me they can hear everything being said.

'I heard her daughter is so ugly, they're afraid to ever send her back,' Roselle says.

'Can you imagine?' Izra shudders at the very prospect. 'Although recently they've been letting all sorts into the palace.'

I ignore the barb, instead wondering which of my half-sisters they're referring to. I don't know where either of Aelia or Fausta's daughters have been sent to grow up, but I do know Aelia's daughter is seven and Fausta's is only two, so how they can sit here and call either one of them ugly is beyond me. I glance over at the two wives and wonder whether their friendship stemmed from the grief of missing their daughters, an alliance which allows them to separate themselves from these cruel-tongued women and hurt in peace.

'Thank goodness my Urso is the eldest,' Izra's saying. 'She gets the best match in marriage. He's incredibly rich.'

Urso doesn't look as if she shares her mother's enthusiasm. Her ears burn a little too red at the edges. I wonder if she's sent her letter yet. Or had a reply.

'I'm sure Sennan will get an equally eligible match,' Roselle says.

Izra laughs. It sounds too shrill, too high-pitched. 'I doubt the Emperor is likely to bestow such an honour on *her.*'

Roselle's eyes narrow. Interesting how she's happy to draw her claws alongside Izra when others are the targets, but less happy when her illegitimate daughter is on the receiving end. I'm fairly certain Roselle would take a knife to Izra's back and bleed her dry if she could get away with it.

How the palace has changed over the years for these two. At first, there was only Izra, the Imperial Empress, beloved by all. But when she failed to provide a male heir, the Emperor took a mistress, and elevated her to the same status as his wife. How they must have hated each other.

But Roselle failed him too, and so he sought a new wife. The stars warned him a holy union was the only way he would produce a son. The prophecies guided him to my mother and her arrival served to push Izra and Roselle down and, subsequently, together. They loathed each other, yes, but that was nothing compared to their joint hatred of my mother. And once the Emperor had got rid of one wife, it became very easy to do it again, until the rooms began to overflow with wives that could only birth girls and were all doomed to live together for ever.

Roselle clearly needs an outlet for her anger, and her gaze falls upon me. She drops her needle, very deliberately, on to the floor.

'Oh, Marzal, be a dear and pick that up for me, would you?' Her voice is taunting, mocking.

There's a collective snigger from the other women, but I smile and bend down to pick it up.

'Here you are, Aunty,' I say, handing it to her.

Once I'm seated, she drops it again.

'Marzal?'

Oh good. A new game.

I retrieve it for her and pass it back.

Izra decides any bullying should be led by her, and this time it is she who drops her needle.

'How clumsy of me! Marzal, fetch.'

Allowing myself to look a little flustered, so they believe I'm upset, I dutifully reach for the needle once more. But this time, while I'm stooped down, Izra kicks me hard, knocking me to the floor.

Laughter erupts from the women, though the loudest cackles certainly come from Izra and Roselle, once again bonded by their hostility towards me.

This is what Izra wanted; me on all fours like a dog at her feet. I know exactly what she's doing. How weak people need to make others look small if they are to appear powerful. The Mother Superior was just like that, always pulling others down to make herself feel better. It was Sister Kala who opened my eyes to what was really happening and, in doing so, gave me an armour that was impenetrable to taunting.

How I wish Kala was with me now. I can just imagine what she would make of these women and their backstabbing. She would despise them. She showed me the importance of solidarity between women in a world where men want to control us. Though she only came to live at the convent a few years ago, she quickly became my closest friend there, and taught me everything I know.

I miss her terribly.

But I'm alone here, and so must endure this torture. I imagine sticking the needles I'm forced to retrieve into Izra and Roselle, envisaging how the metal would snag in their skin and draw blood from their tongues, how the points would glide smoothly into the jelly of their eyes. And soon they grow tired of baiting me, moving on to their next target, which happens to be the palace cook. Apparently, his meat is too tough, more than their crumbling teeth can manage.

'It's as if he wants us to starve,' Izra moans.

The veins in my head pulse hard under the strain of not showing any emotion, but my blood is on fire. Izra knows nothing of starvation. I've seen it first-hand. Seen how a body can fold in on itself before it gives up altogether.

We did our best at the convent to help those we could, but there simply wasn't enough to go around. I want to drag Izra by the hair out into the world beyond the palace walls and show her true suffering, I want to scream at her for being so ridiculous, I want to make her hurt the way she's hurt me.

But I do nothing. The rest of the day passes in simpering subservience, allowing Izra and Roselle to make jokes at my expense, while smiling at their cruelty towards others, and showing without question that I know my place.

When the time comes to leave, Izra gets to her feet, placing her embroidery on her chair.

'Bring it to my room,' she says to me, with a look of distaste.

I curtsey and then watch her sweep out of the hall, with Roselle following close behind. But as I bend over to pick up the cloth, someone touches my hand, pushing a small square of paper into it. When I look up, I'm alone in the room. With no one to see what I'm doing, I unfold the note.

Meet me in the library after prayers.

There's only one person who would write this, and I smile to myself.

Urso wants to talk.

MARZAL

Every day as the sun begins its descent from the sky, we all gather at our altars. Some of us go to the temple for a communal offering. Others prefer to pray in solitude. At the convent, we would sit together before the main altar, candles burning, their flames carrying the silent words from our lips to the heavens.

We each have our favourite God. Some direct their prayers to Ganeen, the Goddess of dreams; others prefer the God Jhish, who watches over family and friends. The Mother Superior worshipped Pralu above the others, for it is he who commands rules and law, and who oversees all other Gods. Personally, I've never really had much time for the deities, but whenever I have sent up my prayers, they're always to Sypka, the Goddess of justice. She is the smallest, the youngest, the most overlooked of all the Gods, but in my eyes, she is the fiercest.

All the images of the Gods are overshadowed by the image of the Emperor. It has become written into lore that over half our prayers should be blessings to his name. A man whom most of those living in Vallure will never meet. A man who cares nothing for anyone but himself. Quite how he has managed such a feat escapes me entirely.

I pray alone. Partly because I was never allowed such privacy at the convent, but mainly because I don't actually do any praying. I will not waste my time and energy on such a pointless activity when there's so much to do. Prayer hour is my time to think.

Today, I'm considering why Urso wants to meet me. It's fair to say I do not trust her. She loves her mother, and I certainly wouldn't put it past Izra to use Urso to spy on me. I must be guarded in what I say – but then, I always am.

Brewing tea helps clear my mind and so I prepare some. It is ready just as the bell rings to signal the end of prayers and I pour it carefully into a cup, resting a lace handkerchief over the top to preserve its heat.

And then I walk as fast as the hot liquid in my hands will allow towards the library.

There are two palace libraries. One I have never seen and never will. It is my father's library, and only men are deemed worthy to enter and read the books inside. The second, smaller library is the one I am heading for now. The one where women are permitted. The one where the books have been carefully selected, lest any put ideas in our pretty little heads.

It may be smaller than the men's library, but the selection is still much bigger than the convent's. There we were permitted only a handful of books, chosen specifically to aid our prayers and devotions. The content wasn't of particular interest to me, but even so I read them all from cover to cover, many times over. This library may not be considered as special by my father but, apart from the herb garden, it's my favourite place in the palace.

I don't think the other women have even noticed that our choices here are controlled, for they seldom show much interest in reading, preferring to spend their time stitching and finding ways to passive-aggressively crush each other. If Urso doesn't want anyone to see us talking, she picked the ideal place.

There is a silence in a library that doesn't exist anywhere else. A silence that is full of dust and parchment and knowledge, the collective sound of a thousand books holding their breath, just waiting for the moment they can release their words into the world.

When I push through the door, I take a moment to listen to the hum and embrace the stillness, but my burning fingers remind me I'm here for a reason, and I begin to search the aisles for my sister.

I find her hiding in the furthest corner, her veil covering her face, which I imagine is an attempt at anonymity, though all it does is draw attention to her.

'You got my note,' she says as I approach, her voice hushed but pleased.

Well, I could hardly miss it since she shoved it into my hand. But I simply nod and say with a warm smile, 'Here, I thought you might enjoy some tea.'

Her own smile falters slightly, but she takes it from me, sipping it politely.

'Still find it bitter?'

'A little.'

'You will grow used to it, I promise,' I say, before asking, 'How are you? Are you well?'

She slips her free hand around mine. 'Oh, Marzal, I know my mother doesn't want us to talk, but I just had to let you know.'

'Know what?'

'I took your advice; I wrote to my friend.' Her face flushes red at the mere mention of him. 'He wrote back.'

She pulls a tattered piece of paper from her sleeve, so

creased I can tell she's already devoured every word of it several times over.

When I simply stare at it, she thrusts it towards me. 'Here, read it.'

'Are you sure you want me to? Isn't it personal?'

Urso hesitates. 'I'm ... uncertain what to do next. I need your advice.'

I reach forward to fold her hand around the note. 'You reply, of course. And I know you don't need me to tell you what to say.'

A self-conscious smile pulls at her mouth. 'Do you think I should?'

I shrug, deliberately casual. 'Why not? You're simply corresponding with a friend, are you not?'

'Yes,' she says, her smile broadening. 'A friend.'

'Though be careful,' I say. 'Izra, perhaps, would not understand.'

'I will,' she says, her smile fading a little. 'I should go. If Mother sees me with you . . .'

'It's all right. I understand. It was nice to see you briefly, especially looking so happy.'

'Dear sister,' she says, leaning to kiss my cheek. 'My mother's just doing what she thinks best. Once she gets to know you better, I'm sure she'll change her mind. Fear not, we'll see each other soon.'

She opens the door slowly and hesitantly, making a big show of peering through a small gap before opening it more widely, which yet again only makes her conspicuous. And then she's gone, leaving me alone with the books. I want to stay and browse the shelves, but I know Ama will be waiting and wondering where I am. So I give Urso a minute's head start, and then I return to my room.

Ama is standing there, hands on hips, her face creased with annoyance. 'Where've you been?'

I glide past her. 'Nowhere.'

She follows me. 'Which means you've been somewhere.'

'It *means* I don't want to tell you.'

She sighs. 'Because you've been doing something you shouldn't.'

'*Because* it's none of your business.'

I pick up my stitching and take a seat. The best way to defuse Ama is to ignore her.

'Too many secrets, that's your problem,' she says, giving in and sitting beside me.

I smile to myself. She has no idea.

The knock on the door that comes a moment later is unexpected, and Ama and I look uneasily at each other. I don't get a lot of visitors, and instantly I'm worried Urso's told her mother of our encounter.

'Were you supposed to be somewhere?' Ama asks, with a hint of accusation.

'No.' I place down my embroidery and pinch my cheeks so I look my best, while Ama goes to open the door.

Standing there is one of the last people I expect to see: Special Advisor Rom.

'All hail the Emperor,' I say, rising quickly to my feet and bowing my head in greeting.

'All hail the Emperor.'

'What can I do for you?' My voice is sweet and willing; I'm painfully aware of Ama watching from where she's discreetly withdrawn behind me.

'I have a message for you from the Imperial Empress. She requests your presence in her chambers.'

My surprise is entirely genuine. 'Me?'

'I am to escort you at once.'

My eyes flick briefly back into the room to meet Ama's, full of questions and apprehension, before I follow Rom out into the corridor.

I haven't actually been alone with him since I first arrived at the palace, but feel I know him well from my nights spent watching him. I'm aware of his reluctance to believe prophecies over Generals; I know the secrets he keeps from my father. He is by far the most sensible man in that chamber, though his common sense is mostly overlooked. And yet I can say nothing about it, as I must not risk exposing myself.

'It's an unexpected pleasure to see you,' I say. I hope it's not too forward, but I've been wanting to carve Rom out as an ally since I first arrived. Opportunities to do so have been few and far between, so I must take what I can.

He glances down at me. 'You have settled in well, I trust.'

'Everyone has been most kind.' If he believes that, he'll believe anything.

'I considered your mother a friend, you know.' This is about the last thing I was expecting him to say. 'When she lived here.'

The mention of my mother is a barb to my heart, but I lock away all feelings from his sight. 'You did?' My tone is light, as if the topic is a pleasant one.

Rom nods. 'I did.' He stops walking. 'I would like you to know I consider myself a friend to you too.'

I meet his eyes, before lowering my gaze demurely. 'Thank you,' I say. 'That is a great comfort to me.'

Rom stares at me for a moment longer before he clears his throat and starts walking once more. Apparently, that conversation is over but, though it was short, it was pleasingly fruitful. I had imagined it would be harder to gain his attention, but his affection for my mother has made things considerably easier. Perhaps the fact I look so like her has helped.

As our journey continues in silence, I wonder what reason the Empress has to summon me – and to her private chambers at that. I wonder too what Izra will say when she hears. Because she undoubtedly will. You have to take great care if you want to avoid whispers making their way back to Izra, and choosing Rom to escort me is far from discreet.

I don't have long to think as we soon arrive at an ornate door, where Rom stops. Before he knocks, he says, 'You can find your own way back?'

'Yes, thank you.'

He nods in satisfaction. 'Then I shall bid you farewell, Princess Marzal. For now.'

'I look forward to the next time.'

Once again, his mouth fails to form the smile he's trying for, but this time there is a gleam in his eyes. I've pleased him.

There's no time to dwell on this achievement though, because he is already knocking on the door, and a moment later I'm ushered in by one of the Empress's handmaidens.

The world of men is shut firmly behind us as I'm escorted through a beautiful, vast living area, and into a boudoir fit for the wife of the great Emperor. Luxurious it may be, but it is dark too, silk curtains draped everywhere to offer privacy. I weave between them until I finally reach the centre of the maze; a large bed swathed in velvets and furs, in which the Empress lies, propped up by a wall of pillows. Turns out I was wrong to believe Izra had the finest rooms.

When the Empress sees me, she reaches out. 'Marzal, you're here at last.'

I hurry towards her and take her hands into my own. 'Are you unwell, Highness?'

The darkness had hidden it, but as my eyes adjust to the dim light I see what I'd failed to notice before. The smile on her face.

'No, quite the contrary.'

And now I understand why I'm here. 'You're with child?'

The Empress nods, biting her lip as if she can't believe her luck. 'And it's all thanks to you. That's why I wanted to tell you myself.'

'I'm honoured.'

Her smile fades a little. 'I have another favour to ask of you, if I may.'

'Anything.'

'The Emperor has insisted I remain here in isolation until our son is born, for his safety. I was wondering whether you would be willing to keep me company from time to time?'

I struggle to hide my shock. 'You're to be bed-bound for the whole pregnancy?'

She nods, clearly unhappy.

My father is such a bastard. He has no concern for how such confinement will affect his wife, how lonely it will make her, how miserable she will be without her daily walks in the garden, how ill she will become without the fresh air.

'It would be a pleasure to visit you. I'd far rather embroider here than have to endure Izra's taunts.'

The Empress smiles. 'Then my prison shall become your sanctuary as often as you wish.'

'Thank you. I shall bring tea.'

'Do you have a blend that will help my baby grow strong?'

'That's the best thing about tea,' I say. 'There's a blend for almost anything.'

'Then I shall drink it gratefully.' The Empress pauses. 'I know Izra makes life difficult for you sometimes, and my absence will only embolden her. I want you to know that my guards can provide any protection you need. Those loyal to me are loyal to you. You simply have to ask.'

She has no idea what such an offer means to me.

MARZAL

The rain falls as though the heavens themselves are weeping for the suffering below. No one has ventured out into the gardens today for fear of being washed away. No one, that is, apart from me.

A herb garden never smells more alive than when it rains, the earthy scent of soil never richer. The way the rain hits the leaves mesmerises me. Sometimes the drops hit explosively, other times they glide down with grace, while others cling stubbornly before inevitably dripping to the ground. Traits which remind me of the women in the court.

I'm picking lilyturf, as the roots – which I require for my teas – are easier to remove when the ground is soaked. They will store well once dried and I'll put them aside for the Empress. They help stimulate milk production and I want to be prepared for any needs she might have.

'My Lady?'

The sound of Zylin's voice makes me jump. I hadn't expected to have any company today.

'Advisor Zylin,' I say, getting to my feet. 'Whatever are you doing out here on a day like this?'

'I was about to ask you the very same thing.'

I gesture to my basket. 'I like to make my own teas. And some things just taste better when picked in the rain.'

He smiles, and I wonder what he's doing here. We have

met several times since our first introduction, enjoying pleasant conversations, but always by prior arrangement. Did he come here hoping to find me unexpectedly?

'Ah,' he says. 'And are you well?'

'All the better for seeing you,' I reply with a smile. 'Though I am soaked to the skin. Will you walk with me back to the palace?'

'I would be honoured, but aren't you concerned we might be seen?'

I gesture to the quiet gardens. 'I don't believe there's anyone here to see.'

He fails to hide his enthusiasm and becomes my willing escort as we head in the direction of the palace. Despite the weather, we do not walk fast.

I'm conscious that my dress is sticking to me, the outline of my figure emphasised, my breasts almost visible through the sheer material. I see Zylin steal a glance before looking away, his neck flushed.

We reach a pergola, covered in honeysuckle, that overlooks the lake now mottled by thousands of raindrops, and I stop walking to gaze at the view.

'It's beautiful, isn't it?'

'Very,' he says, standing close beside me. I know he's not talking about the lake.

A tear slides down my cheek, and I look away from him.

'What is it?' he asks, his voice thick with concern. 'What's wrong?'

'It's just this . . .' I say, gesturing around me. 'This moment right now, it makes me wish . . .'

When I trail off, he says, 'What? What do you wish?' His voice has dropped to a whisper now, our bodies moving slightly closer together.

I look up at him. His adoration is undisguised. 'That I didn't have to leave one day to marry a stranger. That I could stay here for ever. Make my own choices . . .'

His face glows with hope. Cautiously, he raises his hand and softly brushes my tear away. Our faces are close now, our lips practically brushing, but I pull back. 'We mustn't,' I say. 'If anyone was to see . . . It's dangerous. Think what could happen.'

'For a kiss from you, I'd endure any punishment they might give me. Even death,' he says fervently.

My eyes widen. 'Please, don't say such a thing.'

'No, I'm sorry.' He's quick to comfort me. 'It's just that I would do anything for you, you must know that.'

I stare into his rich-brown eyes and move close to him again, my breasts grazing his chest. My pulse quickens. Then once again, I step back. 'Would you . . .' I start, before trailing off.

'What?' Zylin is only too eager to please.

'Would you really do anything for me?'

'Yes,' he says earnestly, his eyes intent on mine.

'Well,' I say, 'I do have something I need help with. Something I can only entrust to the most loyal friend.'

'There is no more devoted servant to you than I,' Zylin says. 'Simply ask, and I will do anything for you.'

I take his hand in mine. 'Truly? I would require absolute discretion; a guarantee of secrecy.'

'I would take your secrets to the grave.'

'Then, I wonder, would you help deliver a letter for me?'

The simplicity of the task takes him by surprise. 'A letter?'

'Yes. Nothing more. But I have to trust it would be delivered safely, you understand. It's very important to me.'

'Consider it done,' he says. 'On my honour.'

'Thank you. I'm in your debt.'

I can see he's thinking about trying to kiss me again, and a shiver runs down my spine.

But perhaps he remembers where we are, for the moment passes. 'We should get you inside, before you catch a chill,' he says, and I don't argue, allowing him to escort me back to the palace.

'I should go in alone,' I say when we reach the doors.

'Of course,' he says. 'I'll see you soon?'

'Tomorrow, in the herb garden?'

'I look forward to it.'

As I bid him goodbye, I give him a lingering gaze, and the smile stays on my lips long after the door is shut behind me.

*

Each night it's easier and faster to navigate the tunnel that joins my room to my father's. And each night, I'm more eager than the last, thirsty for every detail I can tuck away for whenever I might need it. Some nights I slide back to my bed with nothing, other nights are a feast of information. After my day with Zylin, I have high hopes, until I reach the grate.

My father isn't there. This is a first. He's always there. I wonder if he's tending to his young wife now that she's carrying his child.

The room isn't empty, however. Rom and Loris are poring over maps and star charts, and their agitation is palpable.

'You're sure?' Rom sounds disbelieving.

'Certain. The prophecy speaks of a woman. It is she who will end his life.'

'You must be mistaken.' Rom shakes his head fiercely, as if the movement will rid his head of such a ludicrous notion.

'There's no mistake. Should we warn him?'

'No!' The word echoes around the room. 'No. He wouldn't believe you, even if you told him. Besides, the threat is far from imminent. We have other things to deal with.'

Loris looks at Rom with concern. 'The leverage?'

Rom shakes his head. 'Still missing. Our contact has men searching, but nothing yet.'

Loris hangs his head with the weariness of one who lives constantly with fear. 'Please tell me you have something good we can report to him. He won't be shitting all day.'

Charming. I should have known better than to think he might be caring for the Empress.

'I heard from General Tygh. It seems he might have a lead with the sword.'

Loris brightens up. 'He has the blade of blood?'

'Not yet. But he gives me his word he soon will have.'

This is clearly music to Loris's ears. 'Then it doesn't matter what the stars say about a woman. If the Emperor possesses the blade, he's safe.' I'm not sure I've ever seen a man so relieved. How he must fear for his life every time he reads for my father.

Rom, as ever, is more pragmatic. 'He doesn't have it yet.' The words are barely audible, but I hear them.

I repeat them to myself later when I lie in bed, processing all I've heard.

He doesn't have it yet.

I think of what I overhead Loris say too.

The prophecy speaks of a woman. It is she who will end his life.

And the thought makes me smile.

RAYN

They force me to work in piss-blistering chains.

It's not easy to bang iron into shape when your wrists are bound together, the skin rubbed raw beneath the rusty metal. But at least I know now why the Commander brought my tools with me.

It was never just about the blade of blood. Like any other battalion, they need a blacksmith to keep them ready for battle. Commander Stone wasn't exaggerating about how desperate they were for repairs. Since General Tygh threw me out of his tent, I haven't had a second to begin work on forging his special sword, as I've had to cope with the deluge of weaponry and armour his men have dumped at my feet.

We left the camp after a couple of weeks and have been on the road for the past few days. The travelling forge they've given me is decent, so though my days are brutally exhausting, at least I'm not battling poor equipment.

I make as many mistakes as can pass unnoticed. I want their blades weak, overheated, fractured. When they fight, I want them to lose.

We stopped close to a river last night and seem to be staying here for a day or so, while the horses rest. I've been working the forge all day. I have no idea where we're going or why. No one tells me anything. I've learned nothing of use to Drake yet, and barely have the energy to think beyond my duties.

Sensing someone's coming, I look up from my anvil. When I see who it is, my heart sinks to my stomach. The soldier – whose name I don't know but who I have christened Weasel based on his features – comes by most days to make me miserable. He's young, but already cruel. I imagine when he was a child he was the kind to pinch other kids when there was no one around to stop him, and stamp on insects just for the hell of it. A cowardly bully. Now he's a bully with a sword, and I've watched him relentlessly persecute other soldiers, those he considers weaker than him, or less important.

Normally, he approaches with a cruel smile and a weak insult, perhaps something referencing the fact that I'm a girl, as if such information would be shockingly new to me or cause me embarrassment. But today I notice a different set to his jaw. He's angry. And I know why.

'How's that new blade working out for you?' I ask as he storms my way.

In a heartbeat, he's grabbed me roughly by the throat and throws me backwards, slamming me into the cart. 'You piss-whore. You think you can mock me and get away with it?'

It was petty, I know, but I simply couldn't bring myself to sharpen his sword last time he brought it to me, tormenting me at the same time, of course. I dulled it instead. Didn't even bother hiding what I was doing, but he was too stupid to notice. After seeing how he likes to throw his weight around, not just with me but with the younger soldiers, I thought he deserved a taste of his own medicine.

'Actually, yes,' I say, my smile visibly infuriating him.

'Because if you hurt me, I can't fix it, can I?'

'You don't need your face for that,' he says, and then his fist crunches into my cheekbone, sending me staggering to the ground.

The pain is hot, instant, and I'm almost grateful for it. It's a reminder that I'm not entirely dead inside.

Weasel's pulling me up by my hair now, his fist raised for a second strike when a voice stops him dead.

'What are you doing?'

Weasel lets go of me, and though I struggle to regain my balance, I manage to stay on my feet.

Commander Stone stands before us, staring at Weasel with a look of pure contempt.

'She blunted my sword,' Weasel pants, his residual anger leaving him breathless.

The Commander turns to me with an expression that hints at exasperation. 'That true?'

With an effort, I draw myself up to my full height, ignoring the pounding in my face. 'Yes.'

He stares at me a long while before he takes Weasel by the shoulder and pulls him slightly away.

'I ordered that the prisoner was not to be harmed. Yet you've defied me.'

'Sir, but you heard her! She—' Weasel looks stricken. He truly is a snivelling wretch.

'I don't care what she did. You obey *me*. Do you understand?' The Commander is speaking softly, reasonably, but even I can hear the threat in his voice. The chain of command is not to be questioned. Ever.

'Yes, sir.' Weasel knows when he's defeated.

'Raise a hand to her again and I'll remove it myself. Now, go.'

Weasel flashes me a venomous glare, but does as he's told. I wonder how long it'll be before I suffer for this humiliation.

I can worry about that another time though. Right now, the Commander is coming back towards me and I brace myself for my punishment.

'You all right, Smithy?'

I'm too surprised to answer as he lightly touches my chin and turns my head for a better look at my cheek. 'Could be worse,' he says. 'It's not broken.'

'What a consolation.'

His eyes narrow, but he says nothing. Instead he grabs one of the filthy rags I have lying around and soaks it in the bucket of cold water next to the forge. Folding it into a pad, he presses it against my skin. The relief is instant.

'Hold that,' he says. 'Don't want your face swelling so much you can't see.'

I don't mention that I already can't see out of that eye. It's just as well Weasel didn't hit the other side. 'You're not going to punish me?'

The Commander picks up the blade I was working on before Weasel interrupted me and inspects it. 'Did you have a reason for dulling Private Bane's sword?'

'I don't like him.'

'No one does,' the Commander is quick to reply. 'But then, I doubt you like any of us. Maybe it's not only Private Bane's weapon you sabotaged?'

And the look he gives me is challenging.

I accept it. 'I'm only here because you kidnapped me, remember? I'm your prisoner, not your guest.' And I hold up my shackled wrists in case he needs an extra reminder.

He has the decency to look guilty, even if only for a

second. But then his expression hardens again. I wonder what's happened in the past few days to erase his smile that was always close to the surface before.

'Where are we even going?' I ask him, wanting to take advantage of that glimmer of guilt.

'To fight,' he says, his jaw clenched.

'I thought you were here to search for blacksmiths?'

He faces me then, and I wonder if he might look amused if he weren't so tired. 'You think I can put up with more than one?' He sighs. 'Our orders have changed. There's a stalemate over at an important settlement on a key route. We've been drafted in to assist.'

At last I understand why he's angry. His men are exhausted and ill-prepared for battle; he knows he's sending many of them to their deaths.

My mind drifts back to the night of the attack on my battalion. Of the eerie silence I met on my return. Of Luc's body slumped in a pile of filth and blood. My anger is quick to rise.

'I won't help you,' I say. 'I won't give any advantage to my enemy.'

He stares at me. 'Us? The enemy?' Apparently, his anger isn't far behind mine. 'Your country started this war. Everything that's happened is on you.'

'That's a lie,' I bite back. 'Your Emperor wants our gold and he'll do whatever it takes to get it.'

'You attacked first! Our villages on the border suffered for *years* as your governor tested our defences, hoping to take advantage while the Emperor was weakened from his campaign in the east. You're lucky we didn't retaliate sooner.'

I have no idea what he's talking about and can feel doubt spreading its roots in my veins.

He sees it too. 'Didn't know that, did you? Your country's not as perfect as you think.'

Growing defensive, I lash out. 'My country's the one being invaded, the one suffering. We're the ones with the losses.'

He looks up at me sharply, eyes blazing with fury and grief. 'You have no idea what I've lost.'

We hold each other's gaze, and I'm surprised to see my anger, my hurt, my confusion reflected back at me.

Eventually he blinks and the moment is gone. 'I'll be checking your work more carefully from now on,' he says, emotionless. 'Make sure it's good. I won't let you, or anyone else, risk the lives of my men.'

He starts to walk away, and I cannot bear for him to have the final word. 'Then you took the wrong blacksmith!' I shout at his retreating back.

Despite my fury, I do make an effort with the quality of my work for the rest of the day. If I get myself killed, I'll be no use to anyone. And I owe my father and Graylen more than that.

Unexpectedly, Commander Stone returns that evening, as the men are eating their supper. I'm still busy working, with several hours ahead of me before I can rest.

'If you want that sword sharpening, it'll have to wait its turn,' I say, glancing briefly up at him.

'Actually, I came to apologise,' he surprises me by saying. 'I shouldn't have taken my anger out on you earlier.'

When I raise my eyes to meet his, I see the faint hint of his smile has returned.

It softens me.

'You were angry?' I shrug. 'Didn't notice any difference, to be honest.'

He gives a slight chuckle. 'Thought you might be hungry,' he says, holding out a piece of bread. It's mouldy but still the most substantial food I've seen in a long while.

'Where did you find this?' I ask, taking it from him and starting to nibble the edges.

'It was no longer good enough for the General,' he says with a wry smile.

'Ah. Well, I'll happily take his rejects.'

'We're setting off again tomorrow,' he says. 'Thought you should know.'

'Thanks.' And I mean it. The warning means I'll be packed up and ready to leave before I sleep tonight, avoiding a frantic panic in the morning.

He looks like he's about to say something else, when a young soldier approaches, saluting the Commander.

'What is it, Private?' he asks.

'Just came to ask if you wanted any more bread, sir.'

I pause in my eating and stare at Commander Stone, whose head tilts slightly in my direction, though he doesn't go as far as to look at me.

'No, thank you, Private.'

'Will there be anything else I can do for you tonight, sir?' the eager-to-please soldier asks.

'No, go and get some rest. I'll join you soon. We have a long day ahead of us tomorrow.'

'Thank you, sir.' And the soldier salutes again before hurrying away.

'This was *your* food?' I ask Commander Stone, once we're alone again.

He sighs. 'You're working harder than any of us. I thought you might need it more than me.'

He's my enemy. I should be happy to take food from his

mouth, even dry, mouldy crusts. Instead, I tear the bread and offer him one half.

'We all need to eat what we can,' I say. 'Can't have you fainting away.'

The Commander takes the bread with both reluctance and gratitude. 'I would have thought you'd be happy to weaken your enemy.'

'Can you imagine having to explain to people I was kidnapped by the soldier who swooned on the battlefield?' I wince. 'I'd never live it down.'

This time he laughs. 'I'll try very hard not to embarrass you then.'

He starts to walk away, but I call after him.

'Leave your sword.'

He frowns. 'What?'

'You need it sharp before you fight.'

He raises an eyebrow. 'Careful, I might start to think you care.'

I fix him with my most exasperated look. 'If you die, then there's no one to stop Weasel or the rest of them hurting me. So, like it or not, I need you around.'

And long after he's gone, as I sharpen the edges of his weapon, I'm still convincing myself that is the only reason I'm helping him.

*

We reach the edge of a large forest two days later, with no stop for rest. The men are exhausted, and so am I. But not far to the east is the settlement where the battle is taking place and there's no time for luxuries such as sleep.

All around me, men frantically prepare themselves for

warfare. Horses are readied and Commander Stone barks orders at the troops, motivating them, rousing them for what lies ahead. General Tygh is notably absent. I wonder if he's afraid, if that's why he allows a man young enough to be his son to lead in his stead. Or does he simply not care what happens to his troops?

Though these men fight for my enemy, the fear of what's about to happen is infectious, and my insides fuse into anxious knots. So much killing, and for what?

Why would the Commander tell me our country started the war? He seemed genuine in his belief, but it couldn't possibly be true. And yet, the nagging tug of my gut suggests Drake hasn't been entirely honest with me ... if he even knows the truth himself. Truth seems an intangible thing these days, caught on the wind, existing in mere snatches depending whose hand it's held in.

Perhaps the Commander senses me watching him, because he turns to look over at me. For a moment, we're connected across the chaos. Not as enemies. Rather, two lost souls who wonder how the hell they ended up here. Tangled in emotions too many to escape.

And then he's gone. The men, whipped up into a frenzy, are unleashed into battle, while I can do nothing but wait and see how many return.

It's eerie to be alone in camp. I can hear the fighting in the near distance – the screaming reaching me like ghostly wails. I busy myself with work, trying to drown out the noise with my own, pounding the iron too hard so that sparks fly.

If only General Tygh had gone with them, instead of holing up in safety back here. I need to search his quarters. It's not enough to know the Emperor wants a blade of blood . . . I need to know *why*. And every instinct tells me if there are answers to be found here, they'll be in that tent.

The day drags by, and the fear that infected me earlier festers. If they all die, what happens then? Would Tygh take me with him, or kill me without a second thought? And what if they do survive? How long am I fated to stay here?

As the afternoon draws to a close, the men return. Spattered with blood, they look haunted from the horrors they've just witnessed and, in that moment, I don't see soldiers. I see boys, young men, their innocence stripped from them. I wonder how different they really are from the soldiers returning on the other side.

My thoughts are disturbed by nearby shouting. Four men are carrying a wounded soldier whose screams pierce my skin and burrow into my soul. He's trailing blood where the lower part of his left leg once was.

Not far behind, Commander Stone is running to catch them up, and I have never seen him look more furious. I ignore the relief that rises at the sight of him alive.

'What in the hell are you doing?' I'm surprised by his anger and watch as the men lower their friend to the ground. 'You should have left him to die where he fell!'

'We couldn't leave him, sir.'

'Why not? He's dead anyway.'

'We can fix him up,' one of the soldiers argues.

'If blood loss doesn't kill him, then infection will. Do you see a healer anywhere?'

The Commander's words are harsher than I'd expect.

While they stand over the poor man's body, debating his fate, I stare at his face, ashen with shock, his screams trailing off now as his body shuts down. He's so young. *Too* young.

I grab the nearest blade, thrust it into the forge, and when it's glowing red, I walk over to where they're gathered as fast as my chains will allow. Before they even realise what I'm doing, I press the sword hard against his open wound.

His screams reignite and he shrinks away from me. The soldiers grab me, thinking I'm hurting him, but it only takes the Commander a moment to realise what I'm doing. Our eyes meet and he nods.

'Let her go and hold him down. Now!'

They hesitate for the briefest of moments but do as they're told, and I try to resume my work.

'Get these shackles off me,' I shout as I struggle to hold the blade firmly with so little freedom.

'You heard her,' the Commander says, and someone moves forward to release me.

When the wound is cauterised, I get to my feet. 'Infection may still kill him, but at least he won't bleed to death,' I say, before I shuffle back to the forge, the smell of burning flesh clinging to my clothes. My hand is steady, but inside I'm shaking.

Later, the Commander comes to see me.

'How is he?' I ask.

'Alive, thanks to you, Smithy. Unconscious though.'

'Probably for the best.'

I don't think either of us imagines he'll ever wake up.

I hold out my wrists, assuming he's come to put the shackles back on, but he shakes his head.

'I think you've earned the right to work without chains.'

Interesting. I look at my ankles. 'Any chance you're going to take these off too?'

There's that almost-smile again. 'Don't push your luck, Smithy.'

After a moment, he says, 'Thank you. For helping him. That man is a friend of mine.' I must show my surprise, because he says, 'You're wondering why I told them they should have left him behind?'

No point in pretending. 'Yes.'

'There's no honour in dying slowly and painfully in a camp with no healer. Better to bleed out on the battlefield.'

'Neither are good options,' I say, my voice quiet.

I don't think he's going to answer, but then he says, 'You shouldn't have come here. War is no place for a woman.'

'War is no place for anyone.'

We stare at each other, and we may be from different countries, but we're bonded by that simple truth. None of us should be here.

He clears his throat, breaking the gaze. 'You'll be pleased to hear we won, by the way,' he says, starting to walk away.

'Why would that please me?' I call after him.

'We're moving to the settlement.'

'So?'

He turns, and this time there's no disguising the smile. 'They have a proper forge.'

RAYN

I hate that I love the forge. It doesn't belong to me. Who knows where the rightful owner is? They either died or fled. But their sacrifice has become my gain.

I should not be here, but I am. And what's worse, I'm glad to be.

I hate it all.

The settlement is on a key strategic route and having control of it will make it far easier for the Emperor's troops to spread like an infection through our country. Though I am here as a spy, ostensibly working for my country, every repair I make, every tool I create still aids the enemy. I feel like I've betrayed my own people.

I haven't seen Commander Stone since the day of the battle. I presume he's been as busy as I have, but I find myself disappointed whenever someone approaches who isn't him. I hate that too.

So when I glance up one morning to see him striding my way, I'm surprised to discover I'm nothing but annoyed.

'Enjoying the forge, Smithy?' he asks as he walks in.

I glare at him. 'It's Rayn. My name is Rayn.'

He ignores me, instead inspecting the many tools around the forge. 'You have to admit it's better than what you had before.'

'It's not mine,' I snap. 'Just another thing you stole from

innocent people.' He ignores that too.

'Look, did you want something?' I ask, not bothering to hide my irritation. 'I've got a lot to do.'

'You always have a lot to do. Perhaps you're not as good as you boasted?'

He's teasing me but I am not in the mood. I reply with cold silence.

'I've had nicer welcomes,' he says, fiddling with a pair of tongs hanging on the wall. 'After I've been kind enough to give you time to settle.'

'Oh, is that what you were doing?' *What's wrong with me? Why am I so upset with him?*

He grins broadly. 'Miss me, did you?'

I hold up my hammer. 'Like a hole in the head.'

'You're especially grumpy today,' he finally observes. 'Is there nothing you like about your new home?'

'This isn't my home!' I shout, before calming myself with a deep breath. 'Still, at least Weasel hasn't bothered me since we came here.'

'That's because he's dead.'

That shuts me up. I look at the Commander, who nods. 'Died in the battle.'

I stare at him. I expected such news would bring me pleasure. Instead, I feel nothing. Just numb.

'Look,' he says, all humour gone from his voice now. 'I didn't come here to upset you. I need to talk to you about—'

'Commander!'

We both look out to see a messenger galloping fast into the settlement, waving his arm to attract the Commander's attention.

'Excuse me,' he says, his forehead creasing into a frown.

He hurries over to hold the horse's reins steady as the rider offers him a piece of paper.

Intrigued, I watch as the Commander takes the note and tears it open. I see the way his frown deepens as he reads it, the way he glances nervously around, before crunching the paper into his fist. Whatever the message said, it's clear he doesn't want anyone else to see it.

For the first time since I arrived, it occurs to me that perhaps I've been too trusting of the wrong person. Maybe it's not General Tygh I should be spying on. Maybe it's the Commander.

*

When he returns later that day, I'm prepared to tread carefully.

'Twice in one day? To what do I owe such an honour?' I ask, as I hammer out an axe blade that had become misshapen.

'Don't get excited. I told you earlier I need to speak with you.' He's not in a good mood. 'General Tygh wants an update on your special commission.'

I turn to plunge the blade into the heat. 'I have nothing to update him with.'

'What do you mean? You've had ages to work on it.'

'Horseshit. Since I've been here, we've been on the road, and you've expected me to work on everything else that needed doing to prepare you for battle. I know you'd have me forgo both food and sleep but, even then, I only have one pair of hands.' I do nothing to hide my irritation.

'That sword is a priority.' He's not hiding his either.

I remove the glowing blade from the coals and return

it to the anvil, firmly beating out the desired shape. The Commander steps back from the sparks that fly, but I don't flinch as they land on my skin.

When I'm done, I turn my attention back to the Commander, leaving the metal to cool. 'Then give me time to work on it.'

We hold each other's gaze – me defiant, him considering.

'Fine,' he says in the end. 'From now on, you do only the repairs I allow.'

'And what am I supposed to do when the soldiers bring me their blades? If I refuse, I get punished.'

He knows I'm right; I can see annoyance all over his face. 'I will guard you until it's done.'

'You?' I raise my eyebrows. 'You'll be my personal bodyguard?'

'More like your gaoler.'

And for a glimmer of a second I see it – a hint of amusement behind his eyes. I decide to take advantage of it.

'I'm going to need materials,' I say.

The Commander looks around the forge. 'Isn't there enough iron here?'

'Iron, yes. But I'm going to need blood.'

'Blood?'

'It's called a blade of blood for a reason, you know.'

'Whose blood?' he asks.

'Anyone's,' I reply. 'An animal's, yours, drain the dead if you wish. But without blood, I'd just be making you another sword.'

I think it's finally dawning on him quite what it is they're asking of me – that this is no ordinary task.

'Perhaps . . . perhaps it's best if you work on this at night, when there's no one around to see.'

'Best for who?' I can already sense that sleep won't be featuring much in my immediate future.

He simply smiles at me. 'You can start tonight. I'll make sure you have all you need.'

And he's true to his word. As the sun fades, he appears, accompanied by two men carrying a heavy barrel. Once they place it down, the Commander dismisses them and gestures to his gift.

'I hope this is enough.'

Meeting his challenging gaze, I lift the lid of the barrel and, though the failing light means the fluid inside looks like it could be anything, the smell of iron and death leaves me in little doubt as to what it is.

'Should be.'

The Commander settles down on an upturned bucket and folds his arms behind his head.

I frown at him. 'You're staying?'

'I'm your gaoler, remember?'

I look around the quiet settlement. 'I'm not exactly fending off work at the moment.'

'No, but this sword is of the utmost importance to the General.'

Now I understand. 'And you've been ordered to watch and make sure I do it properly.'

He chuckles. 'Something like that.'

It takes me a while to prepare the forge for what lies ahead. Orange heat won't be enough for this job, and I pile the coals high. When it's ready, I work the bellows, pumping the flames to a higher temperature. For this, I need white heat.

Wiping the sweat from my brow, I reach for some iron, place it between my tongs and slide it into the heat. 'You know this whole process is going to take a while, right?'

'How long? Days?'

'Days?' I scoff. 'More like weeks – maybe months. Depending on the quality you want.'

'Why so long?' he asks, frowning in suspicion. 'Are you buying yourself time?'

I glare at him. 'Should I be? Am I dead the moment you have what you want?'

'No.' He's serious. 'I'm not in the habit of killing people for no reason.'

'So when I'm done, you'll return me to the forge you took me from?'

'I'll escort you there myself.'

I really shouldn't trust a soldier from Vallure, but for some reason I do. I believe him completely, and that's unexpected.

'Truth be told, I'll be glad when we get rid of you, Smithy,' he says. 'Might finally get some peace and quiet.'

He's smiling again, and I look away determinedly. The flames are fizzing and spitting little sparks – the metal is ready. I bring it to the anvil, folding it over and hammering with gentle precision, molten metal flying off in all directions. I can't remember the last time I smiled, not a real smile. And I hate the way this man, my enemy, has brought me close to doing so, time and again.

'Don't touch that.'

He's reaching for the half-forged sword I was working on before, and he looks up at me in surprise.

'Why not?' he asks, frowning. His hand still hovers, frozen in mid-air.

'It's hot,' I say. My tone suggests that it's the most obvious thing in the world and his frown only deepens.

He looks from me to the piece of iron, and back again. 'But it's not glowing.'

'Touch it if you don't believe me.'

For a moment, he holds my gaze and sees the challenge there.

And he touches the iron.

'*Piss-flame*,' he hisses, quickly pulling his hand away

I smile to myself. I knew he wouldn't be able to resist. 'It's black heat. The warning glow has gone, but it's still scorching. That it looks safe is what makes it so dangerous.'

He gives me a withering look.

'You might want to get some water on that burn, Commander,' I say, amused.

But even while he's tending to his raw skin, his eyes follow my every move.

Sensing his genuine curiosity, I say, 'You want to know why it takes a long time to make a blade of blood? First, we fold.' I gesture to what I'm doing. 'Then, we fire-weld.' I plunge the iron back into the heat, and when it's sparking once more I remove it again, striking to fuse the metal together from one end to the other. It isn't quick, and I'm back and forth between the forge and anvil multiple times before the iron begins to bend to my will and forget its former shape.

What I'm making is known as Naperone Steel. The technique to forging it is a fiercely guarded secret, a sacred knowledge passed through the generations to only a rare few. My master Jorge was one of those chosen to be trusted with the method, and it was an honour that he then taught it to me. It is a slow and painstaking process but a wonderous one too. It roots me to the long history of blacksmithing in my country, connects me to smiths of the past. They live on through the passing of their wisdom.

As I work, I talk, albeit guardedly. Partly because I can't bear the silence, but also because it's been so long since anyone showed any interest in what I do, and it's refreshing to share what I'm passionate about with someone else. Someone who's listening.

'When I was an apprentice, my master told me about how this technique would make a strong sword, one that wasn't brittle. He also told me that quenching the iron in various substances could strengthen it further. He sometimes used oil when forging. From the legends I've heard . . . your blade of blood follows the same principle.'

I carry the iron over to the barrel and submerge it in the blood, which bubbles at the sudden heat.

'So you're coating it in blood, rather than oil?' The Commander has got to his feet now, coming closer to get a better look.

'Exactly. And then I repeat the process over and over and over again, until I end up with a layered, virtually unbreakable sword.'

'The Emperor's blade of blood,' he whispers.

I nod. I wonder whether I should be doing this, putting such a weapon into my enemy's hand when I have no idea of its ultimate purpose.

'What does the Emperor want with it?' I ask as nonchalantly as possible.

The Commander shrugs. 'You think someone like me knows that?'

Interesting. Do I detect a hint of irritation aimed at his leader? 'Sorry, Commander. I just thought—'

'Oh, stop with the formality,' he says. 'Call me Ilian.'

'Why, is that your name?'

He smiles. 'Yes.'

'Will you start calling me Rayn?'

'Why would I do that, Smithy?' he replies, his eyes flashing with mischief. He's baiting me to get a reaction, but I refuse to give him the satisfaction.

Besides, the iron has been in the blood long enough now, and it's time to begin again. I return to the forge, but find that it is cooling too quickly. If I try this in orange heat, it will be too cold and the layers would come apart.

'Want to give me a hand here?'

Ilian looks surprised. 'What do you need?'

'Heat.' And I gesture for him to man the bellows.

'You normally do all this yourself?'

'You haven't given me anyone else, so yes. But it'll be quicker if you keep the forge hot.'

To his credit, he doesn't argue, doesn't suggest such labour is beneath him. He just quietly gets on with it, and while we work, our conversation ceases. As I concentrate on my craft, I think about the last time I did this.

About the blade of blood that already exists.

When I was young, my mother got sick. For weeks on end she lay in bed, a prisoner of her illness, and we all knew it was only a matter of time before she died. I was already an apprentice to Jorge at the time, my father having quickly recognised how I fitted into that environment better than one of ballrooms and silk dresses. Jorge was old with no children of his own and, like my mother, he sensed the call of approaching death.

He worked me doubly hard, making sure he taught me all he knew before he died. I was to forge a sword to complete my training, and I didn't want to just make any sword – I wanted it to be a way for a part of my mother to stay with us. So when the doctor bled her, I always made sure I offered to dispose of the bowl. Then I mixed it with animal blood and coated the sword I was making with it. Every layer strengthened and protected by my mother's blood. A talisman that I gave to my father after she died, so that she'd always be by his side.

That's what Graylen's message to me meant. He was telling me whoever killed my father also took his sword. Drake thinks the message was simply a way to earn my trust. But the longer I've had to think about it, the more certain I am that Graylen was telling me how to find those responsible for the betrayal.

Find the blade of blood, find answers.

What worries me is that, somehow, the Emperor knows this too, and is searching for my father's sword to silence those who might expose the truth. In which case, making a replacement might buy Drake and his men more time.

And so I forge, with resolve and determination, and the sense that I'm playing in a dangerous game without a single clue of the rules.

ELENA

I have no idea where I'm going. To start with I do nothing but walk, fear propelling me blindly forward, my only thought to keep moving. At night, I sneak into barns or fields, anywhere I can find a cow or goat to milk. I hate that I'm stealing, but I always leave the udders still swollen, taking only what the baby needs, with just a taste for myself.

I'm terrified we'll be discovered. If I hadn't seen it with my own eyes, I wouldn't believe anyone capable of killing infants, not even our enemy. But they did, and I don't know why. Are they murdering all children, or was it just uncontrollable bloodlust that day?

All I want is to travel unnoticed, and to keep this boy entrusted to me safe. Days slip by and still we live. Still we run. I follow close to the road, and when it forks, simply guess which way might be north.

At night, I dream of Aliénor and wake sobbing, my face damp with grief. I feel lost. A ship without a captain, floating aimlessly on the water. Eventually though, the cold shock of what happened to my home, to Aliénor, begins to thaw. Not a lot, but enough for my survival instincts to kick in. If I want to make it safely to the town where Aliénor's sister lives, then I need a plan.

And so I start to divert away from the road into fields

and hedgerows, collecting plants and herbs to bunch into little posies. Then, when I reach the next village, I knock on every door, asking whether any remedies are required. I have no way of making ointments or tonics, and I'm reluctant to be separated from the precious ones stowed in my bag, but I sell what I can. Yarrow for wounds. Mint, wormwood and oregano for stomach aches. Lavender, sage and chamomile for a headache. I don't ask much, and if they have no money to spare, I take milk or bread dipped in honey for the baby. If they don't have that either, then I pass over my remedies in exchange for directions.

The life of a pedlar woman is a hard one. Doors are slammed in my face. Sometimes, I'm spat at. Occasionally, I'm called a shitwitch, though that's hardly new. But I sell enough to keep us alive. And no one questions the baby I carry.

Maybe that is because each village, each town is veiled with a familiar sorrow. Haunted by an unnatural silence – a lack of younglings' cries. I do not ask if they suffered the same fate as our town, for I haven't the courage to hear the answer. Besides, the way people well up at the sight of the boy tells me everything I need to know.

In one town, an old woman allows me use of her stable in exchange for a mixture of henbane and hemlock for her aching joints, and for the first time since I left my home, I stay in one place for a few days, the allure of clean straw and some warm milk being more than I can pass up. There are other, unexpected, bonuses too. Word spreads about the town that my remedies work, and soon those who didn't give me the time of day at first are seeking me out, searching for something to soothe their ailments. If I don't have what they require in my limited supplies, I tell them what they need and where they might be able to find it, and most people are grateful enough to slip some food my way, or some fresh water, in return for advice.

It feels like an escape to focus on my skills for a while. Aliénor raised me to be more than just a midwife. We had to know how to treat all common maladies, because ours was the door everyone came to knock on in times of trouble. Gathering and distributing the same herbs and plants I did with Aliénor makes me feel close to her, softens the hard edges of my grief.

I am her legacy. I have to make her proud.

Since the massacre, the baby and I have formed a silent bond. I can't even describe it, but when his little eyes look up to mine, it's as if we both know we depend on each other. He's so quiet. Even more than he was when the mercenary first brought him into our lives. I worry that too much horror has imprinted on his soul at such a young age, so I hold him close as much as possible. In my arms, or in the sling, our hearts pressed together. Sometimes, I sing to him, but I find that sends me back to the times when Aliénor would soothe me with a lullaby and the pain soon becomes overwhelming. More often, I hum, just beneath my breath. I think it calms him. I hope it does.

I am not a parent. I have delivered children, changed them, fed them, healed them, but never loved one before. Yet this small, sweet baby whose life I've sworn to protect is beginning to capture my heart. What's left of it.

From what I can gather, I've come almost two hundred miles north of where I started, with far more than that to go. It hasn't helped that I haven't taken the most direct route, having made a number of wrong turns in those early days when I was numb and merely guessing where to go. No wonder I'm exhausted. How easy it would be just to seek a new life in a new town. The people here seem accepting, and it's not like I've ever met Aliénor's sister. They weren't close and Aliénor rarely spoke of Anaïs.

And yet, they were family. And Anaïs deserves to know what happened to her sister. She lost her son so recently, perhaps she'll be willing to take on a daughter.

I decide I'll only stay a few more days in the warm stable and then I must move on. I have the names of the next few towns on the route, so my course is set.

But as I'm sorting through my basket, full of a day's pickings, a woman bursts through the door. I recognise her as someone I sold a bunch of St John's wort to a few days ago.

'What's wrong?' I ask, instantly transported back to Aliénor's kitchen, where we were frequently interrupted by emergencies.

'It's my sister,' she says. 'She's dying. Please help.'

Throwing my bag over my shoulder, the baby already in his sling, I hurry after her, running through the streets to a small cottage. I don't need to follow the lady to know where to go. I can hear the screams a long way off.

'What's wrong with her?' I ask, as we get closer.

'She's with child. It's not coming out right.'

My heart flies to my mouth. Childbirth. This is what I know best. But I've never done it without Aliénor before. I was only an apprentice. Selling remedies is one thing. Delivering a baby is another.

But what else can I do but try?

The scene that greets us is carnage. Three women are already attending the girl, who is lying on her back, writing with agony, her brow beaded with sweat and the sheets about her soaked in blood.

I wish they'd thought to fetch me earlier.

'How long has she been labouring?' I ask, as my eyes locate some water and oil with which I can cleanse myself.

'Two days.' The girl's sister looks distraught. She should.

'What's her name?'

'Elsette. Please, can you save her?'

The other women look as pleadingly at me as the sister, and a cold dread grips me. I'm used to Death waiting in the corner during childbirth, but here he practically fills the room. How I wish Aliénor was here with me, to take charge and tell me what to do.

But she isn't. There's just me, a dying girl and her worried family.

I start to unwrap the sling, reluctant to let the boy out of my sight, but I can't work with him at my chest. Not this time.

I pass him to the oldest of the women in the room. 'Keep him safe,' I instruct, and only move away when she nods.

Then my attention is solely on Elsette.

I take her hand in mine, a gesture of comfort that also gives me an opportunity to glide my fingers across her wrist and feel the strength of her pulse. It's barely there. Hiding my growing concern, I smile at her. She looks hardly older than me, and she's petite.

'I'm Elena,' I say to her in calm tones. 'I'm going to look after you.'

'My baby,' she sobs quietly. 'Please help my baby.'

'I'm going to look after both of you.' It's a promise I'll do my best to keep. 'I'm going to have a look, is that OK?'

She whimpers but agrees, and I lift her nightdress to

feel her swollen belly. There is no movement coming from inside, no kicks, no elbows, and the contractions are barely there. My heart sinks. I'm almost certain the baby is already dead. If I don't hurry, the mother will be too.

When I examine her internally, I can feel the baby's head, but when I move my fingers about, I realise the cord is wrapped fast around its neck. If I had been here sooner, when she started labouring, I might have been able to assist in its delivery. But it's too late now. And Elsette is losing a lot of blood.

I finish my examination and take Elsette's sister to one side.

'The baby is dead, I'm sorry.' I speak quietly, not wanting Elsette to hear. 'We need to get it out quickly, or I won't be able to save Elsette either.'

For the first time since I've been on the road, I reach for my bag. One of the bottles I salvaged has a tonic made up of ivy leaves and berries, sage, feverfew and dittany, all boiled in wine. I pour some out and take it to Elsette.

'Drink this. It'll help.'

Then I take a drop of a strong decoction of hyssop and add it to some boiling water from the fire. I force it down Elsette, though it's scalding hot. Both remedies should help bring away the dead baby.

The rest I can do myself.

Many other midwives would not hesitate to dismember the dead baby to remove it from its mother, but Aliénor taught me only to rely on such methods if all else failed.

'We have two hands,' she used to say. 'Use them wisely, and they're all you need.'

I'm able to reach inside and wrap one of my hands around the baby's head, the other across its back, and then I pull, ignoring Elsette's screams. The trick is to apply pressure, but not too much. I don't want to damage Elsette's birthing canal, so I slowly and carefully ease the baby from her.

But with the baby out, the blood starts pouring faster.

I wrap the lifeless child quickly in a blanket and lay it to one side. One of the women sobs, the others just look stricken, but there's nothing I can do for the little girl. Right now I need to save Elsette.

'Get me linens,' I say, and when they arrive I start trying to pack the uterus. 'Elsette?' I call up to her, but she doesn't answer. 'Stay with us, Elsette!'

But there are no remedies in the world that can save her. The excessive bleeding refuses to be stopped and within minutes Elsette is beyond my reach, leaving to be reunited with her baby daughter in another, perhaps better, place.

I close my eyes, shaken. My first delivery on my own. My first death on my own.

I wipe my hands on a cloth, trying to shut out the wails of the women in the room, and take my baby boy from the grieving woman's arms.

'I'm sorry,' I say quietly. 'Truly, I am.'

They don't hear me though, too lost in pain, and I slip out of the door.

Tears threaten to blind me as I rush back to the stable, where I quickly gather together the food and coins I've accumulated these past days.

When the immediate grief passes, the family will want someone to blame. They'll turn on me in a heartbeat. I'm a stranger in this place, with no reputation to support me.

It's no longer safe for us to be here. And so, once again, we run.

MARZAL

My sleep is dreamless, just a deep blackness where I lie in wait, biding time until the next day begins. But I hear Ama's voice breaking through the darkness, and blink my eyes open to see her leaning over me. The sun hasn't fully risen yet.

'What is it? What's wrong?'

I sit up, noting the stray hairs escaping from Ama's normally immaculate bun.

'It's Urso,' she says, her voice quivering with both fear and excitement.

'What about her?'

'She's been sending letters to a man. *Love* letters. They were intercepted and taken to the Emperor.'

A shiver runs down my spine. 'She's ruined?'

Ama nods. 'Utterly. They say the Emperor was furious beyond all measure.'

I can imagine, can almost see the way his face would have bulged with the sheer audacity of Urso's actions.

'When did this happen?'

'Not two hours ago,' Ama says. 'It's all anyone can talk about, so I thought you should know. The day will bring nothing good with it.'

And Urso will seek me out, I'm sure. It no longer matters whether Izra approves of me or not – Urso will need an ally.

'Help me get dressed.' I throw back the covers and set about preparing myself for the day.

I'll have to tread carefully.

'Izra's on the warpath,' Ama says, chattering away brightly as she dresses me. Perhaps it's a relief that for once, *we're* not the topic of the daily gossip. Today, we are not the pariahs. And Ama has no more love for Izra than I do.

'Did she know?'

'Izra? Not from what I've heard. She's almost as angry with Urso as she is with whoever betrayed her.'

'And do they know who that was?'

Ama moves to stand in front of me, straightening my sleeves. 'No, but heavens help whoever it was when Izra finds out. Her daughter's reputation is beyond redemption.'

I say nothing, considering what is likely to happen now.

'Some think this is Roselle's doing,' Ama continues. 'That her jealousy has finally driven her to make a mistake.'

'Hmm.' To say anything at this dangerous time would be unwise. Better to watch how things unfold before offering an opinion.

'But I wonder if it's Sennan,' Ama prattles on, mistaking my silence as willingness to listen. 'She's lived in Urso's shadow all her life. Maybe she grew jealous of Urso's impending marriage and hoped to win the prince for herself. Girls can be singularly determined to get their own way and are often happy to let others take the blame if it works in their favour. Mark my words.'

I can't disagree with her, but still I say nothing. The delicate balance of harmony between the women of the inner court has long relied on a tenuous hierarchy. There hasn't been any kind of scandal since my mother's, and I suspect there's a reason for that. Uncertainty is a disease in this sort of community. If power unravels, who might grab the loose threads? Now that Urso's position is very much under threat, what might happen? Maybe nothing. Maybe chaos. For now, it's wisest to keep my own counsel, my thoughts remaining secret.

When Ama finally tires of speculation, she retreats to do her work, and I set about mine. Urso will come to me, of that I'm certain. So I begin making some tea.

It's ready and brewed by the time the frantic knocks break my peace. Bracing myself for what's to come, I move to the door.

The moment I open it, Urso falls into my arms, sobbing on my shoulder.

'Hush,' I say, smoothing her hair. 'It's all right.'

'No, it's not,' she cries. 'They know. *Everyone* knows.' One look at me and she can see I'm included in the everyone. 'Oh Gods, I'm ruined.'

'But how were you discovered?' I say, guiding her to sit with me. 'I thought you were being careful.'

'I was,' she says, sniffing. 'But someone must have discovered one of our letters.'

'Your messenger?'

Urso shakes her head. 'No, he's one of Mother's men. He wouldn't betray us.'

'Then who?'

She glances slowly at me, and I see it then. Her doubt, her mistrust.

'You think *I* betrayed you?'

'No,' she lies too quickly. 'But I wondered if perhaps you said something to someone? Even unintentionally?'

'No one is more careful with their words than I am,' I say icily.

She looks guilty now. 'Of course, I'm sorry. I'm just so scared, Marzal. Prince Junus has already called off our wedding, and I've shamed the Emperor's name. What will become of me now?'

I reach out and take her hand. 'How about some tea? Nothing ever seems so bad after a cup of tea.'

She manages a small laugh and nods. 'Thank you.'

I go over to the pot and pour a generous cup for her. 'Here you are,' I say, watching as she lifts it to her lips.

'You know, I think I'm finally getting used to this blend of yours,' she says, even though she still furrows her brow a little.

I smile. 'I told you so. And your skin has never looked better.'

'That's something, I suppose. My whole life may be falling to pieces, but at least I look flawless.' And although she laughs, she's only half joking. We both know our appearances are our most powerful commodity. Men will overlook almost anything for a beautiful face.

Her humour fades quickly. 'Oh, Marzal, what am I going to do?'

I sigh. 'I thought you were simply friends. What madness made you write anything incriminating?' My tone is gentle; not chastising, but sympathetic.

Urso buries her face in her hands. 'I know. You told me over and over again to contact him only as a friend, it's just . . . I love him so much. I couldn't help myself.' Her sobs return quickly. 'I'm sick with worry.'

I lean forward to rest my hand on her arm. 'It'll all work itself out,' I reassure her. 'You'll see. One minute something can seem like the end of the world, but I'm sure by the time you wake up tomorrow morning, it'll all seem unimportant. There's never a day here without new gossip, and if there isn't, I'm sure your mother will create some.'

'You are such a good friend,' she says, wiping away tears that refuse to be stopped. 'You always make me feel better.'

'Would you like to stay here today?' I ask. 'Hide away from the world with me?'

'Thank you, but no. I'm supposed to be confined to my chambers, but I simply had to sneak out to see you. If my mother knew I was here, it would only make things worse.'

'Well, if you need me, send for me.'

The moment Urso's gone, I sigh. 'You can come in now, Ama.'

I knew she'd be listening at the door, hoping to pick up any new morsels of gossip. She rushes in at my words, not even bothering to pretend she wasn't eavesdropping.

'Well? What news?' Ama is ravenous for scandal.

'Nothing that you do not already know,' I say, clearing the teacup from the floor.

'So she's ruined? Truly?'

Carrying the teapot, I drift to the window and open it, breathing in the fresh air. 'Oh, I suspect Izra will concoct some story or other to save her.' I pour the cold leftover tea on to the flower bed below.

'I'm not sure even Izra can save this situation,' Ama says, more than a little gleefully. 'Want me to rinse that for you?'

I hand her the pot, and when she's gone, I remain in the window seat, the breeze caressing my skin. The room feels very quiet now, with just me and my thoughts. I feel sorry for Urso. Her upbringing at the Winter Palace was kind, gentle. Too much so. She had no training in how to fight the war raging within the palace walls, all the betrayal and manoeuvring women have to do simply to survive. And as the Emperor's heir, she was an obvious and easy target.

In many ways, we all go into hiding for the day, everyone afraid of what might happen next. When I take tea with the other women, both Urso and Izra are missing, and their absence is deafening. We sit in silence, scared even to gossip when so little is known.

The Empress politely refuses a visit from me, perhaps too sick with uncertainty to entertain company. By the end of the day, I am eager to disappear into the tunnels and find out what my father is planning, but when I reach my spying place, my father is asleep, and only Rom is with him, quietly scribbling out orders on scrolls that I cannot read from such a distance.

By the time I retreat to my bed, my insides feel scratchy, the anxiety impossible to ease.

Next morning, the word is that Urso is unwell and the healer has been sent for. I sit with the other women, stitching our embroideries, nervously waiting for any news.

'What's wrong with her?' Sennan asks one of the handmaidens when she brings in fresh tea. 'Is she actually ill, or is she just hiding?'

'I don't know, my Lady.' The girl sounds afraid. 'But her mother says it's the shame.' She glances anxiously towards Roselle, and Sennan follows her gaze.

'She blames my mother?' Now Sennan sounds afraid.

The girl flees before we can ask her anything else, and Sennan turns to me. 'Why would she blame my mother?'

I gesture at her to keep her voice down and guide her to a corner. 'I don't know. But someone had to know about the letters, and little gets past your mother.'

'But what purpose would it have served her to tell the Emperor?' she asks, defensive and confused all at once. 'It's not like Prince Junus would ever be promised to me.'

'Perhaps that's the very reason. Your mother loves you; it must be hard for her to see Urso continually elevated so far above you.'

Sennan has never been a friend of mine, but even I feel a pang of sorrow for her as her face drains of all colour. 'What can I do?'

'Pray to all the Gods that Urso recovers her strength.'

But the Gods appear deaf to Sennan's prayers.

Over the next two days, Urso's condition deteriorates, the healer declaring her sick of spirit, and the soothsayers claiming the stars speak of her weak constitution and an early death.

The stars, for once, are right.

Urso dies three days after her scandal broke.

We hear Izra's cries from down the corridor. The sound of someone's soul being torn from them. A primal noise heard when the bond between mother and child is broken.

A period of mourning is declared, and all the colour in the women's quarters is muted to grey.

Izra shuts herself away, but no walls can contain her sobs, and I listen to her suffering wherever I go. The loss of her only child has shattered her, previously the strongest of us all, with one swift blow.

Everyone can feel the shift, the balance of power and hierarchy teetering on the brink. What happens now will depend on who makes the first move, and I watch as several of the aunties lust after a power grab.

While they plot and scheme, my observations have never been more important, so the following night I venture into the tunnel. I know how the death of Urso has affected the women – now I want to see what impact it's had on the men. I fear very little. And I'm not wrong.

Whereas all our colour has been extinguished along with Urso's life, my father's room is as bright as ever. While we all fast for her soul, the Emperor continues to feast to excess. It's not only me he doesn't love. It's all of us. His forgotten girls.

Tonight, there is no talk of war. I must be too late for updates and am annoyed with myself. I want to know every battle he fails in, every time the Naperones drive him back. I thrive upon his weakness, as if it feeds my own strength.

Instead, they're discussing grain supplies and the empty coffers, tedious matters, and my mind wanders, until the mention of a man loyal to them on the enemy's side catches my attention. This man, whom they do not name, has promised them supplies of food and gold in exchange for . . . something. I cannot think of what my father could offer beyond power, and so despite most of the talk boring me, I stay, hoping to glean more interesting information.

But the conversation changes direction again and, finally, they speak of Urso.

'Don't forget we have the funeral to plan,' Rom is saying, checking through his long list. 'The death of a princess is something the people will want marked.'

The Emperor scoffs. 'You'd think they'd have better things to worry about.'

I can only assume he's referring to the death and starvation his subjects are facing. So he's not unaware of it, he just chooses to do nothing.

'Nevertheless,' Rom says, 'should I commence arrangements?'

The Emperor shifts in his throne and strokes the fur laid over his lap. 'Tell me, Rom, do we honour the deaths of those who defy us? Who openly disobey my commands?'

'No, of course not, Majesty.'

'And did the princess not, despite being betrothed to a man I chose for her, seek to romance another behind my back?'

Rom hangs his head, silent. He knows where this is going as well as I do.

'She'd still be doing it now, if she hadn't been discovered. But she *was* discovered, and the shame drove her to her grave. So I say we make an example of her. Even those joined to me by blood will not be forgiven treachery.'

The room is silent. Urso was probably the most well liked of all the women at court, for she was so kind to everyone.

'There will be no Imperial funeral. I shall not waste precious resources on the little whore.' The Emperor pauses, a new and amusing thought occurring to him. 'Find the boy she wrote to, and when you do, execute the turdshitter for treason. They claimed to love each other, then let them be together in death.'

He laughs, but no one else does. The most anyone can manage is an uncomfortable smile.

'And what of Prince Junus?' Rom asks. 'Should we delay his invitation?'

'And lose the gold he pledged?' My father is outraged at the mere suggestion.

'What do you propose?'

'I have plenty of other daughters, do I not? Give him one of them. Who's heir now?'

For a moment, I catch a strange shadow pass over Rom's face, like he doesn't want to answer. 'The Princess Marzal.'

I hardly dare breathe, waiting for my father's response.

'Then let them wed. It hardly matters to me which one he has, so long as I get his gold. Though I don't envy Junus if she's as frigid as her wart of a mother.'

This time, everyone joins him in laughter. Everyone, that is, except Rom, his jaw clenched nearly as tight as mine.

The thought of being foisted off on that slimy worm just so my father can get gold makes my blood boil. But more than that, I'm angry that they're mocking my mother.

Their laughter burns in my ears long after I've returned to the safety of my room. I hadn't expected I would inherit Urso's rejected lover. I should have foreseen it. I can't afford such mistakes.

I recall the way Rom fought back his own anger in the throne room. He does not agree with many of my father's decisions; perhaps it's time to use that to my advantage. But I will think about that tomorrow.

For now, my mind is too full of Urso, Izra's wails, and the way my father scorned my mother. All I can do is lie in my bed, with nothing but pillows to muffle my screams.

RAYN

My nights are long. And yet, I find myself looking forward to them. Whatever the reasons that brought me to this point, I am creating a thing of beauty, something I can be proud of, and I haven't had this opportunity in the longest time.

Weeks have passed and still Ilian keeps me company through the dark hours. Sometimes we're silent, with him pumping the bellows so I can work faster; sometimes we talk. But I'm beginning to doubt he knows anything useful that I could pass on to Drake. Though he is from Vallure, he seems to be a good person. He cares deeply about the men he's responsible for, and it's clear he wants to keep them as safe as is possible in a time of war. Often, I've seen him share his food with others, as he once did with me.

And yet I frequently catch him looking troubled, restless. The sword is nearly finished, so I'm running out of time to discover why.

'How long are you and your men going to be stationed here?' I ask him one night.

'I don't know. General Tygh says the Emperor will send more troops to relieve us eventually.'

'And what then?'

'We move closer to Eron, I imagine,' he says without enthusiasm.

'Does it not bother you that the General sits warm and happy in his fancy tent, while the rest of you fight and die?'

Ilian sighs. 'I've known the General a long time, Smithy. He has my complete loyalty.'

Interesting.

'You've fought together before?' I ask nonchalantly, as if I'm making polite conversation rather than interrogating him.

'He trained me.'

I glance up at him but apparently he isn't going to expand on that enticing nugget of information. I'm going to have to try another tack.

'Tell me about your family.' It's a risky question during times of war, but I need to provoke him, make him talk.

He looks sharply over at me. 'I don't have one.'

I know exactly what that means. 'What happened to them?'

His strong arms keep pressing the bellows, up and down, but he's not paying them any attention. He's drifting into the past now. 'We lived near the border in the south. I told you before that your governor sent men to attack us first. I know that because they came to our village. Looted it for food and supplies.' He pauses. 'They murdered my mother.'

I hadn't wanted to believe him before, when he lashed out in anger that Naperone started the war, but I know him better now and know he wouldn't lie.

'I'm sorry,' I say. 'I had no idea that was happening.'

Ilian looks over, and he's angry, but not with me. 'Why do you think so many of us are willing to fight the Emperor's war? Because the Naperones need to be stopped.'

I say nothing. If I ever see Drake again, I'll be demanding

an explanation for this. I've always thought the Emperor's invasion was entirely unjustified, but perhaps I'm yet another foolish, naive pawn who's been deceived by those she trusts. After all, why should the corruption have only come after the war began?

'General Tygh was one of the men who came to pick up the pieces. My brother and I left with him to fight.' Ilian's still in the past. 'And my sister . . . well, she got sent away. I have no idea where she went, or if she still lives.'

'What happened to your brother?' I'm not asking as a spy any more. I'm asking as a friend. A realisation that unsettles me.

Ilian stops firing the forge now, taking a break. I think perhaps I've crossed the line with my question, but he moves a barrel to sit close to me.

'Do you remember when there was an attempt at peace talks a while back?'

My heart hisses, like it's hot steel and he's thrown ice water over it. 'Yes.'

'My brother, Adrien, he was part of the envoy protecting Captain Occius. They were betrayed by the Naperones escorting them and were murdered before they could reach your capital.'

No.

Fate cannot possibly be so cruel; to bind our brothers' destinies in such a way before bringing us together.

But when has Fate ever been kind? I so desperately want to tell him the truth. That, in this at least, my people were innocent. That we both lost loved ones that day. That I share in his grief. But I can't. Despite everything, he is *not* my friend. He is my enemy. I am his prisoner, and if I told him what I know, he wouldn't believe me. He would kill me.

So I simply say, 'I'm sorry.'

He stares at the ground. 'Me too. I'm tired, Smithy. Tired of being angry all the time. Tired of being denied my vengeance.'

I'm regretting ever starting down this path and return my attention to my work.

'How about you?' Ilian's looking up at me now. 'Where are your family?'

'They're dead.'

He nods in understanding and thankfully doesn't press me. We don't speak much after that. Nor the next night. Or the night after that. Perhaps we both sense that we've strayed into territory more personal than is wise. Instead, he watches through the long hours as I perfect the sword. It's so nearly ready, the edges bevelled, the blade sharp.

Almost a week after our conversation, in the dark hours when night and morning blur, the last hammer strike falls, and I look on my creation, content.

With little to do in these last stages, Ilian has fallen asleep, and when I shake him awake, he looks up groggily. 'What? What's wrong?'

'Nothing. It's done.'

That wakes him up. 'Where is it?'

I hold it in my hands before him. 'One blade of blood.'

'You did it, Smithy.' He's impressed. 'May I?'

I hand it to him with the reluctance of a mother passing over her newborn, wondering whether I'll ever see it again.

He runs his hands over it, then holds it out, slashing through the air to test its balance. 'It's something else,' he says to me with a grin. 'I'll keep it safe tonight and deliver it to the General in the morning.'

'And then you'll take me home?'

His smile fades. 'What?'

'You said when it was done, you'd escort me safely back to where you found me. Remember?'

I'm testing him, really. I know he won't be allowed to keep his word, even if he wants to.

Ilian at least does me the courtesy of not looking me in the eye when he replies. 'I'll talk to the General about it when I deliver the sword.'

'Goodnight, then.'

He shifts awkwardly, his guilt unmistakable. 'Goodnight.'

Once he's gone, I settle down as if I'm going to sleep, but sleep is the furthest thing from my mind.

Not for one second do I think Tygh will release me. If I'm lucky, they'll keep me here to continue forging for them. If I'm unlucky, I'll be disposed of. If I had to place a bet, I'd go for the latter.

Which means I have to escape. Tonight. The settlement is quiet, the men resting. I'm never going to have a better chance than this.

I reach down my top for the narrow key I forged long ago, the one that opens any lock. It comes everywhere with me, nestled safely in my supportive binding. I could have released myself long ago, but I've been waiting for the right moment. It's now.

In seconds, the shackles and chains fall free from my ankles. And then I pick up the dagger I set to one side for myself when we first settled here. I've had plenty of time to prepare, to plan, which is why I run towards General Tygh's tent without hesitation. I'm not leaving here without discovering what he's up to. I intend to be gone long before he or the camp wakes up. And once I've got what I need, I'll steal a horse – I've shod them all and know exactly which one can outgallop the rest.

The camp sentries are playing dice and drinking ale. None of them notices me slip through the streets towards the tent. Outside the entrance, a pair of soldiers are on guard. Unfortunately for the General, they're asleep, and so there's no one to stop me from sliding silently under the canvas.

I hold my breath.

General Tygh is lying on the floor, covered in furs and snoring loudly. On the far side of the tent is his desk, which is covered in papers. My heart races. There are so many documents here, something has to be useful, but there's almost too much. It's hard to know where to begin.

I search quickly but silently, desperate to find something that isn't mundane, and at the bottom of the third pile, I see it. A letter just like the one I found in Lord Norvill's study. One bearing Governor Franklin's seal.

'Coordinates as requested. Guard changes a tenth past the hour. Approach from the south-east for cover.'

For a moment I can't breathe. It looks like whoever's working with Norvill is also working with General Tygh – and gave them all the information they needed to successfully take this strategic settlement we've been staying in.

I'm so stunned to have found it, I fail to notice that the snoring has stopped until it's too late. General Tygh has approached on my blind side and his blade is pressing firmly at my neck.

'Drop your knife.' He presses his own harder into my skin, leaving me in no doubt as to what he'll do if I don't obey.

My dagger clatters to the ground.

'I wondered how long it would take you to come here,' Tygh breathes into my ear.

I can feel the warm trickle of blood from where he's broken my skin. Nothing life-threatening, just a taste of what's to come if I retaliate. So I do nothing as he throws me roughly against the central tent pole.

'Honestly, I thought you would do it sooner,' he says, his eyes searching my face. 'The question is, why didn't you?'

Ignoring him, I hold up the letter that's still in my hand. 'You're working with someone in Eron. I want to know who.'

He laughs. 'I'm sure you do. I'm afraid I shall have to disappoint you.' And he snatches the paper from me. 'Guards!'

The sleepy men stumble in, so unprepared for danger I wonder why the General has them there at all. They stare at me as if I'm an apparition.

'Tie her up. And fetch Stone.'

I glare at Tygh as his lackeys bind me roughly to the pole. When they make to leave, Tygh grabs one of them by the arm. 'Once Stone is here, you two disappear. Understood?'

They nod, more than a little nervous, and flee.

As soon as they're gone, Tygh lights the candle on his desk and holds the paper over it. I can do nothing but watch as the evidence folds in on itself, disintegrating to ash. When there's nothing left, Tygh picks up the candle and carries it over to me, bringing it so close that the flame is almost touching my face.

'You like fire, don't you?' he says, his voice a whisper. 'So do I. It devours everything in its path. Like I do.'

The smell of burning hair hits me hard, and I realise he's singed my eyebrow.

Tygh's interrupted by Ilian striding into the tent. As he quickly assesses the scene before him, our eyes meet and I know he sees my fear.

'Sir?'

Tygh steps away from me, to face his former pupil. 'Ah, Commander. It seems our blacksmith friend here is more than she appears.'

Ilian frowns. 'What do you mean?'

Tygh gestures to his desk. 'Caught her snooping through my personal correspondence. Turns out, she's a godsdamn spy.'

Do I imagine the hurt in Ilian's face as he glances at me?

'A spy? Her?'

Tygh laughs. 'Yes, I agree it's hard to believe, though perhaps we should have suspected such a thing from a woman who can forge.' His humour melts instantly away. 'Perhaps *you* should have suspected it, since you've spent so much time in her company.'

The accusation is unmistakable.

'You think . . .' Ilian shakes his head in disbelief. 'You think I knew?'

'I didn't say that,' Tygh says. 'I'm simply wondering whether you've allowed your guard to be lowered by a pretty face.'

Ilian looks over at me, and I hold his gaze. I'm as interested in his answer as Tygh is.

'Sir, I had no idea. I have done nothing but what was asked of me. I watched her when I was told to. Any conversation we had was merely for my own amusement.'

It shouldn't sting to hear him say that, but it does.

'So she means nothing to you?'

Ilian clenches his jaw. 'Less than nothing.'

Tygh smiles. 'Good.' He folds his arms. 'Kill her.'

I tighten my fists, the rope biting into my wrists. If I'm going to die, I really don't want it to be by Ilian's hand.

Ilian doesn't look overly keen either. 'Why me?'

'Because I want you to.'

'Sir, she's an unarmed woman.' Ilian gestures pleadingly. 'I can't kill her in cold blood.'

'She's an enemy spy. Execute her.'

I've been holding my breath for too long and am starting to feel light-headed.

When Ilian still hesitates, Tygh sighs and pats him on the shoulder. 'It might help if I told you who she really is.'

Ilian looks sharply at me and all I can do is shake my head, a small gesture to beg him not to listen.

Tygh continues. 'In fact, I'd wager I'm doing you a favour by letting you kill her. Given your quest for revenge.'

Ilian turns his gaze back to his mentor. 'What are you talking about?'

Tygh's grin is cruel now. 'Oh, didn't you know? It was her father and brother who slaughtered the peace envoy. Who killed Adrien.'

His revelation has the desired effect. Ilian's eyes darken as he turns to me.

'It's not true,' I protest, willing him to hear me, trust me.

'She would say that, wouldn't she? The daughter of traitors. Can a single word she says be believed?'

Ilian's conflict is obvious. I should have told him when I had the chance. My previous silence condemns me, but I hadn't wanted him to look at me the way he does now. With cold malice.

'Tell me,' he says, and I'm not sure whether he's asking me or Tygh, but it's Tygh who answers.

'This is Lady Rayn of Grynn. Did she never introduce herself properly?' Tygh laughs. 'Unsurprising, given her family are wanted war criminals.'

I glare at him. 'You knew? All this time, you *knew*?'

His smile fades as quickly as it appeared. 'Of course I did. You're not the only one capable of spying.'

He turns his attention back to Ilian. 'Remember all the nights we sat up drinking, talking of how you wanted to hurt the people responsible for your brother's death? Of what you would do to them in his name? Here's your chance. They might not be here, but she's the next best thing. Do whatever you want to her. I shan't judge.'

Ilian's grip is tightening on the hilt of his sword, his anguish all too clear.

'Ilian.' I say his name to remind him we're friends. To will him to hear me. 'It's true, my father and brother were part of the peace envoy, yes. But they weren't responsible for what happened. They were falsely accused.'

His eyes flash with betrayal, the pain of wanting to believe me. But he doesn't.

Tygh senses it too and continues to needle his protégé, mocking my desperate claims of convenient innocence, stirring Ilian's need for vengeance.

I'm in trouble. My eyes flick to the hilt of Tygh's sword, protruding from its scabbard, and I wonder whether there's any way I can free myself in time to steal it. But my hands are bound tight. It's useless.

Despite my precarious situation, something's niggling at me. I look back at the sword in disbelief. I hadn't noticed it before, because why would I ever expect to see it here?

But there it is. It's been here all along.

'Why have you had me forging a sword with blood?' My sudden outburst causes Tygh and Ilian to pause.

'For the Emperor,' Tygh says, and I can practically hear his mind racing to catch up.

'But why? When you had one all the time?'

He understands me now, a wry smile tugging his lips as he shakes his head. '*You* made it?'

'Of course I did.' My voice is raw with the fresh wave of emotion that's surfaced.

Ilian looks confused. 'What's she talking about?'

This time, I'm the one to answer. 'His sword; it's my father's.'

Tygh must have taken it after he left him for dead.

'Why did you do it?' I ask Tygh quietly. 'Why did you kill your own men?'

As hard as it was for Ilian to believe I was his enemy, it's nothing compared to the suggestion that his mentor, his friend, the man whose orders he has followed without question, could be responsible for the death of his brother.

Tygh doesn't answer, and I wonder whether he too senses the shift in the atmosphere. Instead, he pours himself a drink of wine and takes a leisurely sip.

Ilian grows impatient. 'Tell her she's wrong! Tell me she's lying!'

When Tygh finally speaks, he addresses Ilian as if I weren't here. 'We are soldiers, Stone. We follow orders, not question them.'

Ilian's reaction is physical. He flinches as if Tygh has punched him in the guts.

'The Emperor wants Naperone, Ilian. He's quite prepared to do whatever it takes to get it.'

'Whatever it takes.' Ilian echoes the words back as if they will haunt him for ever. And as he slowly starts putting the pieces together, a shadow passes over his face. 'Like attacking his own people along the border, to create a desire for war?'

The air is sucked out of the tent as Ilian's world collapses around him, and my hatred for the Emperor grows.

Tygh puts his wine down and steps closer to Ilian, offering a hint of comfort to his protégé.

'Did it never strike you as odd that so many women and girls were killed, while the boys survived?'

Ilian stares at him with cold loathing, as the truth sinks in. 'The Emperor wanted to create a whole generation of men who would willingly fight for him.'

Tygh nods. 'You have to admit, it's ingenious. After conquering the countries to the east in his bid to expand the empire, his men were battle-weary. So he found a way to inspire his troops for years to come.'

'He murdered his own people!'

Tygh shrugs. 'All wars have casualties.'

'And the diplomats? My brother? Just casualties?' Ilian is incensed.

'Blame Captain Occius for that whole fiasco. He initiated those peace talks with Governor Franklin without authority from the Emperor.' Tygh refills his glass of wine and just as quickly drains it dry. 'The Emperor has no interest in peace, but Occius was adamant that the war should be ended, if it could be. The Emperor merely turned it to his advantage – making the Naperones look responsible only motivated his troops further.'

'And you?' Ilian asks. 'Were you simply following orders when you murdered my brother?'

'Yes. Though I had no idea that Adrien had been assigned to the convoy. It was . . . regrettable.'

To my ears he doesn't sound regretful. He almost sounds proud.

'You killed your own men.' Ilian's voice simmers dangerously.

'I did what was necessary.'

'And now, so must I.' Ilian draws his sword. Tygh looks at me as he pulls my father's sword from its scabbard. 'How will it feel to watch the sword you made take his life, right before it takes yours?' he asks me.

I pull at my restraints, desperate to crush the air out of his throat, but I'm bound too tightly. There's nothing I can do but watch as Ilian strikes first.

My father's sword meets his with force, and I see Ilian stagger backwards. Tygh's blade is a good one; it was never intended to be in his hands.

'This is not how I wanted things to be,' Tygh says, as Ilian regains his balance.

'Should have thought of that before you betrayed us,' Ilian snaps as he attacks again.

With the strength of his superior blade, Tygh is soon able to gain the upper hand, so that Ilian is the one on the defence. He's struggling, but there's nothing I can do to help him as the fight rages around the tent.

Tygh duels with the confidence of a man who tastes glory. But he's forgotten something. Though he may have the better weapon, Ilian is fuelled by love for his brother – something altogether more powerful.

Maybe that's what sustains him as he parries blow after blow, until at last he's able to turn things to his advantage. Tygh is older, his skills rusty from avoiding front-line action, and Ilian exploits every weakness.

Dodging the sweep of Tygh's blade, Ilian leaps on to the desk, scattering papers everywhere, and kicks Tygh hard in the neck. Tygh chokes, staggering backwards, and Ilian pounces, knocking him to the floor. Without hesitation, he stabs Tygh in the guts, kicking my father's sword out of his hand and towards my feet.

Tygh stares up at Ilian, his mouth too full of blood to speak.

'Funny thing about a blade of blood?' Ilian says. 'It doesn't make you invincible, no matter what the Emperor might think. It's just a sword. But you . . . you taught me to avenge my family above all else. Thank you for that. This is for them.'

This time Ilian aims straight for Tygh's heart, and silences him for ever.

I'm trembling, blood pounding loudly in my head. 'Are you all right?' I ask awkwardly. Stupid question. He's clearly not.

Ilian stands up and walks to me. He looks lost.

Our eyes meet.

'You're a spy?'

I nod. 'I am.' It's time for the truth.

'What were you looking for?'

'Evidence that men inside both our governments are working together for personal gain. Proof that this war serves only the interests of the few.'

'And then what were you going to do?'

'And then I was going to stop the traitors. Or try, at least.'

He looks at me for a long time. I cannot read him at all, his thoughts far beyond my reach.

And then he leaves the tent, not looking back even as I call after him.

I cry out in frustration. He's left me for dead. The moment I'm discovered with Tygh's body, it's over.

It's time I remembered who I've always relied on – myself. I look up at the roof of the tent and wonder if I can push the pole over somehow. No, even if I managed it, they'd catch me in the resulting chaos long before I could disentangle myself. There's nothing for it but to hope I can wriggle free from the rope, and so I twist and turn, the coarse fibres gnawing at my flesh.

'That won't work.'

He came back.

But the hood of his travelling cloak hides his face as he pulls the sword from beneath it. Not his usual sword this time, but the blade of blood I've spent so many hours making. He went back for it. I have no idea what his intentions are now.

'I don't know who you are,' he says, his voice heavy with sorrow. 'I'm not certain about anything right now. But whoever you are, spy, thief, traitor, there's one thing I do know. You are not my enemy.'

And he brings the sword down on the ropes, freeing me.

RAYN

We ride hard under the cover of night.

I don't know where we're going – for now I'm willing to follow Ilian wherever he leads me.

Before we left the tent, we raided it for anything of use. A travelling cloak for me, some food, a handful of coins. And of course my father's sword, which is at my side where it belongs.

Everything else we left, including all my tools. We took the best horses and fled, hoping for a few hours before the inevitable pursuit. The men had far more respect for Ilian than they did for General Tygh, and though they will believe him to be a traitor, they may still just allow him a slight head start out of loyalty. I doubt they'll be mourning the General.

We don't speak, though there's much to say. We avoid the road wherever possible, Ilian seemingly experienced in travelling unnoticed. It isn't until we settle in a well-concealed copse the following night to rest that we finally run out of reasons not to confront what's happened.

We're huddled around a fire, desperate for warmth, the horses tended to and the air still. A few morsels of food have been shared and now we need to sleep. It's my turn to rest, while Ilian takes the first watch, but my mind won't settle.

'How are you?' I ask. His world's been shattered and he killed his mentor. It's a lot for anyone, even a battle-hardened soldier.

He looks up at me across the flames. 'I've been better.'

Fair enough. 'Any regrets?'

Ilian picks up a twig and pokes it into the fire, watching the end catch light. 'Hundreds. But not about Tygh. Or about being here now.'

A little of my tension slips away.

'Can I ask you something?' I feel slightly safer bringing this up now.

'If I said no, would it stop you?'

At first, I think he's annoyed, but then he lifts his eyes to meet mine, and there's a glint of mischief there.

'You already had your doubts, didn't you? About Tygh?' I watch him closely, to see if my suspicions are correct. Because while I once thought the note he received from the messenger all those weeks ago might incriminate *him*, I'm now wondering if it was something else entirely.

'What makes you say that?'

'The day that messenger brought you a letter. Whatever information it contained, you didn't want anyone else to see it. What did it say?'

He stares at the twig turning to ash in his hand, then shakes his head with a wry laugh. 'A spy, indeed. You don't miss much, do you?'

I say nothing, wanting to give him space to open up.

'Someone with access to the Emperor contacted me with concerns.'

I frown. 'What concerns?'

'Concerns that the Emperor is no longer making decisions with his people's interests at heart. If he ever did. That . . .'

He sighs deeply. 'That recently, Naperone soldiers swept through Vallure, killing baby boys in every town or village they passed. Only they weren't really from Naperone.'

Oh Gods.

'I didn't believe it. Couldn't believe it. But I couldn't forget it either.'

'And so you started watching Tygh more closely?'

Ilian nods. 'I started to notice small things. Nothing incriminating, just signs that he wasn't quite the man he had once been. But then you tried to escape and lit a match to my life.' He gives a hollow laugh. 'Only a fool could have ignored the truth after that. My country and its leader are corrupt. Evil.'

It's a heavy weight to bear, finding out everything you've ever fought for is based on a lie.

'There's corruption in my country too,' I say, and not simply because I want to comfort him with the fact he's not alone. 'The rebels I'm working with? They know that someone powerful on our side helped the Emperor to sabotage the peace envoy, someone close to the Governor. That's why I let you capture me. We knew Tygh was loyal to the Emperor and thought he might have information about who in our capital has betrayed us.'

He raises his eyebrows. 'You *let* me capture you?'

Though all the world seems bleak, I find myself smiling for the first time in years.

'Of course I did. You thought you just got lucky, finding me that day?'

He smiles at me. 'I *was* lucky, Smithy.'

Heat creeps up my neck that has nothing to do with the fire.

'So what do we do now?' I ask, wanting to shift the

conversation to safer ground. 'Tygh burned the only letter I could find linking him to the traitor I'm looking for. I can't go back with nothing.'

'You have me.'

I glance up at him sharply, and he clears his throat.

'I mean, you have my testimony. And my contact.'

'And you think you can trust this contact? I mean, why did they choose you?'

Ilian hesitates. 'I'm not sure. I need to check out their credibility. If the story they gave me can be confirmed, then they could be a crucial asset to us.'

He chooses not to expand on what that story might be, and I don't push him. I have my own thoughts forming.

'I need to go to Eron,' I say.

'Why? Surely you want to return to your superior?'

'I have no idea where he'll be now,' I admit. 'I stayed far longer with you than either of us expected. Honestly, he probably thinks I'm dead at this point.'

'Why Eron though?'

'Because whoever the traitor is, they're using the Governor's seal. They must be in the capital and I'm going to find out who it is.'

'And then what?'

I stare into the fire, the flames like fangs, its heat like venom.

'Then I kill them.'

I'm half expecting him to protest, to tell me I should report back to Drake and let him deal with things, or for him to insist he's coming with me. He does neither.

'Then we may as well keep travelling together. For now. You can find out who your traitor is, and I'll find out if my contact can be trusted.'

For now.

The words remind me that though we are together, we are not a team. Only two people going the same way.

I force my confusing emotions aside and focus on the most important thing. At last, I have a plan.

*

We run into trouble a few days later. My horse throws a shoe and starts to go lame, while Ilian's horse is showing signs of serious fatigue. We're forced to give them up, selling them to a farmer for a few coins.

We'll need to buy new horses at some point, but as we're undoubtedly being hunted, for now we decide to travel on foot and take a narrow, rocky path through the mountains. Those pursuing us think we're on horseback, and as it would be an impassable route to ride, they won't come this way.

After three days of walking through the most inhospitable terrain, where the ground likes to slip away beneath us, I'm wishing *we* hadn't come this way either.

My boots are falling apart, my feet becoming blistered and swollen, and as the incline grows steeper, pain shoots through them as I struggle to keep up.

'Need me to slow down, Smithy?' Ilian asks with a smile.

I shove his arm. 'I'm not unfit, you ass. It's my feet. They bloody hurt.'

He looks at my tattered boots and frowns.

'All right, sit down,' he says.

'I'm fine.'

Ilian gently pushes me to the ground. 'Come on,' he says. 'Let me look.'

'You really don't want to do that,' I say. I suspect it's not going to be pretty.

'How long have you been wearing these things?' Ilian says, peeling off my boots.

'Too long.' They were old when I joined the army and have been sorely tested these past few days. I'm surprised they haven't fallen apart before now.

Ilian inspects my blistered feet with concern. 'You should have told me they were this bad.'

'I'm fine,' I repeat, not entirely convincingly.

'You're not, and I can't afford to be slowed down.'

I laugh. 'And here was me thinking you cared.'

He smiles back up at me, before glancing around. 'Wait here.' He fixes me with his firmest 'do-as-you're-told' look and begins scouring our surroundings.

'What are you doing?' I call.

He doesn't answer but returns minutes later with a clump of moss in one hand and a snail in the other.

I raise my eyebrows. 'And what, exactly, are you going to do with that?'

'Well,' he says, kneeling down in front of me. 'I may not be an expert, but you don't spend your life travelling and not pick up a few tricks.' He takes my right foot carefully in his hands. 'Good, they've aired out nicely. We need to keep them dry and warm.' Then he lifts the snail up, pausing briefly to say, 'Don't move. This might feel weird.'

I don't have time to question him before he's pressing the snail to my painful skin, smearing me with its sticky mucus. It burns like the fires of hell, and yet the sight of him rubbing the creature on me until my raw skin glistens is too ridiculous not to laugh at. 'What are you doing?'

He shrugs. 'Don't ask me why, but it works. I guess the slime stops the snails from tearing themselves to pieces on the ground, so it must act as some sort of barrier?'

I shake my head, half in disbelief, but mostly impressed. 'If you say so.'

But when he starts to remove his own boots, I reach forward to stop him. 'No.'

Ilian looks up at me. 'You need to give your feet a break, and we only have one pair of decent boots between us. So you're having mine.'

'No, I'm not.'

He pulls the boots off. 'Yes, you are. Stop arguing, Smithy.'

I can tell there's no dissuading him, so I watch as he unwraps the cloth from around his feet, and then starts arranging the moss in it.

It hurts when he presses it to my tender skin, and I draw in a sharp breath as he begins to bind the cloth up. But he's gentle, and when he looks up to see how I'm doing, I think we both realise the intimacy of the situation.

Ilian clears his throat. 'You can probably do this yourself,' he says, standing.

Smiling a little, I finish wrapping my feet, before sliding them carefully into his boots.

'They're a bit big,' I say, wanting to lighten the mood again. It works, as he turns and laughs at the sight of me.

'You ready to get going?'

I look at his bare feet. 'Are you?'

'I'll be all right,' he shrugs. 'I'm sure we'll find someone soon enough that I can kill for their boots.'

'Oh, my hero.'

He does a mock bow, and it's good to be with someone

who smiles and makes me smile in return. He's the first person who's managed that in a long time.

'Thank you,' I say, my feet already feeling better from his remedy.

'Don't thank me,' he says. 'If they don't improve, I may have to amputate.' And he winks at me as he picks my old boots up by the laces and slings them over his shoulder.

That night, we do our best to repair my old tattered boots, tearing off some material from my travelling cloak to line them.

'When we reach the next village, we'll find some new ones,' Ilian says, as I pass him back his boots.

'And when will that be?'

'Tomorrow, I hope. Maybe the next day. I think there's a small hamlet just beyond the next ridge.'

'Do you think we can get horses there?'

'With a bit of luck.'

Through the day, I've been snatching clumps of ribwort wherever they've been growing. Now I distribute them between us.

Ilian frowns. 'What are these for?'

'Chew on them. We've got to eat something.'

He bites into one and screws his face up in disgust. 'Oh, it's bitter.'

I roll my eyes. 'It's better than starving.'

That's another reason we need to reach civilisation. Our supplies are diminished, and if we don't find a water source soon, my sore feet will be the least of our worries.

The rain arrives shortly after our meal is finished. At first, it's a relief, and we leave our flasks open to be refilled. But relief turns quickly to misery as it becomes clear sleep will be a challenge.

We're huddled on the uneven ground, our travelling cloaks failing to keep us warm or dry under the assault.

'Here,' Ilian says, shuffling over to me. 'We should sleep back to back. Like the first time we met, remember?'

I look at him through lashes heavy with droplets, shivering. 'Feeling nostalgic?' I ask, my teeth chattering.

He ignores my teasing. 'We can put the cloaks around us, trap some heat in. Come on.'

I do as I'm told, mainly because I'm too cold to argue, and soon our backs are pressed together, our cloaks draped over us for shelter.

'Just like old times,' he says when we're settled.

But it isn't. Last time we were strangers, and every muscle in his back was tense. Now he is relaxed beside me and his warmth brings me comfort.

'Listen,' he says, raising his voice to be heard over the weather. 'I think once we find new horses, we should go our separate ways.'

I'd known it was coming, but still, dread settles in my chest, a heavy ache I resent.

'Your road leads west,' he says. 'Mine east.'

What I want to say is *no*, that I don't want to be alone again, that I don't want to say goodbye. But all I manage is, 'All right.'

'Depending how much the horses are, there should be a little coin left for us to share. Do you have a plan for when you reach Eron?'

I've done nothing but plan. If I'm going to gain access to the Governor, I need to look the part. Unthreatening. A woman of the court.

'I'm thinking it's time I embraced my heritage,' I say. 'It's time I become Lady Rayn of Grynn again.'

He's quiet, and for a while only the relentless patter of rain can be heard. 'Tell me, how *did* someone of your position end up working a forge?'

'Because I had the best of fathers. He let me choose my path, even though it wasn't exactly considered proper. Never forced me to be anything other than myself.'

'You must miss him.'

'I do.' My voice catches in my throat.

Ilian shifts slightly, and I realise he's lowered his hand to his side, reaching back towards me. Nervously, I do the same. Our fingers brush, but neither of us moves them away.

'I don't miss my father,' he says, quieter now. As if sensing the change of mood, the rain lessens to a drizzle. 'He was *not* the best of men.'

At this, the rain stops entirely as if all the world is holding its breath, both wanting to know how this story ends and fearing it already does.

Ilian sighs, the memories clearly painful. 'The scar on my cheek? That was a gift from him.'

'What?' It's more a gasp than a word.

'I was a daydreamer as a child. Trailed Adrien around everywhere, doing whatever he told me. My father said I was too soft. That I needed to become my own man – though I was barely six years old. So he dragged me to the fire and held my face in it. To toughen me up.'

I close my eyes, trying to shut out the horror. I know enough about burns to know they don't toughen a damn thing.

'Exactly,' he says to my unspoken words. 'I nearly died from the resulting fever, and if not for my mother, the infection would have killed me. But here I am now, my own man.' He laughs humourlessly.

'You must hate him for what he did.'

'Once, maybe,' Ilian says. 'But years later, during our first battle in Tygh's battalion, I saw him get decapitated. That muddied my feelings a bit.'

My fingers reach closer to his, and he laces them through mine.

'I'm sorry. For all of it.'

He lets out a long, weary sigh. 'Me too.' He leans his head back to rest on my shoulder, his hair soft against my neck. 'I've been angry for so long now. First at my father. Then at the men who killed my mother. Those who took Adrien from me. Killing Tygh hasn't even dulled the edges.'

I lean my head against his. 'It's because he wasn't your enemy. Not really. He simply followed orders. It's the Emperor who's the true enemy. It's always been the Emperor. He's the one I curse with every fibre of my being. He's the one we'll make pay.'

'I hope so, Smithy. I truly do,' he says, squeezing my fingers tight.

I realise I don't want to fall asleep, don't want another dawn to come. Because each passing moment brings me closer to the one when Ilian and I must part. I tell myself I simply don't want to be alone, but I can taste the lie. The truth is harder to admit.

That here, in the cold, dangerous night, I have never felt safer.

MARZAL

U rso is buried on a dismal, unremarkable day.

Not since my arrival has the whole court been assembled in one place. Even my father has begrudgingly been carried out, his weight almost crippling the ten men who carry his chair.

If Urso had died under any other circumstances, then there would have been a service in the temple. But the Emperor has forbidden it. Instead we are outside, in the palace graveyard, where those not deemed worthy of the Imperial mausoleum are laid to rest.

It is Loris, the chief soothsayer, who speaks a few words about Urso. 'Few' being the operative word. Her beauty is mentioned but little else. I imagine my father has refused to let any other complimentary things be said about her, as he considers her a traitor.

I watch Izra closely. She has been a shadow of her former self since the loss of her daughter. Oona and Vita stand to her left and right, holding her up, comforting her. They're both using their positions in Izra's circle to elevate their status now.

Izra stares at the ground, and it's as if all her spirit is being buried along with her daughter.

Sensing I'm being watched, I stop scrutinising the others and resume a position of respectful mourning.

Who would be looking at me on such a day? After a few moments, I dare to steal a glance.

It's Zylin, and he nods when our eyes meet. I quickly lower my gaze. No one must suspect our relationship; I cannot have Rom, or anyone else, knowing about us. Just look at what became of Urso.

All in all, it is an underwhelming send-off for the Emperor's eldest daughter. When it's over, the Emperor is carried away, and only then does the rest of the crowd disperse, heading back towards the palace.

Carefully, I manoeuvre myself until I fall into step beside Advisor Rom.

'It was a beautiful ceremony,' I say, offering him a grateful smile.

Rom hangs his head. 'I would have liked there to be more, but with the war, the Emperor felt it insensitive, you understand.'

I do – more than he could possibly imagine. 'Of course.'

'Princess Marzal, there is actually something I wished to speak with you about,' he says, and I know he's going to tell me about Prince Junus. How he's going to be inflicted on me now.

'And I you,' I say, eager to speak before he has a chance. 'Would you take a walk with me?'

At first, I think he's going to refuse, but then he smiles and nods. 'Of course.'

We walk in silence to begin with, Rom's arms folded behind his back, his body rigid as he accompanies me away from the others. Once he mentions Junus, he controls the conversation. It's essential I get there first.

'Imperial Advisor Rom,' I begin, but he interrupts.

'Please, call me Rom.'

I acknowledge the offer with a small nod. 'Rom. Though it pains me to speak of my sister's death, especially after only just returning her body to the earth, I fear I must accept the situation I find myself in. That I am now heir to the throne.'

Though I stare straight ahead, I see Rom look sharply down at me from the corner of my eye.

'You are indeed,' he agrees, his tone emotionless.

'I hope you will forgive me for being so direct,' I say. 'But, as my sister was betrothed, I would imagine that my dearest father will now search for a match for me.'

'Your marriage will need to be . . . discussed, yes.' Rom is choosing his words carefully. Good.

'Again, I hope you will forgive me for voicing my thoughts. I know I am merely a woman, and will of course happily marry whomever my father desires. But it occurs to me that, for the good of our beloved country, my husband should be someone intimately familiar with how my father likes things done. Someone who has served at his side, who is respected by the people, as well as those within the palace.' Now I stop walking to look very deliberately at him, in case he has any doubt about whom I speak. 'Someone who *deserves* to potentially rule in my father's stead.'

Rom stares at me, his eyes calculating my words, searching for sincerity. I can tell all thoughts of Prince Junus are gone from his mind.

'Surely,' I continue, 'a marriage to someone suited to power would be in the country's best interests?'

What I do next is a risk. But a necessary one. I reach my hand forward and rest it lightly on his chest. He tenses at my touch, and I quickly pull back.

'Forgive me,' I say. But I know I don't need to.

He's looking at me with such intensity, I can almost hear the power and desire rushing through his body. I've just offered him everything he's ever wished for in one pretty package.

'Princess Marzal,' he begins. This time, I interrupt him.

'I think you can call me Marzal,' I say with soft sweetness.

His moustache twitches in another of his failed attempts at a smile. 'If I've understood you, and I think I have, I must concur ... a marriage between us could be most advantageous. For the country.'

'Yes, for the country.'

Rom starts to walk again, deep in thought, and I match his step.

'Of course, we would need your father's blessing. And he has other ideas for your marriage at the moment,' he says. 'I fear if *I* were to suggest our union, it would be considered a grievous act of presumption. It is not my place, or any man's, to question the Emperor's wishes.'

'What if we were to delay my engagement?' I say it lightly, as if the idea has only just occurred to me and not, in fact, been planned meticulously in the dead of night. 'Wait for the war to be over? In his moment of glory, my father might be more willing to grant our request.'

Rom is silent as he considers my words. I decide to add a little extra incentive.

'While I will gladly do whatever is asked of me, I cannot deny I would prefer to marry for love, and not duty alone.' My voice is soft, alluring, as gentle as any caress. I continue, 'Since the moment we met, the truth is I have found myself drawn to you. I find myself dreaming of you. Longing for you.' As soon as the words are out my mouth, I wonder if I have gone too far.

But Rom is looking at me with a mixture of astonishment and delight. I have done just enough, I can sense it.

We are entirely alone now, and Rom clasps my hands in his own. 'I long for you too, Princess. Your happiness is everything to me. We shall persuade your father of our union, but you are right. The Emperor is on the cusp of victory and will be far more responsive to such a request once he has prevailed.'

'Does that mean no one should know of our feelings?'

Rom pulls my hands close to his heart. 'We must keep them a secret . . . for now. First, I must ensure you are not promised to another. Leave everything to me.'

I nod meekly, as if I am nothing but a besotted girl, wanting to marry a handsome man.

Part of me is astounded that I have won the heart of such an intelligent man so easily. I'm not arrogant enough to believe that it really has anything to do with me, of course. It's my position and all that comes with it – what a marriage to me would give him – that draws him like a moth to a flame. It is strange how men believe us women to be riddled with weakness, but theirs can be exploited with only a few honeyed words.

'We should return before we are missed,' Rom says.

'When will I see you again?'

My eagerness pleases him, I can tell. 'Soon, my love,' he says. 'Soon. You must trust me. You do trust me, don't you?'

Not even for a second. 'With all my heart.'

I think perhaps he's going to kiss me but before he can, we hear the screams. Exchanging a quick look of concern, we hurry back to where we left the scattering court.

The moment I see what's happening, I gasp in shock.

Izra's fingers are wrapped around Roselle's throat. It's her screams and curses we'd heard; the sounds Roselle's making are choked and unintelligible.

Izra's killing her. And no one's trying to stop it, too frozen in shock to move.

Ever composed, Rom strides forward and takes charge immediately.

'Stop this at once,' he says, his voice authoritative as he beckons guards over who quickly part the women.

Izra spits on Roselle as she's finally dragged away. 'It's her doing. All hers! She murdered my daughter.' And she breaks into sobs.

Roselle coughs and clutches her neck as she looks around, fear glinting in her eyes. 'I did nothing,' she protests in a hoarse whisper. 'She's mad with grief.'

'Liar!' Izra screams. 'You've always hated us, both of us. But I'll make you pay, I swear it.'

'Izra.' Rom positions himself between the two women, his tone firm. 'What grounds have you for making such a serious accusation?'

'She found out about the letters. She betrayed Urso. My little girl . . .' Her voice breaks, and only returns on a wave of anger. 'She may as well have stabbed Urso with her own knife. And now . . . my baby is dead. Dead.' Izra's anger is spent now, and she collapses to the ground, inconsolable and broken.

Roselle looks stricken as all eyes turn to her. 'I have no idea what she's talking about. Truly.' She falls to her knees before Rom, her hands clasped as she begs him. 'You must believe me. I mourn the loss of Urso as much as anyone.'

Rom surveys the horrified crowd, and then gestures at Izra. 'Someone take her back to her chambers.' Oona and Vita rush to assist their friend, who has nothing left to fight them with. It's quite a sight to see the once all-powerful Izra so frail.

'As for you,' Rom says to Roselle. 'Get back inside. I will speak with you later.'

She nods, more grateful than perhaps she should be. 'Thank you, yes.'

I watch Sennan hovering on the sidelines, unsure whether to stand by her mother, or if that alliance is now too dangerous.

It's something we all feel acutely, the need to choose a side in this new war. The dynamics have now changed irrevocably. With no obvious leader among the women, there's no one to tell them how to think, how to act. From the way they're all considering each other with caution and suspicion, it seems to be a prospect that makes them afraid.

But not me. This is precisely the opportunity I've been waiting for. I am now heir to the throne. Few of the women hate me or are threatened by me.

It's time to make my move.

ELENA

It feels like I've walked for ever. I've covered hundreds of miles, and the baby has grown so he no longer fits comfortably on my chest, which means I've had to rearrange the sling to carry him on my back.

While he has grown, my own body feels like it's shrunk, worn down from travelling and grief. Peddling my little medicinal bunches has kept our bellies from shrivelling to nothing, but I am warier now, scarred by what happened with Elsette.

I don't linger, I don't get involved and I keep well away from pregnant women.

Elsette fills my thoughts every night. Should I have done more; could I have saved her? My head knows she was already doomed by the time I reached her, but my heart says I failed. Failed her, the baby . . . Aliénor.

The thought that I have let Aliénor down burns more fiercely than all the others, and I no longer feel fit to call myself a midwife. Any confidence I ever had drained away with Elsette's life.

As the light fades on another cold day, I finally reach the town I've been walking towards. Relief warms my bones. Last night I found nowhere to shelter, and we nearly froze to death under the stars.

After knocking on only a couple of doors, I find a man

willing to talk to me in exchange for a few coins, and he knows of Anaïs. Apparently, she's the only immigrant from Metée here.

I thank him and head towards the edge of the town, to the cottage with the rose rambling up its wall.

I know as soon as she answers the door that it's the right house. Anaïs is so like Aliénor that for a moment I think it is her, and am filled with happiness, only to immediately realise my mistake and deflate so deeply it hurts.

'Yes?'

I manage to smile at the woman before me.

'You're Anaïs?'

'Depends who's asking.' She's harder around the edges than Aliénor, but it doesn't deter me.

'I'm Elena. I was Aliénor's apprentice.'

Her face barely moves, but the slight twitch of her eye and tightening of the lip betray her.

'You'd best come in then.'

I step into her cottage, grateful to be out of the night air, only to find it's little warmer in here.

Anaïs gestures for me to sit down near the small fireplace. I untie the sling and carefully bring the baby round to sit on my knee.

'Hungry?'

I'm starving, but I simply nod politely.

'Don't have much,' she says, placing a pot over the fire to heat. 'But you're welcome to it.'

'Thank you.'

While the gruel warms through, Anaïs takes a seat. 'How did Aliénor die?'

So direct, so blunt, that I'm too startled to reply.

'That's why you're here, isn't it? To tell me she's gone?'

Once I catch my breath, I say, 'We were attacked. Soldiers came for the children—'

'And she died protecting them,' Anaïs finishes with a nod. 'That sounds like Aliénor.'

'I thought you would want to know.'

Anaïs gives me a long, considering look. Then she stands up to dollop out the gruel and passes me the bowl. 'And you walked the length of the country, with a little one in tow, just for that?'

Dipping my finger in the gruel, I hold it up for the baby to suck, which he does ravenously. I'm not sure how to answer.

'What were you to her?' Anaïs asks, when I remain silent.

'I told you, her apprentice.' She gives me a scathing look and I wilt under her scrutiny. Swallowing back my sorrow, I add, 'And a daughter.'

'Hmm.' She considers me for a long moment. 'Is he yours?' Anaïs gestures at the boy.

I hesitate before answering. 'No.' He's all I have left, but he isn't mine.

Her eyes narrow as if she can see right through me. 'I'd have thought Aliénor would have taught you better than to take in a stray. Perhaps she grew too soft in her old age.'

'We weren't exactly given much of a choice,' I say, prickling to defend Aliénor.

'We never are.'

Anaïs stares into the fire, her grief softening me towards her.

'I was sorry to hear about your son.' When she says nothing, I add, 'So was Aliénor. She regretted never meeting him.'

I worry that I've ventured somewhere too raw, but Anaïs slowly lifts her head to look at me.

'Did she ever tell you why we were estranged?'

'No,' I admit.

She gives a mirthless chuckle. 'No, I didn't think so. Proud to the end.'

For a moment, I don't think she's going to tell me either, but then she lets out a long, weary sigh.

'It was because of a man.'

I try to hide my surprise and fail. I'd always assumed romance had passed Aliénor by.

'Wipe that look off your face,' Anaïs says, half smiling. 'She was a midwife, not a nun.'

Blushing, I look away.

'He was a farmer, and she loved him. Unfortunately, so did I. Aliénor knew her path wasn't compatible with marriage, so she stepped aside so that he and I could be together. We were to be married. And then I met someone else, and ran away with him. She was never able to forgive me for it.'

'For breaking her heart?'

'No,' she breathes, lost in a memory, 'for breaking his.'

That sounds like Aliénor. She lived her whole life putting other people before herself. I'm not even half as selfless as she was.

Anaïs prods the fire absently with a poker. 'It all seems so pointless now. We missed a lifetime because of a man. We were both fools. Bloody fools.'

The baby is falling asleep, content, his tummy as full as it's been in a long while. His peace serves to calm me, though everything feels so dark.

'It would have destroyed our mother to know we let a

man come between us,' Anaïs says, shaking her head. 'She always taught us the power of sisterhood, how together women are stronger.'

My grief is expanding, threatening to swallow me whole. I thought I knew Aliénor, but I realise now I knew her only as a teacher, a mother. It never occurred to me to know her as a woman, with her own past, her own disappointments, her own demons.

And now I never will.

'She always was the strong one,' Anaïs says.

I know that feeling. That lost sense of confusion now that the person you relied on is no longer there.

'They came here too.' She looks over to me then, her face haunted. 'The soldiers. They came here for the babies too.'

I close my eyes in horror. Every town, every village; the Naperones have left none untouched. The scale of their wickedness consumes me.

'I hid when they came here,' she says. 'Aliénor died trying to save them, and I hid. That tells you everything you need to know about the two of us.'

When I open my eyes, I see the regret in hers. The shame.

'I hid too.'

Anaïs nods her head slowly, in understanding. Then her gaze lingers on the sleeping baby in my arms. I wonder if she's thinking back to when she cradled her own son like this.

'You can stay, if you want. I've a goat out the back, so there's milk for the child.'

'Thank you.' Tears spring to my eyes, I'm so relieved.

'I'm afraid I don't have much else. Since Artemis died,

I've found myself struggling. I have no income. But the Empress lived in this town, before she was summoned to the palace, and she sends money back every now and then. Her family distribute it to those in need. So I've managed.'

She looks at me appraisingly. 'You know the town no longer has a midwife. She died last winter. Maybe you could take on those duties?'

Fear and panic grip me, the memory of Elsette flashing vividly in front of my eyes. 'I can't,' I say quickly. 'I never completed my training. But I have some remedies to sell, if you think anyone would be interested?'

I reach into my bag and hold out a posy for her. She takes it, giving me a curious look. I think she knows I'm lying – but she says nothing.

'I'll certainly recommend you to my neighbours. You might earn us a crust or two.'

Night draws in and Anaïs gathers fresh blankets for us. As I settle down in the safety of the cottage, I decide not to look to the future or the past. Both hold too much fear. If I dwell only on this moment, right now, I can at least say I've done what Aliénor told me to do.

Today we lived. Today we survived. That's the best I can do any more.

MARZAL

Assuming the position of power among the women is not to be attempted with force. Vita learned that the hard way when she made her move straight after the funeral, by adopting an arrogant manner and making demands from us all. In short, she tried to act like Izra, without earning the position first.

The women didn't stand for it, ignoring her, belittling her and rounding on her as a group until she retreated, tail between her legs.

If she knew anything of group dynamics, if she had spent years in a convent watching and learning the intricacies of human behaviour, Vita would have known a gentler approach would be much more effective.

Since Urso's death, I have taken the time to speak to all the women, individually and occasionally in small groups. I have asked them how they are, how they're feeling, if there's anything I can do to ease their pain. Teas of every variety have been blended and shared, and now, when they think of something they need, they come to me. Their friend. The quiet, caring princess, who endured such torture from Izra and Roselle, and yet still has only kind words to say about them both. The one who is always ready with a listening ear, and a morsel of advice.

This is how you assume true power. You gain their respect. And their love.

The atmosphere in the hall when we gather is lighter now. We no longer split into various groups, choosing instead to sit all together. Since the funeral, Roselle hasn't left her room and Sennan sits warily among us, laughing a little too hard at jokes in an effort to ingratiate herself.

But when the door opens one day and we see Izra there, we all fall silent. She hasn't joined us in the hall since Urso died. Lilah, her handmaiden, supports her as Izra shuffles into the room. She is a pale reflection of her former self. Her hair is wilder, her face unpowdered. We've all heard rumours that she can't sleep and, seeing her, I believe them. Dark shadows lie beneath puffy skin, eyes glazed with exhaustion and loss. Lilah escorts her to a chair near the window.

'See, it's your favourite view,' the handmaiden says, her voice so patronising even I cringe.

Izra stares out of the window, though I doubt she's seeing anything beyond it. How the mighty have fallen.

'Will you excuse me?' I say to my companions.

I can sense their curiosity as I leave the hall. Perhaps they think I dislike Izra so much I can't bear to share the same space as her. Or maybe they think seeing her reminds me of the sister I've lost.

So when I return, carrying a pot of tea, they watch me intently.

I walk over to Izra and smile at Lilah, who's eyeing me suspiciously.

'Hello, Aunty,' I say softly to Izra.

Izra doesn't acknowledge me in any way.

'I brought you some tea,' I say, pouring the blend I've prepared into a cup. 'It will help you sleep. There's chamomile in there, and passionflower.' And valerian, but I think it's best not to mention that.

Now Izra looks at me, searching for the trick, waiting for the sting.

'And I picked this for you.' I rest a sprig of lavender on her lap. 'Place it on your pillow. It will help.'

I leave her with a warm smile and return to my seat. I say nothing, but I can feel the women's approval. Apart from Sennan. She's glaring at me the way Roselle used to glare at Izra. She can sense I'm gaining power and she doesn't like it one bit.

'Why don't we all take a turn around the gardens?' I say, needing to escape this room.

Sennan stares at me. 'It's windy.'

'But the sun is shining; it shall be pleasant enough.'

Everyone agrees that this would, indeed, be a welcome diversion, and we tidy away our embroideries.

I smile at Sennan as we walk out of the hall. In our minuscule power struggle, one so small that no one else even noticed it happening, I won.

She's right though, there is a gale whipping up outside, and our dresses and veils billow in the wind so that we look like a flock of crows swooping along. But the air is fresh, reaching into our lungs and filling them with life. Coming outside was a good decision. Izra's presence in the hall left everyone too on edge.

And things improve further when I see Rom approaching us with a determined stride.

'All hail the Emperor,' he says to greet us.

'All hail the Emperor,' we chorus in unison.

'Princess Marzal, would you mind if I steal you away from your companions? There is a matter I must discuss with you.'

A few weeks ago, I would have been mortified if he'd spoken to me in public, would have feared the repercussions of being singled out so. But not any longer. It's yet another seal of approval on my character.

'Of course,' I say, and bid farewell to the other women, whose eyes I can sense on my back as I walk away.

'You are well?' Rom asks when we are out of earshot.

'As can be expected at such a difficult time.'

'Indeed.' He clears his throat. 'That is what I wish to speak with you about. The rather delicate matter of Izra and Roselle.'

'You mean their altercation at the funeral?'

Rom nods. 'It surprised me. I thought they were friends.'

Friendship is a fragile thing in this palace. 'I think they had a grudging respect for one another, but no. I don't think Izra and Roselle have ever been friends.'

He weighs up this information. 'Obviously, no one believes that Roselle actually killed Urso. The girl's shame was her own. But Izra is searching for someone to blame and I have been charged with resolving the matter.'

I decide to say nothing, offer nothing, until directly asked. Every game played within these walls is dangerous, and this one is no exception.

'Do you know how the Emperor learned of Urso's indiscretions?'

I shake my head.

'An anonymous note was sent to one of the advisors.'

I glance up at him. 'And Izra thinks Roselle was the one to send it?'

Rom nods. 'Exactly. So I wanted to ask you what you thought.'

'Oh . . .' I allow an uncertain pause. 'I'm not sure I'm the right person to ask.'

'And yet it is your opinion I seek. Do you think Roselle was the one to betray Urso?'

He stops walking, blocking my path, and gives me his most searching gaze.

I sigh, as if answering pains me deeply. 'I can't tell you whether she did it, but if you're asking me do I think she *could* have done it – then yes. I believe she is capable.'

'Then perhaps that's enough to provide a solution. Izra is demanding justice and the Emperor wants it all to go away. This will appease them both.'

I swallow hard. 'What will happen to Roselle?'

'Banishment, probably. Anything more will cause too much embarrassment for His Imperial Majesty.'

And we couldn't have that, now, could we?

I glance towards the other side of the gardens, where the women still battle against the elements. 'And Sennan?'

'I think I have no choice but to send her with her mother.' He pauses. 'You are the heir now, and if they wanted to hurt Urso, we must consider that they may also want to hurt you.'

I nod, as if this is painful for me to learn.

Discreetly, he holds out a jewelled case. 'This is for you. In case anyone should try and harm you.'

Lifting the lid a fraction, I glimpse the dagger within and shake my head with disbelief. 'I wouldn't know what to do with such a thing.'

'And I hope you never have cause to use it,' he says. 'But until we are wed and I can protect you myself, I don't want you vulnerable. Please, take it. For me.'

Reluctantly, I accept his gift, concealing it under my cloak.

'Go now. And say nothing about Roselle and Sennan to anyone,' he says. 'I want to deal with this as quietly as possible.'

'You have my word.'

And he does, because I'm the last person I want Sennan to hear this from. In fact, I hope the first she knows about it is when Rom arrives to escort her off the premises, because I think if she knew what I'd said to Rom she'd happily strangle me in my sleep given half the chance.

Fortunately for me, Rom has similar suspicions.

It's on a wet afternoon – while we're sitting quietly, drinking tea and stitching, our voices low so as not to disturb Izra, who now joins us every day to stare out of her window – that the men come for Sennan.

They burst in unannounced and we all stagger to our feet.

'What is the meaning of this intrusion?' I ask, stepping forward, the only one brave enough to speak.

Rom sweeps in and points at Sennan. 'Come with us.'

Sennan looks from him, to the others, to me. 'What's going on?'

We hear Roselle before we see her.

'Get your hands off me,' she's screaming. 'Don't you know who I am?'

She's putting up a good fight, but when Roselle's dragged into the room, she looks far from composed. In fact, she looks terrified.

'Imperial Advisor Rom,' she cries, flinging herself at him. 'You have known me since the day I arrived at court.

What is the meaning of such treatment?'

Rom gives her a cold, dispassionate stare. 'You are to be transported to the Winter Palace, where you are to remain for the rest of your days.'

Roselle's face crumples. She knows there's no case to fight here.

But Sennan steps forward. 'What? You can't do that.'

Roselle gives her daughter a warning glance to be quiet, but too late.

Rom turns to address Sennan. 'And you are to accompany your mother.'

At this, Roselle falls to her knees, clutching at Rom's robes. 'No! Please, not Sennan. I demand to see the Emperor. He will let her stay here.'

'These orders come directly from the Emperor.' Rom may as well have cut Roselle's throat, she falls so silent.

She knows that if this is the Emperor's wish, it will be so.

Sennan is still too young, too naive to have comprehended this though. 'Mother, please . . . this is our home.' She turns to Rom. 'You can't do this.'

Roselle gets to her feet and attempts to collect herself. She is the Imperial Mistress – or at least, she was. She understands the importance of leaving with dignity. Her chin tilted high, she reaches out to clutch her daughter's hand.

'Come,' she says. 'It's time for us to bid farewell to our friends.'

She looks at us all standing there, an unwilling audience to this drama, and when her gaze falls on me, our eyes lock.

Does she sense my victory? My great delight in her fall?

I think she does, and what's best is how much it takes her by surprise. Even after all she's done to me, all she did to my mother, it hadn't occurred to her that I might hate her. Might wish for her ruin.

Roselle chuckles humourlessly under her breath and looks away from me. Her realisation has come too late.

Sennan has finally fallen quiet. Like her mother, she's drowning in rage but knows it's a lost cause. The Emperor's word is, after all, law.

Rom nods at me as they leave, a brief acknowledgement that the deed is done and I am now safe.

But it's only once they're gone, the room prickling with a stunned silence, that I look to see how Izra's reacted to this development.

Her eyes are shut, a contented smile on her face. For the first time since Urso's death, Izra has found enough peace to fall asleep.

*

Things return to normal after Roselle and Sennan leave the palace, a sense of relief filling the women's quarters. I write and tell my mother everything. She will be pleased to hear of her rival's downfall.

But there are matters I've neglected over the past few days.

With so much going on, it's been a while since last I saw Zylin, so I enlist Ama to pass a message to him, suggesting we meet after dusk in our usual place, because I know the gardens are deserted then.

In the herb garden, he's waiting for me, jumping to his feet as I approach.

'I feared you wouldn't come,' Zylin says.

'I couldn't stay away if I tried.' I step close to him, so that our skin brushes. 'I have another letter.'

He takes it from me, our hands touching far longer than necessary. 'I will ensure its safe delivery as always.'

'I cannot thank you enough for your assistance.' Our hands are still touching.

'There is nothing I wouldn't do for you, Marzal.'

I smile, before moving slightly away. 'Are you well?'

Zylin looks disappointed that I've placed distance between us. 'Only when I'm with you. I confess, every minute you consume my thoughts. I long for the day when we can be together and not have to hide in secret.'

'I long for that day too,' I say softly. 'Once the war is over, my father will give us his blessing, I am sure of it. In the meantime, you must continue to stay in his favour, do what you can to help him win this war.'

Zylin falls silent for a moment. 'I've noticed Special Advisor Rom looking at you,' he says, and the jealousy is biting. 'I saw you together in the gardens the other day.'

I shall have to warn Rom to watch his gaze. If Zylin has noticed, others may have too. But right now, the last thing I want is for Zylin to doubt my affection. While Rom is old-fashioned and is attracted to a demure, sweet girl with propriety at the forefront of his mind, I think Zylin might prefer other kinds of reassurance.

Closing the space between us, I press myself tight against Zylin's chest and lace my fingers through his. I can feel his shock at such a bold move – and his longing for more. 'Special Advisor Rom shows me only the affection of an uncle,' I explain. 'He talks to me of the weather and architecture. You need not be jealous of him. It is not *him* that I love.'

Zylin wraps his arms around me. 'I am not jealous.' His voice is a soft growl.

My lips graze his. 'Good.' I press my hand to his chest and then slowly move it downwards, slipping past his belt and into his breeches. His breath catches at my touch and he looks at me, startled.

'What are you doing?' He's shocked but excited.

'Showing my gratitude,' I say, my lips purring against his as my hand moves in a stroking motion. Truth be told, I have no idea what I'm doing. I have never touched a man intimately before and know only what Kala once told me, but his body responds nevertheless, his deep moans assuring me I'm doing enough.

With one of his hands, Zylin grabs my breast, squeezing it as I sigh in pleasure to encourage him. He pushes me hard against the high hedging, and with me pinned there, his other hand starts searching for a path through my skirts.

My own hand quickens its motion, which only seems to make his quest to touch me more urgent, but just as he's sliding his way up my thigh, his whole body shudders and he starts to go limp in my hand.

We stay there for a few moments, him panting hard, before I withdraw my touch.

'Your gratitude is most welcome,' he says, giving a soft chuckle. 'My Gods, I can't wait to bed you,' he says, kissing his way down my neck to the top of my breasts.

'Soon, my love,' I promise.

As he catches his breath, he seems to remember where we are, what a risk we've taken, and he moves away, tucking his shirt back in.

'I should return before anyone notices I'm gone,' I say, straightening my own clothes.

'Of course,' he says. He presses the letter I've entrusted to him close to his heart. 'I shall make sure this is taken care of.'

'Thank you.'

'I look forward to the next time,' he says, stealing one last kiss from me. 'Goodnight.'

I walk slowly away, our hands touching until my fingers slip from his. I move silently through the darkness, invisible in my mourning colours, and only when I'm safely back in my room, unseen by anyone, do I breathe again.

I'm surprised by the risk I've just taken. If we had been discovered, we would have suffered the same fate as Urso and her lover. But some things are worth the risk.

Zylin was assured of my devotion, and I of his. In that moment, nothing else mattered.

Still, my night is far from over and there's no time to linger on what I've done. Changing my clothes, I embark on my nightly visit to see my father. If I'm honest, it's been a long time since it was worth venturing into this cold, dark space. My father is often asleep, and even when he is awake, very little happens. But I persevere because, undoubtedly, the one occasion I decide to abstain from my excursion will be the time I miss something crucial.

When I peer into the room tonight, I see it is full of advisors. They're talking among themselves, everyone busy, and I'm surprised when the door opens and Zylin walks in, excusing himself for being late.

Nothing more happens for a while, just the busy hum

of men pretending to be important, until a messenger hurries in.

He bows low before the throne. 'All hail the Emperor.'

My father flicks his finger, telling the man to rise and approach.

'What news?' the Emperor asks lazily.

I see the messenger give Rom a look and a barely perceptible shake of his head. He's not come to deliver good news.

Rom clenches his jaw as he moves to stand closer to the throne.

'General Tygh is dead, Majesty.'

An unsettled silence falls over the room.

'What do you mean, *dead*?' Like it is a personal insult to my father that this man dared to die without his permission.

'Murdered. By one of his own.'

My father's rage is dangerously quiet. 'I see,' he says, and if you didn't know him, you would think he was taking this well. 'And where is his killer?'

'We don't know.'

The Emperor explodes with fury, hurling his goblet at the messenger, who flinches as it strikes him.

'There's more, Majesty,' the messenger continues – bravely or stupidly, I can't quite decide.

My father positively snarls. 'What more could there possibly be?'

'The killer, Commander Stone, took a prisoner with him. A blacksmith.'

This gets my father's attention, his head snapping up sharply. 'What shit-swilling blacksmith?'

'No one of importance, Majesty,' the messenger says hurriedly. 'She's merely a woman.'

The glance between Rom and Loris doesn't escape my attention.

My father, however, remains focused on one thing. 'What. Shit-swilling. Blacksmith?' He punctuates each word for emphasis.

The messenger hesitates before answering. 'Rumour has it she was making some sort of special sword for General Tygh before they absconded. A sword forged in blood.'

The Emperor staggers to his feet, swaying from side to side. He's been drinking. He reaches to pull the sword from Rom's scabbard and plunges it deep into the messenger's chest. The man rolls forward to the ground, death his reward for relaying such bad news.

Now my father turns his wrath on Rom.

'How has this happened? How have you failed me so pus-pissing spectacularly? You said the godsdamn sword would be here soon.'

He reaches forward to grab Rom's shirt, pulling him close. 'Do you want me dead, is that it? Want my throne, do you, Rom? Want to rule yourself?'

My heart is in my mouth. *This is not good.*

'No, Majesty,' Rom splutters, and my father pushes him away in disgust.

'Get out, all of you. Get OUT!'

Nervously, the room empties. He's so forceful, I almost leave myself, before common sense reminds me that he isn't actually talking to me.

As usual, both Rom and Loris stay behind, but tonight my father glares at Rom. 'And you. Get out.'

Rom's ears burn red, he's furious, but he bows nonetheless. 'Of course, Majesty.'

When only my father and Loris remain, the chief

soothsayer steps over the dead messenger to pour my father another drink.

'My enemies are closing in.' The Emperor is afraid.

'No, Majesty,' Loris says. 'The child born on a winter's night? You took care of that. And we will retrieve the blade of blood. At least now we know where to look.'

My father seems a little reassured. 'What do the stars say?'

'That you have no reason to fear.'

It's almost as if he's inflating the Emperor with confidence; I can see my father swelling in stature.

'Rom!'

The doors immediately open, and Rom stands there, ready to serve.

'Yes, Majesty?'

The Emperor takes a long drink of wine, his speech slurring when he talks. 'Contact your man in Eron. It's time we stepped up our plan.'

Rom looks far from convinced but knows better than to argue. 'Consider it done.'

'And find out what's happened to that shitting leverage he promised us.'

'Yes, Majesty.' He turns to leave.

'And, Rom?' the Emperor calls, gesturing to the body on the ground. 'Clear up this mess.'

I don't need to watch Rom be humiliated as his penance, and so I return to my room.

But I can't fall asleep; my mind is too full. I wish I had someone I could talk to. Writing to my mother helps still my thoughts, but at the same time only reminds me how much I miss her. How I wish she were here, so she could comfort me in her arms.

Because it's lonely here at the palace. It was lonely at the convent. My whole life I've lived with lots of people, but I've always been alone.

And tonight, for some reason, I've never felt it more acutely.

RAYN

When I was little, my father would tell me tales about Eron. He visited there from time to time – sometimes alone, sometimes with my mother – to attend court. Whether he was conducting business or there purely to socialise, he would always return with stories to share with me as I fell asleep.

So I'd already known about the vast bridge across the river that leads up to the outer walls. I knew of the many turrets, the archways, and of the cobbled roads that all meet in the city centre, where the government buildings lie. I'd heard how the sprawling courts looked more like temples or palaces than anything political.

I knew all of this. But seeing it is something else altogether.

My father had tried to describe the sheer magnitude of Eron, with its towering walls and labyrinthine streets, but no words he'd used come close. It's the most beautiful place I've ever been. But it's also the most unsettling.

I've spent the past few years travelling the country and have seen first-hand the devastation of the war. Coming here is like going back to a time before the fighting began.

The people are dressed so elegantly, and they look well fed but, even more noticeably, they don't look afraid. They aren't worn down to the quick, wearing grief like a second skin. Everything here is like it was at Lord Norvill's château, only on a much grander scale.

It's unnerving.

I arrived several days ago and quickly secured myself a room in a ramshackle inn, sold the horse I bought when Ilian and I finally emerged from the mountain path, and purchased the least ridiculous dress I could find. I thought it best to explore the capital and familiarise myself with the weaving roads, before transforming into Lady Grynn. I've dared to speak to just a few people, but no one can tell me much about the war. They seem so detached from it, insisting that General Riley will lead us to victory. I hear his name a lot, the leader of Naperone's armies. The people here are very confident in his abilities.

Ilian and I went our separate ways just over a week ago. We said an awkward goodbye; I simply wished him luck, as if we were passing strangers, too afraid to voice anything deeper. I thought it would be less painful that way. Turns out I was wrong.

But I'm here now and I need to focus.

I have to speak to Governor Franklin, but he is proving a difficult man to find.

I've transformed myself from blacksmith to Lady. Thank goodness for gloves, because my calloused hands would otherwise give me away in a heartbeat. My father's sword remains safe, concealed beneath a loose floorboard in my room, but I have a dagger tucked into my boot and my faithful little key remains ever close to my heart.

However looking the part of a fine Lady isn't enough when I reach the government buildings. In fact, it works against me, as no one is willing to take a young woman remotely seriously.

First, I'm told Governor Franklin isn't here. Then someone else tells me he's busy. In the end, I'm finally informed that he is actually in his quarters at the far end of the building, but not to be disturbed.

That's sufficient to send me in the right direction, and I walk purposefully through the corridors, as if I'm meant to be here and not at all trespassing, until I see a distant door guarded by two soldiers. I'd be willing to bet money that's where Franklin is.

I stride up with my most winning smile. 'Good day, gentlemen. I'm here to see the Governor.'

'Governor's busy,' one of the guards says. 'Do yourself a favour and run along.'

My smile remains, but my eyes narrow with irritation. My voice is firmer this time. 'I'm not sure you heard me. I demand to see Governor Franklin.'

The guard looks at me, uninterested. 'Demand all you want. The Governor is not to be disturbed.'

This is ridiculous. I decide to take a risk. 'Look, I have travelled for days, at his request. So I insist you let me in at once.'

'I don't care if you have orders from the Gods themselves. You are not seeing the Governor.'

For a moment, we both hold our ground, staring the other down, but he's clearly unwilling to bend. I'm going to have to find another way in.

'Fine,' I say. 'I hope you're prepared to lose your position over this.' And I retreat, heading back outside to regroup.

Nothing about Eron has been as I expected. Considering troops are marching ever closer to take it and seal the Emperor's success, there's little panic in the air here. There's certainly no indication that they're preparing to endure a long siege. Perhaps they've been too long distanced from the war ravaging the rest of the country. I have to find a way to talk to the Governor and discover what's going on. Urge him to rise up and fight for his people. Warn him that there are traitors in our midst.

'Well, well, well. I didn't expect to see you again.'

I turn to face the man I danced with all those months ago at Lord Norvill's soirée. The man who was there to reprimand the Lord for his frivolity during war. Someone with enough authority to turn the man ashen.

A potential ally.

I smile as we walk towards each other.

'I didn't realise Lord Crouchley was in the city at the moment,' he says.

Ah, yes, the old lecher I'd used to gain entrance to the ball. 'I'm here quite alone, actually,' I say.

'Then join me for lunch,' he says. 'I owe you that at least, for abandoning you on the dance floor.'

I'm hardly full of better ideas, so bow in agreement. 'Thank you. But please do tell me your name, so you're not just "the man I danced with".'

He laughs. 'I'm General Riley. Pleased to make your acquaintance.'

I raise my eyebrows in surprise. '*The* General Riley? Head of our army? That General Riley?'

'Guilty.' And his eyes flash with wicked humour.

Next to the Governor, he's probably the most important man in the whole of Naperone. This might be the first bit of good fortune I've had in a while. As long as he doesn't find out who my family are.

'Forgive me,' I say. 'You don't wear your uniform?'

'Not when I'm off duty. I find it intimidates people.'

How strange. I've never met a soldier who felt off duty in a time of war, let alone the person in charge of our strategies.

'Besides,' Riley continues, as if he can hear my thoughts, 'everyone here knows who I am.'

He escorts me to an inn, and as if to prove his point, everyone we pass salutes him, or offers some sort of acknowledgement. I could be imagining it, but I don't sense he's well liked. Some people seem almost afraid of him.

A table is prepared for us the moment he strides into the inn, and we sit down, only to have a bowl of stew placed in front of us with a tankard of ale. I have to disguise how desperately I want to bolt the food down, acting instead like a Lady who eats frequently.

'I apologise for the slop, but it's the best inn you'll find in Eron.'

There are actual chunks of vegetables in the stew; I'd hardly call it slop. 'I'm sure I can tolerate it.' With as much restraint as I can muster, I take a sip. It's the best thing I've eaten in years, even if it is little more than some potato and carrot in water.

'So tell me, what brings you to Eron?' he asks.

'Safety. The enemy is advancing ever further south and I fear this is the only safe place to be.'

'Not for long,' Riley says, watching me closely. 'This is where they're headed.'

'But surely even with a full-scale assault, Eron's walls cannot be breached?'

Riley leans back in his chair. 'You don't think Eron will fall?'

'It mustn't.'

He chews on a crust of bread. 'You speak a lot about the war.'

'Is there any reason I shouldn't?'

'No.' He shakes his head. 'It's just most women I know prefer to talk about anything else.'

I shrug. 'Maybe they're afraid.'

'And you aren't?' I can sense it's a loaded question.

'Of course I am. I'd be a fool not to be. But I'm also confident that you and the Governor will defend us successfully. That the Emperor's men will eventually be forced to fall back.'

'Indeed.' He sounds like he believes that about as much as I do. This conversation is a maze of deceit – neither of us is being truthful.

'You have family fighting?' When he takes a spoonful of stew, he slurps it off the spoon, leaving drops in his beard.

'I did. They're dead.' Better stick as close to the truth as possible.

'Sorry to hear that.'

The conversation falters awkwardly, and I take the opportunity to eat some more stew. Riley watches me and when I'm finished, he says, 'Now that you're done, why don't you tell me why you're really here.'

I feign innocence. 'What do you mean?'

'The woman I met before showed an obvious dislike for displays of wealth. You've become . . . far more guarded in your opinions.' Now he leans forward, his face creased with concern. 'Are you in trouble? Can I help you at all?'

'You're as perceptive as ever,' I say, choosing my words carefully. 'I did in fact come here with an ulterior motive.'

'Finally, this becomes more interesting.' And Riley smiles at me.

'I was hoping to talk to Governor Franklin, tell him about the hardships his people are suffering and beg him for assistance,' I lie.

'And what assistance do you think he could possibly give you?'

'Allow the people of my settlement to come and shelter behind Eron's walls.'

Riley almost chokes on his drink. 'What makes you think he'd agree to that?'

'Because I'm betting no one else has had the guts to ask.'

That earns an impressed grin from Riley. 'So do it then.'

'Easier said than done, I'm afraid. He's holed up in his chambers and I cannot get past his guards.'

'Well, there, at least, I can help you.' He slides his chair back and rises to his feet. 'Come on.'

I stare at him in surprise. 'You're going to help me?'

'I'm going to get you in to see the Governor. After that, you're on your own.'

I follow him out of the inn, my stomach pleasantly full, my hopes sufficiently raised. It was a stroke of luck to have crossed paths with Riley back at Lord Norvill's château.

We make our way quickly through the city streets, people moving out of the way for Riley.

When we reach the Governor's quarters, the guards immediately stand to attention when they see who's coming, though they cast me an unfriendly glare.

'Let her through,' Riley says, much to the guards' confusion.

'Sir? We have our orders—'

'And now you have new ones. The Lady wants to speak with the Governor. Let her through.'

They do as they're told, though they clearly don't want to, and Riley smiles at me with encouragement.

'Thank you,' I smile back at him. 'I'll see you again?'

'I'm sure of it.'

Bidding him goodbye, I enter the Governor's office.

The drapes are shut, only the thinnest sliver of light seeping through.

'Hello?' I say, my senses on alert. Something's not right.

Sitting in the dark, shrouded in shadow, is the Governor. On first appraisal he seems older than I expected from my father's descriptions, but as my eyes adjust, I see that he's not old so much as exhausted by the weight of war. He looks up at me with suspicion.

'Who are you?'

'A friend, sir. I've come to warn you.'

To my great surprise, he chuckles. 'Warn me?' He laughs more. It's a chilling sound. 'What could you possibly warn me about?'

I sit in the chair across from him. 'There is a traitor in your government. There is someone – or maybe some people – who are working against you in this war, against the country. We need to stop them.'

'We? And who exactly are you?'

'I told you, I'm a friend. I'm working with General Drake.'

He frowns, recognising the name, and slowly it comes to him. 'Ah, yes, Drake. What's he doing working with you?'

What he means is, what's Drake doing working with a woman, but I overlook it.

'We know someone in the capital is sending messages to the enemy. We believe they're sharing strategic secrets, giving the Vallurians an advantage. Who knows what else they've done. But men such as Lord Norvill are working to help the traitor in exchange for protection. All communication has been done using your seal, and we believe they intend to frame you for their crimes, should they be discovered. I'm here to find out who is betraying us all.'

The Governor stares at me. 'You're very young, do you know that?'

I bristle. 'What does my age have to do with anything?'

'When I was young, I saw things in black and white too. Right and wrong. Good and evil. Justice and injustice.'

'And you don't any more?'

He shakes his head. 'You mean well, I don't doubt it, but you and your warning are too late.'

'What do you mean?'

Governor Franklin sighs, like a man who's given up entirely. 'I know there's a traitor.'

Anger builds in me like a furnace. 'You know? Then what are you doing locked away in the dark? Why aren't you trying to find out who it is?'

'They took my boy.' His voice is barely a whisper.

It takes me a few moments to realise what he means, dread quenching the anger. 'What do you mean? Who took him?'

'The Emperor. He sent a mercenary to steal my son. Riley's been trying to get him back for me, but while they have my child, my hands are tied, do you see?'

'The Emperor has your son?'

'It would seem so. I'm waiting for his demands. I imagine he'll want my surrender.'

My anger rises once more. 'And in the meantime, you're just hiding here?'

'The war is lost either way.'

I leap to my feet and crash my fists on to his desk. 'There are men dying out there every day! What are they dying for?'

If my outburst offends him, he shows no sign of it. He shows no sign of any emotion.

'You may have given up,' I say, my disappointment in the man so great I could cry. 'But I won't. This war isn't over. Not yet.'

'It is,' he says. 'You're just too blind to see it.'

Giving him a look that conveys my deep contempt, I leave him to his cowardice and storm out of the room.

I walk straight into General Riley. The guards who were reluctant to step aside are now nowhere to be seen.

The General isn't smiling any more. His former charm has vanished, the mask of a helpful friend now removed. I should have thought more about why the people in the streets seemed afraid of him.

Maybe then I would have realised sooner.

That General Riley is the traitor.

RAYN

I was a fool to miss it before: the calculating confidence of someone betraying everything he should be protecting.

'And how is the Governor?'

It's a trick question, designed to catch me out. 'In low spirits,' I say.

'He told you about his child?'

I nod slowly. 'Yes, he seems to believe the Emperor is holding him to ransom.'

'And what do *you* believe?'

That's when I realise: he's known I was an imposter from the first day he met me. He has listened to my lies in order to search for my purpose.

He's at a distinct advantage.

'*I* believe it would be a shame if the Governor were to discover his true enemy might in fact be closer to home. That the one he's trusting to ensure the safe return of his son is in fact working *against* that outcome.'

Riley sighs. 'Indeed. You know, I fear for our Governor. As you yourself can see, he's not in any fit state to run our country. I've done all I can, but I think it's time to intervene, don't you?'

I have no idea what that means, but I'm certain it's nothing good.

'Since you have such concern for our country, for the

people,' he says, his voice dripping with sarcasm, 'why don't you come with me to talk to the court? I think it's time our politicians were made aware of the situation we're in.'

Before I can answer, he grabs me roughly by the arm, and I can do nothing but let him pull me along while I desperately try to think what to do. For now, there's nothing I *can* do. This whole city is guarded by soldiers and I doubt any will believe me over their General.

Riley holds me close as we make our way back through the building. When we reach the entrance hallway, I try to catch the eye of those passing, but no one's paying any attention to me. Instead they greet Riley, showing respect to the man who's betraying them all.

We climb an ornate staircase I remember my father describing. A staircase that leads to the court, where the men who govern our country meet.

Riley clicks his fingers and soldiers drop into formation behind us.

My throat is dry, my skin clammy. I should never have come here.

The impressive hall is filled with at least twenty men, politicians of the court engaged in heated debate. When we burst in, followed by a dozen of Riley's men, the room falls quiet. One of the braver – or perhaps stupider – politicians clears his throat.

'General Riley, you're here at last. This session began an hour ago.'

'I didn't realise I followed your orders, Henley,' Riley retorts.

Henley looks a little flustered but gathers himself quickly. 'What's the meaning of this?' He gestures to the soldiers looming menacingly behind Riley. Henley ignores me altogether, and that in itself is telling. Ordinarily, a woman walking into the court would cause an outrage.

'I would have thought it was obvious. Governor Franklin has been compromised and needs to be replaced. I have come to take the position.'

There's a scattering of nervous laughter. *The fools, they should be terrified.*

'Don't be absurd,' Henley says. 'Even if what you're saying about Governor Franklin is true, you have no right to assume power.'

Riley smiles. 'I disagree.'

Henley's blustering now; I can sense he's regretting being the one to confront Riley. 'There are procedures, General. There would have to be a vote to relieve Franklin of his authority, and then another to find his replacement. Besides, I very much doubt your name would be put forward. By anyone.'

Riley looks at me then, as if he's somehow teaching me a lesson in this farce. 'You see? You see what I have to contend with?'

Then he turns to Henley. 'Minister, you must be naive to think I'm asking your permission. As of now, you will address me as the new Governor of Naperone.'

Another politician steps forward to join Henley, his indignation compelling him to speak up. 'You may have some control over the army, General. But most are still loyal to Franklin.'

Riley makes a show of looking around. 'But do you see any of them here?'

Now the man finally looks suitably afraid and steps back behind Henley, as if he's somehow safer there.

'Franklin's men are scattered around Naperone, fighting a war they can't possibly win. But my men are all *here*, defending Eron. And the Emperor is very much in favour of my assuming control.'

In the silent room, there is a collective intake of breath at such a revelation.

'So, Minister Henley, you can choose to support me, or you can leave.'

Henley's face has almost turned purple with rage. 'I will never support you.'

With foolish resolve, he strides towards the door. I swallow hard. How does he not sense the danger? How does he not see what's coming next?

Riley's men block the way and Henley is forced to confront the General.

'I choose to leave. Let me pass.'

Riley towers over him, in both size and stature. 'I've changed my mind. There is no choice.'

In one swift move, Riley draws his sword and slices Henley from navel to neck. I stare in horror as Henley spills his innards like secrets before dropping to the floor, spluttering blood across the wooden boards as he dies.

I turn away, wanting to erase what I've just seen, knowing I never will.

Riley grabs my arm again and turns to leave. Without a backward glance, he says to his men, 'Kill them all.'

His soldiers rush past us like a storm, and Riley drags me into the corridor, shutting the door behind us.

'What did you just do?' Though I hate myself for it, I'm shaking.

'What was necessary. Do you understand now? We want the same thing, you and I. To bring an end to the war.'

'The difference being I want us to *defeat* the Emperor, not serve him.' I'm fighting back tears but am determined not to give him the satisfaction of seeing me cry.

Anger flares behind his eyes. 'I don't serve him; I work with him.'

'The Emperor doesn't share power, he takes it all for himself.'

'Oh, but he's been very willing to share his gold,' Riley says with a smirk.

'You think you'll profit, but in the end, he'll kill you too,' I say.

'I don't think so, I'm too useful. But you . . . you know too much.'

The dagger feels comforting in my boot, but it's out of reach. 'You're going to kill me?'

'Actually no.' Riley smiles. 'I'm going to arrest you.'

Now I laugh. 'On what grounds?'

He leans in close to my face, his voice barely a whisper. 'Your father and brother are wanted war criminals. You will atone for their sins.'

My breath leaves me too quickly. He knows who I am. He probably always has.

'They were innocent, as you well know.'

His smile is like a knife to my heart. 'Of course *I* know. Had to keep the focus off me with someone else, didn't I?'

'*You?*' Knowing General Tygh had led the attack was one thing, but it hadn't occurred to me he was working with Riley.

'How do you think Tygh knew where to go?' he asks, grinning. He's actually enjoying this. 'Not that he did a very thorough job. It took me a long time to hunt your meddling brother down, but I managed it in the end.'

'You bastard!' I lunge for my dagger, wanting to strike him down right there for what he's done. But he's anticipated my move and clutches my wrist before I'm able to grasp its handle.

Instead, it's him who pulls the dagger free and holds it up with a look of disappointment. 'Not a very ladylike thing to have on your person.' He clicks his tongue. 'Now I'm afraid I'll have to arrest you for assassinating our Governor too.'

'You're going to kill him.' *Of course he's going to kill him.*

Riley shrugs. 'It'll be your dagger in his heart.'

And as he raises his fist to knock me out, I feel nothing but relief.

Anything to silence the screams that are still coming from behind the door.

RAYN

I don't want to wake up.

As I'm torn away from the oblivion, I desperately try to cling to it. I'm not ready to leave yet. I don't want to think. I don't want to feel. There's peace in the nothingness.

I've failed.

Failed to avenge my father and brother. Failed to stop Riley. Failed to protect my country.

It's all hopeless. There's no end to the layers of deceit, corruption, betrayal. I'd rather stay wrapped in the darkness of my mind and forget everything that's happened.

But I lose this fight too. My body isn't ready to give up just yet, whatever my mind says.

The ground I'm lying on is damp, the cell dark and dismal, and my ankles and wrists are in shackles.

How much time has passed since Riley threw me in here? It's impossible to tell, as there's no natural light, just a lantern hanging from the wall outside my prison. And as I sit there, my despair lifts a little. Instead, a calm resolve settles over me.

I might have failed, but I'm not dead yet.

While I draw breath, there's still a chance for vengeance. While I live, they can still die.

I know what I have to do.

I inspect the shackles around my wrists. If I had made

them, there would be no way of getting out – fortunately for me, these were made by an amateur. A quick inspection reveals that the iron is weak in several places where it's been overheated. Smashing the brittle parts of the iron against the floor, I bring my bound hands down again and again, flinching but absorbing the pain every time my skin meets the unforgiving ground, twisting as much as possible until the iron begins to give, then finally snaps.

Once my hands are free, I'm able to reach the key pressed to my breast and easily unlock the chains at my ankles. Another quick turn and the door is open.

I proceed with caution, listening for anything beyond the immediate silence. The scraping of a chair tells me there's someone behind the door at the end of the corridor, so I'm going to have to fight to get out of here. Unfortunately, since Riley took my dagger, I'm unarmed.

Holding the key between my fingers, I creep closer to the door and listen. There's no sound of talking, so I'm hopeful the guard is alone.

I kick the door open, using the element of surprise. The solitary guard leaps from his chair, but he's too slow, and I crunch my fist hard into his face, the key slicing skin. He falls to the ground unconscious, blood flowing fast from the wound. Searching him, I take his sword and set of keys, then drag him back the way I came and lock him in my cell.

I have no idea whether I'm too late to save Franklin – Riley may have already dispatched him in his coup – but I have to try.

The sunlight blinds me as I emerge from the building into the street. Quickly, I try to get my bearings. I'm a long way from the centre of the city, and so I start to run, a plan forming in my mind.

First things first; I need a real sword. Not this poor excuse for a blade I've just stolen. If I'm going to avenge my father's death, it'll be with his sword. My very own blade of blood.

And I need to get out of this filthy, impractical dress if I'm to stand a chance in a fight.

I head straight to the inn, and once in my room I practically rip my clothes off to replace them with more familiar ones. Then I arm myself, briefly pressing the cold metal to my lips.

'Help me avenge them,' I whisper, calling on my mother's blood. The silence speaks to me.

I'm ready to do this. Or ready to die trying.

But as I run down the stairs, intent on revenge, someone else is running into the inn. The woman is afraid and is shouting at anyone who will listen.

'We're under attack! The Emperor's men are here!'

Panic invades the inn, but I'm confused. Riley's working *with* the Emperor, and he's just taken control. So why would the Emperor need to attack?

While people run from the streets into the safety of their houses, I head towards the centre of the city. To where the fighting is. To where Riley will be.

I take backstreets, keeping to the shadows, trying to figure out what's happening by listening closely and peering around corners as I draw closer to the chaos of battle.

The huge courtyard outside the government buildings is teeming with soldiers. Riley's men are easy to identify by their uniforms, but it takes me a moment to realise who's fighting them and, when I do, my hopes lift with my heart. The townspeople assumed it was the Vallurians attacking, but they were wrong. It's Drake and the rebels. And then I remember he'd spoken of a contact inside the capital – they must have reported the slaughter of the council.

This gives me the chance I need.

Retracing my steps, I take a different route through the city, one that leads me to the back of the main council building, on the opposite side from the fighting. The doors are locked, but the lock is nothing my trusty key can't open, and I slip through the door into what appears to be a cellar. I hadn't realised those charged with running our country needed quite so much wine. I squeeze past numerous barrels until I reach a flight of stairs.

Up in the entrance hallway, everyone is panicked and they offer no resistance as I barge through. They just want to live.

I grab one simpering man and push him against the wall, my sword at his neck. 'Where's Riley?'

He doesn't answer, fear stealing his voice, but he points upwards.

I take the stairs three at a time, running towards the Governor's study, hoping against hope to find him alive.

The door to his room is open and there is no sign of the guards who were here before. Cautiously, I enter, but there's no sign of Riley either.

The Governor is slumped over his desk and I hurry to his side, pulling him back into his chair.

He groans. He's still alive, but won't be for long, judging by the blood pooling in his lap.

'You're all right,' I lie, as I press my hands against the wound in his belly.

With a great effort, he lifts his head to look at me. 'Find my son,' he says. 'Please. For my wife's sake.'

I nod. 'I will.'

'Don't waste your time with me,' he says. 'I'm dead already. Go and make sure that treacherous snake joins me.'

It feels wrong walking away from a dying man, despite knowing I cannot save him.

But I can fulfil his dying wish.

I search every room, on every floor, looking for Riley, but it's not until I reach the roof terrace I see him.

He's standing with his back to me, watching the battle unfold beneath him.

'Can you feel it slipping away from you?' I shout, my voice carrying to him on the wind.

He looks round and doesn't conceal his surprise at seeing me. 'You escaped.'

'Apparently.'

'Well, contrary to what you might believe, my men will overpower yours and this will be nothing but a crease to press out. I will have control.'

'You've already lost it,' I say. 'And now you're going to die.'

He laughs. 'You're a girl. I'm the leader of an entire army. You think this will end any other way than with *you* dying?'

I raise my sword. 'You are responsible for the death of my father and my brother. Today I will avenge them.'

'Not a chance,' he hisses.

I run at him, striking hard, my powerful blade making his shudder. It catches him off guard, but he recovers and soon we are duelling around the terrace with fierce determination.

Unsurprisingly, he's good, his every swing accurate and powerful. But my father's sword is stronger than his. And while he fights only for the power he desperately craves, I fight for something more: vengeance, love, justice. They're what drive me on, though my body is screaming, muscles burning from the effort of absorbing his relentless blows.

He's smiling – he knows he has the stamina to outlast me, can see I'm struggling already. He intensifies his attack, seizing on my weakness, until I can barely parry his strikes. He swings with increased force, and while I manage to keep the blade from my heart, it grazes my collarbone. The sight of my blood only fuels him further, and his next strike slashes my thigh. Neither wound is bad, but if he keeps this up, he'll land a fatal one soon enough.

I can't let him win. I won't. Sheer bloody-mindedness is all that's keeping me standing now. If I die here, it's all been for nothing and Riley, the Emperor . . . they'll win. And they can't win.

So I keep fighting. There's no sound beyond the endless clash of our blades, the blood pounding in my ears, my ragged breathing.

If I am to die here, I will die fighting.

As I tire, his confidence grows. In his mind, he's already won and, bored of the game, he makes his move to finish me. His attack is fierce and my legs buckle as I dodge his blade, causing me to stumble backwards on to the ground. Winded, my sword falls from my hand and I brace myself for Riley to end it.

He stands over me and laughs as I lie there, desperately trying to fill my lungs. 'Pathetic,' he says. 'Dying in the dirt like a coward. Just like your brother.'

My nostrils flare with rage, but there's nothing I can do.

A resounding cheer from the square below shatters the moment. A cry of victory. Chants for Governor Franklin. Riley turns his head, a flash of disbelief across his face. The rebels have won.

I seize the momentary distraction, reach for my sword and plunge it up into his guts.

He looks back slowly to me, a trickle of blood spilling from his lips. I'm on my feet now and I twist the blade hard.

'My family had something you'll never have,' I say to him, as he stares at me in shock. 'They had someone to avenge them. No one will avenge you.'

And using my last remaining strength, I push him over the edge of the terrace and watch as his body falls, before smashing to the ground.

Exhausted, I collapse.

I don't even realise I've passed out until someone shakes me awake, and on reflex I try to stagger up, ready to fight.

But firm, familiar hands are holding me still.

'It's OK, Smithy, it's over.'

I blink several times before I believe it's really him, and when I do, something settles inside me, like I can finally breathe properly again.

'What are you doing here?'

Ilian looks around at the devastation. 'Heard rumours on the road of an attack.' He chuckles to himself. 'I came to save you. Arrived just in time to see you stab the General.'

'Ah.' I manage a smile. 'Thanks anyway?'

'Yeah, yeah,' he says, offering me a hand and pulling me to my feet. 'In my defence, I didn't know you could fight.'

'You never asked.'

To my surprise, he pulls me into a tight embrace. 'It's good to see you, Smithy,' he says.

When I unfold from his arms, I smile up at him, my gaze lingering on his lips for a moment. But then I remember Riley's shattered body on the ground. 'It was him, Ilian. General Riley was the one who was working with Tygh. He's as responsible as Tygh for our families' deaths.'

Ilian's jaw clenches. 'So they're avenged at last?'

I nod. 'They are.' But though I say the words, I don't entirely believe them. Because both Tygh and Riley were only following orders. The man really responsible is still safely tucked up in his golden palace.

'Come on,' Ilian says. 'You should talk to Drake.'

'You've met him? Where is he?'

'Running the country.'

We head back inside the building, where the rebels have taken over, and when I see Drake talking to a group of soldiers, I can't help but smile. This was the last place I expected us to be reunited.

He looks up, perhaps aware of being watched, and excuses himself from the conversation to head over to us.

'When I heard the council had been slaughtered, I didn't expect to find you in the centre of it all. Especially as we'd given you up for dead.'

I shrug. 'Can't get rid of me that easily.' Though all I want is to curl up and sleep, there are important matters to attend to first. 'I have a lot to tell you.'

Drake nods and leads me to a quiet corner. While I relay everything that's happened since we parted, Ilian fetches me some wine and bread. Slowly my energy returns, and as I deliver my report, I feel the weight of all I've carried these past months fall away. My mission is finally complete.

When our business is concluded, I gesture to Ilian. 'So are we all friends now?'

Drake smiles. 'Yes, it'll be good to work alongside a Vallurian. Shows our countries aren't destined to remain enemies, that peace can be achieved.'

'What happens now?' I ask.

'We'll assemble a new council and focus on what's important. Winning this war.'

'And what about Franklin's son?'

Drake looks confused. 'What about him?'

I frown. 'Aren't you going to get him back?'

'There's no need. He can no longer be used for leverage and so the threat no longer exists.'

'Horseshit!' I can tell my outburst surprises Drake, but his callousness has surprised *me*. 'It exists for the boy, for his mother.'

Drake sighs as if he's talking to a child. 'You've been a great asset, Rayn. Graylen would be proud, and so would your father ... but you're a woman. You know nothing about running a country and even less about winning wars. Leave it to us from now on.'

I'm so shocked that these words are coming out of his mouth that I can't speak. He had no problem seeking me out for my help, no issue with sending me to spy for him, no qualms about me dying for the cause, but *now* I'm suddenly the wrong sex to have an opinion?

'The Emperor doesn't have the child.'

I look sharply round at Ilian. 'What do you mean?'

'I heard again from my contact; the child never made it to the palace. It appears the mercenary went rogue. The Emperor has people looking for him, but so far, no child.'

'Then *we* have to find him first.' I'm thinking of the

promise I made to Franklin as he bled to death. This war has already destroyed too many families.

Drake rests his hands on my shoulders. 'Look, we've done it, Rayn. We've rooted out the traitors, put a stop to Riley's plans, avenged those responsible for the deaths of our loved ones. Now we can set the country back on the right path, win this war and stop the Emperor once and for all. *That's* what we set out to do.'

I stare at him. I respect him, but in my heart, I disagree. That's not what *I* set out to do, even if I'm only just realising it.

Gently, I remove Drake's hands. 'Great. Then you do that.' And I mean it wholeheartedly. 'Go win us the war.'

I walk away from them – though I'm bone-tired, though I want to sleep for ever – and head back outside.

There are a group of horses tied up nearby and I run over to them. As I start to tighten the girth of a big bay gelding, Ilian chases after me. 'What are you doing, Smithy?'

I can't bring myself to look at him. If I do, it'll shatter my resolve. Our paths are not the same, I've always known that. And this last stretch I must travel alone. There's no room for anything else, no matter how much I wish otherwise.

'I'm going to find the child and bring him home.' I untie the horse and mount. 'And when I've done that, I'm going to seek true vengeance.'

'What are you talking about?' But he knows what I'm about to say. I can hear the fear in his voice.

'I thought my mission was over, but I was wrong. There's one last thing I need to do. I'm going to kill the Emperor.'

And without a backward glance, I set off at a gallop.

MARZAL

Without the bullying and animosity from Izra and Roselle, my days are almost unbearably quiet and uneventful. There is so little to do, even with my visits to the garden and to the Empress. How we don't all wither away from sheer boredom escapes me.

I miss the Empress's company. Though I visit her every day, it is only for a brief spell before the palace midwife ushers me out. She's a nasty woman. Because she's delivered every one of the Emperor's offspring, she is entitled, and far too outspoken for a servant. She seems as determined as my father to make the Empress isolated and miserable.

When I'm with the other women, I miss Urso. It's taken me entirely by surprise how much I grieve for my sister. I hadn't expected to like her, let alone grow attached, but her absence needles at my heart.

Mainly, I just bide my time before nightfall, when I can sneak off to listen to important and interesting conversations between my father and his advisors – though every time I return to my bed, I cannot help feeling a little more apprehensive than the last. A nagging sense that my time is running out hovers over me like a dark cloud. For all my plans to come to fruition, a great many things need to go my way and at any moment it could all unravel.

I'm so close now. So close. But every step grows more

dangerous, the ground beneath my feet so shaky that sometimes it feels like I'm standing on sinking sand.

The Emperor has been unsettled since the news of General Tygh. His mood has soured further, though I hadn't thought that possible, and even his trust in Rom, Loris and the stars is waning. He eats too much and drinks even more. There is now a sense of unease and distrust in his inner circle that reminds me of how the women acted with each other when I first came to the palace.

The room is full tonight when I arrive, many men enjoying a drink with my father. Whether they've had good news, or just too much wine, I'm not sure, but the mood is more raucous than it's been in a while. Yet, beneath the surface, the room is simmering with tension.

My father is laughing with some men I don't know, but then calls over to Rom, who's been standing apart from the others as he so often does.

'Rom, what's the name of that little filly we saw the other day?'

Rom frowns, but approaches the Emperor. 'Majesty?'

'You know, the one with the large tits who was with Duke what's-his-face? At the banquet?'

'Do you mean his daughter?' If you pay attention, you can hear the hint of disapproval in Rom's voice. But my father's not paying attention.

'Yes, her. Why don't you arrange for her to come and stay at the palace?' The Emperor looks at his faithful hangers-on and smiles. 'Think I'll enjoy planting my cock in her. She'll certainly make a tasty change to that fat wife of mine.'

I'm not sure whether I want to scream or vomit. Maybe both.

'Majesty, she's barely fourteen.'

The Emperor glares at Rom and a nervous hush descends on the room.

'What's your point?' My father's voice has gone deadly soft.

Rom knows it too and quickly alters the course of his comment. 'I simply mean she's a little young to come to court unaccompanied. Perhaps I should invite her father too?'

'Tell him she can bring a chaperone. And tell him if he wants his daughter to be the next Empress of Vallure, he'll do as he's blood-blazing told.'

The next Empress? He's already planning to ditch his pregnant wife, even before the child is born?

'You intend for her to be your bride?' Rom looks unimpressed.

'If she's as tasty as those tits promise.' The Emperor laughs and all the men but Rom guffaw, and I hate them.

'Speaking of marriage, Prince Junus is asking about arrangements for the wedding. Didn't I ask you to see to it?'

The Emperor's still angry with Rom, I can tell from the way he speaks to him. But I watch Rom closely now, because his reaction will be very telling.

'Yes, Majesty. I simply haven't had the time—'

'*Make* the time. You do still follow orders, don't you?'

After a beat, Rom bows. 'Of course, Majesty. Leave it with me.'

I was right to suspect my time is running out. For all that Rom may wish to marry me and claim the throne for himself one day, he cannot outright disobey an order from the Emperor. Anxious nausea spreads through me. If I get married off to Prince Junus, all my efforts will be for nothing, my plans ruined before they can be completed.

'To marriage,' the Emperor says, holding his glass up in a toast. 'May each wife be younger and more cock-worthy than the last.'

The men are glad to laugh again, dispelling the tension from the exchange with Rom. It's time for me to leave, and I'm just beginning to shuffle away when I sense a change in the atmosphere, and crawl back to see what's happened.

A messenger has arrived. The last one I saw came with news that my father's contact inside the Naperone capital had slaughtered the council – I hadn't seen him so happy in a long time.

But I fear this news isn't so good. Rom is reading the scroll, his face darkened by a shadow of disbelief.

'There's been an attack on Eron.'

The Emperor looks confused. 'I didn't issue any such order.'

Rom shakes his head. 'They discovered Riley was working with you, Majesty. The attack was on him and his men. He's dead.'

The Emperor is quivering with rage, his skin turning quite red, and I'm waiting for him to explode. But when he speaks, he's dangerously calm.

'Dead? Then who's in charge? Franklin?'

'No, he's dead too. Someone named General Drake.'

My father stares at Rom. He knows him too well, knows he's holding back. 'And what else? What are you not telling me?'

Rom has never looked more reluctant to speak. 'Riley was killed by the blacksmith who escaped Tygh's custody.'

That gets my attention. Things just got interesting.

'The same blacksmith who stole my blade of blood?' My father is incredulous.

Rom nods. 'And there's more. The blacksmith is now searching for the child. She knows we don't have him.'

For a moment, they consider this and then realisation dawns on them.

'How could they have known that, unless . . .' Rom looks around him.

'. . . unless we have a traitor among us.' My father finishes the thought, looking from one shocked face to another.

Everyone is suddenly a potential enemy.

'One of you piss-boiling shitholes has betrayed me.' The Emperor's voice is soft, menacing. 'Confess now and I will grant you a quick death. Delay and you will be made to suffer.'

No one answers, and I realise even I'm holding my breath.

'Get out.' My father says it quietly and then screams it. 'Leave, you TRAITORS!'

They all make it out alive, which is a miracle in itself, and when I decide to follow, my father is throwing and smashing anything within his reach as he vents his rage.

All his scheming, all his plans, they're falling apart. Maybe, like me, he feels his time running out. The prophecy spoke of his death, after all. Perhaps by trying to avoid his fate, all he has done is make it inevitable.

The woman blacksmith with the blade of blood is out there, and she is the key to my father's undoing.

The thing about having a plan – the *most* important thing if you hope to see it through to the end – is that sometimes you have to adapt.

Which is exactly what I'm going to do.

RAYN

It's strange to think that not so long ago I feared being alone. Now, travelling across the country with the wind at my back, I've never felt so alive. Having my father's sword at my side feels like my parents are with me, and my sense of purpose drives me in a way I haven't known before.

While finding the child is potentially a fool's quest, I knew it would be easy to get information if I asked in the right places. Though there aren't as many of us as before the war, blacksmiths still exist, and we see and hear everything. Every soldier or traveller who uses our services reveals some secret, intentionally or not, and all I need to do is find the pieces that tell a story and put them together.

There were many sightings of men that could have been mercenaries, but when one blacksmith mentions a man travelling alone with a baby, I pay attention. He clearly did his best to disappear, but even a mercenary trying to become invisible needs to have his horse shod on such a long journey. And while blacksmiths can usually be relied on for discretion, it's different when they're talking to one of their own.

All I've heard has brought me to Vallure, but now information has dried up. Partly because the blacksmiths here don't trust me as readily, and partly because the mercenary seems to have vanished into thin air. And

I have had to be much more careful since I crossed the border three days ago. My accent makes it obvious I'm not from here.

I had hoped Ilian's contact was wrong about the slaughtering of children – that it was a mistake. But it's horribly true, and the grief is still palpable in every town I pass through.

It makes me keep to myself all the more, for fear of retribution. The Vallurians are angry, and rightly so. Unfortunately, they're angry with the wrong people. It's their own ruler they should turn their fury towards, the soulless bastard destroying all our lives.

My travels become much more about keeping an ear to the ground, eavesdropping at inns or when passing through settlements. It's surprised me how dangerous it is in Vallure, considering they're not the occupied country. But food is in short supply, and grief and hardship have left the people bitter. I wonder who exactly is prospering from this war, and again I picture the Emperor safely tucked away inside his palace.

Does he know how his own people suffer? Does he care?

I eventually hear whispers that might set me on a new trail. Not about the man I've been hunting so far, but of a young woman with a child at her breast who has been passing from town to town, selling remedies before moving on. Maybe the mercenary isn't working alone, but with a female partner who'll attract less attention. Certainly she sounds like someone who doesn't want to be seen.

It may be nothing, of course, she may simply be a mother protecting her child in a country where they're being slaughtered, but it's all I have. So, like a hound who's caught the scent of blood, I follow.

I trace her to a town in the north of Vallure, which sadly has no blacksmith to answer my questions. So I take a risk at the inn and ask about her there. The owner says a girl selling remedies arrived a while back, with a young one in tow who she keeps close at all times. He says she lives with an older woman and describes where. I thank him for this information with an extra coin for the gruel.

Then I find the cottage and watch.

After less than a day, I'm certain she's the girl I'm looking for. She's constantly on edge, always checking over her shoulder, and guards the child in a way that borders on obsessive. There's no sign of the man, but he could be in hiding, hoping his accomplice will be less conspicuous.

I form a plan to steal the child back. At night, when the town is asleep, the girl fetches a small scoop of grain from the stable across the way for the goat outside her cottage. The child comes with her, as it always does.

Tonight, I will be waiting for them.

*

The stable offers many shadows to hide in. I wish I could hide as easily from my thoughts, which give me no peace. I've been so certain that I've found the right person, the right child, but what if I'm wrong? What if I'm about to attack an innocent mother? My instincts and fears clash wildly with each other.

But then the girl opens the door, and there's no more time for doubt. She comes straight over to the barrel, lifting the lid, her back to me.

Silently I emerge from the darkness, slipping my hand around her neck so the blade of my knife presses against her skin. I sense her fear, hear her gasp and grab her tightly.

'Give me the baby,' I say, applying a little more pressure to her neck to convince her to obey me.

She's shaking, but her answer is firm. 'No.'

I'm still hoping we can do this without me having to kill her. A mercenary can usually be paid off. 'That child is not yours,' I say, wondering how much I'll need to offer.

'And he's not yours either,' she says, her voice trembling. 'I'm sworn to protect him.'

That's unexpected. 'A caring mercenary? You're a rare breed,' I hiss into her ear.

'I'm no mercenary,' she says. 'I'm a midwife. And you'll have to kill me before you harm a hair on his head.'

Now I spin her round to face me, still pointing the knife at her throat. 'Who are you?'

She doesn't have a chance to reply. At that moment, the door bursts open and three men stride in.

In a heartbeat, I recognise them. I saw them drinking at the inn last night. They must have followed me. Damn it. Three against one are not the best odds, but I cannot let them know I'm afraid.

'What do you want?' I say to them, drawing my sword with my free hand.

'Same thing you do. Thank you for leading us straight to him.' The man's face is a tapestry of scars. I think I've found the real mercenaries. Or, more accurately, they've found me.

'You think you're taking the child?' And I laugh.

'Don't see anyone here who's going to stop us.'

My smile evaporates. 'Then I must be invisible.' I lean to whisper in the midwife's ear. 'Get behind me.'

She hesitates for half a second, and then clearly decides I'm her best chance. I hope she's right. Still clutching the boy tight in her arms, the girl shelters at my back while I step towards the men, knife in one hand, sword in the other.

'I suggest you gentlemen leave before anyone gets hurt.'

Apparently, I don't intimidate them. There's not a doubt in their minds that they will kill us both and claim their prize. Their confidence and arrogance ignites the rage in my blood.

'Tell me, do you work for the Emperor or for General Riley?'

There it is. A flicker of doubt that I know such names.

'Because I should mention, Riley's dead. I killed him. And I intend to return this child to his mother if it's the last thing I do.'

The three men glance at each other. But presumably they decide leaving me alive is not an option, because they come for me hard and fast.

The first man is the easiest to kill because he's simply not expecting me to be capable of anything. My sword slips between his ribs with ease and he drops to the floor with a thud.

It rattles the other two for a split second, but then they adapt, obviously outraged by my continued existence.

I kick the closest man in the chest so that he stumbles backwards, far enough away for me to be able to concentrate on his friend for a moment. He's a competent fighter, but carelessly confident, and when he allows his defences to slip, I seize the advantage to bring my knife fast across his neck.

The final mercenary is back on his feet now. He has

eyes colder than ice, and he doesn't seem bothered that his companions are dead, but smiles at the sight of their bodies.

'More money for me,' he grins.

'Is that all you care about?'

'There's only one thing I care about more than money,' he says. 'And that's more money.'

Hilarious.

I flick my knife, but only succeed in slicing his chin. He's quicker than his friends, and I have to be careful to keep blocking the girl and the baby. He's trying to get past me, his only real goal snatching the child. But I won't let him.

With every swing of my sword I manage to push him further back, away from the two people I'm protecting, and eventually I pin him against a wall of straw bales.

'You should have found something else to care about,' I say, and I stab him in the guts.

Relieved, I turn to check the girl and child are still safe.

'Look out,' she shouts at me, but it's too late.

Once again, my blind spot has proven my weakness. I couldn't see the man reach for the dagger in his belt, or make it his dying move to strike me.

His blade glides into my stomach as if it were made of silk.

Shocked, I stare at his battered face and he grins at me as he dies, cruel until his very end.

Once he's drawn his last breath, I stumble forward, clutching my wound, my body struggling to work properly.

The midwife is at my side now.

'You're OK,' she says. 'Just stay awake.'

My bloody hand searches for hers and when I find it, I

grip it urgently. 'You have to run.' It's a struggle to get my words out. 'Keep him safe.'

'No, no, no,' she says. 'We're going to do that together. Just hang on, you hear me? What's your name?'

I blink. She seems far away now. I'm losing consciousness. 'Rayn.'

And then the pain hits, hot and fierce, seconds before I pass out entirely.

ELENA

For a moment, a very real moment, I'm tempted to leave her. But then I imagine what Aliénor would say about that, and curse under my breath. One way or another, I'm going to have to help her, this woman who just saved our lives.

But I have no idea how.

Before I can figure it out, the door is thrown open once again and I find myself staring at yet another soldier. I'm frozen with fear as he takes in the messy tableau before him, his eyes settling on the dying woman at my feet.

'Smithy!' He rushes forward to sit beside her and looks up at me. 'Is she . . .?'

His concern melts me into action. 'No, she's alive. She saved us. Help me help her!'

He seems to gather himself. 'Tell me what to do.'

'Bring her and follow me, quickly.'

He scoops her carefully into his arms and I clutch the baby tightly to my chest as we return to the night, silently moving unnoticed across the track to the relative sanctuary of our little cottage.

Anaïs is asleep by the fire, but wakes with a start when we burst in.

'Here,' I say, resting the boy down in her arms. 'There's been an accident.'

'What kind of . . .' She trails off as the man comes into the cottage with Rayn bleeding in his arms.

I slam the door behind him and point towards my room.

'I'll explain later,' I say to Anaïs, before hurrying to strip all but one sheet from my bed, not wanting them to get blood-soaked. I'll have need of them before the night's out.

'Lay her down here,' I say to the man carrying Rayn.

He does as he's told, his face tight with fear.

I'm used to reassuring men who are watching their loved ones slip away from them, have spent a lifetime doing it. 'What's your name?' I ask him, as I roll up my sleeves.

'Ilian. I know her.'

I smile gently. 'I guessed. I'm going to need water, lots of it. The well's down the road, towards the inn. Bring me as much as you can carry.'

He nods, grateful as they all are for a job to occupy them.

But this isn't like those other nights, when I was delivering life into the world. Tonight, I must stop death.

Rayn's bleeding badly, and if I do nothing, I know she'll be dead within minutes. Maybe less. Panic grips me. This isn't what I'm trained for. I have no idea how to heal such a wound, and with every second's hesitation she edges closer to death.

Aliénor's words whisper in my mind like a reassuring touch. *We help where we can, how we can. We can't always defeat death, but by Gods, we'll try.*

Rayn's shivering now, her skin ashen as her body empties before my eyes, and it stirs me back into action. I reach for my bag. Ultimately, I need to try and sew the wound closed, but the first thing I have to do is stop the bleeding. After that, I need to clean it, or infection will kill her as surely as any blood loss.

'Where do you want this?' Ilian stands in the doorway with two buckets of water.

'On the fire. Heat it up, and when you're done, gather up those sheets and start tearing them into strips.'

While he does that, I pour some vinegar and oil on my hands to cleanse them, and then I press down hard on the wound, feeling the warmth of blood soak up through the material. There's nothing to do now but wait. If an artery or any major organ's been hit, the bleeding won't stop and she'll die. I close my eyes.

Ilian returns with the boiled water, and I instruct him to take my place. I'm going to think positively and start preparing an ointment that I can use to heal her. It makes sense to use the same ingredients I would use to heal ladies' tearing: crushed root of arnica, St John's wort and a dash of vervain on a base of chamomile, yarrow and prunella. I just hope it's enough.

I move to sit beside Ilian. This is it. The moment of truth. I gently brush him aside and lift the padding. And breathe a sigh of relief. The bleeding has all but stopped. There's hope yet.

Even unconscious, Rayn flinches as I place a steaming-hot cloth on to her ragged skin, and I don't envy her the pain that'll be seeping through to her dreams.

I add some vinegar and oil to the hot water and flush out the wound as best I can. Once I'm satisfied it's as clean as it can be, I smear the ointment over the cut. Then I press some of the strips of sheet on it.

'Hold this,' I say to Ilian, who's been standing watching me anxiously.

As he takes my place, I reach for one of my poultices, deciding to add some extra ingredients because of the severity of the injury. Quickly, I crush up thyme and woundwort to fight potential infection, as well as the slightest dash of monkshood and hemlock. They'll help with the pain a bit, should Rayn wake up.

Once the poultice is ready, I nudge Ilian out of the way and place it over the tear in Rayn's stomach, securing it with long strips of material.

It's all I can do for now, and I let out a long sigh of relief.

'Will she be all right?'

Ilian's looking at me for reassurance I can't give him right now.

'I don't know. But I've done my best. I just hope she doesn't get a fever. If she's still fine by morning, I'll sew her up.'

His eyes don't leave Rayn and he asks, 'So what do we do now?'

'We wait.'

I go through to the other room to check on the baby, who's sleeping soundly in Anaïs's arms.

She looks at me, communicating all her fear without a single word.

'It's a long story,' I say. 'But I think she'll live.'

'Elena, who *is* she?'

I run my fingers through my hair, my every bone aching with weariness. 'I don't know.'

'She's come to take you away.' Anaïs sounds so sad, and so certain.

I rest my hand on her shoulder, but it's all the comfort I can give. I'm not sure what will happen now, but I too sense things are about to change.

'Try to rest. It'll be a long night.'

Picking up a stool to take to Ilian, I head back into my room.

Then I sit by my patient and place a cool cloth across her forehead. She's too warm, and a fever is the last thing we want.

'How do you know her?' I need the air to be filled with sound tonight, to crowd out my many fears clamouring to be heard.

Ilian chuckles to himself. 'I captured her. She was my prisoner. And then I set her free.'

As answers go, it wasn't the one I was expecting.

'Thing is,' he says. 'That's not really true. It was her that set me free.'

He's disappearing into his own thoughts, and I don't want to lose him to them. 'So whose side are you fighting on now? If she's from Naperone and you're a Vallurian?'

'We're both fighting for the same thing. For the people, for peace. Our countries aren't enemies, only the men in charge of them are.'

An anger I've spent months suppressing crawls out across my skin. 'But her country, her people, they came and butchered our children. How can you say they're not monsters?'

Ilian sighs. 'Because it wasn't her people who committed that atrocity. It was ours.'

It's like he's squeezed the air from my lungs, I can't breathe. Not only because I recognise the truth in his words, but also because it means Aliénor was right – as always. It's not the Naperones who are monsters. Just our Emperor.

'I've been protecting the child,' I say. 'Because he's an innocent in all this. And now I know what the Emperor is prepared to do to innocents.'

Ilian looks up sharply. 'That's Governor Franklin's child?'

I nod. 'Rayn thought I was a mercenary. I think she would have killed me if the other men hadn't arrived.'

'She's been searching for the child to bring him home safely. I've been trying to catch up with her, but have always been one step behind.' He sounds admiring. Then he looks at me with suspicion. 'But who are you? How did the child come into your care?'

'I'm a midwife. My name is Elena. One day, a man knocked on my door and handed me a baby, made me swear to keep him hidden, keep him safe. That's what I've been doing ever since.'

And, for the first time, it dawns on me that they're here to take the child home. To take him away from me and suddenly I'm standing on the edge of an ocean of grief that's just waiting to drown me.

'What should we do about those men in the stables?' I ask, needing to change the conversation.

Ilian looks as though he'd forgotten about the three dead men. 'I'll go and deal with the bodies,' he says.

I don't ask him what he intends to do with them, trying hard to forget the image of the mercenary's body disappearing into the black depths of the river when Aliénor and I had to get rid of him. His dead eyes still stare at me in my nightmares, a reminder of the promise I made to him. To Aliénor. To keep the boy safe. And now I'm healing the woman who wants to take him away?

I glance at my patient with concern. Her temperature is rising, but there's nothing I can do now. The poultice is still my best chance of drawing any infection out.

Throughout the night I place cold cloth after cold cloth on her forehead, trying to break the fever. I get no sleep, changing poultices regularly, wiping the ointment away each time before refreshing it with new paste. I hold Rayn's head up as I pour a strong brew of feverfew and thyme into her, but still her fever doesn't abate.

By the time Ilian returns, his deed complete, Rayn is sweating and trembling in a way that makes me fear she'll never wake. Ilian doesn't say anything. He just fetches fresh hot water before silently joining me, stroking Rayn's forehead to soothe her as she tosses and turns.

But by the time dawn breaks, so does the fever. Slowly Rayn's body grows still, her breathing more regular, and I sigh in relief. The worst has passed.

I'm checking her poultice when I hear a slight murmur and look up to see Rayn's eyes flickering open.

'Welcome back,' I say with a smile.

She holds my gaze for a moment, hers full of fear, and then she sees Ilian and fear is replaced with relief.

'You're here,' she whispers.

Ilian smiles. 'Hey, Smithy. Sorry I was late.'

'Again,' she says, and it sounds like she's teasing him. She tries to move and immediately grimaces.

'Stay still,' I say. 'Until I've stitched you up, you're going nowhere.'

She watches me cautiously, trying to remember who I am, assessing whether I'm a threat. And then her hand grasps my arm. 'Thank you.'

I smile. 'Thank you for stopping those men.'

'You have the child?'

Sighing, I sit beside her. 'Yes.' And I tell her what I told Ilian, the story of how the boy came to be in my care.

'And now you need to take him.' My words are dull and emotionless, because I cannot bear to think of it.

Rayn looks at me with pity. 'I promised his father I would take him home to his mother.'

I think of Aliénor, and the hole her absence has left in my heart. I think of Anaïs, who has been hollowed out by the loss of her son. I will not be responsible for another mother's grief.

'I understand. When you've recovered, you have my blessing to take him.' I cough, trying to disguise the way my voice catches in my throat. 'In the meantime, you are welcome to stay here. Both of you.'

'Thank you,' Rayn says again.

I shift uncomfortably. 'But right now I need to stitch you up,' I say apologetically.

'All right.'

'It's going to hurt,' I warn her.

Rayn clenches her jaw. 'OK. Let's get it over with then.'

I gather what I need from my bag, trying to forget all the times I've tried to stitch a woman's stomach back together. They had all died. But then there is a certain brutality to the act of tearing a woman open and ripping the life from within it. They weren't actually expected to survive such desperate measures. Rayn has every chance of survival now.

I take the largest of the two needles I have and hold it in the candle's flame for a moment, before threading it with cord.

'Ilian, hold her down.'

'*What?*' Both Rayn and Ilian say it at the same time.

'When I start this, I need you to stay still,' I explain. 'And trust me, you won't want to.'

Rayn holds my gaze for a moment before relenting. 'Fine.'

Ilian tentatively rests his hands on her shoulders, and I swallow hard.

'Ready?'

'Ready,' Rayn says, closing her eyes. Ilian nods, resolute.

With the first stab of the needle, Rayn's whole body jerks upwards in objection and she stifles a scream. Gritting my teeth, I focus on the job that needs doing and ignore every gasp, every cry that Rayn emits until the final stitch is in place.

The wound closes well despite its jagged edges; my poultices have kept the skin from becoming infected. Still, there'll be a scar.

'All done,' I say, squeezing her hand. 'I think you'll live. Ilian, why don't you fetch her some water?'

I take a moment to step back and think about what I've done.

I saved a life.

After the loss of Elsette, I wasn't sure I could do it, but Rayn is living proof. For the first time since Aliénor died, something sparks inside me. Hope.

'You should rest,' I say to Rayn, her breathing ragged. 'How do you feel?'

'Oh, just like my insides were gouged out.' But she manages a weak smile. 'How long until I can travel, do you think?'

'A week, at the very least. Longer would be better though.'

Ilian returns with the water. 'A week will give us time to come up with a plan. I'll see if my contact has anything to help us.'

I look from one to the other. 'What plan?' I thought they were just here to take the boy.

Rayn winces as she shifts her position. 'Now that I've found the child and we can return him to his mother, there's something else I need to prepare for. It's time to stop the person responsible for all our suffering.'

I frown, uncertain what she means. But then it hits me with perfect clarity, like a blow to my guts, and I have to reach out to steady myself. One look at the resolution in her eyes confirms my suspicions.

Rayn is going to kill the Emperor.

MARZAL

The Empress's belly has swollen impressively over the past few months. So much so that, despite my rubbing oil on it every day when I visit, her skin has marked where it's stretched.

She's lonely. She's scared. My father hasn't come to visit her once since he confined her to her quarters, and she misses her mother.

I know how that feels.

She's not been sleeping, her mind too full of worries, her body too uncomfortable from its incapacitation. And so I've spent the whole afternoon with her, for once undisturbed by her midwife, who's been unable to leave the latrine since I slipped some senna leaf into her tea earlier today.

I'm curled under the covers with the Empress and have enjoyed the hours of escape from the rest of the court. Alone together, I feel something approaching safe – I can laugh with her and talk more freely than with anyone else. It's the closest I can come to being myself.

'Why don't you write home?' I say, trying to cheer her as the evening draws in and our time together grows short.

'It makes me too sad. You know my mother has not been invited to the palace,' she says. 'And until I produce a healthy boy, I have nothing with which to persuade the Emperor.'

Given that he's already courting his next bride, possibly not even then.

'No, I know. But you could request the town's midwife attends to you, rather than that old windbag.' I nod towards the curtains, in the direction of the tyrannous midwife who would have already thrown me out if she weren't shitting herself uncontrollably. 'Surely the Emperor could not object to that? And she can bring news of your family, comfort you at this time.'

Her eyes light up at the prospect. 'Do you think he would allow it?'

'I can't see that he would mind.' What I mean is, I can't see that he would care. But I didn't want to sound too harsh. 'I'm sure Imperial Advisor Rom oversees such things anyway, and I can put your request to him, if you'd like?'

'Oh, Marzal, I simply don't know what I would do without you,' the Empress says, her hand finding mine and squeezing. 'You have been such a true friend.'

'As have you. I wish there were more I could do for you. I hate to see you so unhappy.'

'I have been happier since you arrived than any time before.' And a tear escapes from her eye, gliding down her perfect cheek. An unexpected impulse to lick it from her skin strikes me, but she brushes the tear away before I can act on it. 'Ignore me, I'm so emotional at the moment.'

'When did you last sleep?' I ask her softly.

'Oh, I don't remember,' she says, her voice shaking even as she tries to laugh it off. 'I am too afraid all the time, I cannot relax.'

I once said something similar to a girl back in the convent and she helped me, comforted me, soothed me. Gained my trust.

I shift closer under the covers to the Empress until my breasts press against her, and I slip my leg between her thighs, parting them slightly.

'What are you doing?' she asks, and she's scared. I can feel her body tense with fear as I slip my hand up her nightdress, gently caressing her skin as I reach for the warmth between her legs.

'I won't hurt you,' I whisper. 'I promise.'

True to my word, my touch is light, soft, and slowly I feel her relax, her breathing quickening with something that has nothing to do with fear.

'We shouldn't be doing this,' she says, though her voice lacks conviction. 'What if we're caught?'

'It's our secret,' I breathe into her ear. 'No one needs to know. But say the word and I'll stop right now.'

Her only reply is a moan of bliss as her body twists, rising to my caress.

Every movement, every touch takes me back to the convent. Of endless nights lying with Kala. She taught me what pleasure my body was capable of giving, how loving someone could bring such exquisite escape from the world. I never imagined I would be so intimate with another woman again, but the truth is I'm not doing this because I love the Empress. I desire only to further deepen her love for me and secure her loyalty.

And I enjoy having someone so vulnerable and at my mercy.

Because I lust for the power.

It doesn't take her poor, deprived body long to climax under the right guidance, and she cries out with pained delight as her back arches and her body writhes. I remove my hand and smile at her.

'Was that all right?' I ask coyly, brushing the hair from her forehead.

Her cheeks glow as she meets my gaze. 'What did you do to me?' She's breathless, almost giddy.

'Only what you deserve. And it should help you sleep.'

'You promise you won't tell?'

I lean over and kiss her softly on the lips. 'I promise.' I pull the covers back and climb out. 'Now you need to rest.'

'You'll come back soon?'

'As soon as I'm able.'

As I leave, I realise my dress is crumpled from hours in bed, and so I quickly divert back to my room to change. I want to see Rom as soon as possible and don't want my appearance to cause him to ask any questions.

Once I'm decent, I seek him out. Since my father demanded he begin arranging my marriage, we've had to be more careful. I told Rom to put wheels in motion for the preparations, but I have no intention of seeing them through. I've assured Rom of that. I just don't wish my father to cut him from his inner circle.

Rom is in his office, a room so full of books it could be a library itself. He is reading through scrolls, scribbling down notes, and it takes him a moment to realise I'm even there before he looks up.

'Princess Marzal,' he says, maintaining a public formality between us. 'How may I be of assistance?'

'I have a request from the Empress.'

He gestures for me to take a seat, and I explain about her situation, taking care not to be too unkind in case anything should somehow make its way back to the midwife and cause her to take out her anger on the Empress. When I've stated her case, Rom considers it.

'I would be happy to make that request,' he says, after a while. 'It does no harm to anyone.'

'Thank you,' I say.

He glances up at me. 'You are well? You look a little flushed. I hope you're not sickening with a fever?'

'I'm well,' I assure him. 'Simply pleased to see you.'

It is all we dare say to each other in a place where we could easily be overheard or interrupted. His longing has not abated, I am reassured of that. All I can satisfy him with is a smile full of promise before I leave him to his work.

When I return to my chambers, I reflect on my precarious situation. I am sewing a tapestry with my plans and schemes, threads of all colours in use, and I cannot afford to let one loose. It's nearly finished now, but as with all things the final step will be the hardest, with the most to lose, as well as gain.

I think of my mother. It is always her I think of when I'm afraid. She alone knows my thoughts, she alone spurs me on. She makes me brave.

*

Days pass without incident. But then, one night, I hear an interesting discussion between my father and Rom. They are alone, still trying to uncover the traitor in their midst. They haven't got very far.

'These are the ones I think most likely,' Rom says to the Emperor, handing him a list.

I cannot see my father's face but I hear him muttering under his breath as he scans the names. 'Zylin? You think that prick weasel smart enough to be a traitor?'

'I have seen him looking at your daughter in a way you would not appreciate.'

My heart starts to beat faster. Zylin, you fool. I knew you were being too obvious.

'Then interrogate him first.'

'I'll do it tomorrow.'

My heart is racing now. Zylin will break quickly under questioning, I have no doubt. If Rom finds out about us, we'll both be dead by sunset.

'I thought I would intercept any messages to and from the men on the list, Majesty,' Rom says. 'I may catch them in the act.'

'Good. But do it to all messages that leave the palace, not just theirs. If anyone's sending out information, we'll know.'

I hurry back down the tunnel as fast as I can, my mind racing. I'm going to have to move quickly, bring forward a part of the plan I'd hoped to leave a little longer.

Once I've changed my clothes into my nightwear, I scrawl a short note, and then open my door, peering out into the corridor. It's late, and the women are all modestly tucked up tight in their beds. So there's no one to see me slip through the shadows and hurry to where I know Zylin's quarters are. I'm taking a huge risk, coming here like this. If anyone sees me, I will struggle to explain what I'm doing, but I'm desperate.

I slip my note under the door and tap lightly, before fleeing the scene, managing to return to my room without meeting a single soul.

And then I wait.

The knock on my door comes not half an hour later. I've managed to regain my composure and prepare myself for this meeting. For what must come next.

'Who is it?' I whisper at the door.

'Me.' Zylin smiles broadly as I let him in. 'Were you expecting someone else?'

'Of course not.'

He drinks me in with his eyes, my sheer nightdress hinting at the silhouette beneath. 'I cannot tell you how happy I was to receive your note. I came as soon as I could,' Zylin says, his face flushed with excitement. 'No one saw me.'

'You're certain?'

He nods. 'Of course. You know your honour is too important to me to put it at risk.'

I smile. 'You have been most loyal,' I say. 'And I've been more than grateful for the way you've assisted me in delivering my letters. But I fear we might soon be exposed.'

Zylin looks confused. 'How so?'

'I may only be a woman, but we hear rumours, you know.'

'And what rumours are you hearing?'

I glide my finger across the bedsheets. 'That the Emperor grows suspicious of those in his circle. He fears that someone is betraying him.'

There it is, the glimmer of panic in Zylin's eyes. But he quickly blinks it away.

'You know you shouldn't believe everything you hear,' he says in a soothing voice. 'And you have nothing to worry about. I told you I would take your secrets to the grave.'

An easy promise to make when you don't know what those secrets are.

He steps forward and wraps his arms around me. He wants to finish what we started in the herb garden. He wants his reward for all he's done for me. For all the messages delivered. That's why he came, to claim it.

'I love you,' he says, kissing my neck, his hands hungrily spreading out over my body.

Empty words.

'I know,' I say. 'And I'm sorry.'

He tilts his head back to give me a puzzled look. 'What for?'

I answer him with the blade that I push into his gut, twisting as it severs flesh and life.

He stumbles backwards, his confusion apparent as he clutches at the wound I've just made. Slippery hands try to stop the blood spilling through his fingers, but it's pointless. It's just a matter of time.

'Marzal?' He falls to his knees, before collapsing to the floor.

I kneel beside him, looking into his terrified eyes.

'I really am sorry,' I say softly. 'You've proven a most valuable asset, but it was always going to end this way. If you want to blame anyone, blame your father.'

He blinks, not understanding. 'Father?'

I reach my hand out to caress his face. 'It'll be over soon,' I say. 'And I am most grateful for everything you've done, truly I am. You played your part admirably, but I no longer have a need for you.'

Zylin coughs, spraying blood up on to my face, my clothes. 'Marzal?' He sounds as if his heart is broken.

'Time to take my secrets to your grave.'

They are the last words he hears before he dies. Once the last breath has left his body, I scream. Loudly.

Ama bursts into my room, and then she too screams.

I run to her embrace, sobbing, while she strokes my hair. 'Are you hurt?' she asks, clutching me close to her bosom.

I shake my head. 'You need to fetch Rom,' I say. 'Now.'

Her eyes widen. 'What? No.'

There isn't time for this. 'Yes. We can trust him. Please, Ama, go now.'

She gives me a look that conveys she hopes I know what I'm doing, and then she hurries out of the door, leaving me alone with the man I've just killed.

I do nothing. Touch nothing. Feel nothing. I simply wait.

The moment Ama returns with Rom in tow, my tears start flowing again.

Rom's eyes widen as he takes in the scene, and I throw myself into his arms, which wrap protectively around me.

'Get out,' he says to Ama. 'You saw nothing, understood?'

Ama nods and, giving me an anxious glance, flees to the safety of her room.

Once we're alone, Rom pulls me away from him. 'What happened? Tell me everything.'

'He came to my room,' I say, through heaving breaths. 'I refused him, told him it wasn't appropriate for him to be here, but he forced his way in. Then he . . . he tried to . . .' I dissolve into sobs once more, gesturing to the bed so that Rom is in no doubt of my meaning. 'I didn't mean to hurt him. I just wanted him to stop.'

'And did he hurt *you*?'

I shake my head. 'I stopped him before . . . before he could do anything.'

Reassured that my honour is still intact, Rom grips me by the shoulders. 'I will take care of this,' he says. 'Don't you worry.' And he kisses the top of my head. 'Go to Ama and get yourself cleaned up. I will let you know when it's safe to return.'

I nod, staring up at him with wide eyes. 'Thank you,' I say.

'I would do anything for you,' he says, his eyes flashing with sincerity.

Resting my hands on his chest, I tilt my chin upwards, inviting him to lean towards me. He accepts and presses his lips hesitantly against mine. They're rough and cold. His moustache grates against my skin. His tongue slides in, parting my teeth until it rests on mine. He pulls me closer and I feel his body stirring.

Finally, he separates from me, breathless from the kiss. There's something else in his eyes now. Lust. Desire. But Rom is smarter than Zylin. He knows he can only possess me fully *after* marriage if he is to truly get what he wants. The throne, after all, is the real prize.

'Go now,' he says. 'All will be well.'

I do as I'm told, and Ama says nothing as she wipes the blood from my face. She asks no questions and I'm certainly not offering any explanation.

And when I return to my room later, there is no sign of the body or the blood it spilled all over my floor.

It's as if nothing ever happened.

RAYN

Thanks to Elena, my wound is healing well. Though my recovery has taken longer than I would have liked, I'm now up and about, and almost back to full strength. We've fallen into a comfortable routine, the four of us and the boy. Elena and Anaïs have welcomed us as family, sharing the little they have with us.

I can tell it's breaking their hearts, knowing we'll be taking something precious away from them, but never once do they make us feel their pain.

Elena's out selling remedies, and Anaïs is milking the goat, so Ilian and I are preparing some stew for dinner. It's the first time we've been alone, so I take the opportunity to ask about what happened after I left him for Eron.

'Did you find what you were looking for?' I ask him. 'Is your contact reliable?'

Ilian nods.

'Do you remember I told you I had a sister?' he says.

His use of past tense is ominous.

'I do. You said she got sent away?'

After the attack that killed his mother. The one that was done by his own people, ordered by his own Emperor.

Ilian nods. 'She was . . .' He searches around for a word to describe her, his face illuminated with affection. 'Fierce.'

'I like the sound of her.'

Ilian laughs. 'She would have liked you too, you're very similar. Brave, smart, and you both refuse to let the world keep you quiet.' He falls silent, stirring the broth that's heating on the fire. 'I never knew what happened to her after she was taken. But the letter I received was from someone who had been her friend. My sister had told her about me, and once her friend tracked me down, she reached out to me. She too has been trying to put an end to the injustices of this war and thought I would want to aid her. Especially once I found out what happened to my sister.'

I frown in surprise. 'Your contact is a woman?'

'I assume so – because of where she met my sister. In a convent. She might have been a servant there before she went to the palace, I'm not sure. Anyway, turns out my sister was sent there because she'd fallen pregnant out of wedlock. The father's family was wealthy and didn't want a scandal so they sent her into a . . . well, a prison to keep her quiet. She lost the child but still wasn't allowed to leave. That's where I went when we split up, to speak to the Mother Superior and find out if it was true that my sister had been there.'

'And had she?'

Ilian nods unhappily.

She . . . died there?' I ask, though I fear I already know the answer.

Ilian sighs, a sound hollow with grief. 'Yes. I'd always suspected she was dead, but I had hoped . . . After this stupid war was finished, I planned on finding her. It's too late now though. Like everything else.'

I rest my hand on his arm. 'I'm sorry.'

He blinks back tears and clears his throat. 'The point is,

I believe my contact has been telling the truth. She truly seems to have loved my sister, and now she needs help.'

'What kind of help?'

'I don't know,' he says. 'I wrote to her when you were first injured, let her know where I was so she could contact me here. But she only wrote back to say communicating via letter wasn't safe any more. I'm not sure what happens now.'

'We'll figure something out,' I promise.

We're interrupted by Elena returning home, the boy riding on her back. She looks exhausted.

'Good day?' I ask her, as Ilian lifts the child down from her and starts playing with him on the ground. He's grown very fond of the little boy since we've been here.

Elena rubs her forehead with her arm. 'Not great. I only sold one posy.' The weight of responsibility bears heavy on her, especially now there are two more mouths to feed. But there's something else bothering her today, I can tell. I just don't know what it is.

Anaïs clatters into the room with a full bucket of milk. 'Don't worry,' she says to Elena. 'We'll manage.'

Elena forces a weak smile, but it's not until we're eating the thin stew, while the baby eats milky gruel, that she tells us what's on her mind.

'I was approached by someone from the big house today.' The big house which is home to the Empress's family. I watch Anaïs closely to gauge her reaction because I don't know what this might mean, but there's only the smallest narrowing of her eyes to observe.

'Why?' Anaïs asks casually before slurping the stew from her spoon.

'The Empress is with child and has requested a midwife from home be sent to aid her delivery.'

I glance over at Ilian, who meets my gaze but says nothing. This conversation isn't for us.

Elena looks miserably at her food, which she's barely touched. 'They wondered if I might have any such skills, given that there is no midwife here any more.' She pauses. 'They offered me a lot of money, but I'm not a midwife, not really . . .'

Anaïs is shaking her head. 'You've been running from this too long. When will you admit that you *are* a midwife? My sister would never have wasted her time with you if you weren't.'

'I was just an apprentice,' Elena says, her voice breaking, tears pooling in her eyes. 'I can't do it.'

'You *were* an apprentice. Since then you've travelled hundreds of miles with a baby and kept both yourself and him alive. You brought Rayn back from the brink of death. You're no longer an apprentice.'

Elena shakes her head, dislodging the tears so that they spill down her cheeks. 'You don't understand . . . There was a girl . . . I couldn't . . . She didn't . . .' She can't quite bring herself to say it, but we all know what it is she's not saying.

Anaïs gets to her feet and walks to Elena, taking her hand. 'How many women could Aliénor not save? One loss does not make you a failure. Being a midwife doesn't mean you'll be able to save every woman and baby who come into your life. But it does mean that you *try* to save them, and you try with everything you have.' Her voice is gentle, but irrefutably firm.

For the longest time, Elena doesn't answer. And then, 'I'll go.' It's a whisper, almost a prayer.

Anaïs leans down and kisses Elena on her head. 'That's my girl.'

She shuffles back to her seat and resumes her stew.

But a thought has taken root in my mind, and as we continue to eat, it grows, until eventually I can no longer be silent. 'I'm going with you,' I say.

They all stare at me.

Ilian's frowning. 'What?'

'This is my best chance,' I say. 'I can accompany Elena as her assistant and I walk straight into the palace. Once I'm there, I kill the Emperor.'

'It's too dangerous,' he argues. 'You go into that palace, you won't leave alive.'

'I know.' I meet his eyes. 'But it's a small price to pay to end this, once and for all.'

'And what about Elena? It places her in danger, being associated with you.'

Elena looks up at me, her brave face determined. 'I agree with Rayn. He needs to be stopped. He needs to die. I'm not like Rayn. I know I'm not a soldier. But I don't need a sword to fight for what's right. And if I can help, then I will. No matter the cost.'

Ilian gets to his feet, agitated. 'And what am I supposed to do?'

'Return the boy to his mother,' I say. 'Make sure that once the Emperor's dead, Drake reaches out for peace. End this war.'

He shakes his head, eyes wide, as if what I've suggested is ridiculous. Then, running his hands through his hair, he storms out of the room.

I look over at Elena, who shrugs. 'He's your friend,' she says.

Sighing, I follow after him. I don't want to. I don't want this to be harder than it already is.

He's pacing outside, and when he sees me, he turns all his anger on me.

'Why are you doing this?' he hisses. 'Acting like you've got nothing to live for?'

'I'm not,' I say, hurt that he even thinks that. 'But this is bigger than me.'

When he says nothing, I add, 'Do you think I'll fail? Is that it?'

Ilian laughs then. A sound without humour. 'No, you'll succeed. If anyone can, it'll be you.'

'Then what? What's your problem?'

'*My* problem? When are *you* going to stop running?'

'I'm not running,' I say, bristling.

'No? Because I came to Eron to find you, only for you to flee without a second glance. I've chased you across two countries already, and I would go a lot further if I had to.'

'I never asked you to do any of that!'

'You didn't have to! I did it because—' He hesitates and I pounce on his silence.

'Because what?'

'Because I love you! *There*, are you happy?' He shouts the words and falls silent as soon as they've escaped.

Pressure builds in my chest. All the things I've been avoiding, hoping they could wait until another time, another life, have caught up with me. Time has run out.

'You're a fool, Commander,' I say softly. 'There's no place for love in war.'

'*You're* the fool,' he replies. 'Always sharpening your edges to keep everyone away. But you can cut me, bleed me dry, it won't stop me. I've lost everyone else that mattered. I won't lose you too.'

His words are fire, melting my iron heart. I walk to him and cup his face in my hands. 'I don't want to lose you either,' I say, my voice barely a whisper. I hardly want to admit to myself what he means to me. It terrifies me. But he's right, I *have* been running, and now the road has come to an end.

I brush away the strand of hair that has fallen over his eye, my thumb lingering on his cheekbone.

'I love you too.' I thought it would be hard to say, but the words come easily and true.

'Then stay with me,' he says, resting his forehead on mine.

'I wish I could. I'm not doing this because I want to.'

His lips brush my cheek, his breath warm on my ear. 'What *do* you want?'

I close my eyes and melt into him. 'I want to go home.' And for a moment I allow myself to imagine it. Returning to the lands my father loved, where I grew up, watching my own children learn to forge a blade, Ilian beside me, smiling in the way he does that brings light to the shadows.

I want it so much it chokes my heart.

But I can't have it – at least not yet – and we both know it.

'We're at war,' I say. 'What we want doesn't matter. We have a duty we can't escape, and this is an opportunity we can't ignore. You know I'm right.'

'Of course you are. I just wish you weren't.' Ilian sighs deeply. 'I'll do my part, but on one condition.'

'What?'

'That you come back to me. If there's any chance, come back to me, Rayn.'

The tear escapes from my eye without permission, and I wipe it away.

He said my name.

'Done.'

I mean it, I truly do, and yet when we steal our first kiss, for all its sweetness and longing, it tastes like goodbye.

RAYN

The journey to the palace has been uncomfortable, the wheels bumping over the uneven ground of the roads, which are all in need of repair. I'd far rather be riding or walking, but when the Empress sends a carriage for you, you don't refuse.

Leaving was almost unbearable. For Elena, saying goodbye both to the child and Anaïs left her broken. She just sat sobbing opposite me for the first day. I keep my pain inside me. Ilian and I had said all we needed to during our last night together, memories I hold close to my heart.

Now we must all focus on what comes next.

Elena and I have talked strategy. She is going in an official capacity and I will present myself merely as someone from the town who volunteered to chaperone her on the dangerous journey. That should leave her as uncompromised as possible, so that if I succeed, she isn't implicated and can say she had no idea what I was planning. Her main focus is safely delivering the Empress's baby. Mine is killing the Emperor. She deals in life, I deal in death.

When we arrive at the palace, all our fears are temporarily forgotten. It's staggeringly beautiful, but it's a façade. A pretty face disguising the evil within.

'It's like something out of a dream,' Elena says.

Or a nightmare.

The carriage clatters through clean streets, which are all teeming with well-fed people. It reminds me of Eron. Yet another protected place for the elite to remain uncontaminated by the violence of war.

We come to a halt in front of the gleaming palace, and suddenly the reality of why we're here strikes home.

Elena squeezes my hand, and then together we take a deep breath.

There's no turning back now.

She climbs out of the carriage first, and I follow right after, our bags tightly clutched in my hands.

A group of women wait to greet us, flanked by soldiers. My heart beats faster. This could all be over far more quickly than I'd like if they insist on searching us.

The girl who steps forward to greet us looks young, younger than me, but radiates a certain authority. She is impossibly beautiful.

'Welcome,' she says to Elena, as I hover behind. 'I'm Princess Marzal. The Empress asked me to come and greet you personally. I hope your journey was tolerable?'

Elena curtseys deeply before the princess, while I wonder what we did to earn this honour. 'Thank you for inviting us. It is a privilege to be here,' Elena says.

The princess looks over Elena's shoulder at me, with a questioning glance.

'Oh, forgive me, Princess. This is my chaperone. She is an immigrant from the south, whose parents came to live here during the occupation. She lives in our town and volunteered to accompany me so I would not have to travel alone.'

'I see. It is brave of you both to travel during these

difficult times,' the princess says with a small nod. 'The Empress is very grateful. Does she speak Vallurian?'

'Very little,' Elena says, though her smile is nervous. Though I can just about pass as being from Metée, we've decided to take as few risks as possible, so I will talk only when absolutely necessary. 'We hoped she could stay here with me,' Elena goes on. 'Assist me if needed. And then accompany me safely back home after the baby has arrived.'

'As you wish,' the princess says. 'Let me show you where you are to sleep.'

But as I step forward to follow them, the guards block my path and gesture for me to open our bags, clearly intending to search them. If they do that, they'll no doubt search me too.

Sweat trickles down my back as I weigh my options. Should I fight, make a run for it or plead ignorance?

All my instincts say fight, so that's what I'm bracing myself for, when the princess turns round and sees what's happening.

'These women are invited guests, here at the invitation of the Empress herself! I do not think we need insult them by searching them, do you?'

The guards hesitate and look over at me, as if trying to decide whether I look like a threat. They see what all men see. A woman. An insignificance. A nothing.

And I'm allowed to pass unchallenged, walking into the palace with my sword beneath my cloak.

So it begins.

*

Princess Marzal escorts us to our rooms, which are situated opposite the Empress's chambers, and though I'm sure they are small and plain compared to the Empress's, it's been a long time since I've seen anything so luxurious.

'You can sleep here,' she says to me, before turning to Elena. 'You, however, are to speak with the Empress before settling in. If she wishes it, you will sleep on the floor in her room, in case you're needed.'

Elena nods. 'May I meet her now? I would like to examine her as soon as I'm able.'

'Come with me. She longs to hear news from home.'

'I'd be happy to give it.' Elena glances at me. 'Why don't you get us unpacked?'

I nod obediently, and hand Elena her bag full of medicines.

The two of them leave me alone in the room and once they're gone I immediately remove my sword from under my cloak and tuck it beneath the mattress. I breathe easier once it's hidden.

I set about unpacking the little we brought with us, clothing and such, and at first don't notice the note that's slipped under our door.

Uncertain who it's from, I pick it up, unfolding it with shaking hands.

When the Empress gives birth, the Emperor is alone. It is tradition that he waits for his son's arrival in private, and unattended. All others are sent to pray for a safe delivery.

Folded with the note is another piece of paper with a crude map on it. Directions to the throne room.

It tells me all I need to know. If I want to kill the Emperor, my best chance will be when the Empress goes into labour. This note must be from Ilian's contact – word of our arrival has clearly spread quickly.

It's a while before Elena returns, but as soon as she does, I'm on my feet, desperate for news.

'How long does she have?'

Elena shakes her head. 'Could be a day. Could be a week. She's very close, but she's been shamefully neglected. Her previous midwife bled her, and so she's very weak.'

I can hear the fear in Elena's voice. She's afraid of losing another baby. Another woman.

'You can do this,' I say to her. 'You saved me, remember.'

She doesn't look convinced. 'I think I should stay with her,' Elena says. 'I daren't risk leaving her.'

I can hear the apology in her voice, because it means abandoning me. So I show her the note.

'I don't think I'll be on my own for too long,' I say. 'My opportunity's coming sooner rather than later.'

When she's read it, Elena stares at me. 'It's really happening, isn't it?'

I nod, my stomach twisting into knots.

Elena pulls me into a tight embrace. 'I'm so glad we met, Rayn,' she says.

'Me too.'

I release her and look squarely into her eyes. 'We can do this. You have your job, I have mine. And we're both going to succeed.'

Over the next few days, we settle into life at the palace. Elena is almost constantly by the Empress's side, trying to build up her strength before the baby comes.

It gives me plenty of time to become familiar with the building.

A little exploring reveals the map to the throne room shows a route through the servants' quarters. I am able to wander the narrow passages, which run parallel to the main corridors, unseen. I silently thank the hubris of the men who decided that even seeing handmaidens or other servants was beneath them.

The women who work here don't like me one bit. I'm not sure whether it's because they think I'm from Metée, because I refuse to speak to anyone, or because Elena has replaced one of their own. But it means they leave me to myself, allowing me the freedom I require.

Every day, I wake with a sense of urgency. I don't know when my chance will come so I must be prepared for it at any time. And yet the longer I'm here, the more afraid I become. There's so much at stake. Not just my life, but the lives of countless others.

On the sixth night, Elena returns to our room even later than usual, too exhausted to say much.

'It will be soon,' she warns me as she lies back on her bed.

She's been saying that since we arrived, and it doesn't bring me any comfort. If anything, it leaves me even more on edge.

'Are you scared, Rayn?' Her voice cuts through the darkness. 'Of what might happen to us?'

'I'm not afraid of dying itself,' I whisper truthfully. 'But I am afraid of missing life. All the things I'd never get to do. All the weapons I'd never forge. Of all the people I'd leave behind. I know how much it hurts to watch someone you love go where you can't follow.'

She doesn't reply. She doesn't need to. Some things cannot be healed, some fears never allayed. We are both afraid and must carry on regardless.

I'm close to falling asleep when an urgent knock on the door makes us jump.

Elena looks at me, and we share a moment. We both know this might be it. She stretches over to take my hand and squeezes it.

And then she hurries to the door, where she's greeted by a frantic handmaiden.

'Come quickly!' she urges. 'The Empress is dying.'

ELENA

I run into the Empress's chambers and can taste the fear in the air.

'Please,' she whimpers. 'Help me.'

'You're all right,' I assure her. 'I need to see what's happening. Will you let me?'

She nods. 'I'm bleeding.'

I force a smile to my face. 'Let's have a look.'

She lies back and a handmaiden assists me in draping a blanket over her knees to protect her modesty. I sigh with relief at what I see.

'You're not bleeding. Your waters have broken, that is all.'

Her eyes are pleading as I meet them. 'The baby's alive?'

'Yes, there's nothing to fear. It just means it's time.' I turn to the handmaidens. 'Fetch me hot water and plenty of fresh sheets. And can you let my companion know the Empress is in labour, please? I may need her help.'

Of course, that isn't true. I just want to let Rayn know it's time for her to do what she came to do, but I can't think any more about that now. It terrifies me too much.

I rinse my hands in vinegar and oil. 'I'm going to see how far along you are,' I say, giving the Empress my undivided attention.

The Empress gives a sharp intake of breath when I touch her, though I'm as gentle as I can be.

'You have a little way to go yet,' I say. 'I think we have a long night ahead of us.'

At this point, there is nothing I can do but keep her comfortable and provide herbs for the pain. I rub salve on to her belly, and when the contractions come I hold her hand, mop her brow and even rub her feet so that she doesn't feel alone.

The hours pass and the contractions grow stronger. I try so hard not to think of Rayn and what she's doing. She's on her own now, as am I. And I can't let the Empress down. She's a woman who needs my help, and helping women is what Aliénor taught me to do from the moment I was born.

I can almost feel her with me now, standing in the corner, reminding me to be prepared, to have instruments clean and ready should they be required. The only certainty with any delivery is that anything can happen.

As the sun begins to rise, I stand and stretch my aching limbs. 'Come on,' I say, taking the Empress's hand. 'You need to get out of this bed. Your baby will come a lot sooner if you walk around.' I'm concerned she may be too weak to stand after such prolonged bedrest, but I don't want this labour to stall.

'I can't . . .' She's afraid.

'Of course you can,' I say, though I'm far from certain that's true. 'I've got you.'

With my help, she manages to rise to her feet, and though she's shaky, she's able to stand. The effect is immediate. I can almost see the baby drop inside her.

'There you go,' I say. 'Come, kneel on the ground and

lean on the bed. Then you don't have to support yourself.'

I lie soft cushions down for her knees, and she obediently does as she's told.

'Open a window,' I say to the handmaiden hovering nearby.

'My old mistress said it should remain warm and dark in here, like a womb.'

Her old mistress was a fool. 'Well, she's no longer here and I'm telling you we need some air.'

'Do as she says,' the Empress growls, when the girl continues to hesitate.

I squeeze her hand by way of thanks, comforting her as she moans low through the pain.

When the Empress grows agitated, complaining of nausea, I know the baby is ready to be born.

'All right, Highness,' I say to her. 'You're going to need to push now.'

'Please,' she says, already exhausted from the labour. 'Can you call me Sabina? I haven't been called by my name since I arrived here.'

I smile. 'Of course, Sabina. Now, I'm not going anywhere. I'm right here with you and we're going to get through this. Together. OK?'

She nods, a steely determination on her face. I've seen it hundreds of times. There is no one stronger than a woman in labour, no warrior fiercer.

Though her body has been neglected, forced to lie for months in an unnatural position, Sabina gives her all to every push, while I watch the birthing canal for progress.

It's taking longer than I would expect.

When she grows tired, I rest my arm around her shoulders. 'I need to take a look and see where baby is.'

'You want me back on the bed?' She sounds like I've asked her to climb a mountain.

'I'm sorry,' I say. 'I haven't got a good enough view like this.'

She begins to sob, broken by the exertion, the exhaustion, but allows me to guide her so that she's lying down once again.

In between contractions, I find out what's wrong. The baby's hand is lying against its cheek. It's going to be tricky to get out.

'Sabina, your baby is in a difficult position,' I say gently to her. 'I can help you, if I make a little cut.'

'Will it hurt?' She stares at me with wide eyes.

'Yes.' I won't lie to her. 'But if I don't, you will tear anyway, and this will be easier to heal, and make the delivery quicker.'

She closes her eyes. 'Do it.'

Swallowing hard, I take a blade from my bag and hold it in the fire to cleanse it.

I call the handmaidens over to help me. 'Take a knee each,' I say, instructing them to hold the Empress's legs up, folded into her chest.

'Right, Sabina,' I say. 'Let's meet your baby.'

I make the cut as swiftly and cleanly as I can, smearing ointment all around to keep it from infection, and then tell the Empress to push with all her might.

Carefully, I guide the baby's head down, the hand still pressing against the cheek. If I hadn't pre-empted this, the poor woman would have torn herself badly. 'Right, the head is here,' I say, stroking Sabina's leg. 'I need you to give a last, small push now, very gently, and the rest of the baby will be out.'

When the contraction comes, she pushes again and the body slides out. For a moment, I stare at it. I've done it. The baby is delivered. Everyone's alive. And then I get back to work. There's still a lot to do, the placenta to deliver, but as the newborn's screams rattle through the air, I can't stop smiling.

I am Elena. And I am a midwife.

RAYN

I wait for Elena to return, but she does not. Instead, a handmaiden delivers the message that the Empress is in labour and my presence may be required. I can only hope that too much will be happening in the Empress's room for anyone to notice when I don't show up.

Because this is it.

I have no idea how many men might be guarding the Emperor. I must be prepared for whatever I find.

The sword I stashed beneath my mattress is quickly retrieved and hidden under my cloak once more.

And then, I run.

I know the route I must take, the hidden passageways designed to keep servants invisible, allowing me to be the same. When I reach the point where I must venture out into the main palace, I meet no one. As my contact indicated, they've all taken to their quarters to pray to their Gods.

There is one solitary guard protecting the Emperor's location. He blocks my way as I approach.

'You aren't supposed to be here.'

'I have a message about the Empress,' I say, hoping to buy myself time.

He hears my accent and frowns. 'You're not from—'

I don't wait for him to finish the sentence. I hit him,

knocking his head against the wall and rendering him unconscious.

I don't have long – someone will walk by and find the guard soon enough. As I burst into the throne room, I hear – even from this distance – the faint wails of the Empress, but then the doors shut firmly and her screams are silenced.

The Emperor is sitting on his throne, slumped forward.

At first, I wonder if he's praying, but there's something about the angle of his head that gives me pause. Something is wrong.

Cautiously, I take a step closer and it's then I see the blood that's pouring from his neck, spilling down to stain his chest.

Raising my sword, I search the room for the killer, but I'm alone with the Emperor's dead body. Whoever did this is gone. I reach to press my fingers into the blood. It's still wet, still warm. This can't have happened more than mere minutes ago. So how could the killer have disappeared?

I'm still standing, stunned, by the Emperor's body when the door opens and a man rushes into the room.

It doesn't take him long to drink in the scene. I know I look as guilty as hell, standing over the Emperor with a sword as his blood pools over the marble floor.

'I didn't do this,' I say, thinking fast, holding out my sword, both as a warning and as evidence. 'See, no blood. He was dead when I arrived – we need to find the killer.'

The man has no chance to respond before half a dozen bodyguards burst in behind him, their swords drawn.

'Don't move,' one of them says. 'Imperial Advisor Rom, you and your accomplice are under arrest for the murder of the Imperial Emperor.'

'How dare you?' The first man is indignant. 'This is outrageous! I don't even know this girl.'

'And I didn't kill him,' I protest, but it falls on deaf ears. We're clapped into irons and escorted from the room.

I manage one last look at the body slumped in the throne. I have no idea who killed him and am furious to have had the opportunity to do it myself stolen from me. I wish I knew who got here first. I don't know whether to thank them or curse them.

MARZAL

I am Marzal. I am a daughter and a lover, and I came here with only one goal.

Revenge.

All I have said and done since I arrived has been for this purpose. Every kind word, every misleading deed, all calculated and intentional. Every string I have pulled, every person I have manipulated, all with one aim.

And I have succeeded.

The tunnel seems longer than normal and as I hurry through it to reach the safety of my room, I slip and slide in blood.

Don't worry, it's not mine.

My father's face floods my mind. His shock, his incomprehension. He hadn't heard me creep out from the vent, his focus so entirely on his longing for a son. He made it too easy. Unguarded, unprotected. Believing himself invincible, free from danger. I was behind him within seconds and had thrust the blade Rom gave me into the folds of his neck before he even had time to look up.

The memory is still vivid, the way he stared at me, disgust and disbelief mingling, his hand trying to stop his life spilling from him.

'Who—' He struggled to say the word, blood spitting

from his mouth. 'The hell. Are you?' It was the worst thing he could have said.

'A child born on a winter's night, when moon was full and land was bright.'

The way his eyes had widened then, his first hint of fear, despite the fatal wound that was already causing him to drown in his own blood.

'*You?*'

And I'd smiled. 'Yes, me. A girl. Your daughter. Your heir.'

He still couldn't believe it. Even though it was happening, his brain just couldn't comprehend the situation. It was almost funny. *Almost.*

'Why?' The word was barely a whisper, his lungs running out of air to form it.

'For my mother.'

And I'd stabbed him again, this time right in the throat, leaving the blade there until I saw the light fade from his eyes for good.

I'd had to run then, taking care not to drip any blood for fear of leading people to my secret tunnel. It's vital I return to my room as quickly as I can to rid myself of the weapon and these bloody, incriminating clothes.

I've done it, Mother. Everything I promised to do. They didn't suspect a thing, and still don't. For how could a mere girl be capable of such duplicity, such cunning? Their ignorance has made it all so easy.

I got away with killing the Mother Superior, after all. My practice run. She deserved it, every last moment of pain I inflicted on her. Those thieves that came to the convent? Who took everything they wanted from the kitchens? Well, that included the Sister who worked there.

They raped her and beat her until they were bored and she was dead. So Mother Superior decided to put someone else to work in the kitchen, someone who'd already lost their womanhood, someone she considered damaged goods, someone who, in her opinion, deserved what would happen to her if the thieves ever came back.

And they did. This time it was Kala, my beloved Kala, who was brutalised, and I was the one who found her the following morning, barely alive and wishing she wasn't. And as she was the one who taught me about oleander and its poisonous qualities, it seemed only fitting that I should use it as a means to avenge her after she slit her own wrists.

It's a bitter poison, oleander, and so I made a harmless but foul concoction for the nuns for a few weeks, so they would suspect nothing when the time came. And then, one day, I laced the Mother Superior's tea with the poison and watched from afar as it claimed her life.

I applied the same strategy with Urso, of course. It was a shame she had to die, but how else could I really hurt Izra but to take her daughter from her? How else could I inflict the same pain on her as she did on me? The bond between mother and daughter is tied tight in the veins, and as she slashed ours, so did I hers. And then to make Roselle take the blame? Well, that was necessary too. After all, she played her part, did she not? With her jealous whispers and spiteful tongue.

As for Zylin's crime? Well, it was not his, but his father's, and sadly just as I've paid a price for others' sins all my life, so too has Zylin paid for his father's.

And Rom? The man who masterminded the whole sordid tale at my father's request? Well, his comeuppance will be any moment now.

I will destroy the bundles of letters stashed underneath my mattress, each one lovingly written to you, my darling mother, but never sent. Zylin only delivered my letters to Ilian, Kala's brother, the one other person in the world who cared enough to avenge her death. Writing to you was simply a means to comfort myself, keep me focused. After all, really, there was never anyone to send them to, was there?

My whole life, I've planned this. From the moment you were executed. Killed because you produced a daughter, not a son. Killed because my father was bored and wanted a younger woman. Your death sealed by the first wife, who hated your kind heart, and the mistress, who feared being replaced. The lies they told to Rom to ensure your execution were never forgotten. Rom, who loved you, betrayed you to appease my father, spinning a tale of falsehoods and fabrications, to condemn you to death. And Zylin's father was the man to bring the blade down on your fragile neck and take you from me.

Your last letter reached me though, even in the convent. Told me the truth. And I swore I'd avenge you or die trying. And so I have.

*

I just have one part of my plan left to execute.

It is only when I wriggle out on to my bedroom floor that I realise quite what a mess I am, but that's the least of my worries. As I turn from the wall, I discover to my horror that I'm not alone.

Ama stares at me like I'm a ghost, and honestly an apparition probably wouldn't be more terrifying than I am right now, stained red and holding a knife that still drips my father's blood.

Silence fills the space between us, and I'm wondering what to say when Ama steps towards me.

Gently, so gently, she lifts my dress over my shoulders, and I daren't move as she strips me naked, removing every last trace of evidence. When she holds her hand out for the blade, I hesitate, but her hand remains there, open and waiting, and eventually I give it to her. She wraps it in the bloodied material, and then leans down to stuff the bundle into the vent, letting the tapestry fall back to hide my dark secrets.

Still not speaking a word, she fetches fresh clothes, and I stand there, more exposed than I've ever been, until she returns to my side and covers me once more.

As she wipes the last of the blood from my skin, I open my mouth. I want to thank her. I want to ask her why she's helping me. But as I start to speak, she raises her finger and presses it to my lips, quietening me.

Her eyes glisten with tears. 'I loved your mother too.'

It's all she says, but no other words are needed. I wonder if she knows everything I've done. Has she known all along? Maybe one day I'll ask her, but not today.

'There,' she says, when I'm presentable. 'Go now. Finish what you've started.'

I kiss her on the cheek and smile.

I intend to.

RAYN

I have no idea what has happened. The Emperor is dead, but not by my hand, and I realise now I have been tricked. I am about to be blamed for something I have not done – though I wish I had, so perhaps I am guilty in a way.

There's a rattling of keys, and I look up sharply.

To my surprise, it is Princess Marzal. She is about the last person I would expect to see here.

She steps into my cell, and I scramble to my feet, even as she gestures for me not to bother.

'I thought you might be hungry,' she says, passing me the bowl she's carrying so carefully between her delicate, clean hands.

'Thank you.' I take it from her and slurp down a few mouthfuls of the watery soup.

'We've met before,' she says. 'I'm Marzal. Heir to the throne.'

There's something in the tone of her voice that stops me eating, and I look over the edge of the bowl at her. 'I didn't kill your father. He was already dead when I got there.'

'But you intended to kill him, did you not?'

There's no point lying now. 'Yes. For every terror he unleashed, he deserved to die.'

Marzal steps towards me, and I'm trying to read her, but I cannot. The girl is unfathomable. 'I don't disagree with you,' she says, her voice soft. 'My father was an evil man. Which is why I fed you and Ilian as much information as I could to enable you to gain access to him.' She pauses, taking in my stunned silence.

I can't speak. My mind is busy trying, and failing, to catch up.

'I'm so glad it was you that came, that it was a woman who was prepared to do the job. Men underestimate us at their peril, do they not?'

And she smiles at me.

'You're Ilian's contact,' I breathe. I can't quite believe it. 'Why would you want your father dead?'

'Trust me,' Marzal says. 'I had good cause. I think in another time, another place, we might have been friends, you and I. It's a shame it has to end this way.'

'I told you, I didn't kill him. Nor did the advisor you arrested. You should be looking for the actual culprit.'

'And yet, you're hardly innocent, by your own admission.'

I fix her with an icy glare. 'I could say the same to you.'

'You're the blacksmith, are you not?'

'I am.'

'And the sword you carried, was it not forged in blood?'

I swallow hard, my throat dry. She knows everything. 'It was.'

'I am sorry,' she says. 'Truly I am. I wish you did not have to be another casualty of this war. But you came here expecting this fate; I merely give it to you.'

My heart is racing too fast, and something's not right. Maybe nothing is. 'What are you talking about?'

'You killed the Emperor. That is how history will remember you. Some will thank you for it, others won't. But at least you will be remembered.'

'I didn't kill him,' I insist.

She waves a hand dismissively. 'That is nothing more than a technicality.'

My legs buckle and I fall to the floor. My skin is sweaty, and my insides are churning.

Marzal crouches opposite me. 'Are you feeling unwell? I'm sorry, it won't last long.'

I meet her eyes and see it then. The coldness. When I glance towards the bowl of soup, she smiles.

'It was unwise to drink so readily from the enemy's dish.'

I stare at her. 'What have you done?'

'What was necessary. You see, even *you* looked at me and saw no danger. I must say, I'm disappointed.'

She's right, I'm a fool. I've spent my life around black heat – I know when something appears harmless it only makes it more dangerous. And this time, my mistake is going to cost me everything.

'You see, the story is simple,' Marzal says. 'Rom, the man my father trusted most, betrayed him by leaking information to the enemy. He allowed you access to the palace, and together you assassinated the Emperor. You even carried the blade of blood prophesied to carry out the deed. It's poetic, really.'

The feeling in my legs has all but gone now. 'But it was you, not Rom. He'll reveal the truth.'

'I think not. I was careful enough to leave a trail of clues leading back to him. Including the scroll they'll find on your body, with his seal on it.'

It's hot in here, and airless. I'm struggling to fill my lungs.

'Why?' I can barely speak. 'Why have you done all this?'

Marzal leans close to me now, our faces almost touching.

'Because my mother was betrayed. Murdered. She loved Rom and he loved her. But to save his own neck, he sacrificed hers and so I've made it my life's work to destroy *everyone* who hurt her. Including my father.'

My vocal cords have shrivelled and I can no longer speak, but my eyes are still able to widen as she looks down on me and smiles, leaning over me to tuck a piece of paper into my pocket. Paper that will condemn an innocent man. Well, innocent of this particular crime, at least.

'I am sorry,' she says again. 'As I said, in another life, we could have been friends. In this one, you were simply in the wrong place at the wrong time. But because Ilian cares for you, and because Kala loved him, your death will be quick. My gift to you. Rom will receive no such mercy.'

Marzal stands up, and I am helpless to do anything but look at her.

'Goodbye, blacksmith,' she says, and then she bangs on the door for the guards to release her.

Marzal glances back at me one last time, and then she's gone, leaving me with nothing but the cold floor and the poison in my veins for company. I can feel it, working its way through my body, closing every door behind it.

I stare at the ceiling and think of my father. My brother. Luc. All waiting for me. I think of Elena and hope she is safe, that she won't be punished too. I think of Ilian and of what might have been.

A warm tear spills on to my cheek and then I think no more.

MARZAL

An unfamiliar sensation passes fleetingly through me as I shut the door on the blacksmith. A hint of guilt? No matter, I cannot regret it. She came here prepared to die for her cause, and I have simply facilitated that. The poison I chose for her was painless and swift, and a death like that is more than most can hope for. It's more than Rom will receive.

It is his cell I go to next, hungry for his suffering.

When he sees me, his eyes lighten, his body relaxes. When he looks at me, he sees an ally, a way out, a saviour. Unfortunately for him, I am none of those things.

'Marzal,' he says, rushing towards me and clutching my hands in his. 'Thank you for coming. I've been asking for you ever since they threw me in here, but I wasn't sure they'd pass on my message.'

The arrogance of the man. To think I'm only here on his summons.

I pull my hands away from his.

A frown creases his confident face. 'Marzal? Surely you know I had nothing to do with your father's death? That I had nothing to do with that woman?'

'I know no such thing.'

My coldness stuns him. He has never seen this side of me. I have never let him. Fear creeps over him like vines strangling a tree.

'My love?'

I laugh, and it is a hollow sound. 'Love? What do you know of love?'

He stares at me, the beginning of understanding dawning in his eyes. He tries once more. 'What of our plans to marry? With your father dead there is nothing to stop us now. You must know I would do anything for you.'

'I do not doubt that you would do anything to claim the throne,' I say. 'That is why you truly wished to marry me, and we both know it.'

Panic is taking hold now, and Rom alters his approach. 'My whole life I served your father; I would never betray him.'

'Why not? You betrayed my mother.'

I raise my eyes to meet him with the challenge and see his disbelief shining back at me. I've pulled the thread and now shall enjoy watching him unravel.

'Your . . . mother?' His voice shakes slightly.

'Yes, the woman you loved, remember? The one you swore your life and soul to? You could have protected her from my father, but instead you sealed her fate. Surely you haven't forgotten her? Surely you see her blood on your hands every time you wash them?'

Rom searches for words but finds none. I've rendered him speechless. How fitting for what I have planned next.

'Guards?' I call, and within seconds three of the Empress's men have joined us in the cell.

'This traitor is spreading lies. I think we should silence him, don't you?'

Rom's eyes widen as the men grab hold of him. He tries to fight them off, shouts that I'm a liar, that he's innocent, but it's no use. These men are not his, nor the Emperor's. They are loyal to the Empress, and she is loyal to me. Love is always more powerful than fear.

They hold him down and grab his tongue. I watch with the greatest satisfaction as they slice it off, Rom's muffled screams penetrating the air. He will not be able to spread unwanted lies any more.

Afterwards, he sits there, curled in a heap, moaning in pain as blood dribbles down his chin. As afraid as a child alone in the dark.

'Was it your idea to accuse her of being *spoiled*? Or was that Izra's work?' I ask, once the guards have stepped outside again.

That was the case Rom built against my mother, that before she had wed my father she'd been with many other men. A 'spoiled' flower. Nothing would anger my father more than believing he'd been promised a virgin and given a whore. And Rom, whom my mother loved even though they could never be together, took the lies spread by Izra and Roselle and made them into fact by fabricating the documents that doomed her. He may as well have killed her with his own hands.

'Why would I want to share the throne with you?' I say, leaning close to him. 'For too long, men have taken everything they can from us women. Our bodies, our children, our lives. I will not let you take my power.'

He stares at me, utterly hopeless.

'Let me tell you what will happen now. The young woman you found with my father's body? She was Rayn, the blacksmith. And she was armed with a blade of blood.'

I can see the confusion in his eyes, confusion that I would even know about such things.

'We searched her body and found a letter bearing your seal, instructing her on how to kill the Emperor. Oh yes, you're not the only one who can fabricate evidence. You will be tried for your crimes and you will be found guilty. Your body will be subjected to a hanging before you're drawn and quartered. It will be slow, brutal, agonising. And I will delight in every moment of it.'

I stand up, looking down at his pitiful body. How quickly these powerful men can be destroyed.

'Oh, and one last thing,' I say. 'The prophecy was wrong. It wasn't referring to a blade made *of* blood. It was a blade wielded *by* his flesh and blood.'

He can't believe it. That I am the one who killed my father. Seeing his shock is more satisfying than I can say.

I leave him then to his despair, giving the guards explicit instructions that no one is to enter the cell apart from me.

My whole body tingles with fire as I walk back towards my chambers. I have never felt more alive.

Then I see her, the midwife that so usefully enabled me to get Rayn into the palace. Once Ilian had told me where they were, it was easy to suggest to the Empress that she summon a midwife from home. It didn't matter that I could no longer communicate with letters. I knew Rayn would take the bait.

'You.'

The midwife stops walking, and even from this distance I can see that she's trembling. To her credit though, when she faces me, she's defiant.

'The blacksmith. She came with you, did she not? You brought an assassin into the palace.'

She swallows hard, and the blood drains from her skin, but she says nothing.

'Did you know? Were you in on her plans? Or were you simply manipulated?'

'I knew.'

Her honesty surprises me. I'm so used to people scheming and lying and cheating to survive, it's refreshing to be faced with such transparency.

'Then why? Why would you want our Emperor dead?'

'Do you know the noise a mother makes when she loses her child?' she asks, and I nod, thinking of Urso and Izra. 'Imagine that amplified by the hundreds. Your father ordered babies to be killed. Slaughtered like animals. And I can't silence them in my head. I will never be able to. So that's why. For the women. For their pain. For my own.' Rage flickers behind her eyes, and in that moment, she reminds me so much of Kala that I want to hold her.

It is time to repay honesty with honesty. 'You're right to hate him,' I say. 'He was a monster.' She's as stunned by my honesty as I was by hers. 'I don't blame you for wanting him dead.'

'Am I to be arrested?' she asks.

'No. I think enough people have suffered because of him, don't you? It is time for this war to end, for a new age of peace. And as heir to the throne, I shall make sure of it.'

'And what of Rayn? Will you free her too?'

She hasn't heard then. 'I'm afraid Rayn is dead.' I watch as the midwife's eyes fill with tears. 'My father's guards killed her before I could intervene. I'm sorry.'

The girl fights away her grief, locking it up until she can release it in private. 'She knew the risk,' she says, trying to comfort herself.

'And she will be honoured by all those who wished for an end to this war. The truth will become known about my father's part in the atrocities. Rayn may be dead, but her name will live for ever. However,' and I pause, altering the tone of my voice from sympathetic to one of warning, 'you must never speak of your part in what happened, or of this conversation. I cannot be considered weak for letting you live.'

The midwife nods. 'All I want is to help people.'

'Then do so with my blessing.' As an afterthought, I ask, 'The Empress? Is she well?'

'Yes, she delivered a healthy baby girl.'

I suppress my smile. Another sister is no threat to me.

*

By the time I return to my room, I'm giddy. I've succeeded. My enemies are all dead and nothing can prevent me from becoming Imperial Empress. I risked everything and now I shall reap the rewards, ruling this country in a way that would make my mother proud. All I want to do now is share my victory with the only person I can – Ama.

She's lying on my chaise longue, fast asleep, which isn't like her at all, but it has been a particularly intense day.

'Ama,' I say, wanting to wake her. 'Ama, I did it.' I still can't quite believe it. I've been wearing the mask of revenge for so long, I didn't realise how good it was to breathe without it on. I laugh – a real, true laugh – and it sounds strange to my own ears. I do it some more, because it feels so wonderful.

I look down, and still Ama sleeps. Irritation disturbs my joy. 'Ama.' I scold my governess for her lethargy.

Then I see the bowl on the ground, the half-eaten soup staring back at me accusingly.

And my heart stops.

Slowly, as if it was even possible to disturb her now, I kneel beside Ama, pushing the poisoned soup away, cursing myself for not disposing of every last drop once I poured a bowl for the blacksmith.

'Ama?' I take her hand in mine but it's cold. Lifeless.

How often did I imagine doing Ama harm to punish her for vexing me? No one irritated me, bothered me or annoyed me as much as she did. And yet, too late, I realise that I loved her. That because of her, I was never truly alone. I am now.

When the tears come this time, they are not pretend. They are horribly real. The screams that follow are equally raw. How could I have been so *stupid*? All this time I've taken meticulous care over the smallest action, only to fail at the very end.

And as I sob beside the woman who raised me when I had no mother to do so, I am not an Empress. I am a little girl.

I have everything I ever wished for. All it cost me was everything I had left.

ELENA

For a girl who once had never left the town she grew up in, I have certainly travelled a great distance. But while my journey from my old home through Vallure to reach Anaïs was treacherous, the journey from there towards Eron has been less terrifying.

This is partly due to the fact that I've been on horseback rather than walking, and also because I'm no longer alone.

When I returned to Anaïs's house, I was surprised to discover Ilian and the boy still there.

He had wanted to wait for Rayn.

At the news of her death, his eyes had dimmed. Without a word, he'd walked out of the door and was gone for several days, so long that we weren't sure if he was ever to return. But eventually he did, insisting that he escort me and the boy safely back to Eron.

The light still hasn't returned to his eyes, however. I'm not sure it ever will.

It was Ilian's last promise to Rayn that he'd see the Governor's child reunited with his mother. It was my last promise to Aliénor that I would do the same. Together, we are finally fulfilling our vows.

The boy is growing big now, and is less content being strapped to my back. He pulls at my hair and wiggles unbearably, but still, I cherish these moments. They are to be our last, for Eron is within sight, and before the day is over our mission will have reached its end.

'It will be hard for you,' Ilian observes as we ride along our final stretch of road. 'To say goodbye to him.'

'Yes. I love him as if he were my own.'

'If you wish, I can speak with General Drake and the child's mother. See if you can be his official governess?'

I don't answer him immediately. The temptation to accept is strong, but my visit to the palace taught me something important about who I am. I was not saved from an early grave to care for only one child. Aliénor gifted me with more than just life – she gave me a purpose. One that I can no longer run from.

'Thank you, that's very kind,' I say. 'But my place is with Anaïs. The town has no midwife and I can help there. It's time to accept who I am, to stop running.'

Ilian falls quiet. I'm certain he's thinking of Rayn.

'Do you want to talk about her?' I ask gently. I've tried to give him space to grieve privately, but in the end none of us can escape our loss.

When he doesn't reply, I think that's his answer. But after a few moments, his voice reaches me, soft on the wind.

'To start with, she was like a blister. Always there, always bothering me. My world had been dark for a long time, but there she was, a light that refused to stop shining. It annoyed me that someone from Naperone could be so clever, so brilliant. That of all the people who would wake me up from my non-existence, it would be her.'

Tears fall down my cheeks. His grief calls to mine, setting it free.

'She was like nature; wild and strong. A cat with nine

lives.' He chokes on his sorrow. 'How can she be gone, after everything she survived? What cruelty took her at the very end of things? When we were so close to happiness.'

There are no words I can offer him that will ease his pain, so I say nothing. Besides, he doesn't need my response, he needs to speak and the words spilling from him cannot be stopped now.

'Would I change it if I could go back? Perhaps I should wish I never met her. Save myself this pain.' He considers his answer before saying, 'No. I would not have missed one moment of our time together. I loved her long before I realised I did. I love her still.'

And then he starts to cry. He makes no noise, but his shoulders shake and tears dampen his skin. If we were not on horseback, I would reach to console him. But it is not my arms he longs for.

Eventually, he lets out a deep sigh. He's back with me.

'At least you can take comfort knowing she died a hero,' I say. 'She single-handedly altered the course of this war.'

'I take more comfort knowing she died having claimed the vengeance she sought.'

The boy at my back struggles to escape the sling, crying out in frustration when he fails.

'Someone wants to walk,' Ilian says, glad of the distraction, and he smiles at the child.

'Soon he'll be riding on his own,' I say, laughing as small fingers wrap around my face, poking my cheeks.

'Maybe I'll stay in Eron. Teach him to ride. Keep a close eye on him.'

'Won't you want to return home?' I ask, surprised.

Ilian glances over at me. 'What home? There's no place for me in this new world.'

'Of course there is. You will be an important part of the peace talks, of reuniting the two countries. And whatever happens, you will always have a home with Anaïs and me. We're your family now.'

He offers me a small smile and nods his head gratefully. I'm not sure he could speak if he wanted to.

As little hands move to prod my lips, I kiss them gently. The war has taken so much from me – from all of us. But it has also given in unexpected ways. My time with this sweet child, finding Anaïs, meeting Ilian and Rayn. As this part of my story comes to an end, I cannot regret all that has happened. I will forever mourn Aliénor, but I will honour her by living. By carrying on. Just as Ilian will do for Rayn.

There will be many hard times to come. Leaving the child today will be one of them. But I will do what I must. Because to start a new season, the old one must be left behind. And before all new beginnings, first must come goodbyes.

My last moments with the boy are slipping away, like air from my lungs. I will steal one final heartbeat just for us. I kiss the small hands again and close my eyes.

Goodbye, my sweet boy.

MARZAL

The throne is huge, and while my father filled it, I'm like a bird on a perch. And yet, sitting on it, I feel invincible, strong.

The world is already changing. Soldiers are returning home to their loved ones and families are reunited. I have met with the new leader of Naperone, Governor Drake, and have agreed to take no retribution for Rayn's actions. We both want this war to end and a treaty has already been drafted. I have seen to it that Ilian will be rewarded with both money and position.

The aunties have been reunited with their children and are free to choose where to live now. I wish them nothing but happiness. The Empress has already returned home with her daughter, though she has left behind many of her loyal men to serve me. She has promised to visit whenever she is able, and I am glad of it. She was the only real friend I made here.

I have rebuilt a council of advisors, made up equally of men and women. I want to have balance in my new order, and together we will rebuild our country and restore our people.

But despite all my father did to destroy Vallure, it's hard to step out of his shadow. I am young, and many see that as a weakness. Even those I've given a voice to seem to want to use my youth against me. I understand now how my father felt – that vultures always circled, wanting power for themselves. Perhaps, if I am to survive, I shall have to find another way to rule.

The door opens and a woman is escorted in.

'Thank you,' I say to the soldier, who shuts the door behind him.

'You wanted to see me, Majesty?'

'I did. Your father, Loris, was a soothsayer, was he not?'

She nods. 'He served your father faithfully for many years.'

'Good. I believe you have the same gift?'

'No,' she says. 'Begging your pardon, Majesty, I am better.'

I raise an eyebrow. 'How so?'

'The stars do not lie,' she says. 'But my father often misunderstood them. Made mistakes. I do not.'

Mistakes that cost *my* father everything. Believing the child was a baby born within the past year. Confusing the role of the blacksmith in his death. Failing to see my part at all. His interpretation was close, but fatally wrong.

I smile and get to my feet.

'Then you shall henceforth be my High Priestess.'

I look upwards. One thing I never saw from my grate all those times I spied on this room was the window high up in the ceiling. It was there for my father and his soothsayers to gaze directly at the stars.

I stare at them hungrily now, desperate to discover their secrets.

'Tell me,' I say to the girl. 'What does the future hold?'

ACKNOWLEDGEMENTS

Yet again I've had the opportunity to work with the absolute best people and it is an honour to take a moment to appreciate them all.

Davinia Andrew-Lynch – my fabulous agent who goes above and beyond for me every day. Thank you for picking me up whenever I'm down and carrying me onwards.

Lena McCauley and Nazima Abdillahi – what an editing team you are. Thank you for believing in my girls – and in me.

The brilliant folk at Hachette – how wonderful to work with you again. Special thanks to Ruth Girmatsion, Bec Gillies, Sarah Farmer and Hazel Cotton. Also to Jennifer Alliston for designing, and Leo Nickolls for illustrating the beautiful cover.

A special thank you to Lisa Wisdom, whose blacksmithing insight was invaluable. And also to Steven A Wilson of SAW Forge – you were so helpful to me all that time ago when I came asking questions. Any inaccuracies are entirely mine.

The bookish community – your support means the world to me, and I cannot thank you enough. Extra special shoutout to writer friends who have encouraged me on: Mich Kenney, Holly Race, Kat Dunn, Menna van Praag, Katharine Corr, Liz Corr.

To my amazing family – thank you for letting me disappear so often into my own world . . . and for still being there when I return. I love you all.

THE EPIC
ISLES OF
STORM &
SORROW
TRILOGY

Seventeen-year-old Marianne is fated to one day
become the Viper, defender of the Twelve Isles.

But the reigning Viper stands in her way. Corrupt and
merciless, he prowls the seas in his warship, killing with
impunity, leaving only pain and suffering in his wake.

He's the most dangerous man on the ocean . . .
and he is Marianne's father.

She was born to protect the islands. But can she fight
for them if it means losing her family, her home,
the boy she loves – and perhaps even her life?

A brave heroine. An impossible dilemma.
An epic fantasy trilogy set on the high seas.

Marianne has never wanted to be a fighter, but hopes
for peace in the Eastern Isles are being frustrated.
The corrupt King remains on the throne, bandits are
proving hard to stop and Marianne is not sure who
among her crew she can truly trust.

For the islands to prosper, the invisible bond
that once existed uniting land and sea must be reinstated.
There's only one way that can happen – the return of
magic. To do that Marianne must put aside all her fears:
she must return to her roots, the Western Isles,
and call on the power that runs in her blood.

She must become a Mage.

Only then, can she possibly command the army
needed to finally take down the King.

Having exposed herself to the darker
side of magic, Marianne is struggling.
The magic within her is nearly impossible
to control, and she becomes cruel and
violent, mercilessly pursuing those who have
harmed her in the past, ignoring the pleas
of those closest to her to remember what's
really important: saving the islands.

Everything she's fought for has come down
to this. Will Marianne be able to fulfil her
promise to bring peace to the islands when
she can't even bring peace to herself?

Conquer the darkness.
Control the magic. Save the Isles.

Raised on a healthy diet of fantasy and fairy tales, Bex Hogan has spent much of her life lost in daydreams. Writing her stories down was a natural progression and now she enjoys sharing her time between living in the real world and escaping to her imagination. A Cornish girl at heart, Bex now lives in Cambridgeshire with her husband, two beautiful daughters and a fluffy cocker spaniel.

Follow her on Twitter @bexhogan
or visit her website at bexhogan.co.uk